IN
FIRM
PURSUIT

PAMELA SAMUELS-YOUNG

In
FIRM
PURSUIT

sepia™

IN FIRM PURSUIT

A Sepia Novel

ISBN-13: 978-0-373-83040-4
ISBN-10:　　0-373-83040-8

© 2007 by Pamela Samuels-Young

www.kimanipress.com

Printed in U.S.A.

To my husband, Rick.
Thanks for loving me and for constantly cracking me up.

Don't be afraid of the space between your dreams and reality. If you can dream it, you can make it so.
—Belva Davis, journalist

Acknowledgments

After many years of working toward this goal, it is indeed nothing short of a blessing from above that I am a twice-published author. In addition to thanking God, I also owe a debt of gratitude to a boatload of family and friends.

My first thank you goes out to five very special men. To Jerome Norris, thanks for delving into my manuscript and helping me keep it real. When this brother from the hood gave *In Firm Pursuit* a big thumbs-up, I knew it was ready to roll. To Rafael Medina, the biggest movie buff I know, thanks for your astute critiques and ever-present enthusiasm. To my cousin Donny Wilson and his fellow Raytheon buddy, Frank Harris, thanks for that last-minute critique and your manly insights. To Karey Keenan, the coolest white guy I know (you must have been a brother in another life), thanks for your constant praise and top-notch editing skills.

To my loving parents, John and Pearl Samuels, no daughter could have had two better book promoters. To my wonderful stepchildren, Tonicha Haythorn, Tanya Knight, Goldman ("Ricky") Young, III, and Shelby Young, thanks for all the pub!

Many thanks to my cheerleader friends who publicized my first novel, *Every Reasonable Doubt*, by telling all their friends, buying several copies, setting up and attending multiple book signings and hawking the novel as if it were their own: Olivia Smith, Rachell Jackson, Jackie Hilson, Lisa Gooden Campbell, Tina Fisher, Sharlene Moore, Linda Teems, Geneva O'Keith, Roosevelt Womble, Syna Dennis, Alicia Tilque, Russana Rowles,

Carla Burhanan, Bettie Lewis, Sara Finney-Johnson,
Felicia Henderson, Monique Brandon,
Linda Rosborough, President of Black Women
Lawyers Association of Los Angeles, my Coro buddy
Jennifer Davis, my uncle, Eddie Stephens, my college
roommate Donna Lowry (you really hooked me up in
Atlanta!), my homey, Edna Browder (thanks for the
great home cooking in Gary, Indiana), my Compton
homey Dewitt Tolbert (thanks for being my chauffeur in
Boston), Al and Alice Coombs (thanks for the hospitality
in Boston) and my Compton High School government
teacher, Walter Bodle (thanks for the room and board
in Seattle as well as setting up all those appearances).
And an extra-special thank-you to Naomi Young,
Johnine Barnes and Betty Southard Murphy, three
partners with the law firm of Baker Hostetler. That
elegant book-signing party you hosted in my honor
in Washington, D.C., has yet to be matched.

To my amazing Toyota supporters, Alva Mason,
Lynda Martin, Gay France, Kathy Fairbrother,
Michelle Ramos, Lisa Williams, Nichelle Norris,
Diane Mackin, Sophy Woodhouse, Judy Simmons,
Alicia McAndrews, Molly Byock, Charles Zacharie,
Michael Gutierrez, Midge Waters, Karin Accomando,
Marsha Silady, Pat Trytten, Shirley Price,
Linda Coleman and Jackie Boss, your passionate
support, pats on the back and encouraging e-mails
warmed my heart. To the Nubian Queens Literary Club
of Los Angeles, especially Gwen Jones (who made the
time for a second read on very short notice), thanks for
sending me back to the drawing board, which resulted
in a much better product.

To the members of my writing group, Adrienne Byers,
Jane Howard-Martin and Nefertiti Austin, every author

needs to be surrounded by other truly supportive writers. Thanks for all those gentle critiques. And to my agent Sha-Shana Crichton and my Kimani Press editor, Glenda Howard, thanks for getting me to this point.

Finally, I am especially blessed to be surrounded by a circle of extraordinary people whose giving spirit has helped me grow in so many ways. I consider these individuals my personal board of directors: Cheryl Mason, who provides me with both spiritual guidance and remarkable literary insight; Ellen Farrell, my motivational coach and literary sounding board; Brian Dunn, my self-appointed promoter, who came out of nowhere and made so many things happen that I'm still scratching my head; Debbie Diffendal, Jewelle Johnson, Sauti Baraka, Ginger Heyman, Cynthia Hebron, Halima Horton and De'Borah Letbetter, the best critics/champions an author could have; Virginia Gonzales, my new friend and editor extraordinare; Carolyn Holt, my superb publicist; Laurie Robinson of Corporate Counsel Women of Color, a smart, dynamic young lawyer who constantly pushes me to dream big; Shunda Leigh, my energetic Atlanta publicist, from *Booking Matters* magazine, who always makes things happen; and last, but most certainly not least, public speaking/marketing guru Mike Rounds, who generously shared both his time and talent and who is constantly making me feel as if I'm something special. You have all aided me on this journey in immeasurable ways.

Please stay tuned. I'm just warming up!

PROLOGUE

Karen Carruthers had never thought much of women who filed sexual harassment claims. A woman who couldn't hold her own with a man—any man—simply didn't have balls. But now, Karen was one of them.

Gripping the gearshift of her convertible Mustang Cobra, Karen pressed down hard on the gas and didn't let up until the speedometer hovered near eighty-five. At this time of the day—only minutes before sunrise—L.A.'s 405 Freeway resembled the flatlands of some Midwestern highway. The road was all hers, so she took it.

Whenever trouble loomed, Karen did the one thing that soothed her. She drove. For the past few weeks, anxiety had crept into her every thought and buried itself there. But during her freedom drives, as she liked to call them, she felt fearless. Invigorated. Fulfilled. All those *empowering* words her therapist insisted that she *embrace*.

As the Mustang glided past ninety, the crisp air fanned Karen's face and she inhaled a healthy gulp that a New Yorker would have considered warm for a February. Despite the cool temperature, she felt a hot exhilarating rush. Not all that different from what she experienced during sex. Really great sex.

Zooming past the Santa Monica interchange in a nearly drunken state of euphoria now, Karen almost missed the Mulholland exit. Imitating a stunt she'd seen in a Bruce Willis movie, she laterally zipped across three lanes, just in time to make it to the off-ramp. As Karen ascended the short incline to the traffic light ahead, she combed her fingers through her thick mass of strawberry-blond hair, then rubbed her emerald-green eyes.

When Karen first reported her allegations of sexual harassment against Henry Randle, she had expected that the man would be fired. But she had not anticipated that Randle would turn around and sue Micronics Corporation. Now Karen was her company's star witness in his wrongful termination case. A case she wanted nothing to do with.

Leaning forward, Karen pressed the CD button and began singing along with Faith Hill. Not until she had made a left onto Skirball Center Drive and a right onto Mulholland, did she notice the black sedan a couple of car lengths behind. A longer glimpse in her rearview mirror told her that the car was a BMW with a lone occupant inside. Karen punched off Faith mid-chorus and picked up speed. Her pulse did the same. She passed the University of Judaism at close to seventy. The sedan sped up as well. And then it hit her. *The documents!* Karen snatched her purse from the passenger's seat, fished out an envelope and stuffed it down her sweater and into her bra. She had known all along that they would eventually come looking for the documents. Feeling them against her skin sent an icy chill through her body.

Karen inhaled and tried to think clearly as trepidation gradually sucked the air from her lungs. The two-mile stretch of Mulholland that lay ahead was interspersed on both sides with outrageously expensive homes and cliffs with made-for-Hollywood views. A sharp turn down one of the long driveways would leave her trapped, making her an easy target for her pursuer. A wrong turn in the opposite direction could send her into a nosedive off one of the cliffs, finishing the job for them.

Though fear now coursed through every vein in Karen's body, an odd smile graced her lips. There was no way the BMW would be able to keep up. Her breathing slowed ever so slightly after another glance in the mirror confirmed that her pursuer was losing ground. Karen had cruised Mulholland so many times she could almost drive it blindfolded. She only had to make it down the hill to Beverly Glen. Somebody was bound to be walking a dog or taking an early morning jog. *They* would not want witnesses.

Karen patted her breast, confirming that the envelope was still there. Still safe. Just then another car shot out of a driveway several hundred yards ahead and Karen's heart slammed against her chest. Instinct told her the BMW to her rear was not working alone. She anxiously felt for the envelope again and concentrated on her next move.

She took another quick glance in the rearview mirror. *The BMW wasn't there.* When she looked to her left, her eyes bore across the empty passenger seat of the BMW and directly into the barrel of a gun.

Time froze for a second, then a piercing scream left Karen's lips, reverberating into the early morning air. Karen stomped on the brakes and the BMW, unprepared for her sudden stop, darted ahead, just as she had anticipated.

What happened next, however, had not been part of Karen's plan.

She jerked the steering wheel sharply to the left and hit the gas. But instead of making a full U-turn, the Mustang headed off the road, straight toward a thin patch of bushes where a guardrail should have been.

Karen's hands flew to her face, barely muffling her futile screams.

For what seemed like minutes rather than seconds, the Mustang floated across the reddish-orange sky like a wonderfully woven magic carpet. After a moment of calm, Karen felt the sharp pull of gravity, then braced herself for a landing that turned daybreak into darkness.

CHAPTER 1

"This case should be settled," barked the Honorable Frederick H. Sloan. The judge's demanding baritone required a response even though no question had been posed.

I looked over at Reggie Jenkins, my spineless opposing counsel, seated to my left in the judge's private chambers. The petrified expression on his face told me I would have to speak for the both of us.

"Your Honor," I began, knowing how much judges loved to hear that salutation, "we're just too far apart. My client is ready and willing to try this case."

Judge Sloan rolled up the sleeves of his crisp white shirt, revealing more of his flawless tan. Most of the federal judges who sat on the bench in California's Central District did not fit the typical stereotype of a jurist. Sloan was both tall and handsome and had probably hit the gym during the lunch hour. If it weren't for his lush gray hair, it would have been hard to tell that he had bypassed sixty a few years back.

"How about you, counselor?" The judge swiveled his chair away from me and zeroed in on my opponent. "Are you prepared to try this case, too?"

Jenkins inhaled and scratched the back of his neck. A

chubby, middle-aged black man, he had chronically chapped lips and wore a short Afro that always looked uncombed. His beige linen suit needed a good pressing and his tie was as crooked as he was.

"Oh, no, Your Honor." Jenkins cracked the knuckles of his right hand against the palm of his left. "I don't like wasting the taxpayers' time and money."

I wanted to bop Reggie on the head with my purse. He settled all of his cases because he was too incompetent to go to trial.

Judge Sloan swung back to me and smiled heartily. "I've seen very few cases that were slam dunks. You sure you want to try this case, little lady?"

Little lady? I hated it when judges talked to me like I was some bimbo. After only eight years of practice, I had some pretty impressive stats on my Bar card. I was a senior associate at O'Reilly & Finney, one of the most respected trial firms in L.A. I had also won a five-million-dollar verdict in a race discrimination case and defended a high-profile murder case. But taking crap from judges was par for the course.

Before I could respond, the judge returned his focus to my rival.

"Mr. Jenkins, what's your client looking for?"

"Your Honor," I interrupted, "my client really wants to try this—"

Sloan held up a hand the size of a dinner plate, but did not look my way. "I'm talking to Mr. Jenkins right now." He grabbed a handful of roasted almonds from a crystal dish on the corner of his desk and tossed a couple into his mouth.

"W-well, Your Honor," Jenkins stuttered, "my client, Henry Randle, was fired based on trumped-up charges of sexual harassment. He was really terminated because he's a black man and because he refused to turn a blind eye to the company's fraudulent billing practices. He—"

I couldn't contain myself. "That's not true. Your client was fired for grabbing Karen Carruthers in an elevator and trying to kiss her. And there's absolutely no evidence that—"

This time the judge cut me off with a raised hand *and* a stone-hard glare. "Ms....uh..."

"Henderson," I said, annoyed that he couldn't even remember my name. "Vernetta Henderson."

"Ms. Henderson, you will speak only when I ask you to."

I locked my arms across my chest and slumped a little in my chair. When a federal judge called for order, he usually got it.

"Mr. Jenkins," the judge continued brusquely, "I know the facts. Let's cut to the chase. Make Ms. Henderson an offer."

Jenkins looked timidly in my direction and took a long moment before speaking. "I believe I could get my client to accept five hundred thousand," he nearly squeaked.

"Out of the question," I said, ignoring the judge's gag order.

Judge Sloan leaned forward and stroked his chin. "I'm afraid I would have to agree. Give us a more realistic number, Mr. Jenkins. What's your bottom line?"

Reggie looked down at his hands. "I...uh...I guess if my client received something in the neighborhood of thirty thousand, he might accept it."

Thirty thousand. I mindlessly doodled on the legal pad on my lap. That was a good offer. My client, Micronics Corporation, would easily spend ten times that in attorneys' fees by the time the trial was over. But Micronics's litigation philosophy mandated trying winnable cases, even when they could be settled for nuisance value. They firmly believed that if a plaintiff's attorney litigated a case for months or years and netted nothing for his efforts, he would think twice before suing the company a second time, knowing the battle that awaited him.

Truth be told, I was psyched about trying the case for reasons of my own. If everything remained on schedule, my anticipated victory in the Randle case would come about a week before my law firm's partnership vote. Having another big win under my belt days before the vote would cinch things for me. I would soon become O'Reilly & Finney's first African-American partner. I was not about to let Judge Sloan steal my thunder.

"Your Honor," I said, looking him fearlessly in the eyes, "my client isn't interested in settlement."

Sloan propped an elbow on the desk and pointed at me with a finger the size of a wiener. "You *and* your client are making a big mistake," he said with a controlled fury.

I swallowed hard and said nothing. Pissing off a judge, particularly a federal judge, would mean hell for me the next time I appeared in Sloan's courtroom. He could be as retaliatory as he wanted with no fear of repercussions. One of the many perks of having a job for life.

Sloan snatched a legal pad from his desk and started writing. "You want to try this case?" he said with a cruel smile, "then you've got it. I'm expediting the filing of the pretrial documents. I want the trial brief, the jury instructions and all motions filed by Monday morning. And I'd like to see you two back here Tuesday afternoon for another status report."

"Your Honor!" Jenkins whined, cracking the knuckles of both hands this time. "I'm a solo practitioner. There's no way I can get all those documents drafted in four days." He took a Chap Stick from his jacket pocket and nervously dotted his lips.

"That's not my problem, Mr. Jenkins. Perhaps you'll be able to talk some sense into Ms. Henderson before Monday morning." The judge grabbed another handful of almonds. "You can leave now."

As I followed Jenkins down a long hallway that led back to the main courtroom, a flutter of apprehension hit me. *What if I didn't win?*

Luckily, the flash of self-doubt did not linger. Reggie was a lousy attorney. Going up against him would be like trying a case against a first-year law student.

The Randle case was going to trial and I was going to win it.

CHAPTER 2

Reggie Jenkins made it back to his office on the low-rent end of Wilshire Boulevard in less than thirty minutes. Instead of getting to work drafting the pretrial documents for the Randle case, he gazed out of a window clouded with years of grime and sulked.

He could not understand why Vernetta Henderson was so adamant about trying the case. Especially after he had made a perfectly reasonable settlement offer. Women attorneys, particularly the black ones, always made everything so personal. The girl acted like she wanted to punish him for even filing the case.

The view of the alley two floors below did nothing to lighten Reggie's sour mood. To the right, three bums nodded near a metal trash bin overflowing with debris. The stench managed to seep into Reggie's office even though his windows had been glued shut for years.

Reggie regularly fantasized about having an office with a real view, in a swanky downtown high-rise with marble floors, round-the-clock security guards and windows so clean you could see yourself. His name would appear on the door in fancy gold letters: *Reggie Jenkins, Attorney-at-Law*. Or better yet, *Jenkins, Somebody and Somebody*.

His secretary, paralegal and sometime girlfriend, barged into his office without knocking. "I just wanna make sure you gonna have my money on Friday," Cheryl demanded. Her fists were pinned to a pair of curvy hips.

Reggie's teeth instinctively clamped down on the toothpick dangling from his thick lips. "I told you I would, didn't I?"

"You said the same thing last month, then you didn't show up at the office for three straight days."

Reggie snatched his checkbook from his briefcase and scribbled across one of the checks. "Here," he said, thrusting it at her. "Just don't cash it until tomorrow."

As Cheryl sauntered out, Reggie shook his head and frowned. One day, he was going to have enough cash to hire a real secretary.

He stared down at his cluttered desk, realizing that he was about to lose another one and there wasn't anything he could do about it. Although he had promised Henry Randle his day in court, Reggie had never actually intended to make good on that vow. It was much easier to settle cases—the winners as well as the losers. He'd only had six trials during his thirteen years of practice and had lost every single one of them. He thought about calling Randle to update him on today's court session, but what would he say? *You'll get to tell your story to a jury, but you're going to lose.*

Reggie had checked around and learned that Vernetta was an excellent trial attorney. *He* clearly was not. Juries unnerved him. Whenever those twelve pairs of eyes focused on him and him alone, something inexplicable happened and he turned into a bumbling idiot. If a witness responded with an answer he had not expected, it startled him and he froze up. When an opposing counsel yelled *Objection—hearsay* in the middle of his question, it wrecked his rhythm, causing him to stumble like an old drunk taking a step off of a curb he didn't know was there. By the time the judge had ruled on the objection, Reggie did not know what to say next because he could not even remember what question he had asked.

He rummaged through the unruly stack of papers in front of him and pulled out the *Randle v. Micronics* complaint. The day Henry Randle had walked into his office and told his story, Reggie felt like someone had handed him a blank check. He had never had a case with allegations of race discrimination *and* whistle-blowing. Randle swore that he had never even laid eyes on Karen Carruthers before running into her in that elevator, and he certainly had not grabbed the woman or tried to kiss her. And Reggie fully believed his new client's claim that Micronics trumped up the whole thing to silence his complaints about the company's fraudulent billing on some multimillion-dollar contract with the Air Force.

But as the litigation progressed, Reggie's enthusiasm for the case waned. Just as it always did. Now he simply wanted his thirty-three percent of whatever settlement he could get so he could move on to the next one.

He turned on his ancient computer and prepared to get to work on the pretrial documents. Before he could open a blank screen, an idea came to him and his dour mood immediately brightened. After mulling it over for a few minutes, Reggie grabbed his car keys, checked his breast pocket for his cell phone and rushed out of the door.

If his brilliant little plan actually panned out, he was about to turn the tables on Ms. Vernetta Henderson *and* her scheming client.

CHAPTER 3

After being released from detention in Judge Sloan's chambers, I headed back to my office, where I checked my voice mail messages and quickly browsed through twenty-three new e-mails. Finding nothing that couldn't wait, I made my way to Haley Prescott's office on the other side of the twelfth floor.

Haley was a second-year associate assigned to assist me with the Randle case. She had only been with the firm for six months, having clerked for a federal judge in D.C. after graduating from Yale Law School.

The sweet smell of lavender prickled my nose the minute I stepped inside Haley's office. The place smelled like a florist's shop. The oversized bouquet sitting on the corner of her desk looked like it had just been picked from somebody's garden. Haley's fingers were gliding across her computer keyboard, her eyes glued to the monitor in front of her.

"Hey," she said flatly, not bothering to look my way. Haley saved her more enthusiastic greetings for male attorneys. The partners in particular.

"I just got back from court," I said as I walked up to her desk. "I hate to deliver bad news, but Judge Sloan wants all the pretrial documents in the Randle case filed by Monday."

Haley's fingers froze in place. "That's not possible. I'm spending the weekend at my condo in Mammoth."

As hard as I tried to like the girl, she never failed to get on my last nerve. What bothered me most was her air of superiority, something that was no doubt bolstered by having a mother on the Ninth Circuit Court of Appeals, a politically connected father and the looks of a runway model. Almost every attorney in the firm—partners and associates alike—treated her as if she were rainmaking royalty. Considering the potential clients she would likely attract to the firm because of her parents' connections, she probably was.

But ruined travel plans came with the territory. So I ignored her grousing. "Which documents have you drafted so far?" I asked.

Haley rudely went back to typing. "None of them."

"I thought you told me you had already started drafting the trial brief and jury instructions," I said.

She paused to tuck one of her curly blond locks behind her left ear. The girl had long, feathery, Pamela Anderson hair. And from what I could tell, it was the real thing, not that dull, pasty shade that came from a peroxide bottle or years of overexposure to the sun. It was no doubt the only genuine thing about her.

"This isn't the only case I have," Haley snapped. Her voice took on a Bostonian pitch that hadn't been there a second ago.

"I don't know what other cases you have," I snapped

back, "but I'm sure they aren't going to trial in a matter of weeks."

All I could do was stare at the girl. It was times like this that I really missed my friend, Neddy McClain. She'd been the only other African-American attorney at O'Reilly & Finney besides me. Neddy and I had started out on rocky ground, but ended up getting pretty tight after defending a big murder case together. She had recently moved to Atlanta, where her new fiancé, a former police detective, had opened his own private investigations firm. I would've loved to see Haley give Neddy the kind of attitude she was throwing my way. Neddy would've had Haley running from her own office in tears.

Haley's lips remained pursed into a tight pout. "Like I said, I really can't work this weekend."

My right hand went to my hip. "And, like *I* said, the documents have to be filed by Monday."

As far as I was concerned, the fact that Haley's mama was one step below a Supreme Court Justice did not mean she didn't have to work just as hard as everybody else. I was actually glad to be throwing a wrench in her plans.

Haley allowed several beats to pass, then fixed me with an infuriated look that didn't need translation. "Fine," she said tightly.

I turned to leave, but Haley stopped me. "I forgot to give you this." She shoved a document at me. "One of the secretaries from Micronics's HR Department faxed it over this morning."

I quickly scanned the four-page fax and felt a heavy pall come over me. It was a memo to file written by Bill

Stevens, Micronics's former in-house attorney. When Stevens left the company, the Randle case was transferred to O'Reilly & Finney. The memo briefly summarized allegations of sexual harassment made against six Micronics employees, not including Henry Randle, during the past five years. Most of them had been accused of misconduct far more egregious than what Randle was accused of doing. One of the men allegedly grabbed a woman's breast. All six were white. To my dismay, even though an HR investigation confirmed the charges against each of them, none had been fired.

I looked at the date in the upper left-hand corner of the page and thought I was seeing things. "This document was written months ago," I said, more to myself than to Haley.

"The secretary said the memo was misfiled with another case," Haley explained, her full attention still on her computer screen.

"Why didn't you call me the minute you got this?" I paused and tried to collect myself, not wanting Haley to pick up on my rising stress level. "You knew I had a court appearance in the Randle case today."

Haley huffed out a breath of air. "Actually, I tried," she said. "But you apparently didn't have your cell phone on. I didn't leave a message because I figured you were already in court."

I felt a light pounding in my chest. I walked over to close the door, then turned around to face my subordinate. "I just passed up a chance to settle this case," I said. "Something I probably wouldn't have done if I'd known about this fax."

Haley shrugged. "I was out when it came in and I didn't

think you'd be discussing settlement at a pretrial conference. It wasn't scheduled until two o'clock. If you'd come into the office this morning, you would've known about that fax."

"I had a dental appointment," I said testily. *Why was I explaining myself to this child?* It took most junior associates until their third or fourth year before they stopped being intimidated by the partners and senior associates. But my senior status apparently meant nothing to Haley.

She tucked another loose curl behind her ear. "How much did Jenkins want?"

I exhaled. "Thirty thousand. And I should have taken it."

"I thought you were so eager to try the case."

"I *was.*" I waved the fax in the air. "But this changes everything. This memo basically proves Randle's discrimination case. Every one of these guys—who all just happen to be white—got off with a mere slap on the wrist. We can't take a chance of going to trial with these facts."

"Well, I can tell you one thing, Porter's not going to be happy when he finds out you passed up that settlement offer."

Tell me something I don't know.

Porter was the partner in charge of the Randle lawsuit. He'd been riding me ever since we got the case, something he seemed to enjoy doing to most associates.

"Well, look at the bright side," Haley said. "That document is attorney-client privileged so we don't have to produce it. And the odds are pretty good that Jenkins won't find out about those cases on his own. He didn't even ask for information about prior sexual harassment claims during discovery. The man is totally incompetent."

I suddenly felt protective of my fellow black brother. *I could call him incompetent, but I didn't like hearing him criticized by this pompous little sorority girl.*

I reread the fax and my rage slowly shifted from Haley to Micronics. *Why hadn't somebody at Micronics told me about these other cases?* I was certain that I had asked HR about prior sexual harassment claims. *Hadn't I?*

"If you ever get another fax or letter or telephone call or anything else with important information about a case I'm working on," I said, "I want to know about it. Right away."

"No problem." Haley gave me a Cover Girl smile.

I headed for the door and did not bother to look back. "I'll expect to see a draft of the trial brief and jury instructions by noon on Saturday."

CHAPTER 4

The CEO of Micronics Corporation strolled down the spacious hallway of the Cypress Club with a decided, purpose-filled gait. His eyes bore straight ahead, ignoring his elegant surroundings. The rich wood paneling, the expensive Oriental rugs, the Picassos and Monets that lined the walls. Any other time, J. William Walters would have taken notice of the Pavarotti aria wafting from the expensive Bose speakers. Not today.

A casual observer might have assumed that Walters's brain cells were consumed with annual reports, stock prices or one of his company's newest inventions. But in reality, unshakable images of newspaper headlines and prison cells had been his primary focus for several weeks now. At night, it was becoming increasingly impossible to shake the visions—he refused to call them nightmares—of SEC agents raiding his posh office, slapping handcuffs across his meaty wrists and taking him on a preplanned perp walk as cameras from all the major networks shined blinding lights into his eyes.

Making a sharp left, Walters headed for the Ronald Reagan Room, one of a dozen or so private meeting places reserved for the Cypress Club's most exclusive members. Exclusive in Walters's world meaning not just rich, but rich and powerful. When he reached his destination, he did not bother to knock before thrusting the door open and stepping inside.

It took a second for Walters's eyes to adjust to the near darkness. The ominous room seemed more suitable for a late-night poker game than clandestine corporate decision-making. He nodded in the direction of the room's sole occupant, sitting in a red velvet club chair. Rich Ferris, Micronics's Vice President of Human Resources, was a fair-skinned black man who was as buttoned-up as a born-again preacher. Ferris nodded but did not otherwise greet his boss of the last seven years. Instead, he quietly took a sip from his second vodka of the evening.

The CEO was a long-time member of the Cypress Club. Thanks to Walters's connections, Ferris had recently been extended an invitation to join the elite society. Unlike some of his colleagues, Walters had not raised a fuss when the club finally gave in to outside pressures and began actively complying with its nondiscrimination provision. No matter how many blacks or Jews walked through the door, it would have no tangible impact on his life. Certain people were impervious to change. At least, that was how it had been.

"Well, let's get to it," Walters said, wishing he had a drink, too. He eyed the fully stocked bar in the far corner of the room. The thought of getting up to fix one for himself had not occurred to him. An attendant would arrive shortly. He would wait.

"How're we going to fix this?" Walters's harsh eyes rested pointedly on his subordinate.

Ferris did not rush to respond to the question. In his

own right, he was a well-educated, impressive business-man whose innovative workforce strategies had earned him profiles in publications like *Forbes, Black Enterprise* and the *Wall Street Journal.* At the moment, though, he looked like a scared little boy.

The CEO let the silence linger to the point of punish-ment. "You don't have any ideas?" The sarcasm in Walters's voice failed to mask his anger. "Let's not forget that we're in this together. If the feds come calling for me, they're eventually coming after you, too. So I'll ask the question one more time. How do we fix this?"

Ferris sat forward and cleared his throat. "I've taken care of it," he said. He raised his glass to his lips but did not take a sip. "In fact, everything is well under way."

"Go on," Walters said.

"I don't think I should say any more than that. The less you know the better."

The CEO grimaced. He wanted to hear the specifics, but Ferris was right. If somebody sat him down in front of a polygraph machine, he liked the idea of being able to honestly plead ignorance. Too bad he had not taken that approach months ago.

"When will we know for sure that everything's been resolved?" Walters asked.

"A month at the most, maybe less."

"What about the media?" Walters absently rubbed his jaw. "Are you certain there's nothing out there that some overambitious reporter won't uncover?"

"There's no paper trail to speak of," Ferris said. "We've covered our tracks."

Walters wanted to explode. Ferris had just lied to him. Intentionally, no doubt. There was indeed a paper trail. A very troublesome one. But Walters had already put his own clandestine cleanup plan into motion, knowing he could not leave something this serious up to his circle of incompetents. If and when real trouble surfaced, the minions he had carefully positioned on the front lines would be there to take the fall.

The CEO had personally picked each of his nine direct reports as much for their shrewd business acumen as their unique personal frailties. They were all yes men. Brilliant yes men, but clearly followers, not leaders. Intellect without strength. At the time, Walters had not wanted an equal among his inner circle. Now he could have used one in the room.

"What about the Randle case?" he asked.

"That's being taken care of as well." Ferris spoke with genuine confidence for the first time.

Walters nodded again. "Who's handling it?"

"O'Reilly & Finney. If something goes wrong, it'll look better if an outside law firm has a hand in it."

"Good," Walters said, nodding.

"I had them assign the case to Vernetta Henderson. She handled that wage-and-hour lawsuit at our Long Beach facility last year," Ferris said proudly. "She also defended a big murder case a few months ago." He paused. "And she's African-American." Ferris actually preferred *black* over *African-American,* but was trying to sound politically correct.

Walters had made it known that he liked having

African-American attorneys heading up Micronics's defense team when black plaintiffs sued the company. In the CEO's mind, having a black mouthpiece diffused the issue of race for the jury. Ferris wholeheartedly agreed.

"Good," Walters said again. He glanced at the door. He could not wait much longer for his drink.

"The trial's just a few weeks away," Ferris continued. "According to Ms. Henderson, a defense verdict is all but a certainty."

A stunned look glazed Walters's face. It took a moment before he could speak. "Are you out of your mind? That case can't go to trial."

Ferris unconsciously balled up his left fist, then set his empty glass on the table to his right. "We already gave Ms. Henderson the go-ahead to try it." His voice came out in a near whimper. "It's going to look pretty strange to suddenly ask that it be settled."

"Not half as strange as you and me sharing a prison cell!" Walters yelled. "If this thing gets out they'll hang us all out to dry!"

Ferris pinched the bridge of his nose. "Ms. Henderson's a real go-getter. She's going to ask a lot of questions."

"I don't care about her questions," Walters said through clenched teeth. "Just get the damn case settled. Now!"

CHAPTER 5

I left Haley's office and nearly ran to mine. After reading that Micronics memo, I was anxious to confirm that I was not the one who had screwed up. Finding out how your client handled similar claims—no matter what kind of case—was Employment Law 101.

Snatching open the middle drawer behind my desk, I pulled out two file folders. As I perused my handwritten interview notes, I could feel the pace of my breathing escalate. I had asked every question *except* that one.

I was close to full-scale cardiac arrest when I finally found what I was looking for on the fifth page of my interview notes with Kathy Fairbrother. I fell into my chair and let out a loud sigh. *Thank God.* My notes reflected that the HR Representative had told me that Micronics only had three significant allegations of sexual harassment in the past few years. Each one had been investigated, but HR had been unable to substantiate the charges. None of the cases listed in the fax were among them. *Had Fairbrother intentionally lied to me?*

I picked up the telephone and dialed Fairbrother's number. To my surprise, a secretary informed me that she was no longer with the company. Rich Ferris would be handling all inquiries concerning the Randle case.

It was quite unusual for the VP of Human Resources to serve as the point person on a run-of-the-mill employment case. Somebody at his level only got involved in high-exposure litigation. I asked to be transferred to Ferris, but he was out of the office.

According to my interview notes, Fairbrother had only been a Micronics employee for four months at the time I interviewed her. Maybe she didn't know about the other cases either. But she claimed she had checked.

I reluctantly closed the folder and thanked God a second time. Haley was right. Reggie had done a piss-poor job during discovery and probably would not discover this information on his own. And we had no obligation to voluntarily provide it to him since his original discovery requests had not asked for information about similar claims.

Just to make sure, I pulled out the pleadings file and scanned Reggie's discovery requests. He had only served a single request for production of documents and a set of twenty interrogatories. His questions focused solely on Henry Randle's work history and the specifics of the allegations made by Karen Carruthers. Thank God for shoddy legal work. I breathed another sigh of relief.

Despite the inferior legal talent of my opponent, this evidence made the case far too risky to take to trial. I had to get it settled.

The telephone rang, interrupting my thoughts.

When I picked up, I was happy to hear my husband's voice. "Don't kill me," Jefferson said, "but I'll have to work Saturday *and* Sunday, so I won't be coming home this weekend."

For the last three months, Jefferson had been living in San Diego during the week and coming home on weekends. The small electrical company he owned with his partner, Stan, had won its first big commercial job— a strip mall about two hours south of L.A. Our young marriage did not need the separation. We had recently survived a short breakup, caused primarily by my demanding work schedule. But now Jefferson's work was keeping him even busier than me.

"Don't sweat it," I said. "I have to work all weekend, too." I was about to tell him about my crazy day, when my secretary, Shelia, knocked on my open door.

"Mr. Porter wants to see you in his office." Shelia made a face that said she felt sorry for me. "Immediately."

CHAPTER 6

"Man, at the rate we're going, I'm never gonna get home to see Vernetta again." Jefferson Jones stared down at the blueprints spread out in front of him on the rickety card table.

His business partner, Stan Parks, stood next to him at the rear of the trailer that served as the on-site office for Jones-Parks Electrical. They had been studying the blueprints for the last twenty minutes, trying to figure out exactly what had gone wrong.

"Don't freak out yet," Stan said. "I think the problem is someplace over here." He made a circle with his index finger in the northwest quadrant of the blueprint, then dumped his two-hundred-fifty-pound frame into a cheap metal chair that could barely hold him. Stan was a dark-skinned man in his mid-forties who smiled a lot because he liked showing off the gold tooth he had front and center.

"And like I keep telling you," Stan continued, "you don't need to be running home to your wife every weekend. Let that woman miss you. Absence makes the heart grow fonder, my brother."

Before Jefferson could respond, the trailer door opened and LaKeesha Douglas walked in. A sophomore at San

Diego State, LaKeesha had been working part-time as their office assistant for just over two weeks.

"What's up, boss men?" She dropped her book bag on the floor near one of the two desks that sat on opposite sides of the trailer. She had micro-thin, shoulder-length braids that were pulled back into a loose ponytail. Her Baby Phat jeans were so tight, the seams along her hipline threatened to rupture at any second. She was braless underneath a thin, red-and-white tank top, making it hard for Jefferson and Stan to keep their eyes above LaKeesha's neckline.

"What you guys got for me to do today?" She forced her hands into the front pockets of her jeans, which gave her bosses an even better view of her erect nipples.

Jefferson realized he had been staring and abruptly turned back to the blueprints. "We need some more supplies. Coffee and sugar for one." He pulled his wallet from his back pocket and took out three twenties. "Check to make sure we have enough cups and napkins, and stop by Staples to pick up a case of paper for the printer."

"Aye-aye, captain," LaKeesha said, giving him a salute. She grabbed her book bag from the floor, took out her keys and a small purse and headed out of the squeaky trailer door.

Stan shuffled over to the window and watched LaKeesha walk away. "That little tenderonie is gonna hurt somebody one day. Too bad it can't be me."

"Get your mind out of the gutter, man," Jefferson laughed. "She's barely legal."

Stan remained bent at the waist, peering out of the window. "Where I come from, twenty-one is old enough to do a whole lot of fun stuff. She might not want my fat ass, but she would definitely give you some."

Jefferson grinned. "I'm a happily married man, remember?"

"We're talking apples and oranges, my brother. One thing ain't got nothing to do with the other."

Jefferson shook his head, then rolled up the blueprints and stuffed them into a long plastic tube. "C'mon, man," he said, opening the trailer door. "Let's go fix this problem."

LaKeesha returned while they were out and restocked the supplies, cleaned the coffeemaker and straightened up the desks.

A short while later, Jefferson entered the trailer. When he made a move toward the coffeemaker, LaKeesha jumped in front of him.

"I'll get it for you," she said.

"You don't have to do that, LaKeesha. I can fix my own coffee."

"I don't mind," she persisted. "You guys have been working pretty hard out there."

Jefferson relented and sat down at his desk.

Seconds later, LaKeesha sauntered over and set a cup on his desk. "Just the way you like it. One cream and two packets of sugar."

Jefferson took a sip. "Thanks," he said, enjoying the personal attention. He caught a pleasant whiff of her perfume.

Stan had insisted on hiring LaKeesha over his objections. Jefferson thought it would be too much work trying to keep the guys off of her, but the girl had no trouble fending for herself. She seemed pretty streetwise and admitted blowing a couple of years after high school hanging out and partying before finally deciding to go to college.

As LaKeesha walked over to the miniature fridge to the left of the coffeemaker, Jefferson could not help staring at her ass. Breasts were nice to look at, but he was an ass man. In his younger days, as long as a woman had a decent face, a small waist and a big behind, not much else mattered. And LaKeesha had a whopper.

Jefferson watched as she bent down to open the fridge. She held the pose far longer than necessary, which made him smile. The girl was obviously messing with him. But he was well past the age when he could be played by some youngster.

He took another sip of coffee, then lowered his head to the desk and rubbed the back of his neck. Before he knew it, LaKeesha was standing behind him massaging his shoulders. Jefferson stiffened at her initial touch, but quickly relaxed.

"Your trapezius muscles are really tight," LaKeesha said, kneading her fingers along the base of his neck. "You have quite a bit of tension in your shoulder area."

Jefferson knew he should stop her, but it felt far too good. "You sound like a professional masseuse," he said.

"I was for a while," LaKeesha replied. "Had to give it up, though. Ran into too many perverts." She used her right elbow to press deep into Jefferson's shoulder. "You've got quite a bit of lactic acid buildup on your right side, but I think I can break it up."

And after several minutes, she apparently had because he felt great.

"So how does it feel now?" LaKeesha asked.

Jefferson twisted his head from side to side, then rotated his shoulders. "That definitely hit the spot. I think you're in the wrong business."

LaKeesha beamed with satisfaction.

Jefferson's cell phone rang and he grunted. "Now what?"

"I'll get it." LaKeesha grabbed the phone from the desk before he could reach it.

Jefferson listened as she politely and professionally explained that he was not available, jotted down a quick message and hung up.

"You're pretty good at that, too," Jefferson said.

"If you want, I can screen your calls for you," LaKeesha offered with a coy smile.

Jefferson did not ponder her offer long. "Sounds like a plan." This time he smiled. It had been a long time since he'd had a female as young and as fine as LaKeesha shooting him vibes and it felt pretty cool. But he knew what was up and he was not stupid enough to screw up his marriage over a five-second orgasm with some kid.

"Just let me know if you need another massage," LaKeesha said, walking back over to Stan's desk. "I have quite a few tricks up my sleeve."

Jefferson smiled to himself. *I bet you do.*

CHAPTER 7

A bad feeling began to rattle around in the pit of my stomach as I made my way to Joseph Porter's corner office five doors away.

Porter was one of those lawyers who had a brilliant legal mind, but no people skills. His gruff, all-business demeanor made him about as approachable as a freshly watered cactus. I was the senior associate on three of his cases. I just prayed he wasn't summoning me to his office to talk about the Micronics case. I needed more time to plan a graceful way out of my predicament before being subjected to one of his grillings.

I paused just outside his door and took a deep breath before marching in. I did not expect a greeting and I didn't get one.

"Haley just advised me that you rejected an extremely reasonable settlement offer in the Randle case today," he said, the second I appeared in his doorway. Porter was a tall man—basketball-player tall—with dark, thinning hair. He did not look up from the brief he was editing.

That little cow! Haley must have blabbed to Porter the minute I left her office. I felt like I was standing in the principal's office. And, basically, I was.

I took a seat without being invited to. "I'm sure you're well aware of Micronics's position on settling cases that have a solid defense," I began. "Micronics had given me the go-ahead to try the case." *And so did you.*

"Well, that fax we received this morning certainly changes things, doesn't it?" His head remained bent over the brief.

I couldn't disagree with that, so I said nothing. Porter's attitude didn't surprise me. When a case appeared to be going south, lawyer logic required finding someone else to take the blame. And I was Porter's someone else.

I looked around his office and tried not to wince. Although every O'Reilly & Finney partner received a generous stipend for office decoration, Porter had rejected his, calling it a waste of firm resources. He had never married, so there were no smiling family portraits to provide a personal dimension. Art did not interest him, so the walls were bare. His office had only the basic ne-cessities: a wall-to-wall bookcase and matching credenza, a dated oak desk and two small chairs. Rumor had it that he had inherited his furniture from another partner who had died of a heart attack at his desk.

Porter finally put down his pen and looked up at me. "How come you didn't know about those other cases?" he asked, his face flooded with disapproval. "Didn't you inquire about past practice during your initial interviews?"

"Of course I did." I was glad that I had taken the time to double-check my interview notes. "But, Kathy Fair-brother, my contact in HR, neglected to mention them. Frankly, I'm concerned that Micronics may have inten-tionally withheld that information from us."

Porter shrugged. "Wouldn't be the first time."

It only figured that Porter would be willing to hang me out to dry while letting the client off the hook. I wanted to push the issue, but that would have been a mistake. I had learned early in my career that when a case blew up in your face, you just had to suck it up and concentrate on putting the pieces back together. Complaining about it would only make you look like a whiner. And whiners didn't make partner.

There was another reason I didn't want to make any waves with Porter. Jim O'Reilly, the firm's Managing Partner, was my mentor and staunchest supporter. He had personally recruited me from another Los Angeles law firm two years earlier. For reasons nobody understood, Porter and O'Reilly despised each other. Porter would love to have a valid reason to derail the partnership chances of an O'Reilly loyalist.

"Let's get back to that offer you turned down," Porter grumbled. "You should've checked with the client before doing that."

I sat up straighter in my seat. "I had planned to let them know about the offer, but based on my conversation with HR last week, they were adamant about trying the case and teaching Reggie Jenkins a lesson." I paused. "Anyway, I'm sure his offer is still on the table."

"Good." Porter picked up his pen again. "I just got a call from Rich Ferris, the VP of Human Resources. He wants the case settled. That fax you got this morning was the first he'd ever heard of those other cases."

And you believe him? I had only met Ferris a few times,

but I knew he was a micromanager. That kind of boss knew everything. He was the only African-American client I had not been able to forge a bond with. African-Americans in corporate America, by virtue of their limited numbers, tended to reach out to one another. But Ferris had seemed more and more standoffish every time we met. So I finally gave up.

"Ferris sounded pretty antsy about getting the case resolved right away," Porter said. "In light of that memo, thirty grand is a steal."

I had to agree, but I didn't want to call Reggie right away. "I think we should wait a couple of days," I said. "If I call Jenkins now, he's probably going to up his offer."

"No," Porter said. "Call him now. Micronics wants the case settled as quickly as possible. They don't care how much it costs."

"They don't care how much it costs?" I said, amazed. "Since when? We can't be talking about the Micronics I know."

Porter waved his hand as if he were swatting at a gnat. "Just get it settled."

I struggled to get up from the small chair in front of Porter's desk. His guest chairs were so low to the ground that anyone sitting in them, no matter how tall, had to look up at him. Everybody knew Porter was dying for a judicial appointment. His seating arrangement was apparently his substitute for feeling like he was sitting on the federal bench.

"Too bad the Randle case isn't going to trial," Porter muttered before I got to the door. "Haley did a great job on that trial strategy memo."

I looked over my shoulder at him, my brows arched in confusion. "What trial strategy memo?"

"You haven't seen it?" Porter rotated his chair, picked up a document from the credenza behind his desk and handed it to me.

As I skimmed it, my face grew hotter with each passing millisecond. I was the senior associate on the case. Haley should have reviewed the document with me before giving it to Porter.

"Excellent legal analysis," Porter said.

"What?" I had briefly zoned out.

"That memo there. Stellar work for someone at her level. Don't you agree?"

"Yeah," I said. "Wonderful." I handed the document back to him and left.

I was sitting at my desk, steaming over the Micronics fax, Haley's big mouth and her little trial strategy memo, when the firm's Managing Partner popped his head into my office.

"Why the long face?" Jim O'Reilly asked, walking inside. O'Reilly was a big, firmly built man who had the swagger of an Irish cop strolling the beat. He also made fifty-two look like forty.

"My Micronics case just went south," I said.

O'Reilly closed the door behind him and took a seat. He was wearing a light blue shirt with a navy blue pin-striped suit. Either Armani or Valentino, the only labels he owned. He was by far the best-dressed man in the building.

"What happened?"

I quickly recapped the latest on the Randle case.

"That was an extremely reasonable settlement offer,

Vernetta," he said. "Sounds like you took a pretty big gamble."

"I wasn't gambling," I said. "We had a strong case and Micronics had instructed me to try it. I could have won it, too."

O'Reilly chuckled. "I like your chutzpah, but there're no sure bets when you're in the hands of a jury. You shouldn't have dismissed an offer that low out of hand."

I started to defend myself but decided to let it go. "I was just about to call the opposing counsel to accept his offer when you walked in."

O'Reilly stood. "Good idea," he said. "And be careful. You can't afford any screwups before the partnership vote. You know how much of a nitpicker Porter can be."

I nodded, then glumly turned to my computer to look up Reggie's number.

CHAPTER 8

I had been on hold for far too long when Reggie finally came on the line.

"Jenkins here." His greeting was a welcome contrast to the snippy woman who had answered his telephone.

"I've had a change of heart," I said. "I think Judge Sloan was right. Your offer was pretty reasonable. So I guess we have a deal."

Reggie chuckled. "Do we?"

I sighed. I was not in the mood to play games. "I can get a draft of a settlement agreement faxed over to you in a couple of hours," I said.

My words were met with prolonged silence.

"Are you there?" I asked after a moment.

"Yep, I'm here," Reggie said. "But I'm not so sure that offer is still on the table."

The man was so sleazy. "C'mon, Reggie. I have a lot of other cases to deal with and I assume you do, too. If this case goes to trial, chances are pretty good that I'll win." *Provided you don't find out about those other sexual harassment cases.*

"Maybe *I'll* win," he said.

I heard an unfamiliar bravado in his voice. "Only if you know something I don't."

"Maybe I do."

I choked back a gasp. There was no way Reggie could know about those other cases. *Was there?* "You just offered to settle the case a few hours ago," I said coolly. "Now you're turning down a guaranteed thirty grand? What's up, Reggie?"

"I've had an opportunity to reassess the value of my case," he said, "and I no longer think that's a viable offer."

I chuckled derisively. "Okay, Reggie, let's hear it. How much do you want?"

"Oh, that's interesting. You flatly reject my offer and now you're asking me to name my price? Why don't you tell *me* what's up, Ms. Henderson?"

"I never said my client would pay more. I was just curious to find out what you were looking for."

"What we're looking for is a jury verdict in our favor," Reggie said. "Mr. Randle wants his day in court so he can tell the world how your client railroaded him."

I inhaled. "Reggie, you have a very weak case and you know Judge Sloan's going to have a fit when he finds out that you reneged on your settlement offer."

"I'll handle the judge," he said, sounding more and more comfortable with his newfound confidence.

"I can't believe you really want to try this case," I said.

"Actually, I do. See you in court on Tuesday."

I heard a click. The slob of an attorney had hung up in my face! I was about to hit the redial button, but changed my mind and dropped the receiver back into the cradle.

Micronics wanted the case settled. I could not afford to start a fight. I knew the game Reggie was playing. He didn't want to spend all weekend drafting the pretrial documents any more than I did.

I glanced at my Bulova. Reggie would probably call back in an hour asking for another ten or twenty grand and the case would be a done deal.

CHAPTER 9

Unfortunately for me, Reggie did not call back.

When I walked into Judge Sloan's courtroom Tuesday afternoon, I was shocked to find Reggie already there. During prior court appearances, he was usually rushing in at the last minute, looking winded and disheveled. Today, he was sitting in the front row of the gallery, both arms stretched along the back of the wooden bench, seemingly poised and relaxed. He turned around and acknowledged me with a slight nod and a big smile.

What in the hell did he have to look so happy about? I still planned to say something to him about hanging up in my face.

I took a seat across the aisle from him, two rows back. Reggie was dressed in a nice gabardine suit that was actually pressed. We were first on the court docket and the clerk called our case just minutes after I sat down. I rose from my seat and stepped through the swinging gate that led into the court's inner sanctum. I was pulling documents from my Coach satchel when I noticed a man standing next to Reggie at the defense table.

"Your Honor, I'll be associating in another attorney," Reggie said, puffing out his chest as if he had already won. "Mr. Hamilton Ellis will be taking over as lead counsel."

I stared across the courtroom in disbelief. How in the hell had Reggie convinced Hamilton Ellis to sign up for *this* case?

Hamilton had the double blessing of being one of the best trial attorneys in the state as well as quite nice to look at. He was six-two with large hazel eyes and a neatly trimmed goatee. His warm smile and dazzling personality radiated manliness. Women wanted him. Men wanted to be him.

Judge Sloan waved his hand in the direction of the court reporter sitting down below him. "Let's go off the record," he said.

I exhaled. *Thank God.* The judge was going to lambaste Jenkins for bringing in new counsel so late in the case.

"Mr. Ellis," the judge said, smiling, "I just want to say it's great to have you in my courtroom. I read that feature article about you in last month's *California Lawyer.* Congratulations."

Hamilton flashed the judge an even bigger return smile. "Thank you, Your Honor."

I looked around the courtroom as everyone stared at Hamilton in awe. Most of the spectators probably remembered him as a star running back for UCLA. A knee injury ended his football career five months into his first season with the Oakland Raiders. Luckily, he had brains to fall back on. He later graduated from Stanford Law School at the top of his class.

I leaned forward and tried to steady myself, pressing all ten fingertips against the defense table, making two little teepees with my hands. I wanted to object. But to what? The judge kissing the plaintiff's attorney's ass and the plaintiff's attorney doing it right back?

"Okay, let's go back on the record," Judge Sloan said. "I see both sides have filed all of the required pretrial documents. How many witnesses does the plaintiff expect to call and what's your estimate for the length of trial?" He looked in the direction of Reggie and Hamilton.

Reggie was sitting down now, his right ankle resting on the opposite knee, glad to have his new co-counsel running the show. "Based on my review of the case," Hamilton began, "we'll have six witnesses, not counting our experts. I'm fairly certain we can complete our direct in no more than four days."

"You've had time to get up to speed on the case already, Mr. Ellis?" the judge asked with a degree of compassion I never knew he possessed.

"Yes, Your Honor."

"Of course you would," Judge Sloan said, smiling again. "I wouldn't expect anything less from an attorney of your caliber. There're a lot of members of the Bar who could learn a thing or two from you, sir."

Sir? I looked at Hamilton, then at the judge, then back at Hamilton again. I had never seen Judge Sloan show any attorney the kind of deference he had just displayed toward Hamilton Ellis.

"Ms. Henderson, are you with us?" the judge said. His voice had hardened considerably. "I asked for your trial estimate."

"Uh...yes, Your Honor." I looked down at a document

in front of me. "About seven days. And I expect to call ten witnesses."

Judge Sloan scowled and pointed that wiener at me again. "That's a lot of witnesses, Ms. Henderson. I'm warning you right now, if the testimony starts to get repetitive, I'm cutting you short."

I almost wanted to laugh. This wasn't happening.

The judge asked a few more procedural questions, then dismissed us.

I stuffed my papers inside my satchel, my mind a muddle of anger, confusion and dread. *How in the hell had this case taken such a crazy turn?*

It wasn't until I looked down at the document I was holding that I realized my hands were shaking.

CHAPTER 10

I stepped outside the courtroom and spotted Hamilton and Reggie standing just a few feet away. They were apparently waiting for me.

"Nice to see you again, counselor." Hamilton extended his hand.

When I offered mine, he clasped it gently, then proceeded to hold on much longer than necessary. I finally had to ease my hand from his grasp.

"Thanks for the heads-up about joining the case," I said, not hiding my frustration.

"Forgive me," Hamilton replied. "If I hadn't been so busy trying to play catch-up, I would've called you."

I rolled my eyes, then glowered at Reggie, who was still all smiles. "When did *your* telephone stop working?"

"I have to run," he said, ignoring me. He extended his hand to Hamilton. "Thanks, brother-in-law."

So they're family. But that still did not explain things. Hamilton was far too concerned about his precious trial record to associate himself with a dog of a case like this one. At least it should've seemed like a dog based on the facts he knew.

"Let's stand over here, out of the way." Hamilton

pressed his palm against my back and guided me from the middle of the busy corridor, closer to the wall.

"I'm really looking forward to going up against you again," he said.

I had won a close case against him five years earlier. I was only a third-year associate at the time, and it had not looked good for such a seasoned trial attorney to be outdone by a novice.

"Don't tell me you still haven't gotten over losing the Byers case," I said. This time I was the one smiling.

"I'll admit that it still stings a bit," he acknowledged. "But that's only part of the reason I decided to help Reggie out with the case. You *can* be quite a handful, you know."

"Oh, so I'm the reason you're on the case?"

"As a matter of fact, you are," he said. "Except I didn't realize you'd been taken." He lifted my left hand and examined my wedding ring. "I'd heard you married some plumber. Tell me it's not true."

"My husband's an electrician," I said, annoyed that he was being so condescending. Hamilton was quite a playboy and had constantly hit on me during the Byers trial. But I never took the bait.

"Six of one, half dozen of the other. You could've done better. You could've had me."

The man was such a jerk. "How's *Mrs.* Ellis these days?" I asked.

"Wouldn't know. I'm back on the market." Hamilton straightened his tie and struck a pose straight off the pages of *GQ.* His black suit, pink shirt and silver cuff links probably cost half my weekly salary. "Even though

Reggie's sister and I got divorced a year ago, he and I are still pretty tight."

Hamilton's blatant leering was beginning to unnerve me. "You guys really don't plan on settling?"

"Not sure yet," he said. "Haven't had time to fully assess the case. But there's one thing I am sure of. It ain't settling for a measly thirty grand. I can't believe you didn't jump at that offer."

I didn't need the reminder. "If we're going to trial, then I guess my record against you will be soon be two and 0," I bluffed.

Hamilton chuckled. "I don't think I'll lose this time."

"Your client grabbed Karen Carruthers in that elevator and you know it," I said.

"Maybe. Maybe not. But it doesn't really matter." He paused for several seconds, obviously for effect. "The judge loves me. And when Judge Sloan loves you, he has an unconscious habit of steering the jury your way."

Hamilton gave me a sexy wink, then walked off.

When I felt my body veer sideways, I was glad there was a sturdy granite wall there to hold me up.

CHAPTER 11

I had just pulled to a stop at a traffic light at Grand and First Street, two blocks from my office, when my Black-Berry rang. I reached over and dug it out of the bottom of my purse, which was sitting on the passenger seat of my Land Cruiser.

When I heard Haley's voice, I wanted to ask God what I did to deserve such a lousy day.

"You told me to call the next time something important came up in the Randle case," she said. "So that's what I'm doing."

After the shocker I had just gotten in court, I could not handle any more bad news. I held my breath. "I'm listening," I said as I made a right and headed into the underground parking garage of the O'Reilly & Finney office building.

"Well, you're going to freak out when you hear this." Haley sounded like a kid who couldn't wait to tell a big secret.

"Just tell me," I said, still refusing to breathe.

But Haley didn't say anything. "I'm listening, Haley," I said again, even more impatient now.

Still no response.

"Haley, are you there?"

I looked down at my BlackBerry. *Shoot!* I had apparently lost my signal when I entered the underground garage. I rounded a curve to the second level, pulled into a parking stall and hopped out of my SUV. I took one elevator to the lobby of the building and another one to the twelfth floor. I squeezed out of the elevator without waiting for the doors to open completely and walked straight past my office and into Haley's. I didn't realize how winded I was until I came to a panting stop inside Haley's doorway.

"I lost you when I drove into the garage," I said, my chest heaving underneath my black Evan Picone blazer. "What's going on?"

She pointed to a chair in front of her desk. "I think you'll want to be sitting down when you hear this."

Something told me not to object. I took a seat, dumping my purse and satchel on the floor next to me. I prayed that Haley was just being overly dramatic. "Okay, let's hear it."

Haley rested her forearms on her desk. "Porter just got a call from somebody in Human Resources at Micronics. Karen Carruthers is dead."

I could tell by the way she looked at me that she expected me to go into meltdown mode. It took a second for me to process her words.

"What do you mean, she's dead?"

"I mean, she's dead. As in no longer alive."

"How?"

"Car accident. Her car went off a cliff up on Mulholland."

My heart instantly went out to the woman. I had only

met Karen Carruthers a few times, but I could imagine the fear she must have felt as her car plunged off that cliff. I had driven Mulholland once during a heavy storm. The street was long and winding with lots of blind curves. Rain or shine, it could be a dangerous strip of road.

"When?" I asked.

"Five days ago. She apparently died the same day you turned down that settlement offer." Haley's eyes were drenched with glee. "Some hikers found her body trapped inside the wreckage."

Every muscle in my body tightened in alarm. I might be able to keep Hamilton and Reggie from learning about those other sexual harassment cases, but I could not hide the fact that Micronics's most important witness would not be testifying at trial because she was dead. There was no way they would settle the case now. They would insist on going forward, knowing that Micronics's case would be severely handicapped by having to rely on Carruthers's videotaped deposition to tell her story.

I stood up so fast I suffered an attack of vertigo.

"I guess you really regret not taking that thirty thousand, huh?" Haley said.

It would have given me tremendous pleasure to reach over and slap the girl. If she had tried harder to reach me when she got that fax, this case would have been settled last week.

"By the way," I said, grabbing my purse and satchel from the floor, "I didn't appreciate you talking to Porter about that settlement offer before I had a chance to."

Haley nonchalantly waved a hand in the air. Her nails were a shimmery lilac. Yesterday they were a soft red.

How in the hell did the girl find time to change nail polish every night?

"Excuse me, but I didn't think it was any big secret." She raked her fingers through her blond curls. "He *is* the partner in charge of the case."

I did not want to argue with the girl. I just wanted her to know that if she was trying to screw me, I knew what was up. "And that trial strategy memo you prepared," I said, "you should've shown it to me before giving it to Porter."

"Didn't I copy you on the e-mail I sent to Porter?" she said with patently feigned concern. She turned away and started pecking on her keyboard. "I certainly meant to. Let me double-check my outgoing e-mails."

I waited as she went through her ruse.

She glanced up at me and shrugged. "I guess I didn't. I'm really sorry. I'll send you a copy right now."

"You should've been spending that time working on the pretrial documents," I said. "If I were you, I'd be a little more careful about how I apportioned my time."

She smirked in response to my scolding. "I don't know if you know it," Haley said, "but my mother's on the Ninth Circuit and my father's a highly regarded political consultant. Both are Harvard Law grads, so I grew up reading legal decisions for fun."

"And your point is what?"

"My point is, I'm far more versed in the law than your average second-year associate. I don't need to be micromanaged."

My vertigo returned. "Haley, I don't have time to micromanage you or anybody else," I said. "Just remember that *I'm* the senior associate on this case. Not you." I walked out before she could respond.

Back at my office, I closed the door and paced. The Randle case was supposed to be my shining moment before the partnership vote, but it was exploding in my face. Even if Reggie and Hamilton never found out about the other cases, there was no way I could win without having Karen Carruthers take the witness stand to tell her story. You needed emotion to sway a jury in a sexual harassment case. Carruthers had been quiet and sullen during her deposition. The jury wouldn't feel a lick of sympathy for her.

I opened the middle drawer of my desk and took out a bottle of Advil, swallowing two of the tiny rust-colored pills without water. I stared out at the L.A. skyline. Something wasn't right. First, an extremely damaging memo that should have been produced months ago, wasn't. Then, the head of HR, who claimed he knew nothing about the memo, wanted the case settled ASAP—at any cost. Add to that, the unexplained departures of both the in-house attorney and the primary HR contact. And now, the only witness who could tell the company's side of the story was dead.

I looked at the clock. It was after five. I picked up the phone and dialed Special, my best friend and confidante. Besides my husband, Special was the only person who could cheer me up whenever I was in a funk.

"Are you going to happy hour at Little J's tonight?" I asked.

"Girl, why're you asking me a silly question?" Special

replied. "It's Tuesday, ain't it? I'm walking through the door right now."

"I'm on my way there to meet you," I said. "I just had the day from hell."

CHAPTER 12

It took me fifteen minutes to make the drive from my office to Little J's at Eleventh and Olive. I stepped into the darkened club and paused near the dance floor and watched for a minute as the thirty-and-over set grooved to the Isley Brothers' "Living for the Love of You." The song immediately eased my anxiety.

I squeezed through the packed crowd and headed down a narrow hallway that led to the rear of the club. A short flight of stairs took me to the second level, which held another spacious dance floor. I spotted Special sitting in a circular booth, snuggled up with an attractive, well-dressed man who was not one of her regulars.

Special yelled out and waved me over. "Hey, girlfriend!"

When I got to her table, she leaned over to give me a big hug. "Meet my new friend, Jesse," she beamed.

I slid into the booth across from them. "Nice to meet you," I said.

Even though Special had a head of thick, shoulder-length hair, she was wearing a short, reddish-brown wig that had a girlish pageboy cut. I had never known anybody who changed hairstyles as often as Special. She was three inches short of six feet and had squeezed her tall, shapely frame into a tight turquoise skirt and a frilly, low-cut blouse.

"Jesse's a Southern boy." Special grinned.

Jesse nodded and smiled, exposing nice white teeth.

When a waitress arrived with drinks, Jesse sent the woman back to get a Diet Coke for me, but not before tipping her five bucks. Special cast me a look that shouted *big spender*.

"Vernetta and I went to USC together," Special bragged. "We go way back." Special neglected to mention, however, that her college career ended early, due to too much partying and not enough studying.

"USC, huh?" Jesse said. "Two college girls. That's real cool. I bet y'all ski, play golf, all that fancy stuff." He picked up a huge strawberry from a dessert plate piled high with hors d'oeuvres and stuffed it into his mouth, stem and all.

"I'm lousy on the golf course," I admitted, "but I can hold my own on the slopes. And Special's not too bad herself."

"I knew it. I knew it," Jesse said, talking with his mouth full. "I bet y'all can learn me how'da ski."

Deep lines of frustration appeared across Special's normally wrinkle-free forehead. She leaned in closer to Jesse. "What did you say, sweetie?" Even in the dim lighting, I could see the horror in my friend's eyes.

"Can y'all learn me how'da ski?" Jesse repeated.

Special spoke her next words slowly and softly, as if she were talking to a first-grader. "No, sweetie, I don't think we're good enough to *teach* you how to ski."

"Aw c'mon." He picked up a cube of cheddar cheese from the plate in front of him. "I learn fast."

Special looked over at me, her eyes signaling defeat. "Vernetta, ain't that K.C. over there?" She pointed a finger across the room. "Jesse, we'll be right back."

Before he could swallow the cheese and crackers he had just chucked down his throat, Special had snatched her purse from the table, slid around to my side of the booth and practically pushed me to the floor in her haste to escape. I had trouble keeping up with her as she stalked toward the stairs.

"I hate grown ass men who can't conjugate verbs!" Special complained as we zipped downstairs.

When we got to the first floor, I took off in the direction of an empty table at the back of the club. But Special stayed put, her arms defiantly folded across her chest. "I don't want to sit way back there," she moaned.

I backtracked and grabbed her by the forearm. "Don't worry," I said, tugging her along, "the men can still see you."

"If I don't meet anybody decent tonight, you're going out with me next weekend," Special said, reluctantly following.

"I'll probably be free," I said. "As hard as Jefferson's been working lately, I doubt he'll make it home next weekend either."

Special pointed a finger in my face. "Girl, I keep telling you, we need to roll down to San Diego and check everything out. One of the secretaries at my job just found out her husband had another wife and kid living up in Bakersfield." Special was about to enter her eighth year as a manager for Telecredit and always had some wild story to tell about one of her coworkers.

We sat down at a cocktail table for two. "Special, I trust my husband," I said.

"Trust my ass," Special said. "You have to keep a brother in check. History should've taught you that."

"History? What are you talking about?"

"Hillary trusted Bill. Kobe Bryant's wife trusted him. And let's not even talk about Jesse Jackson."

"Whatever, Special," I said. "I'm not here to talk about Jefferson. One of my cases is about to explode in my face."

Special instantaneously perked up, always interested in hearing about my legal dramas. She scooted her chair closer to the table.

I leaned in until my head almost touched hers. "First, I'm dealing with this second-year associate who thinks she's superlawyer," I whispered. I told her about the Micronics fax, the strategy memo and how Haley had blabbed to Porter about my missed settlement opportunity.

"That little girl is hella bold," Special said.

"There's more," I continued. "The opposing counsel, Reggie Jenkins, who can't litigate his way out of a paper bag, surprised me in court today by bringing in another attorney as lead counsel. A very, very good attorney."

Special dismissed my concerns with a flick of her wrist. "Girl, stop trippin'. If you can whip one attorney, you can whip 'em all. You're pretty good in that courtroom. I've seen it with my own eyes."

I inhaled. "Wait. You haven't heard the worst part. I just found out that my star witness—"

"Well, well, well. Fancy meeting you here."

When I looked up, my throat constricted at the sight of

Hamilton Ellis, drink in hand, taking up far too much of my personal space. It took all the bladder control I could muster to keep from relieving myself right then and there. *How long had he been standing there?*

I scanned the club. It was too noisy for Hamilton to have heard anything I had just shared with Special. I took a long breath. I definitely wouldn't be discussing another case in Little J's anytime soon.

"Hello, Mr. Ellis," I said, looking up at him.

"Please, counselor, call me Hamilton." He was talking to me, but his eyes were glued on Special. "Aren't you going to introduce me to the lovely lady here?" He took a sip of his drink.

Special treated Hamilton to a smile wide enough to drive a bus through.

"Special Moore, meet Hamilton Ellis, my new opposing counsel," I said dryly, pointing from Special to Hamilton.

"Special," Hamilton said, mulling over her name. "I like that. So are you?" His eyes were sending heat rays directly to her exposed chest.

"My mama and daddy certainly think so."

"Well, that's good enough for me."

I did not like the sparks whizzing past my head. Having Special hook up with Hamilton was a complication I didn't need. I had to cut this short.

"May I have this dance?" Hamilton said, gallantly extending his hand to Special.

Before I could think up a legitimate reason to protest, my best friend obediently clasped hands with my newest rival and pranced off behind him to the dance floor. I watched them do a sexy cha-cha, moving smoothly to the music as if they had been lifetime partners on "Soul Train." With the help of Special's two-inch heels, they were almost eye-to-eye. As Hamilton eased in close enough to bend down and lodge his nose into her cleavage, Special did not give him the usual brush-off she reserved for men she only wanted to tease.

After the third song, they returned to the table, still hand in hand. Except for a few beads of perspiration along her hairline, Special showed no other visible signs of the extended aerobic workout. She could dance up a funk and never get funky. Hamilton slipped out of his jacket and slung it over his right shoulder.

When he took a chair from another table and sat down at ours, I pounced out of my seat as if I had springs attached to my butt. "We were just leaving," I said hurriedly. "You ready, girl?"

Special sat as still as a Macy's mannequin. "I'm not ready to leave yet." She spoke in a pouty baby voice.

I gave her a stern look, but she ignored it.

"Well, just walk me across the street to my car," I said. "I'll drop you back out front so you can return to your new *friend*." Once I got her outside, I could give her the lowdown on Hamilton and nip any puppy love action in the bud.

"Let me have that honor." Hamilton emptied his glass.

"Never mind," I said, snatching my purse from the table. "I'll be fine."

"No, I insist." Hamilton winked at Special. "I'll be right back," he said, pushing his chair back from the table. "You stay pretty."

CHAPTER 13

We walked out of Little J's and across the street in silence. The parking lot had sufficient lighting, but as I glanced up and down the deserted street, I was actually glad that Hamilton had insisted on escorting me out.

"Your girl's really cool," he said, slipping his left hand into the pocket of his slacks.

"That she is," I replied. I was not thrilled about this development, but it probably wasn't worth raising a stink over. Hamilton was a busy man. He would not have the time or inclination to call Special five times a day just to tell her how lucky he was to be with her.

"Look, I'm not one of those lawyers who gets off on clashing with my opposing counsel," Hamilton said.

"Neither am I."

"Then why the cold shoulder?" he asked.

"I didn't know I was giving you one."

"Okay, my bad." He looked at me as if he were trying to determine whether I could be trusted. "Truce?"

"Truce," I said, but my guard was still firmly in place. I hit the remote control button on my key ring, unlocking the driver-side door of my Land Cruiser. Hamilton gently took my elbow and helped me climb inside.

"What a gentleman," I said, smiling. I put the key in the ignition and rolled down the window. "Thanks for walking me out."

"Anytime," Hamilton said, smiling back at me. "You know, I spent some time reviewing Randle's videotaped deposition before coming over here. I have to tell you, he's pretty convincing. This case is going to come down to credibility."

I quietly cleared my throat. He was absolutely right. I could play snatches of Karen Carruthers's taped deposition, but it would not be nearly as effective as having her present in court to tell her story. The jury would be much more apt to sympathize with Henry Randle, who would be sitting right there in front of them. It was imperative for me to get the case settled before they found out about Carruthers's death.

"Karen Carruthers is pretty credible herself," I said.

"We'll see about that. If Randle's story is true, that means hers isn't. Now, I don't usually play my hand like this, but you should know we just retained a private investigator."

"Sounds like you're grasping at straws," I said, laughing cockily. "But if your investigator stumbles across a smoking gun, you be sure to let me know."

Hamilton chuckled. "I like your balls, girl. You don't scare easily. We could use a dynamic sister like you at my firm."

"You making me a job offer?" I asked.

"Maybe. When the time is right."

"No thanks," I said. "I expect to make partner at O'Reilly & Finney. As a matter of fact, the partnership vote should take place a week or so after the Randle trial ends."

Hamilton dropped his head dramatically and stared at the ground. "Losing a trial for a big client like Micronics right before that vote is going to be pretty embarrassing."

I purposely waited a beat. "But *I'm* not going to lose. If I were you, I'd be trying to work out a settlement."

"I have to say, I find it a little strange that you suddenly want to settle after turning down a hell of an offer," Hamilton said.

I shrugged. "As much as I'd like to take you on again, I have to admit that I probably acted a little rashly in turning down Reggie's offer."

"Whatever you say," Hamilton said. "But you should know that if and when we do talk settlement with you again, we'll probably be looking for something in the seven-figure range."

Seven figures! I felt tiny pin prickles along the back of my neck. "You're kidding me, right?" As much as Micronics wanted out of the case, there was no way they would pay seven figures to resolve it.

"I think my boy's allegations about Micronics's fraudulent billing only touched the tip of the iceberg," Hamilton said. "I'm counting on my investigator to uncover what's really going on."

"Whatever," I said, the only response I could think of. I attempted to put the SUV into Reverse, but it lurched forward, causing Hamilton to jump out of the way.

"You trying to win the case by running me over?" he

said playfully. "Truce, remember?" He made a peace sign with his fingers. "This is a job, my sister. Just a job."

Without warning, Hamilton leaned his head through my open window and planted a kiss on my cheek. "In a few weeks, when I'm kicking your ass all over the courtroom, remember that kiss and what a nice guy I really am."

I cut my eyes at him as hard as I could, then screeched off.

CHAPTER 14

On Friday morning, three days after my parking lot conversation with Hamilton, I was standing in line at the Starbucks in the lobby of the O'Reilly & Finney office building when an *L.A. Times* headline caught my attention. *Faulty Micronics Navigation System Blamed for Crash of U.S. Transport Plane in Iraq.*

I started to step out of line and grab a copy of the newspaper, but I was up next. The clerk, who took my order five days a week, gave me a look that said she hated to see me coming.

"Caramel Macchiato with non-fat milk, sugar-free vanilla syrup—four shots—an extra shot of espresso and hold the whipped cream." She hurriedly scribbled my order on the side of a small cup that Starbucks insisted on calling tall.

I paid for my coffee as well as a copy of the *Times,* then grabbed one from the newspaper stand. The article stated that twelve U.S. soldiers had been killed in Iraq when their transport plane crashed outside Baghdad a week earlier. Preliminary reports blamed the accident on a mechanical defect in the plane's navigation system, which was manufactured by Micronics Corporation. I read further and lost my breath when I saw a reference to Micronics's GAP-7 Program.

Alarm bells sounded in my head. *Randle had alleged fraudulent billing on the GAP-7 Program.*

When I heard my name being called, I grabbed my drink and headed for the elevators. For the past few days, I had been racking my brain for a way to get Hamilton and Reggie to the negotiating table without signaling that I was running scared. So far, luck was on my side as far as the news about Karen Carruthers. I found out that Randle was visiting relatives in Atlanta, so he probably had not heard about her death yet. Fortunately, the local media had not reported the accident because a recent spate of freeway shootings had dominated TV and newspaper coverage all week. But I knew I only had a matter of days, if that long, before Hamilton and Reggie found out. Did the *Times* story about the GAP-7 Program add another twist to the case?

I heard the ping of an available elevator car and took it to the twelfth floor. When I arrived at my office, I set my coffee on the corner of my desk, opened a file drawer and pulled out all four volumes of Randle's deposition transcript. Micronics's former in-house attorney had taken Randle's deposition before the case was transferred to O'Reilly & Finney, so I never had a chance to depose Randle myself. I flipped to the index in the back of each volume and wrote down every page that referenced the GAP-7 Program.

An hour later, I had reread every allegation Randle had made about the program. GAP-7 stood for Global

Assisted Positioning system. Randle's complaints were limited to claims that Micronics had overbilled the Air Force for the program. He had made no allegations, pro or con, about the navigation system's technical capabilities. That made sense, of course, since he was an accountant in the Finance Department, not an engineer.

Micronics had always insisted that Randle's allegations of overbilling were untrue. And based on the documentation they had provided to me, that appeared to be the case. An outside consultant brought in to audit the accounts Randle had identified also confirmed that nothing was amiss.

I took a sip of my coffee and was disappointed that it was now lukewarm. I did not know what I had expected to find in Randle's deposition transcript. I was just glad there was nothing about the GAP-7 Program that might further sink my case. Hopefully, if Hamilton or Reggie saw the *Times* story they would not link it to the Randle case. After draining the rest of my cold coffee, I decided to put Henry Randle and Micronics Corporation out of my mind and focus on my other cases.

Just before noon, I was inches from the doorway of my office, purse in hand, when the telephone rang. I had a one o'clock hair appointment and I had just enough time to make a stop at Jack in the Box before hauling it over to the Emerald Chateau in Inglewood. I tried to ignore the ringing telephone, but force of habit compelled me to check the caller ID display. It was Special, so I picked up.

"I think I'm in love," Special swooned.

"And I love you, too," I said, laughing.

"Not you," she said dreamily. "That fine ass Hamilton Ellis. I think this is fate. We were just sitting there talking about your case and Hamilton appeared right before our eyes. The Lord works in mysterious ways, don't He?"

"Special, you just met the man three days ago. I think you need to slow your roll. And I told you he's one of the biggest players in L.A."

"A player can only play a woman who lets herself get played," she said. "I know how to handle my business. The man just sent me four dozen of the most beautiful yellow tulips I've ever seen. He called my secretary and found out my favorite flower. I sure do deserve his ass."

"Just be careful," I said. "I really don't want you to get hurt."

"If anybody's going to get hurt, it's him, not me," Special insisted. "I've already got that brother's nose wide open. We had lunch at the Water Grill on Wednesday and dinner last night at this cute little Italian place on Venice. Tomorrow night we're going to one of your favorite spots, Crustacean."

"I'm telling you, Special, you need to slow down. At least give the man time to breathe."

"This is my fish," Special replied. "You let me worry about reeling him in."

"Okay, whatever you say. Just make sure you don't tell him anything I told you about the Randle case."

"Girl, if you tell me that one more time, I'm gonna pull off my wig and throw it out the window."

"All right, all right."

"Anyway," Special said, "I was calling because I need

to borrow your green earrings with the silver beads. They'll look good with this green leather miniskirt I'm wearing tomorrow night."

"You got it," I said. Maybe Special's hooking up with Hamilton was not such a bad thing, after all. If Hamilton was all tied up with her, he might not be as focused on the Randle case.

"Just drop by before six," I said. "I have a banquet to attend. You're really going all out for Mr. Ellis. I hope it pays off for you."

"It will," she said, full of confidence. "If he's still spending big cash in three months, then it's on."

I laughed. "Girl, Hamilton Ellis is not waiting three months to get with you."

"Oh, he'll wait," Special said, even more emboldened. "A man like Hamilton is all about the chase. And when that brother sees how hot I look tomorrow night, his ass'll chase me for as long as it takes."

CHAPTER 15

A lawyer of Joseph Porter's stature was accustomed to giving orders, not taking them. So he was not pleased about the call from Micronics Corporation demanding his presence at the General Counsel's office at two o'clock on a Friday afternoon.

It further perturbed him that the underling who delivered the message had no information regarding the specific nature of the meeting. Only that it involved a highly confidential matter.

Porter checked his Timex, then picked up O'Reilly & Finney's *New Business Report* from his in-basket and stared at it in disgust. The report listed six new cases for Jim O'Reilly and zero for himself. Client development was not Porter's strong suit. He despised the idea of prostituting himself by wining and dining people he didn't know or care to. It violated his sense of ethics. Good lawyers did not have to beg for work. Clients came to them.

He also loathed the fact that Jim O'Reilly was running the firm. Porter considered himself far brighter and a much better administrator. On top of that, he consistently billed more hours than any other partner in the firm. But when you happened to be the grandson of the firm's founding partner and an egomaniac to boot, some things simply fell into your lap whether you deserved them or not. Unfortunately for Porter, the managing partner title was not the only thing O'Reilly had stolen from him.

Porter tossed the report into his trash receptacle and glanced at his watch again. It was time to leave. He grabbed his briefcase and headed for the door.

As was his custom, Porter arrived exactly fifteen minutes early and was shown into an empty conference room. Porter hated wasting time. In his world, time literally was money. He pulled out a copy of the *Daily Appellate Report* and started browsing the day's new court decisions.

When the door to the conference room opened eleven minutes after the hour, three men with grim expressions stepped inside. Porter recognized Bob Bailey, Micronics's General Counsel, and Rich Ferris, the VP of HR, but not the third man.

"Good afternoon, Joe," Bailey said. "Thanks for coming by on such short notice."

Porter extended his hand and gave him a curt smile. "I prefer Joseph."

"Forgive me," the General Counsel replied awkwardly.

Porter greeted Ferris and the other man, who was introduced as Nathaniel Hall, Micronics's Chief Financial Officer. The three executives sat on one side of the eight-foot table, leaving Porter alone on the other.

Bailey did not waste time with small talk. "We wanted to speak with you about the Randle case," he began. "We're concerned about the fact that Ms. Henderson has not gotten it settled. We—"

"I'm confident that we can get it resolved," Porter interrupted. "Though perhaps not as quickly as you might like." He hated groveling. He wanted to tell all three of them to back off and let O'Reilly & Finney do the job Micronics was paying them to do.

Ferris, the HR exec, gripped the edge of the table with both hands. "It needs to be settled now. Before they learn about Ms. Carruthers's death."

Their high level of anxiety about getting rid of the case signaled to Porter that Micronics probably had something to hide. Something significant. CFOs did not attend meetings involving employment cases. Neither did general counsels.

This was not the first time the company's executives had sat before him sweating bullets over the possibility of having their dirty laundry exposed. After Enron and Sarbanes-Oxley, every top executive in America wanted to avoid even the appearance of an impropriety that might land them in jail.

"Hamilton Ellis is the lead attorney on the case now. He's a pretty savvy lawyer. We can't just snap our fingers and settle the case," Porter said. "But I'll be sure to communicate the urgency of your wishes to Ms. Henderson."

"We've had enough communications," the General Counsel replied. "We need resolution."

Ferris nodded. "You may not be aware of it, but Randle's attorney has been trying to stir up some media attention," Ferris said. Hall, the CFO, had yet to open his mouth.

It was not Porter's job to put a muzzle on opposing counsel. "I don't watch much TV," Porter replied unapologetically.

"Even if you did," the General Counsel said, "you probably wouldn't have seen Mr. Jenkins's performance a few nights ago. He was on some public affairs talk show on one of the local cable channels." Bailey pulled a videotape from a large envelope and handed it to Ferris, who walked over to a TV monitor built into the wall and slipped the tape into a VCR machine. Ferris remained standing while the tape played.

The grainy picture showed Jenkins sitting on a shabby-looking set decorated with a chair and love seat that looked like Goodwill rejects. A dusty fake cactus stuffed inside a straw basket appeared close to tipping over. The whole room had a faded appearance that had nothing to do with the quality of the videotape.

"I know for a fact that Micronics had at least six confirmed cases of sexual harassment in the last five years," Jenkins ranted. "Yet my client—the only black man falsely accused of this heinous offense against women—was the only one they fired."

The host of the show, who resembled a thinner version of Al Sharpton, sat across from Jenkins and pitched him one softball question after another. In response to each inquiry, Jenkins went into a long, repetitious diatribe about how Micronics had bilked the Air Force out of thousands of dollars on an Air Force contract and fired his client based on trumped-up charges of sexual harassment for trying to expose the fraud.

"I think we've seen enough," Bailey interrupted. Ferris hit the Pause button and returned to his seat.

Porter did not wait for the General Counsel's next

words. He had no idea how Jenkins found out about the cases in that memo, but it was not his job to play spin doctor. "I'm afraid we can't keep Jenkins from talking to the media, and I use that term loosely with respect to what we just saw. If I'd known you wanted to discuss the Randle case, I would've invited Ms. Henderson along." Porter could not have looked any more indifferent.

"She's the very reason we called this meeting." The General Counsel suddenly looked uneasy. "We have reason to believe that Ms. Henderson has committed a very serious ethical breach."

CHAPTER 16

I returned from my hair appointment just after four and found my secretary, Shelia, packing up to leave.

Shelia followed me into my office with a worried look on her face. "I have to tell you something that I'm not supposed to be telling you," Shelia said after she had closed the door.

Loyalty was Shelia's middle name. She had worked for O'Reilly & Finney for more than fifteen years and had seen hoards of attorneys come and go. She was only ten years my senior, but still treated me like a daughter. "Just before you got here, I got a call from Joseph Porter's secretary," Shelia began. "She asked me to bring over your cell phone records for the last six months."

I was putting away my purse, but Shelia's words stopped me in my tracks. "My cell phone records? Did she say why?"

Shelia glanced behind her at the closed door. "No, but she did say Mr. Porter was calling from his car, and that he left specific instructions directing us not to tell you about his request."

I had never seen Shelia look so troubled. I sat down behind my desk. "Why would Porter want my cell phone records? And why not ask *me* for them?"

"I think it may have something to do with the Randle case," Shelia said.

"What makes you think that?"

"Right before his secretary called, Haley went into your office and took some of the Randle files. And when I delivered your cell phone records to Mr. Porter's office, Haley was sitting in there with the files."

She waited for me to speak, but I was too stunned.

"I don't know what's going on, but thanks for having my back, Shelia." I gave her a hug.

She walked out, then popped her head in again. "That haircut is the bomb."

"Thanks." I absently ran my fingers through my hair.

What in the world was Porter up to? Had Haley run to Porter with something else to try to screw me? I thought about giving O'Reilly a call to see if he knew anything, but doing that would reveal that Shelia had tipped me off.

I pulled out the drawer behind my desk to see if I could determine exactly which files Haley had taken. All of the deposition transcripts, the pleadings files and my interview notes were gone. Maybe Porter had decided that he would get the case settled himself. But there was no reason for him to do that without telling me first. And that still didn't explain why he wanted my cell phone records.

I tried to finish revising a discovery motion in another case, but I couldn't think straight. Haley and Porter were up to something and I needed to know exactly what it was.

I got up and took off toward Haley's office.

CHAPTER 17

I knocked lightly on Haley's open door, but she was staring at her computer screen and apparently didn't hear me.

I was practically standing over her desk when she finally noticed me. The girl jumped a good ten inches in her seat, then hurriedly clicked out of her computer screen before I could see what she had been reading so intensely.

What in the hell was going on?

Haley swung around to face me. A different bouquet of flowers sat on the corner of her desk. Shelia had told me that Haley had fresh flowers delivered every Tuesday and Friday morning and got her nails done twice a week. She even had a professional masseuse come to the office three times a month to give her a fifteen-minute neck massage.

"I just dropped by to say hello," I said, unable to come up with something more creative. "Since we're going to be working together, we might as well get to know each other."

The look in the girl's bold blue eyes told me she saw right through me.

"Great," Haley said, her voice just as insincere as mine. "Have a seat."

"I finally had a chance to read that trial strategy memo you prepared." I was hoping that a compliment would loosen her up. "You did a really good job. You must've seen a lot of trials when you clerked."

"Yes, quite a few."

Haley evidently didn't believe that my friendly overture was legit and was not about to make this easy for me.

"Too bad we won't be able to take the Randle case to trial," I said. "It would have been a good experience for you."

"Really? I heard it was definitely going to trial," Haley said.

"And where did you hear that?"

"One of my law school classmates works at Hamilton Ellis's firm. Ellis is apparently pretty psyched about trying the case."

I felt my stomach lurch. "Really? What else did your friend tell you?"

"That was about it," Haley said.

I tried to keep my smile from turning into a smirk. "Anything else going on in the Randle case that I should know about?"

"Nope. You're the senior associate on the case. You would certainly know more than me." Haley paused and a contemplative look glazed her face. "How well do you know Mr. Ellis?" she asked.

"What do you mean?"

"I hear he's pretty active with the local African-American Bar association. You ever have an opportunity to interact with him?"

What was she getting at? "That's a rather strange question," I said.

"Oh...well...I just think it's good to learn as much as you can about your opposing counsel. His habits, his weaknesses, his likes, his dislikes. You never know what little tidbit can help you at trial."

"I tried a case against him a few years ago," I said. "None of that ever came into play. I tend to focus on the facts of the case. Not the idiosyncrasies of the attorney who's trying it."

Haley shrugged and twirled one of her blond ringlets around her finger. "I'm just curious. What's he like?"

"If I didn't know better, Haley, I'd think you had a crush on the man."

She giggled like we were best girlfriends. "He is pretty darn hot, don't you think?"

Haley was trying to lead me someplace that I did not want to go. "The only man I'm interested in is my husband," I said.

"Oh, I forgot that you were married," she said. "What does your husband do?"

"He's an electrician."

"Oh, that's nice. It says a lot about you that you could marry a guy who's not on your level."

Did the girl just insult me, my husband or both of us? "Exactly what makes you think my husband isn't on my level?"

"Oh, don't misunderstand me," Haley said. The attitude in my voice must have told her she needed to backtrack. "What I mean is, a lot of women with as much education as we have wouldn't even look sideways at a guy who didn't have a college degree. I think you have to be very secure with yourself to be with a man who's not a professional. The disparity in income alone can create lots of problems in a marriage."

"That's never been a problem for us," I said, with ice in my voice. "As a matter of fact, the company he *owns* is doing all of the electrical work for a big strip mall in San Diego right now. And on top of that, my husband happens to be one of the brightest men I know." I felt stupid for trying to defend Jefferson's worth to this girl.

"Oh, so he owns his own company. Then he *must* be a pretty smart guy. How does he oversee a project way down in San Diego?"

"He stays down there during the week and comes home on weekends."

She gave me a look of sympathy. "That must be hard. You must miss him a lot."

"Work's been keeping me pretty busy," I said.

Coming to Haley's office had been a mistake. A major mistake. I did not like the way she was trying to get all up in my personal business. I got up to leave.

"If you hear anything else about the Randle case, be sure to let me know," I said.

Haley treated me to her trademark bogus smile. "Will do."

CHAPTER 18

When I got back to my office, I was dying to hear my husband's voice. I dialed his cell phone and was thrown when a female answered instead of Jefferson.

"Who's this?" I asked.

"Who's *this?*" the voice fired back.

"This is Ms. Henderson. I'd like to speak to Jefferson."

"I'm sorry. He isn't available to take your call right now. Would you like to leave a message?"

"Yeah. Tell him he needs to call his *wife* as soon as he *is* available."

I heard a quiet gasp, then muffled voices. "I'm sorry. I didn't know you were his wife." She sounded rather young and her tone was much more courteous now. "Jefferson's right here."

My husband's words spilled out quickly, before I could get mine out. "Don't trip, babe," Jefferson chuckled. "That was just LaKeesha, she's the college sophomore we hired to help us out around the office." I heard a loud squeak, then what sounded like a door being shut.

"Why are you walking outside the trailer? You can't talk in front of LaKeesha?"

"C'mon, babe, don't trip. See, you wouldn't have this

problem if you used my last name. When she heard you say Henderson, she didn't know you were my wife."

"Why is she answering your cell phone in the first place?"

"She's screening my calls for me. The phone rings so much I can't get anything done."

The explanation sounded plausible, but I was still concerned.

"C'mon, babe, don't trip. How're you doing?"

"Don't change the subject, Jefferson. You didn't even tell me you guys had hired an assistant. How old is she and what does she look like?"

He laughed again. "What you wanna know that for? Don't you trust me?"

"I trust you. So answer my question."

"Uh, I think she's twenty-one," Jefferson said, stalling.

"Twenty-one? Shouldn't she be almost out of college by now?"

"She got a late start," Jefferson said.

"And what does she look like?"

"I don't know."

"Yes you do."

"If you really wanna know, most of the guys around here say she looks like Beyoncé, but has a body more like Serena Williams. But I don't really see it."

When I went mute, Jefferson started cracking up. "C'mon, babe. I'm just messing with you. It don't matter what she looks like. She's jailbait as far as I'm concerned and that's not my style. You are."

My lips remained locked in an angry knot.

"I think I like this," Jefferson teased. "I can't

remember you ever acting jealous before. This is really good for my ego."

"You still haven't answered my question, Jefferson," I said. "What does the girl look like?"

"And I'm not going to answer it because it's crazy." Jefferson's voice lost its playfulness. "That youngster don't want nothing to do with a tired ass dude like me. She's helping us around the office. That's all. So let's change the subject."

I rarely felt insecure about my marriage. Jefferson had never given me a reason to distrust him and I knew it was silly for me to have such doubts now.

"C'mon, babe," Jefferson said. "You know where my heart is."

"Your heart ain't what I'm worried about," I said.

He laughed again.

"So when do you think you'll be able to make it home?" I asked.

"Not sure yet. We've run into some more problems, so you probably shouldn't count on me coming home this weekend either. But I'm hoping we'll have everything under control soon."

"I really miss you."

"And I miss you, too," he said. "I promise I'll be home as soon as I can. What you got planned tonight?"

"Absolutely nothing," I sighed. "But tomorrow night I have a banquet to go to."

"Aw, sorry I'll miss it," Jefferson said, feigning disappointment. "I can taste that delicious rubber chicken right now."

This time I laughed.

"Anyway, babe," Jefferson said, "I gotta get out to the worksite."

As I hung up, Special's words came back to me. Perhaps I would have to make some time to drive down to San Diego as she suggested. Just to make sure Ms. LaKeesha was on the up-and-up.

CHAPTER 19

"Homegirl, you definitely need a push-up bra. And bad."

It was close to six o'clock on Saturday night and Special lay stretched out across my bed, browsing through old issues of *Interior Design,* searching for home-decorating tips. She had picked up a side job decorating the homes of a couple of friends and from what I had seen, was actually pretty good at it.

"I'm filling out this dress just fine, thank you very much." I took an admiring look at myself in the full-length mirror on the back of my bedroom door. The short black dress that I had purchased on sale at Nordstrom was definitely me.

"Hey, look at this." Special held up the magazine and pointed to a picture of a purple-and-white striped couch. "This is the same fabric I used to reupholster my couch. You have to come by and see it."

"I can't wait." Merely looking at the gaudy thing made me dizzy. "Here're the earrings you wanted." I tossed them to her, then went back to rummaging through my jewelry box trying to find another pair to match my dress.

"What snooty law firm function are you going to tonight?" Special continued flipping magazine pages.

"The Langston Bar Association's annual banquet. They're honoring one of our partners, Jim O'Reilly."

"Ain't that the black Bar association? What they giving him an award for?"

"He was the lead partner on a *pro bono* case the firm handled for some homeowners in South Central last year. He's getting the award for *Pro Bono* Lawyer of the Year."

"I thought you worked on that case, too?"

"I did. But he's the partner and it's the partner who gets all the glory. Shouldn't you be home getting dressed for your big date with Hamilton?" I asked.

"I've got plenty of time. You know I like to keep my men waiting."

"I'm thinking about making a trip down to San Diego to visit Jefferson," I said. "You still wanna go with me?"

Special sprang up from her prone position and crossed her legs into a pretzel. "What happened?"

"Nothing happened. I was just thinking that it would be easier on Jefferson if I went down there for the weekend, rather than having him come here."

Special eyed me suspiciously. "Remember who you're talking to, okay? What's up?"

After a few seconds of stalling, I decided to come clean. "I called Jefferson's cell phone yesterday and a woman answered."

Special dropped her magazine. "Go on," she said.

I told her about LaKeesha screening Jefferson's calls. "I believe him," I said, "but I just want to check her out."

"Good move," Special said, picking her magazine back

up. "I'll be able to call her number the minute I see her. When are we going?"

"Not sure yet. It depends on what's happening with the Randle case next week." I held up a pair of silver-and-black earrings next to my earlobes. "How do these look?"

"They don't do a thing for that dress. They're not big enough."

"I don't know why I even asked you."

After putting on the earrings and checking myself in the mirror one last time, I scanned the room for my purse. I spotted it on the bed next to Special, but when I looked inside, I didn't see my banquet ticket. I walked into the living room and unzipped my leather satchel, which was sitting on the coffee table. The Micronics fax was the first thing I saw. Just looking at the thing irked me. In fact, everything about the case irked me. I threw the fax down on the coffee table and continued searching for my ticket.

I still had not heard anything about why Porter had asked for my cell phone records yesterday. I ran into Haley an hour or so after leaving her office and she barely looked at me. Those two were definitely up to no good. I was just thankful that I had not gotten a call from Hamilton or Reggie about Karen Carruthers's death.

I finally spotted the ticket in a small side compartment.

"I'm running late," I yelled to Special as I opened the front door. "Lock up for me. And don't take all year to return my earrings."

CHAPTER 20

The foyer outside the main ballroom of the Century Plaza Hotel was packed with most of the city's black elite. I spotted several politicians and judges, a couple of local TV newspeople and, of course, hoards of lawyers.

As I was about to head over to the bar for a Diet Coke, I heard a familiar voice from the rear. "Can a brother get a hug?"

I turned around to find James Willoughby, my best friend from law school, standing in front of me with open arms. We embraced like old friends happy to see each other, which we were. Despite being inseparable all through law school, our respective jobs made it difficult to find time to connect. James worked as a public defender out of East L.A.

"Where's your boy, Jefferson?" James asked.

I smiled to myself. James always tried to sound extra hip when he was around other black folks. He was raised in South Central, but was the nerdiest black man I'd ever met. Over the years, he'd blossomed quite a bit in the looks department. A nice suit and a law degree could make even the blandest man alive look a whole lot better in the eyes of some women. Tonight, James was quite debonair in his black Hugo Boss suit.

"Jefferson's working on a big project in San Diego," I said. "Is Melissa here?" I asked, knowing that she was not. James never brought his white wife to black functions.

"Nah, she starts a new trial on Monday and had to work late." A tall, dark-skinned woman in a tight red dress sashayed by and James was practically wagging his tongue. I wondered sometimes if he regretted crossing the tracks.

All through law school, I had painfully watched as James dated one vicious, self-centered woman—all black—after another. When I suggested that he might have better luck if he looked beyond a pretty face and a big behind, he had angrily warned me to mind my own business. Each woman he dated took his kindness for weakness and squandered what little money he had, wiping her feet on his heart on the way out the door. After a stewardess who was a dead ringer for Alicia Keys used his credit card to buy her real boyfriend a new suit, James declared a permanent moratorium on black women.

That decision had set off a heated, unlawyerly like debate that almost ended our friendship.

"You're just a coward," I had argued, feeling personally maligned by his vow to never date another black woman. "You don't see black women giving up on black men just because a couple of brothers dogged them out."

"That's because they're too busy looking for the next guy to screw over."

"Well, white women aren't necessarily the answer." I was determined to change his mind. "I know plenty of white boys with broken hearts."

"They don't have to be white," James said, "just anything but black."

"So what're you saying about your mama?" I asked.

"I ain't saying a thing about my mama," James shot back. "And I hope you ain't either."

Two months passed before we spoke again, but James stuck with his decision and never looked back. A few years out of law school, James met and married Melissa Feldman, an anorexic-looking Jewish woman from Manhattan. She was an assistant U.S. attorney who prosecuted white-collar criminals. Melissa worked only because she wanted to. She was the first person I had ever met who had a trust fund—a seven-figure trust fund. Her great-grandfather had bought tons of prime real estate in Manhattan and Los Angeles in the forties and fifties and parlayed it into a variety of successful business ventures that would support his offspring for decades to come. Once I had gotten to know Melissa, I had to admit that she was a perfect match for James.

In the midst of giving me a recap of one of his latest trial victories, a devious smile eased across James's lips. "Uh-oh," he said, "here comes trouble."

"What are you talking about?" I glanced over my shoulder to see what James was smiling at.

"That dude who broke your heart right before you met Jefferson is on his way over here."

Before I could remind James that *I* dumped Bradley Davis, not the other way around, the man sidled up to me. He slid his arm around my waist and pulled me to him at the same time he leaned in to kiss me on the cheek.

"Hey, baby," he whispered in my ear. "You look even finer than you did the last time I saw you."

I was a happily married woman, but having Bradley Davis so close still caused me to swoon inside. He was tall and muscular with a shaved head and full, luscious lips. The fresh smell of his cologne stirred up memories I felt guilty recollecting.

I was about to say something cute and flirty when I saw his black Bambi standing off to the side. "Aren't you going to introduce us to your date?" I said instead.

Bradley swept his hand in Bambi's direction but kept his eyes fixed on me. "This is my friend, Briana."

"Hi!" Briana said excitedly, as if someone had pulled a string at the back of her neck.

The girl was a stunning, chestnut brown, with long, shiny hair that was probably her own. I pegged her at twenty-five tops, and she couldn't have been bigger than a size two. But Bambi had a vacant look in her eyes that told me long division without a calculator might be a challenge for her.

"Nice to meet you, Briana," I said. I introduced James, who nearly salivated over the woman.

Bradley's use of the word *friend* to introduce Briana hit a distant nerve. I could still recall him introducing me as his *friend*. Never *girlfriend*. Bradley was a successful patent attorney who knew how to put the *r* in romance. When he was with you, Bradley had a way of making you feel like nobody and nothing else in the world could possibly matter. And the sex was incredible. Rose petals in bed, massage oils in every fragrance and slow, supersensual lovemaking. But after an intense weekend of his undivided attention, it could be days before Bradley might bother to call or even favor you with a return call. I soon wised-up and moved on, despite the slamming sex.

The three of us chatted for a few more minutes, while black Bambi had every guy in the vicinity doing a double take. When we made our way inside, Bradley invited me to sit at his law firm's table, but I declined. It bugged me that just looking at the man could still get me all hot and bothered.

After a predictably bland dinner of roasted chicken and scalloped potatoes, O'Reilly graciously accepted the award for *Pro Bono* Lawyer of the Year. The Langston Bar Association's president explained how O'Reilly and a team of attorneys from our firm had assisted a group of homeowners in South Central whose property had been seized through eminent domain. Thanks to O'Reilly & Finney, the homeowners ultimately received fair market value for their houses as well as hefty relocation allowances.

Dressed in his finest Armani, O'Reilly smiled big and occasionally scratched his head. I had seen him go through the same well-rehearsed motions many times. To the crowd, he looked humble and slightly nervous. But it was all an act. He was as cool and collected as the powerful, successful lawyer his résumé proclaimed him to be.

After thanking the association for honoring him, he launched into the altruistic part of his acceptance speech.

"While it's great for our firm and other firms like ours to provide free legal help to those who can't afford it, we know that's not enough," O'Reilly declared. "Despite the rise in minority enrollment in law schools across the country, the partnership ranks at most firms, including ours, remain essentially white and male." O'Reilly paused to glance around the room.

"At O'Reilly & Finney, we're committed to recruiting bright young minority attorneys. And we fully recognize that getting them through the door isn't enough. We must mentor them so that they can successfully make it to partnership." A chorus of applause caused him to take another brief pause.

"I'd like to take a moment to introduce one of our senior associates whom I've been lucky enough to mentor." O'Reilly stopped and looked around the room again, although he knew exactly where the firm's table was located. "Vernetta, could you please stand?"

I rose from my seat, modestly acknowledged all the looks that came my way and quickly sat back down.

"Vernetta Henderson is one of the best young trial attorneys we have, and I hope to be calling her a fellow partner pretty soon. She was raised in Compton and is also an active member of your organization. It's our hope to recruit more dynamic young attorneys like Vernetta so that our firm begins to reflect the full diversity of this community. Thanks again for this honor."

O'Reilly smiled, exchanged handshakes with the emcee, then lingered at the podium, lapping up the applause.

I smiled over at James, sitting two tables away. I was lapping it up, too.

CHAPTER 21

Across town, Hamilton pulled to a stop in front of Crustacean in Beverly Hills and eased out of the driver's side of his silver Mercedes-Benz S600. He watched with pride as the parking attendants drooled at the sight of Special gracefully gliding out of the passenger door.

She had really outdone herself tonight, Hamilton thought, staring over at her. Her leather skirt was both short and tight enough to double as a tube top and her beige fishnet stockings hugged her legs like the skin on a snake. He was a leg man and Special had a pair that would make Tina Turner turn a mean green. Her low-cut Lycra top was so tight he could calculate the diameter of her nipples.

"What're you staring at?" Special said, smiling at him as they walked arm in arm toward the entrance of the restaurant.

"The beautiful lady I have on my arm," Hamilton replied, opening the door for her.

Special leaned over and parted his lips with hers and gently sucked on the tip of his tongue.

Damn, that turns me on! Hamilton loved being with a woman who did not mind public displays of affection.

Denise, his ex-wife, was always worried about appearances. He glanced over Special's shoulder and spotted two guys at the bar staring at her ass. *Sorry, fellas, all mine tonight.*

As the hostess showed them down a narrow aisle to a staircase in the far corner of the restaurant, every man in the place, and most of the women, too, turned to watch Special prance by. Hamilton had never met a tall woman who was as comfortable with her height as Special. He purposefully lagged behind so he could observe the reaction on everyone's face.

The hostess showed them to a table on the second level, handed them menus and left.

"You look gorgeous tonight," he said as they settled in.

"Thank you, counselor." This time she gave him a full tongue kiss.

A male waiter with blond streaks throughout his black buzz cut walked up to their table. Special ordered a Long Island iced tea and two appetizers—the coconut prawns and the California rolls. Hamilton settled for just a cognac.

Staring at the mounds of flesh bubbling up out of Special's top, Hamilton imagined the feel of his lips brushing across her breasts. He definitely could not wait much longer to get with her. Tonight would have to be the night.

"Hey, sweetie," Special said softly, running her hand along his forearm. "Are you listening to me?"

"I'm sorry," Hamilton said apologetically. "It's hard to concentrate sitting here with somebody as fine as you. What did you say?"

"I was asking how your day went."

"Not bad," he said. He paused as the waiter set their drinks on the table. "Just rescuing my clients from themselves."

Special snuggled up closer to him. "I have something I wanted to talk to you about." Her voice was now extra soft and feminine.

Hamilton's shoulders tensed. He hated it when women wanted to *talk*. Whenever Denise had mentioned that word, it usually meant she had something to bitch about. Hamilton hoped Special was not about to corner him about making a commitment this early in the game.

"Sounds serious." He took a swallow of his drink.

"I'm a pretty good cook," Special said. "I was hoping you'd let me prepare a gourmet meal for you some time soon."

Hamilton smiled. A freak *and* a good cook. He had definitely hit the jackpot. "You name the time and the place, baby, and I'll be there."

Special kissed him again, letting her hand rest on his thigh, dangerously close to his trigger point. He glanced at his Rolex and tried to think of something other than Special's beautiful, naked body. It took every ounce of control he had not to guide her hand to his groin and have her jack him off right there. The waiter reappeared and set the appetizers on the table.

"Can I take your order now?"

"Sure," Special said. She picked up the menu with both hands, holding it so close to her chest that it blocked Hamilton's view of her cleavage. "I'll have the Asian

Caesar salad and the lobster for my main course. And can you bring us some more California rolls? And I think I'm about ready for another Long Island iced tea."

Hamilton scratched his forearm. *She had the appetite of a horse!*

"And what can I get for you, sir?"

"I'll have the shrimp, but hold the garlic noodles."

"You must be doing the no-carb thing," Special said, once the waiter left. "That must be how you stay in such good shape." She playfully fingered the chest area of his V-neck sweater.

He took a quick sip of his cognac. Everything about the woman excited him. Nothing in the world could match the thrill of new pussy. Absolutely nothing. He wrapped his arm around Special's shoulder and kissed her neck. Even her scent turned him on. "Why don't you tell me about your day?"

Hamilton zoned out while Special babbled on and on about the headaches of being a supervisor at Telecredit. He had purposely refrained from asking her anything about Vernetta on their first two dates. Now seemed like an appropriate time to find out if she had any worthwhile information to share.

"How does my competition feel about us hooking up?" he asked.

"She ain't exactly happy about it. But like I told her, *she* works for O'Reilly & Finney, not me."

"Now that's what I like. A woman who runs her own show." He leaned over and kissed her on the neck again.

Hamilton emptied his drink and signaled the waiter for

a refill. "I'm really looking forward to going up against your girl in the Randle case," he said.

"Whoooaaa, cowboy," Special said, holding up her hands and forming a cross with her index fingers. "I've been given specific instructions to avoid any discussion of that case."

"Then you do know something," Hamilton teased.

"I don't know a thing. And my girl is hella paranoid, so let's just change the subject."

The waiter appeared with their dishes and began arranging them on the crowded table.

"Do you guys still serve that chocolate lava cake?" Special asked eagerly.

"Sure do," the waiter replied.

Special turned to Hamilton. "Hey, sweetie, you have to save some room for dessert. The chocolate cake here is absolutely incredible!"

"Okay," Hamilton said, grinning. *You eat up, baby girl. 'Cause I want you strong and sturdy for the workout I've got planned for you tonight.*

CHAPTER 22

It was just after nine o'clock when LaKeesha drove her white Honda Civic into the gates of the construction site and rolled to a stop about twenty feet from the trailer that housed Jones-Parks Electrical. As she stepped out of the car, her stiletto heels sank into the soft dirt. Her ruby-red spandex dress fell just a couple of inches below crotch level.

There's no way Jefferson can resist me tonight.

LaKeesha pulled her book bag higher on her shoulder and gingerly climbed the four steps leading up to the trailer. She stuck her key in the door even though she knew it was probably unlocked.

When she stepped inside, Jefferson looked up from a blueprint spread out on his desk. "Hey, LaKeesha, what're you doing here?"

"I was hoping to get some studying done." She resisted the urge to tug at the hem of her dress, which had crept farther up her thighs. "I was at a party with some friends, but I got bored. I figured I could make better use of my time by coming over here to study."

LaKeesha headed over to Stan's desk. "Is it okay? I promise I won't bother you." She kept her back turned and hoped Jefferson was enjoying the view of her ass.

"No problem," Jefferson said.

He sounded preoccupied, but she planned to fix that very shortly. "How about some coffee?" LaKeesha asked, turning around. She was disappointed to find Jefferson's eyes back on the blueprint.

"That would be great," he said, without looking up.

LaKeesha prepared the coffee, then settled in behind Stan's desk. She opened her psychology book and pretended to read. After a couple of minutes, Jefferson yawned and began rolling up the blueprints.

"You're not leaving, are you?" LaKeesha asked with a bit too much anxiety in her voice.

"Not until I have that cup of coffee." Jefferson wrapped a rubber band around the blueprints and placed them underneath his desk. "LaKeesha, it's not a good idea for you to be here by yourself this late at night. Isn't there someplace else you can study?"

How about your place? "Not really," she said. "The library closes at ten on Saturdays. I live with my grandmother, my sister, her son and two teenage cousins. Trying to study there is impossible."

"Where're your parents?"

"My mom died of breast cancer when I was twelve," LaKeesha said. "I never knew my father." Actually, her father's new Bible-thumping wife had put her out nine months ago. The woman insisted that she dress like a nun and spend every freaking night in church and LaKeesha wasn't having it. The part about her mother, though, was true.

She could tell from Jefferson's expression that he felt sorry for her. *Excellent.*

When the coffee finished brewing, LaKeesha hurried over and poured Jefferson a cup, then walked it over to him. She strolled back to the coffeemaker to pour a second cup for herself.

LaKeesha could not afford to wait much longer for things to get rolling with Jefferson. Londell, the married man she had dated for the past year, had started having a guilty conscience and broke it off with her so he could go to counseling with his boring ass wife. But that was going to be a futile effort. From everything Londell had told her, his wife was too evil and too selfish to keep him or any other man happy. LaKeesha did not understand why married women acted so bitchy. Didn't they realize that there were busloads of women out there willing to treat their man right?

"So what's your major?" Jefferson asked.

Getting next to you. "Psychology," she said. "I want to help people solve their problems." She paused, then softened her voice. "Do you mind if I ask you for some advice?"

"Hey, you're the future psychologist, not me." Jefferson chuckled and took a sip of coffee. "I can't promise you my advice will be worth much, but go ahead."

LaKeesha ran her fingers through her braids. "I'm really having a hard time finding a decent boyfriend."

Jefferson grinned. "If *you* can't find a man, then the brothers around here must be crazy," he said. "Just be patient, the right guy will come along. I didn't get married until I was in my mid-thirties."

"Are you saying I should set my sights on an older man?"

Jefferson smiled. "No, that's not what I meant. You should concentrate on getting your degree. Everything will happen when the time is right."

"I wish I could find a man like you," LaKeesha purred. "You're smart, you own your own business and you seem to really love your wife."

"That I do," Jefferson said.

LaKeesha walked over to the coffee machine and pretended to straighten up. "You ever mess around on her?" She glanced at Jefferson over her shoulder.

"Nope." Jefferson said. He was no longer smiling. "My wife is also my friend. And I don't fuck over my friends."

Sure you don't. Men always professed to be so true blue. But not one had turned her down yet. "Don't get mad at me for saying this," LaKeesha said, bent on her mission, "but if you weren't married, I'd definitely wanna be with you."

Jefferson looked away. "Uh…" He stood up, then quickly sat back down.

But not quickly enough. LaKeesha was certain she had spotted undeniable proof that she had gotten Jefferson aroused.

"Hey, LaKeesha," Jefferson said, "I don't know where this conversation is going, but I think we need to cut it short."

"This conversation can go anywhere you want it to go." She glided across the room and perched on the edge of Jefferson's desk. He wanted her. She could see it in his eyes.

"LaKeesha, you're a very attractive girl," he said. "But I'm married. Happily married."

"I can deal with that," she said, sliding her butt farther back on the desk, allowing her dress to rise even higher.

"But I can't." Jefferson fiddled with his empty coffee cup. LaKeesha could tell that he was nervous. "I think it's about time for you to go home," he said.

So he was going to play hard to get. Fine. She needed a challenge. "Well, why don't you walk me out to my car?"

"You'll be fine, LaKeesha. I'll watch you get to your car from the window."

LaKeesha hopped off the desk, put a hand on her hip and cocked her head to the right. "You don't want to stand up 'cause you don't want me to know you've got a hard-on," she teased. "You got excited just thinking about being with me, so just admit it."

Jefferson did not move for several long seconds. Then he gripped the edge of his desk, slowly pushed his chair back and stood up. No erection in sight.

"Since you've been doing such a good job around here, LaKeesha, I'm going to pretend this conversation never happened." Jefferson spoke with a fatherly firmness. "Now pack up your stuff and go home."

The muscles in LaKeesha's face throbbed with anger and embarrassment. The disapproval in Jefferson's voice reminded LaKeesha of her stepmother. She snatched her book bag and headed for the trailer door.

Jefferson stepped in front of her and pushed the door open. "Drive safely."

As she squeezed past, LaKeesha looked up at him with a wicked smile. *I ain't done yet, boss man. 'Cause what LaKeesha wants, LaKeesha gets.*

CHAPTER 23

Hamilton steered his Benz down Buckingham Drive and spotted a parking space directly in front of Special's apartment building, but on the opposite side of the street. He had been a perfect gentleman all evening and now he expected to be rewarded for his restraint.

"Thanks so much for dinner." Special looked over at him with a demure smile. "I had a great time. Why don't you just double-park and walk me to the door?" Her legs were crossed, revealing far more leg than skirt.

Hamilton ignored her suggestion and concentrated on trying to shake off the urge to reach over and ease his hand between her legs. He pulled into the parking space and cut off the engine.

"You're not going to invite me up for a nightcap?" A street lamp directly above the car cast a soft shadow on Special's face.

"I don't think it's time for that just yet," she said.

Hamilton turned away and bit his bottom lip. This was precisely the reason he refused to date women with self-esteem. It was too much friggin' work. "Exactly how long will I have to wait, Special?" He tried not to sound as frustrated as he felt.

"Not long," she said.

He was about to say something, when she leaned over and quieted him with a long, deep kiss. Before he knew it, Special had snaked her hand underneath his sweater. He couldn't believe how soft her hands were, and he loved the way she gently tugged on his nipples and rubbed his chest hairs between her fingers.

"You know, you're quite the little tease," he said, feeling an erection coming on.

"And you know you get off on it, too," she whispered between kisses.

"Yeah, I do," he said. *But this high school petting stuff is getting old.* "Why don't we just go inside and—"

Special put a finger to his lips. "Until the time is right, how about a *special* treat." In the blink of an eye, she had unbuckled his belt and unzipped his pants.

"Baby, this is really nice," Hamilton moaned as she caressed him. "But can we please just take it inside?"

"In time, sweetie. In time. How does this feel? Does it feel good?"

Hamilton grunted. "Hell yeah, it feels good." He hit a button on the side of his seat, causing it to slowly recline.

"Then tell me," Special said softly. "It turns me on when you talk to me."

"Good, baby," Hamilton muttered, struggling for the right words. "Yeah, uh...um...real good. It feels real good." He had never been able to think straight when his Johnson was experiencing a blood rush. That talking crap took too much energy.

Hamilton confined his words solely to moans and

groans as Special slowly massaged him with a soft, almost featherlike touch that took him to the edge, lured him away, then snatched him back again.

Her touch was so sensuous he had to concentrate hard on not coming. "Oooooh, baby! This is nice...real nice. You're going to make me—" Hamilton felt a sharp wave of cold air hit his exposed groin.

"Gotta go." Special hurled the passenger door open. "We'll have to pick this up some other time."

"Oh, hell nah!" Hamilton yelled, as he struggled to rise from his prone position. "Come back here!" He fumbled frantically for the button on the side of his seat. It took forever for the seat to return to the upright position. In his haste to zip up his pants, Hamilton pinched himself with the zipper. "Owww!"

When the pain had subsided enough for him to breathe, he stumbled out of the car and charged across the street. Special was nowhere in sight. He peered through the double glass doors into the empty lobby of the three-story building. He dialed her apartment code, but Special did not pick up.

"Oh, to hell with this!" he shouted, and stormed back across the street. He snatched open the car door, grabbed his cell phone from the center console and dialed Special's number.

She answered on the fourth ring. "Good evening. I'm Special," she cooed.

"Special, I'm too old for these kind of games!" Hamilton said angrily.

She laughed. "C'mon, sweetie, can't you take a joke?"

"I'm not laughing, Special."

"C'mon, sweetie, don't be mad at me," she said with the seductiveness of a phone sex operator. "I really, really dig you, Hamilton. And by the way, you're absolutely huge."

"Don't play me," he seethed.

"I'm serious. I don't think I've ever had the pleasure of being with a man as well endowed as you are. We're going to have a really great time."

"And exactly when is that going to happen?"

"Soon, baby. Soon. And I promise you it'll be worth the wait. There're still some things I need to know about you before we can go there."

Hamilton laughed bitterly. "Just what in the hell do you need to know about me?"

"Lots of things. Like your favorite position, for example. Do you like it from the front? The back? Do you prefer whipped cream or honey? All that stuff is important, you know."

Damn her! Hamilton slammed his head against the headrest and closed his eyes. He could feel himself getting hard again. He turned his key, starting up the engine. "You're something else, you know that?" he said, some of his anger dissipating.

"Yep, I know," Special said smugly. "Hey, hold on a second. I need to slip off my panties and put on my red silk teddy."

Hamilton dropped his chin to his chest. The image of Special's long, smooth legs in a teddy was enough to make him lose it right there. He turned the steering wheel to the left and made a hasty U-turn.

Hamilton laughed. The girl was definitely working him. He could not remember the last time he had been so turned on. But he was a busy man and he did not have time for high-maintenance babes. When she finally gave it up, he would hit it a couple of times and then move on.

As the car turned off Buckingham and onto Slauson, he did a quick mental check of his little black book, trying to figure out who he could call to alleviate his throbbing hard-on. Both Priscilla, a paralegal at his office, and Katie, a cute redhead who had come onto him in the grocery store last week, were probably at home and neither would give him any flack about showing up on their doorstep after ten o'clock on a Saturday night. In fact, they would both be thrilled to see him. Maybe he could talk them into a threesome.

"Are you still there, sweetie?" Special asked.

"Yeah, I'm here," Hamilton replied. "So…you wanna know what I like?" he said, growing excited again at the thought. "When I walk into the room, I want you butt naked, bent over in front of me, touching your toes. I'll take over from there."

"Umm," Special purred. "That's a new one. But I think I can handle that. Now go on. What else? Tell Special everything you like and exactly how you like it."

CHAPTER 24

At eight o'clock on Monday morning, Porter picked up the telephone but did not immediately dial a number. He hated having to report to Jim O'Reilly like he was some lowly associate. But as the Managing Partner of the firm, O'Reilly had to be updated on the Micronics situation.

Having a client as important as Micronics unhappy with the firm's services was not just Porter's problem, it was the firm's problem. O'Reilly & Finney handled Micronics's employment litigation, as well as their corporate deals, intellectual property matters and business litigation. If Micronics fired the firm, it would mean the loss of millions of dollars in legal fees.

Porter grudgingly dialed O'Reilly's number.

"Good morning, Mr. Porter," O'Reilly's secretary chirped.

The woman's excessively cheerful voice had always irked him. Porter asked to speak with O'Reilly.

"I'll see if he's available." The secretary returned to the phone within seconds. "I'm sorry, but Mr. O'Reilly is preparing for an important telephone conference with the Governor right now. Can he return your call later?"

Porter groaned. "No. Tell him my call is important, too."

After a lengthy wait, O'Reilly came on the line.

"Yeah?" There was a definite air of impatience in his voice.

Porter could tell he was on the speakerphone. Porter hated speakerphones. "I'm calling about Vernetta Henderson. There seems to be a problem with a case she's been handling. The folks at Micronics thinks she—"

"I know all about it," O'Reilly said, cutting him off. "I played golf with the General Counsel Sunday morning. I just wish you'd had the foresight to fill me in before that awards dinner Saturday night. You had that meeting on Friday afternoon. You should've called me right away."

Porter's two brows knitted into one. "Well, I'm calling you now. I just wanted to let you know that I plan to meet with Vernetta this morning to—"

"I'd like to be there. Let's have the meeting in my office. How about nine-thirty?"

Porter was speechless. This was *his* case and *his* problem. The meeting should be held in *his* office. O'Reilly was always throwing his weight around.

"Well, does that time work for you or not?" O'Reilly asked impatiently.

"Fine."

"Good. I'll see you then."

Porter squeezed the telephone receiver so hard his hand began to ache. He had planned to resolve this matter quickly and quietly. Now O'Reilly was stepping in and would probably end up taking credit for cleaning up the mess. Nothing had changed since the first time O'Reilly had screwed him more than twenty-five years earlier. Porter's anger over that incident had only intensified over time.

During their first year at the firm, a jury handed one of O'Reilly & Finney's most respected senior partners the kind of notoriety no attorney welcomed—a multimillion-dollar jury award that was not in his favor. O'Reilly and Porter became the two junior members of a post-verdict team charged with coming up with a basis for overturning the embarrassing award.

Porter and O'Reilly were assigned the same legal issue to research. Although instructed to work as a team, both young associates were confident that their own superior intellect and excellent research skills would uncover a multitude of cases on point. So it made no sense to share the glory. The first day's research, which lasted late into the night, produced nothing helpful. By five the next morning, Porter was stationed in his cubicle in the library, well along in his research. O'Reilly didn't stroll in until after seven. While they had verbally agreed that O'Reilly would review treatises on procedural law and Porter would begin with law review articles, both had secretly encroached on the other's assigned turf.

After seven straight hours of research, Porter left the library hoping that some fresh air would energize his brain cells. He was gone just long enough to pick up a turkey on rye at the deli across the street.

As Porter headed back to the library, he was greeted in the hallway by a beaming senior partner. "Did you hear the news?" the partner asked.

"What news?" Porter was too sleep-deprived to worry about the impropriety of appearing uninformed.

"O'Reilly found the case we needed. *U.S. v. Lewis.* We're drafting a motion for a new trial as we speak."

When Porter returned to the library, his appetite gone, he noticed that the papers in his cubicle had been disturbed. The volume of the *Harvard Law Review* that he had just reviewed was no longer perfectly centered on his yellow legal pad where he had left it. It was now sitting slightly askew.

Porter stared at his legal pad and felt sick to his stomach. *U.S. v. Lewis* was the eighth case on his list. He had already crossed off the first six. If he had taken the time to read just two more cases before going out for his sandwich, he—not O'Reilly—would have made the big discovery.

For months, Porter stood quietly on the sidelines as the entire firm sang the praises of the young Columbia law grad who had saved the day. When the verdict was subsequently overturned, everyone began saying that O'Reilly would be twice the lawyer his grandfather had been. One of the partners even joked that he could pull a rabbit out of a hat.

Porter never told anyone that O'Reilly's rabbit had been stolen from *his* hat. Porter kept his suspicions to himself because doing otherwise would have made it sound like he was not a team player. And everybody knew that O'Reilly & Finney attorneys were expected to be superb team players.

Even if they hated each other's guts.

CHAPTER 25

When I got to the office Monday morning, I did not give it a second thought when my secretary told me O'Reilly wanted to see me in his office in an hour. I was still on Cloud Nine after the plug he had given me at the banquet Saturday night. I figured he just wanted to lay it on even thicker.

But when I hit the doorway of his office and saw Porter sitting rigidly on O'Reilly's brown suede couch, my body's internal defense mechanism set off a silent alarm.

O'Reilly stood up when I entered the room. "Why don't you have a seat?" He motioned toward one of the chairs in front of his desk.

Good, I thought. I did not want to sit on the couch next to Porter.

Instead of returning to the chair behind his desk, O'Reilly walked over and closed the door, then took a seat in the other guest chair next to mine. I noticed that neither O'Reilly nor Porter made eye contact. With me or each other.

A dreadful thought sucked the air from my lungs. Associates who would not be considered for partnership were typically told a few weeks before the vote that their names would not be submitted. *They're about to tell me I'm not making partner!*

"Well, I won't beat around the bush," O'Reilly began. His voice was uncharacteristically formal, his body as stiff as a cardboard box. "We wanted to speak with you about the Randle case." He stopped and rubbed his chin. "The folks at Micronics have reason to believe that you may have a conflict of interest."

"What?" I felt my body relax, relieved that partnership was not the subject of this meeting, but still totally confused. I glanced over at Porter and then at O'Reilly. "What're you talking about?"

O'Reilly coughed. "We need to know whether you're involved in a personal relationship with Hamilton Ellis."

I laughed nervously. "You're joking, right?"

"Take a look at these," Porter said gruffly. He leaned forward and extended a manila envelope to me.

I opened the flap and pulled out five eight-by-ten photographs. Seemingly from nowhere a burst of heat exploded in my chest. I struggled to keep my hands steady as I examined the pictures. They were taken a week earlier, when Hamilton escorted me to the parking lot across the street from Little J's.

The first two pictures captured me and Hamilton walking toward my Land Cruiser. In another photograph, Hamilton had me by the elbow, helping me climb inside my SUV. In the fourth, Hamilton's head was leaning into the window and he appeared to be kissing me. The angle of the picture, however, made it impossible to determine whether Hamilton's kiss had landed on my lips or my left cheek. The final photograph showed Hamilton and Special. Both of them sported huge smiles as they walked out of Little J's.

I returned for a second look at the picture that showed Hamilton kissing me. I tried to swallow before speaking, but my throat felt as if it had been stuffed with cotton balls. "This is crazy." I tried to keep my voice level so I didn't sound defensive. "If these pictures are the basis for your accusation that I have some kind of conflict of interest, then you're wrong."

"Nobody's accused you of anything yet," Porter said.

I flung a hateful look his way. "Of course you're accusing me. You're obviously implying that I'm involved in a romantic relationship with an opposing counsel. Well, I'm not. And in case you've forgotten, I'm married."

"Well, can you explain that picture of you and Hamilton Ellis?" Porter snorted.

"There's nothing to explain." I turned away from Porter and intentionally addressed my comments to O'Reilly. "I met my best friend at a nightclub after work last week. Hamilton Ellis just happened to be there, too. Almost as soon as he came in, I left. He offered to escort me to my car and since it was dark out, I let him. This picture is misleading." I shoved the photographs back inside the envelope and tossed it onto O'Reilly's desk before continuing.

"He took me completely by surprise and leaned into the window and kissed me on the cheek—not the lips—which is not evident from the angle of that photograph. He said something about remembering his kiss when the Randle litigation got rough. That was it."

"Okay then, what about that picture of your friend,

Ms. Moore? What's her relationship with Mr. Ellis?" Porter demanded.

"If you're asking me if she's dating him, yes she is. I can't control who my friends go out with."

O'Reilly sighed. "Can you understand why Micronics might have a problem with this whole situation?"

"What *whole situation?* There is no *situation.*" My vocal cords cracked, but I hurled the emotion from my voice. There was no way I would allow myself to break down and cry in front of them. "I haven't done anything wrong."

Porter refused to let up. "I understand your husband's living in San Diego. Are you having trouble in your marriage?"

That little bitch! I couldn't believe I had been stupid enough to talk to Haley about Jefferson. So that was why she had asked me those questions about Hamilton.

I was poised to tell Porter that the state of my marriage was none of his damn business when O'Reilly raised his hand. "Vernetta, forget that question." He gave Porter a cautionary look. "But I have to ask this next one. Just for the record. Reggie Jenkins appeared on some cable TV show a few days ago. It appears he knows about those sexual harassment cases summarized in that fax you got from HR. Micronics wants to make sure he didn't get that information from you."

"You're right," I snarled back at him. "You already know the answer. If you're asking me if I gave Reggie Jenkins, Hamilton Ellis or anybody else a copy of a confidential client memo and in the process committed malpractice by violating the attorney-client privilege and the Rules of Professional Conduct, the answer is no. No, I did not."

"Is there any chance your friend Ms. Moore might've seen a copy of the document?" Porter asked. He was sitting on the edge of the couch now, acting like an aggressive trial lawyer trying to catch his witness in a lie.

I was on the verge of tears. Tears of anger. I clutched the arms of the chair for support. "If you're asking me if I'm in the habit of showing confidential client documents to my friends, the answer is the same. No."

The office fell as quiet as a library after closing hours.

"Well, Vernetta, how do you think we should handle this?" O'Reilly asked.

I knew he was only humoring me. "I assume I'm here because Micronics wants me off the case. Is that what you wanted to tell me?"

O'Reilly reached over and patted my forearm. "Look, kiddo, you just told us you didn't do anything inappropriate, and we believe you. But I'm sure you understand the position this puts the firm in. The best thing for us to do is abide by the client's wishes. We're just fortunate that Porter was able to convince the General Counsel not to pull the case from the firm altogether."

"Fine," I said, standing up, even though they had yet to dismiss me. "Should I assume I'm still being followed?"

"You weren't being followed," Porter groused at me. "Micronics hired a private investigator to trail Randle and his attorneys. The company believes they've been trying to obtain some confidential company records."

I didn't buy that story. "I only found out that Hamilton

Ellis had joined the case a few hours before those pictures were taken. Micronics must've known earlier since they had time to assign someone to follow him. Why didn't they tell us?"

Neither Porter nor O'Reilly had an answer to that question.

"And if Micronics thought Randle or one of his attorneys was stealing documents," I said, "why accuse me of giving them the information about those other cases?"

O'Reilly raised his hand for the second time. "We just had to ask the question, Vernetta."

I started to ask about my cell phone records, but I couldn't risk getting Shelia into hot water. Porter had probably wanted them to see if I had been making regular calls to Hamilton.

O'Reilly got up and put a hand on my shoulder. "Look, kiddo, we're in your corner."

I looked him dead in the eye. "Sure you are."

I walked back to my office in a total daze. My legs felt about as sturdy as two toothpicks. *This is insane.* One of the firm's most important clients was accusing me of misconduct based on a stupid kiss on the cheek.

I was about to enter my office when an awful thought paralyzed me mid-stride. I had left a copy of the Micronics fax on the coffee table in my living room before heading off to the banquet. *Had Special read it and shared the information with Hamilton?*

While part of me knew that what I was thinking was absolutely insane, I could not shake the awful possibility from my head. I rushed over to my desk, grabbed the telephone receiver and dialed Special's office. She answered on the second ring.

"I need to ask you a very important question." My tone was gruff and businesslike.

"What's up with the ugly attitude? You sound like you're ready to take my deposition."

"Did you ever tell Hamilton anything I told you about the Randle case?"

"What?" Special replied. "Of course not. Anyway, you haven't really told me anything."

"Are you sure? Remember that night you came over to borrow my earrings?" I was speaking at a rapid-fire pace, as if Special were on the witness stand, her guilt already determined.

"Yeah, so?"

"I left a copy of a fax about the Randle case on the coffee table in the living room. And somehow, Randle's attorneys found out about it. You didn't happen to look at it when I left, did you?"

"Hold up, girlfriend. I know you're not asking me what I think you're asking me."

"I just need to know," I said. "Did you read the document?"

"That law firm mess has really gone to your head. You really think I'd stab you in the back like that? And over some man? Don't you know me any better than that?"

The insanity of my questions suddenly hit me. They were even more offensive than the ones O'Reilly and Porter had just posed to me. I plopped down in my chair and closed my eyes. "Look, I'm sorry, I—"

"Sorry, my ass. I don't know what's going on down there, but if the tables were turned, I wouldn't have had to ask you the questions you just asked me."

"Wait, Special, let me explain—"

"Save it. Since that law firm is so important to you, call one of them white boys down there the next time you need a friend."

Before I could say another word, she had hung up.

CHAPTER 26

I drove home in a complete fog. I fumbled with my Black-Berry on the Santa Monica Freeway, desperate to reach Jefferson. The first time, my call went to his voice mail. When I called back five minutes later, LaKeesha answered and I hung up.

After nearly rear-ending a silver Jag at a red light south of Exposition, I pulled into the parking lot of the Albertsons at La Brea and Rodeo Road and tried to get myself together. I pressed my forehead against the steering wheel for a minute or so, then walked into the grocery store and bought a six-pack of pineapple-kiwi wine coolers, a party-size bag of Cool Ranch Doritos and a can of Planters peanuts.

When I finally turned into my driveway, I thanked God for letting me get there safely. I had thrown open the door of my Land Cruiser and was about to jump out, when I heard the jovial whistle of my next-door neighbor, Mr. Robinson.

"How ya doin', counselor?" he said, waving as he walked over.

Luke Robinson was a retired bricklayer whose wife had died about a year ago. They had no children and Jefferson and I had somehow become his surrogate family. Whenever we were out of town, Mr. Robinson looked after our house and we did the same for him. He frequently dropped by with a sample of some extravagant dessert he had baked. The other couples on the street considered him the neighborhood busybody, but he was just a lonely old man who had no one to talk to. But today, I was not in the mood.

When he got closer and saw my face, the glee left his. "Counselor, what's wrong?"

"Bad day at the office," I mumbled, gripping my bag of snacks.

"I can definitely see that. Anything I can do to help?"

I tried to smile. "No, Mr. Robinson. But thank you."

He was about to say something else, but I rudely plowed past him. I would apologize later.

Staggering inside, I dropped my purse and keys on the sofa table near the door and headed straight for the master bathroom. After filling up our Jacuzzi tub and stripping off my clothes, I slipped into the warm water and opened up a wine cooler.

I soaked for over an hour, then climbed into bed even though it wasn't even noon yet. I opened a second wine cooler and called Jefferson's cell again. "Hey," I squeaked when I heard his voice.

"What's up?" Jefferson sounded like he was talking through his nose.

"You sound awful," I said. "You okay?"

"Nope. My sinuses are really giving me hell. And I only got about three hours' sleep last night."

I waited for him to ask how I was doing, but the question never came.

"Hold on a minute." I heard Jefferson say something to someone, but I couldn't make out the words.

"Who're you talking to?" I asked.

"LaKeesha just brought me some Sudafed." I could hear him take a gulp of water. "Man, I don't need this sinus crap right now. We're so far behind."

Sudafed? "Exactly what is she? Your secretary or your damn nurse?"

Jefferson exhaled. "Vernetta, I feel like crap and I don't have time for this right now. As long as I'm paying her, it's her job to do whatever I want her to do. So you need to stop trippin'."

This was not the way this conversation was supposed to go. I had called my husband so I could cry on his shoulder, not argue with him.

"Well, I had a pretty messed-up day myself. Remember that sexual harassment case I told you about?" I didn't wait for his acknowledgment. "They took me off of it and I think there's a good chance I'm not going to make partner." The flood of tears I had been holding in check was finally released.

"Hey, babe, I'm sorry," Jefferson said, his voice much gentler now. "That's really messed up. What happened? Why'd they take you off the case?"

"They think I'm having an affair with the opposing counsel," I sobbed.

"What? That's crazy. At least I hope it is. What's going on?"

"It's too unbelievable to even try to explain."

"C'mon, babe, don't cry. If you don't make partner

there, you'll make it somewhere else. That ain't the only law firm in the world."

"But it's not fair."

"Well, life—"

"And don't tell me life isn't fair! That's not what I need to hear right now."

"I know, babe. I'm sorry. I know how much this means to you."

I could hear Stan's voice in the background. "I'll be just a minute," Jefferson called out to him.

"I know you have to go," I said, still teary. "I just needed to talk."

"And I wanna be here for you," he said, "but you caught me at a really bad time. Just let me run out and check on this job and I swear I'll call you right back."

"Okay," I said. "I hope you feel better."

"You, too," he said. "Everything will be okay. I promise. I love you."

"I love you, too."

Out of habit, I started to call Special, then realized I couldn't.

CHAPTER 27

Jefferson called me twenty minutes later and we talked for over an hour. He said everything I needed to hear and I felt much better by the time we hung up. A couple of hours later, I decided to head over to my parents' place in Compton.

Returning to my childhood home always made me feel as if I had been wrapped in a blanket of complete acceptance. It did not surprise me to find the house empty. Only illness—serious illness, not just a cold or an attack of arthritis—could keep my parents away from their Monday afternoon Bible study at Community Baptist Church at 148th and Central.

I smiled as I inspected my parents' tiny living room. The tan leather couch was a fairly recent addition, but the antique coffee table was the same one they had purchased my senior year of college. The carpet only recently changed from eighties mauve to all-purpose beige, but the walls had never known any color other than Swiss Coffee.

Change of any kind came hard for my parents. ATM machines, e-mail and TiVo had yet to become necessities in their lives. Whenever I brought up the subject of them moving closer to my area, they quickly found something else to talk about. It would take a forklift and a truckload of National Guardsmen to force them from the only piece of property they had ever owned.

I walked into the den and sat down in my father's leather recliner, positioned squarely in front of his Sony big screen. Since their simultaneous retirement from the Post Office a year earlier, my parents spent most of their day glued to the television set.

I pulled the lever on the side of the recliner, sending the chair into a horizontal position. I was sound asleep in no time.

An hour later, I opened my eyes to find my parents peering down at me. Identical, worry-stricken expressions plagued their faces.

"Netta, are you okay?" my mother asked, moving her hand from my forehead to my cheek, then back to my forehead again. "You don't seem to have a fever."

"I'm fine," I said, maneuvering the recliner upright. I hugged them both in a single embrace. Time definitely was not slowing for them. With every visit, I noticed a new patch of gray or a hitch in their step that I had not detected the month before.

They remained frozen in place, staring at me as if I were some late-night intruder.

"I'm fine," I said, laughing. "I just dropped by to spend some time with my wonderful parents."

"Oh, I know something's wrong now." My mother took a step back to get a better look at me. "Just tell us what's wrong. Did you and Jefferson have a fight?"

"Mama, please. Jefferson's fine and I'm fine, too." I plopped back down into the chair and pretended to sulk. "If this is the kind of reception I get, then I'm going home."

My father took off his sports jacket and folded it over his forearm. He was still inspecting my face as if he might have missed some important clue.

"Daddy, will you please stop staring at me."

"I'm sorry, Netta. If you say you're okay, then fine. But those dark circles under your eyes are telling a different story."

"Why don't you just go change clothes?" I ordered.

My father stalked into the bedroom, while my mother began busying herself in the kitchen.

"How's work?" my mother asked as she pulled plates from the cabinet. She was still fishing.

"Okay," I said.

"Do you have another trial coming up anytime soon?"

Her question filled me with regret. "Nope," I said softly. My parents loved it when one of my trials received media attention. They bragged so much it was embarrassing. After my big murder case, they had been interviewed by the *Compton Bulletin,* which ran a front-page profile on me.

I got up from the recliner and tried to open the back door, then remembered that I needed a key to get through the steel bars nearly everyone in my parents' neighborhood had barricaded themselves behind. I took the key from underneath the sugar dish on the kitchen table and unlocked the door. Once I was outside, I sat down on the cement steps. The backyard bordered a busy boulevard and I could see the cars whizzing by through the worn fence.

A bird's nest at the top of my father's prized peach tree

caught my attention. I watched as the mother bird went back and forth, fortifying the nest, one twig at a time. After a few minutes, my father joined me outside, crouching down next to me on the top step. It took a few seconds for him to get settled.

"Look," I said, pointing up at the tree. "That bird's building a nest."

"I just hope they don't mess up my tree," he muttered.

We continued to watch in silence as the bird went about its work.

"You know you can talk to us about anything, right?" my father said after a long while.

"Daddy, please. I told you, I'm—"

"Shhhh." He pressed a heavy finger to my lips. "I don't have a bunch of college degrees like you, but I know when something's wrong with my only child."

He wrapped both of his arms around me and hugged me tight. I tried, but failed, to hold back my tears.

"I don't know what's going on and I'm not going to pressure you to tell me if you don't want to, but my gut says it's got something to do with that darn job. Otherwise, you'd be at work today."

"Daddy, I—"

"You just listen for a second," he said, pulling a handkerchief from his back pocket. "Just pretend you're in my courtroom now."

I smiled as he dabbed at my eyes with his handkerchief.

"You want to know what I think?" he said, not bothering to wait for my answer. "I think you're pushing yourself too hard. You always did." He pulled me closer.

"Remember when you were in the second grade and you got that *S* in Science?"

I had no idea what he was talking about.

"Every other grade on your report card was an *E* for excellent but all you could focus on was that *S* for satisfactory. I think you must've cried for a straight week. And me and your Mama were just scratching our heads, trying to figure out why."

He repositioned himself on the step. "Netta, I know being a lawyer is very important to you. You've been talking about making partner from the day you finished law school. But if for some reason it don't happen, don't let it worry you."

He took my chin between his thumb and index finger. "Whatever's going on down there at that law firm, it's not the end of the world. It's not a big deal if you've messed up some case. It's not a big deal if you've lost some client. And it's not a big deal if you don't make partner. And I know you've explained it to me a thousand times, but I'm still not quite sure what that partnership stuff is all about anyway."

I chuckled quietly through my tears.

"The only thing you need to be worried about is being happy with you," he said, tapping my chest with his finger. "You need to stop using everybody else's measuring stick to judge yourself by and find your own darn stick. If you can be happy with yourself, and I mean really happy, it don't matter what nobody else has to say about you, good or bad. And there's no reason in the world for you not to be happy. You got a good job, a hard-working husband and we raised you to have faith in God. And you don't need much more than that. And I almost forgot, you in-herited my good looks."

I smiled and kissed him on the cheek. "Thanks, Daddy."

"Don't be thanking me. I haven't done nothing. Y'all young people go and get all them darn degrees and make all that money, but don't have no idea how to be happy. They need to have a college course called Common Sense 101. I can teach it with my eyes closed.

"C'mon," he said, pulling me up by both hands. "Let's go inside before your nosey Mama comes out here and starts bothering us."

CHAPTER 28

As hard as it was to do, I marched into the office Tuesday morning with my head held high. I had not done anything wrong and I refused to walk around acting as if I had.

I kept my office door closed for most of the day and only left once to grab some lunch and three times to use the restroom. The day seemed to zoom by. Just before six, the telephone rang.

"Ms. Henderson, the delivery guy's here with your food." I glanced at the phone. The call was coming from the lobby.

"You've got the wrong office. I didn't order dinner," I said, though I wished I had. I was planning to work another couple of hours and I could have used a bite to eat.

I heard the muffled voice of the guard talking to someone else, then he came back on the line. "Ms. Henderson, this guy swears the food is for you. He's insisting that you come down here and pay for it."

I slipped on my pumps, hopped on an elevator and charged into the lobby. I was highly annoyed by the unnecessary interruption and I planned to make that perfectly clear to the insistent deliveryman.

When I spotted my husband leaning against the black

marble reception desk carrying two white plastic bags, a torrent of happiness engulfed me. He was wearing black sweatpants, a white T-shirt and a big, goofy grin.

I rushed over to him and threw my arms around his neck. "What're you doing here?"

He set the bags down on the counter, pulled me into his arms and held me tight. "I've got some business to take care of around here," Jefferson said, his voice hoarse from his clogged sinuses. "Where's the dude who claims you're having an affair? I'm here to kick his ass."

I laughed. "Just what I need, a knight in shining armor."

"Damn straight," Jefferson said.

"Well, I don't think I'll be needing you to punch anybody out," I said. "You sound awful. Please tell me you didn't drive up."

"Nah. I flew into LAX, then took a cab to the house and picked up my car. I was gonna wait and surprise you when you got home, but I couldn't wait to see you. And don't be mad, but I have to head back in the morning."

"There's no way I could be mad. You have no idea how happy I am that you're here."

I looped my arm through his and guided him toward the elevators. "What's in the bags?"

"All of your favorites. Yang Chow's slippery shrimp, spicy wonton soup and shrimp fried rice," Jefferson said, quite satisfied with himself.

"I can't believe you went all the way to Chinatown for Yang Chow's. You definitely get the award for Husband of the Year."

An elevator opened and we stepped inside. As soon as

the doors closed, Jefferson set the bags on the floor, pressed me against the wall and kissed me.

"Jefferson, I think they have cameras in here," I said, trying to dodge his kisses.

"Good. Then the little geek who's watching can get his rocks off."

I laughingly squirmed away from him just as the elevator doors opened. When we got to my office, Jefferson placed the bags on the table across from my desk, then walked over to the window. "Every time I come here, I can never get over this incredible view."

"I'm usually too busy working to notice it," I said. I closed the door and began clearing papers and books from the table to make room for us to eat.

Jefferson pointed up at the ceiling. "We just finished installing some recessed lighting just like this in a section of the project we're working on."

I followed his gaze upward. I had never even noticed the lighting before. I was busy opening cartons of food when Jefferson walked up behind me and kissed me on the back of the neck.

"All right," I warned, "don't start fires you can't put out."

"Hey, babe, just show me where the fire is." He grabbed me around the waist, pulling me back against him. "My fire hose is working just fine. Can't you feel it?"

I turned around to face him and we kissed again, softly at first, then voraciously, as if we'd been starving for each other. Several seconds elapsed before we came up for air.

"C'mon, boy, let's eat before our food gets cold." I

reached for his hand and directed him to a seat at the table. "I'll fix a plate for you."

Jefferson sat down while I began piling food onto a plastic plate. He pulled two Sudafed capsules from his pocket and popped them into his mouth, then chased them down with a swig of Coke.

"You really think this thing is going to keep you from making partner?" Jefferson asked.

I shrugged. "I don't know."

"You going to be okay if you don't make it?"

I chuckled. "If you're asking if I'm going to jump out of that window over there, then yes, I'm going to be just fine."

"Can I ask you something?"

I smiled at him warily. "Go ahead."

"Why do you want to be a partner?"

Jefferson's question caught me off guard and no immediate answer came to me. "I just do," I said.

"Okay, but why? I'm only asking 'cause as hard as you work, I don't get the impression that you actually like practicing law."

"That's not true," I said defensively. "I do like practicing law. Do you like what you do?"

"Nope." Jefferson reached across the table and picked up a large shrimp between his thumb and index finger and tossed it into his mouth. "I *love* what I do."

My husband's response surprised me. "And exactly what's so lovable about it?"

"Everything," he said, talking and chewing at the same time. "I get to call my own shots instead of having somebody else tell me what to do. I like watching a building develop from the ground up and seeing all the electrical components come together. I love it when I get to work outdoors. And when somebody needs me to figure out a complicated electrical problem, that's when I really get off."

I laughed, but I quietly envied my husband's enthusiasm for his work. He stuffed a big forkful of shrimp fried rice into his mouth. "I already know you'll make a boatload of money," Jefferson said. "But I still can't figure out what else is so good about being a partner?"

"O'Reilly & Finney is a very prestigious law firm," I said. "And they've never had a black partner before. It would be an incredible achievement if I were the first, okay?"

"But is that going to make you happy?"

I wished Jefferson would stop asking stupid questions. "Yes," I lied. "Yes."

But in reality I did not know the answer to Jefferson's question. He was forcing me to think about something that I had not carefully thought through. Like the fact that most of the attorneys I knew hated their jobs. There were times when I found my cases intellectually stimulating, but I was often exhausted from the long hours. Although I had no close personal relationships with anyone at O'Reilly & Finney, I still wanted to be part of their elite little fraternity.

"You know what I think?" Jefferson said, talking with his mouth full. "I think you give this firm more props than it deserves. Since these white boys haven't allowed anybody with your skin color to make partner, you interpret that as them saying black folks aren't good enough.

But you listen to me." He set his fork down and waited until my eyes met his. "You *are* good enough. One thing I never let anybody do is define how I feel about myself. And you shouldn't either."

Jefferson's words sounded so much like my father's they gave me an eerie feeling.

"I need to take a leak," he said, hopping up from his chair. "I've been here enough times to know, but which way is the john again?"

"Make a right out of the door and then a left at the end of the hallway."

I searched the bottom of the bags for more soy sauce as Jefferson headed out. After about five minutes, I heard loud muffled voices outside my door.

When I peered outside, I saw Jefferson standing face-to-face with a pimply faced white man who barely looked old enough to be out of high school. His navy blue security guard jacket hung off his narrow, hunched shoulders and his run-over shoes needed a good shine.

I rushed over to them. "What's going on?"

"Ms. Henderson, is this man your guest?" the guard asked, his eyes tracking Jefferson's every move.

Jefferson took a single step forward and the security guard flinched. "I already told you, you little—"

"Jefferson, please!" I grabbed him by the wrist and stepped in front of him. "Yes. He's my husband."

"Visitors in the building after hours must be escorted at all times," the guard said.

"I'm sorry," I replied. "It won't happen again."

I pulled Jefferson inside my office and closed the door.

"That little punk didn't have to come at me like that," Jefferson said, still fuming.

"If a guard sees somebody in the building he doesn't recognize, he's supposed to approach them," I said.

"You mean if he sees somebody *black* he doesn't recognize. If I were a white boy, he wouldn't have said shit to me. I can't believe you're actually defending him!"

"Jefferson, please keep your voice down," I whispered. "You're overreacting."

He folded his arms. "I have no idea why you would even wanna work here. They don't want you up in here no more than they want me in here. The fact that we're in the goddamn twenty-first century and they've never had a black partner ought to tell you that."

"You don't have to be mean, Jefferson."

"I'm not being mean, I'm being real. You need to stop running behind these white folks banging on their door, begging them to let you in. If you wanna be a partner then start your own damn firm."

I walked over to the table, picked up my plate and scraped the food back into the container. "I'm not hungry anymore."

"Me neither," Jefferson said. He stayed put as I closed up the containers of food.

"Maybe I should just leave?" he said.

I didn't want him to go, but my lips refused to form the words to tell him to stay. "If this is how you're going to act, then maybe you should."

When Jefferson took a step toward the door, I had a change of heart. "Jefferson, wait. You're overreacting. Just—"

"I'm not overreacting," he said, actually shouting now. "I fly up here to see about you even though I'm sick as a dog and this is the thanks I get?" He snatched the door open. "I'm outta here."

CHAPTER 29

By the time Jefferson's plane landed at San Diego's Lindbergh Field Airport, it was close to nine and his sinus problem was ten times worse. The airplane pressure had clogged his ears and breathing through his nose was almost impossible. All he wanted to do was sleep for a week.

Jefferson trudged down the airplane ramp, then stopped to read the maze of signs to figure out which way he needed to go. Somehow, he managed to make it to the street level and started searching for the cab stand. He felt a tap on his shoulder at the same time a sexy female voice purred, "Welcome home!"

He turned around to find LaKeesha smiling up at him.

"What're you doing here?"

"I knew you weren't feeling well, so after you called me to change your flight, I decided to pick you up so you wouldn't have to catch a cab."

LaKeesha was wearing baggy jeans and a tight-fitting sweater that buttoned down the front. The top three buttons were undone. Jefferson was beginning to think the girl didn't even own a bra.

"You didn't have to do that, LaKeesha," Jefferson replied, but he was actually grateful that he did not have to use what little energy he had left trying to get to the Residence Inn. "I think I might have something more serious than a sinus problem. I hope it's not the flu."

"Poor baby," LaKeesha said. She reached for his duffel bag and he willingly let her have it. As soon as he settled into the front seat of her Honda Civic, he reclined the chair as far back as it would go and promptly fell asleep.

Forty minutes later, LaKeesha had the passenger door open and was trying to shake him awake. "Hey, Jefferson, wake up. We're here."

It took a minute for Jefferson to realize where he was. When LaKeesha extended her hand to help him out of the car, he pulled so hard, she tumbled into his lap. He felt her cheek brush against his.

LaKeesha giggled and climbed out. "Why don't you hold on to the door instead?" she said.

Jefferson gripped the roof of the car and lifted himself out. He now had a pounding headache to accompany his plugged-up nose and ears. LaKeesha stayed close behind him as he wobbled up the stairs toward his room on the second floor of the inn.

They stopped outside his room and Jefferson dug into the pocket of his sweatpants, took out the white card key and slipped it into the metal slot in the door. He pushed it open, flipped on the light and charged straight for the couch, sprawling out across it.

"I'm going to fix you a hot toddy that's guaranteed to make you feel better," LaKeesha said, marching into the tiny kitchenette. "In the meantime, here's some Sudafed."

She set a glass of water and four red pills on the coffee table in front of him. "I think you might need a double dose."

Jefferson sat up. "You just happen to carry this stuff around with you?"

"Nope," she laughed. "I stopped at Vons and picked up some groceries, but you were snoring when we pulled into the parking lot and snoring even louder when we pulled out."

LaKeesha walked back into the kitchenette and began opening and closing cabinets. Jefferson watched as she took three lemons from a grocery bag, cut them in half and squeezed lemon juice into a pan. She added a few tablespoons of honey and turned the burner up high. When the mixture reached a boil, she poured some into a cup, then added a healthy dose of whiskey.

"Did you eat dinner?" LaKeesha asked. She walked over to the couch and handed him a cup and saucer. "I don't want to give you this on an empty stomach."

"Yeah, I ate," he replied, although he'd only had a few spoonfuls of shrimp fried rice before storming out of Vernetta's office. He was already starting to regret leaving the way he had. He would call Vernetta and apologize as soon as LaKeesha left.

The first sip of the hot drink LaKeesha had prepared soothed his throat. "Hey, this is pretty good," Jefferson said. He really appreciated the way LaKeesha was taking care of him. But when she joined him on the couch and picked up the remote, a warning signal went off in his head.

He turned to face her. "Uh, hey, thanks for everything," Jefferson said. "You don't have to hang around."

LaKeesha smiled at him. "I have a history exam tomorrow. Is it okay if I study in the bedroom for a couple of hours? I promise not to disturb you."

Some part of Jefferson's subconscious told him that he should tell LaKeesha to leave, but how could he do that when she had been so nice to him? He knew exactly what the girl was all about and he did not want to give her the impression that he was down with it. But if she was really going to study, there was no harm in her hanging around. He had already nipped things in the bud when he sent her home the other night and she'd been cool since then. Besides, he felt so lousy he would need a jack to prop up his dick.

"No problem," he said.

LaKeesha picked up her book bag and headed into the bedroom. Jefferson stretched out on the couch and was asleep in seconds. About an hour later, LaKeesha opened the bedroom door and stuck her head out. "Hey, boss man, I was about to heat up the clam chowder I picked up at the store. Want some?"

"Actually I am a little hungry," Jefferson said.

When LaKeesha walked past him into the kitchenette he saw that she had changed into a pair of shorts. Actually, hot pants would be a more accurate description. As she stood in front of the sink, Jefferson had a full view of her left butt cheek. He turned away and tried to concentrate on "The Parkers" rerun on the television screen. He was going to let her fix him some clam chowder and then put her ass out. He was too old to be played like this.

He heard the ping of the microwave, then LaKeesha walked over to the couch carrying a serving tray with two bowls and a package of Ritz crackers. "Is anything good on?" She repeatedly pressed the remote and stopped when she got to BET.

After a minute or so of watching three half-naked Generation Xers shake their asses, Jefferson reached for the remote control. *Did the girl really think he didn't know what was up?*

"Let's see what else is on," Jefferson said. He flipped past several stations and stopped when he found a "Seinfeld" rerun.

When he was almost done with his clam chowder, LaKeesha stood up. "I almost forgot to make you another hot toddy."

LaKeesha busied herself in the kitchenette and in what seemed like seconds, handed him a second steaming hot cup of her special brew. When he took a sip, he could tell that she had used twice as much whiskey as before. The buzz felt great.

Jefferson closed his eyes as he took another swallow. *What the hell?* All he was doing was sitting on a couch next to a woman fine enough to make any man's dick turn to steel. It certainly did not constitute infidelity.

They watched the rest of *Seinfeld* and when it was over, Jefferson decided it was time for LaKeesha to leave. But first, he wanted another drink. "Got any more of that hot toddy stuff?" he asked. His head still hurt and he could barely breathe. If he got blasted, at least he would be able to sleep through the night.

In a flash, LaKeesha was standing directly in front of him, her crotch inches from his face, handing him his third hot toddy. Jefferson felt a tingle of arousal. He looked down at his pants to make sure his growing erection was not visible through his sweatpants. He took a sip of the drink. This one was almost pure whiskey. He chuckled to himself. The girl was trying to get him drunk, and she was doing a damn good job of it. He could usually hold his own, but whiskey was not his drink of choice. It was probably the four extra Sudafed capsules he had just taken.

"Hey, LaKeesha, thanks for everything," he said, taking a warm swallow. His words were slightly slurred. "But it's getting late. I think you've wasted enough of your time babysitting me." She was sitting down next to him, much closer than before.

"Yeah, I guess it is about time for me to be rolling up outta here." She eased off the couch and stretched, then bent down to collect the dishes from the coffee table, treating him to another view of her exposed rear end.

Her movements were noticeably measured and Jefferson could tell that she was waiting for him to stop her. Once she had straightened up the kitchen, LaKeesha gathered her books from the bedroom, then returned to the main room and stuffed them into her book bag. She was almost at the door when she stopped.

"Hey, I forgot to ask about your shoulder," she said.

Jefferson rubbed his neck. He did not remember his head feeling so heavy. "Haven't had a problem since that massage you gave me."

"Well, let's see." Before he could object, LaKeesha had dropped her book bag to the floor and darted over to the couch. "Your trapezius muscles still seem a little tight." Her fingers glided up, down and across his shoulders and neckline.

Damn, that feels good. Jefferson lowered his chin to his chest. He was not doing anything wrong, he told himself. She was practically a professional masseuse. He would make her leave as soon as she finished his massage.

Jefferson wasn't sure if it was the whiskey or the Sudafed or the massage, but he was feeling quite mellow. And he suddenly realized that he could almost breathe through his nose again. LaKeesha had lit some incense and a strong, sweet smell invaded the room. Closing his eyes, he became lost in his relaxing massage.

Jefferson could not remember exactly how it had happened, only that it *was* happening. He felt what seemed like a dozen pairs of lips kissing the back of his neck and a dozen pairs of hands roaming his body, sending sparks of pleasure in a thousand different directions. When he opened his eyes, he found LaKeesha kneeling between his legs, using one hand to untie the drawstring of his sweatpants, while her other hand massaged his erection through the thick cotton fabric.

Before he could process exactly what was going on, LaKeesha had already freed him and gently taken every inch of him into her warm, wet mouth. When his brain had finally put it all together, he did not possess the will or the desire to put an end to it. He settled back on the couch and moaned in a way that could only give her encouragement.

When the last of his mental resistance had faded—for no physical opposition had ever surfaced—he gently stroked her head, encouraging her all the more.

CHAPTER 30

Precisely three seconds after Jefferson came, all of his brain cells rushed back into his head with the velocity of a speeding car slamming into an invisible wall of steel.

Oh, shit!

"So," LaKeesha said, grinning up at him, "how was it?"

Jefferson's lips felt like rubber. He tried to speak, but he could not get the words from his brain to his lips. "LaKeesha...I...this really wasn't cool. I...we...we shouldn't have done this."

Jefferson clumsily tucked himself back in and retied the string of his sweats.

LaKeesha, still kneeling between his legs, winked up at him. "Don't sweat it, boss man. I know the deal. You're a happily married man, right? *You* didn't do anything. This was something *I* wanted to do."

You try telling that to my wife!

Jefferson could hear the thumping of his heart and his air supply felt uncomfortably low. All he could do was shake his head in disgust at himself for letting this happen. The haze he had felt from the whiskey, the Sudafed and his congested sinuses had completely vanished and he could see far clearer than he wanted to.

"This really wasn't cool," Jefferson said. "This can't ever happen again. You have to...we gotta..." He could not think straight. "LaKeesha, this shouldn't have happened and it can't happen again. Ever. You gotta leave. Now."

LaKeesha was obviously disappointed, but played it cool. "No problem, boss man." She walked toward the door and bent down to pick up her book bag, pointing her ass directly at him. "I'm off tomorrow, so I'll see you on Thursday. Feel better." She blew him a kiss and walked out.

When she closed the door, Jefferson flung his head back against the couch. "Shit!"

He sat still for several seconds, then glanced at the clock. It was after midnight. He reached for his cell phone and hit the second button on the speed dial. "Man, we have to fire LaKeesha!" he sputtered when Stan picked up.

"Fire her?" Stan said groggily. "For what?"

Jefferson paused. He should have taken some time to think things through before calling Stan. "'Cause we can't afford an assistant."

"What? Man, what're you talking about? LaKeesha's the only reason we've been able to keep track of our invoices. And she's very nice to look at. We ain't firing her."

"Man, I messed up. I messed up bad."

"What're you talking about?"

Jefferson groaned. "Man, she came over here. She fixed me this drink. She got all up on me and—" He paused to take a breath. "Man, I just fucked up."

Stan let out a long, low whistle, letting Jefferson know that he understood exactly what had gone down.

"So we just gotta fire her," Jefferson said again. "We can tell her it's a layoff. That we don't have enough work."

"Aw, man, you lucky dog! You had a slice of that little tenderonie? I told you she wanted to give you some. How was it?"

"Are you nuts? I didn't want this to happen. She kept giving me this whiskey stuff and—"

"Oh, so you saying she got you drunk and took advantage of you," Stan chuckled. "I'm sure your wife'll buy that story."

"My wife won't have to buy that story because she's never going to find out about this," Jefferson said. "That's why we gotta fire LaKeesha. If Vernetta calls the office and LaKeesha says something to her, I'll—"

"Hold on, man. Just calm down. I don't know if firing LaKeesha is the right thing to do. The minute we let her go, she'll probably run back to that temp agency claiming sexual harassment."

Jefferson rubbed his face with his open palm. "I messed up bad."

"Just hold on," Stan said. "Man, please tell me you put on a raincoat."

Jefferson inhaled like it might be his last breath. "I didn't, but—"

"How could you be that stupid?" Stan exploded. "What if she gets pregnant?"

Jefferson's free hand curled into a tight ball. "It didn't go down like that, Stan. She gave me some head, man. I didn't ask for it. She just did it. I swear."

"Head? Is that all? Aw, man, that ain't nothing. That ain't

even really sex," Stan said, chuckling. "If the president can get his dick sucked in the Oval Office, you should be able to get a blow job at the Residence Inn." Stan started cracking up.

"This ain't funny, Stan. And you better not tell your wife because there's no way Vernetta can ever find out about this."

"Man, just cool out. Everything's going to be fine. But I'm not with you on the firing tip. Just play it cool and keep it in your pants for a few more weeks, then you two can go your separate ways. That little girl knew exactly what she was doing. When she comes back to work, everything has to be strictly business."

Stan consoled Jefferson for a few more minutes, then urged him to get some sleep.

Jefferson was about to close his cell phone when he noticed that he had a voice mail message. He knew it was from Vernetta before he even punched in his code.

Hey, Jefferson. I'm so sorry. I really didn't want you to leave and I shouldn't have let you. I know how hard you've been working and I really appreciate you coming home to check on me, particularly since you weren't feeling well. I was the one who overreacted, not you. I love you. Call me.

He flipped the phone closed, then hung his head and did something he had not done in a long, long time.

He prayed.

CHAPTER 31

I tossed and turned for most of the night, worried and upset because Jefferson had not returned my call.

Early the next morning, I was about to call Jefferson again, when the phone rang. My hotheaded husband and I spent the next twenty-five minutes apologizing to each other.

My second day back at work after the Micronics fiasco was uneventful and I actually got quite a bit of work done. I left the office around five and had just slid a Lean Cuisine dinner into the microwave and poured a bottle of piña colada mix into my blender when the doorbell rang.

"I hope you don't think you can buy me off that cheap," Special said when I opened the front door. She was wearing bright orange pedal pushers and bronze sandals with a platinum toe ring on the second toe of each foot. A head full of auburn straw curls had replaced her short pageboy.

I reached out and gave her a big hug. I knew the Mahogany greeting card, the purple tulips and the Ellen Tracy blouse I'd had delivered to her office would do the trick. "You can give me as much flack as you want and I'm taking it," I said, smiling at the sight of her. "I'm so glad to see you."

"Tell me something I don't know," Special said as I pulled her inside.

I threw an arm across her shoulders and led her into the kitchen. "Look, I'm sorry. I never should've asked you those questions."

"Let's just forget about it," she said. "How you doing, girl?"

"I'm alive," I said, "but just barely."

Special pointed at the bottle of piña colada mix on the counter. "Ms. Goody Two-shoes is drinking at home alone on a weeknight? It must be serious. What exactly went on down at the plantation?"

"They took me off the Randle case."

"Why?"

"Said I had a conflict of interest because of you and your boyfriend, Hamilton."

"They took you off the case just because I went out with Hamilton?"

"Not exactly." I stuck a wooden spoon into the blender to sample my brew. "Basically, they implied that *I* was the one going out with him."

"Are you serious?" Special sat down at the kitchen table.

"They had some photographs of me and Hamilton that night we ran into him at Little J's. Remember when he walked me out?"

"Yeah."

"Well, somebody with a camera must've been hiding in the bushes snapping away."

"They had somebody following you?"

"Not me. They were supposedly following Hamilton.

I was just lucky enough to be caught in a few of the shots."

"What the hell were they following him for? And if they took any pictures of me, I'm suing their asses for invasion of privacy."

Taking that cue, I decided not to mention the one picture of Special.

"So what was the big deal with the pictures?" she asked.

"One of them showed me and Hamilton…kissing."

Special shot up from the chair, hands on hips. "Excuse you?"

"Girl, don't worry, I don't want your man." I recounted Hamilton's stupid little stunt and described the photo that caught him in the act. "And then that idiot, Reggie, got on TV and started talking about some information that just happened to be in a privileged memo. Of course, they assumed I was his Deep Throat."

"Oh, so that's why you called me up with them crazy ass questions."

"Uh, let's just forget about that part."

"This is some hella serious undercover stuff," Special said. "Who's handling the case now?"

"That little overachieving, second-year associate, Haley Prescott. The partner on the case thinks she walks on water. They didn't even assign another senior associate to supervise her."

"Oh, girl, I know that pisses you off." Special laughed.

"That's an understatement. How are things between you and Mr. Ellis?" I asked.

Special rolled her eyes. "I had to cut that brother loose.

This world is much too small. Can you believe he was seeing one of the hairdressers where I get my hair done? And she ain't even cute."

"How'd you find out?"

"She had a picture of him and her up in her booth."

"Special, I know you couldn't possibly think you were the only woman Hamilton was seeing."

"No, but I didn't think he'd be bold enough to take us both out on the same night. How tacky is that? He told me we had to have dinner at six because he had to get back to the office to prepare for a deposition. He only dropped my ass off at eight-thirty because he was picking her up at nine. I guess I got dumped off first because I wasn't giving it up. I'm so glad I didn't give his ass none."

I tried not to show how relieved I was.

Special looked me up and down and turned up her nose. "I hate to be the one to tell you this, but you look whipped."

"I've been so stressed out over this stuff with the Randle case. I know they're going to use it as an excuse not to make me a partner."

"They better not or they're gonna have to deal with me."

"This case is turning out to be so bizarre." I paused. "I want to tell you something," I said, "but you have to swear not to mention it to a soul."

Special raised her right hand as if she were taking an oath.

"You know that woman Hamilton's client supposedly harassed?" I said.

She nodded.

"She died in a car accident a few days ago."

Special was quiet for a moment, then her jaw dropped. "You think it was really an accident?"

"I'm beginning to think not. According to the *Times,* the same Micronics program Henry Randle had been complaining about may have been responsible for the crash of an Air Force plane over in Baghdad."

"Dang! You think your case is tied to the war in Iraq?"

"I don't know," I said, handing her a drink.

She took a sip and scrunched up her face. "There ain't enough alcohol in here to fill up a thimble." She got up and grabbed the Bacardi bottle from the counter and doused her glass with more rum. "Girl, Hamilton may've done you a favor getting you kicked off that case."

"Maybe so," I said.

Special's face turned pensive. "I have an idea," she said. "And before you reject it, just hear me out."

"I'm listening," I said warily.

"Remember I told you I was thinking about starting my own investigations firm? Bust-A-Brother. Well, why don't we conduct an investigation and find out what really happened to that woman?"

"Excuse me?"

"It would be fun. We could call ourselves Randle's Angels. Get it? *Charlie's Angels*…Randle's Angels."

"Special, Karen Carruthers is dead, Henry Randle doesn't have a job and if I do what you're proposing, I won't have one either."

"C'mon, girl, maybe that brother really was set up like he said."

"You're crazy. Forget it."

"It would be easy. There's this LAPD detective I know with this serious foot fetish. He was always trying to polish my toenails. He could get us a copy of the police report and I could—"

"Special, forget it." This time my tone was razor sharp.

"C'mon, a police report is a public record, ain't it?"

"I said forget it, Special. Besides, once you tell that detective what you're up to, he'll think you're as crazy as I do."

"Girl, please. If that brother thought he *might* get a chance to touch my feet, I could convince his old ass to run butt naked down Crenshaw Boulevard in rush hour traffic."

"You're talking crazy, so count me out."

"Okay, fine," Special said.

But I knew my best friend. She rarely gave up on one of her harebrained ideas that easily. I pointed a chiding finger at her. "I'm not playing, Special. Forget about this. You're not even supposed to know about the woman's death."

"Okay, okay. I'll let it go," she replied. "But I'm telling you, something is up. I can feel it."

CHAPTER 32

Ninety minutes after walking out of Vernetta's front door, Special was sitting across from Detective Mason Coleman in a back booth at the Ladera Flats Supper Club on La Tijera. It had been a while since she'd had to pour it on this strong, but Special knew how to use her womanly ways to get what she wanted.

"C'mon, sweetie," Special pleaded, "why can't you let me make a copy of these documents?" She picked up a large manila envelope from the table.

The detective grabbed the envelope back. "I already gave you a copy of the police report, and I let you read these papers. But I can't let you copy 'em. I had no business even showing 'em to you."

Detective Coleman was a bear of a man, with a short, thinning Afro. The edge of the table sliced into his large belly, forcing him to shift positions every few seconds. He reached out across the table and took Special's fingers into his massive, liver-spotted hands.

Special liked hanging out at Ladera Flats because she could always count on picking up an older man willing to blow his money on her without her having to actually put out. She could appease men in the fifty-five-and-up range in all kinds of creative ways that did not involve actual sex. Ways a younger man would never accept. She had hooked up with Detective Coleman at the club over a year ago.

"C'mon, sweetie," she begged. "I just wanna show my friend, Vernetta, what they found in Carruthers's car. I'm trying to find out who murdered her."

"Special, I've told you a thousand times," he said, exasperated, "there's no evidence that the woman was murdered. And I just can't let you copy these papers."

Special puckered her lips into a childish pout. When she noticed the detective eyeing her chest, she leaned over the table to give him a better view. She had intentionally worn one of his favorites. Her leopard-skin minidress. But Detective Coleman refused to relent.

"Okay, never mind then," Special said, pretending to be mad. "Excuse me for a minute." She slid out of the booth and headed toward the rear of the darkened club. When she spotted the club's owner, a thin, caramel-colored man in leather pants, she walked up to him and whispered in his ear.

"Special, that man's a cop," the club owner said. "What are you trying to get me mixed up in?"

"Just do me this one favor, C.J." She threw an arm around his shoulders and gave him a sad puppy-dog face. "Pretty please with sugar on top?"

He surrendered within seconds and she hurried back to the table.

"How about one of my *special* massages?" she said to Detective Coleman.

He smiled a wide, toothy grin and started to laugh. "Hee, hee, hee, hee, hee. Girl, you're something else."

Special reached underneath the table and slipped off her right shoe. She then stretched out her leg and began rubbing her toes up and down the detective's hairy leg.

"Hee, hee, hee, hee, hee." He sounded like a hiccupping bullhorn. "Girl, you've got the prettiest, softest toes in the world."

Special began inching her foot higher and higher up the detective's pant leg. She could tell by the way his lower lip began to quiver that he was getting aroused.

"All right now, girl!" the detective sputtered. He glanced around the restaurant. Wednesday was not a very busy night for the club. They shared the room with only three other couples, all of them a good distance away. Confident that no one was paying attention to their little game, Detective Coleman relaxed.

When Special's toes had climbed as far as they could go, she shook her foot free and began a new trek up the outside of his pants. The detective closed his eyes and smiled. When Special's toes reached his crotch, he began to breathe low and heavy. "Hee, hee, hee, hee, hee."

While Detective Coleman concentrated on his *special* massage, Special slid the envelope from the table and quietly dropped it to the floor alongside the booth. Within seconds, C.J. walked over and retrieved it.

Detective Coleman, totally preoccupied with his massage, noticed nothing. His eyes remained tightly shut as Special continued to maneuver her toes to his apparent satisfaction. His breathing became louder and more labored and tiny beads of perspiration dotted his forehead. Special slowed her pace, not wanting to get him too excited.

"You okay over there, sweetie?" she asked. Her toes were beginning to cramp up from the workout. What had initially felt like a lumpy pillow had turned into a mound of clay. She figured he could not get any harder without taking one of his Viagra pills.

"I'm just fine," Detective Coleman said in a husky, contented voice. He had yet to open his eyes.

The club owner abruptly interrupted the detective's special massage. "Does this envelope belong to one of you?"

Special happily dropped her cramped foot to the floor. The detective seemed dazed when his eyes finally popped open. He searched the table and realized that the club owner was holding his envelope.

"Yeah, that's mine," Detective Coleman said, reaching for it. "How'd you get it?"

"Found it on the floor." The club owner gave Special a knowing smile and left.

"How in the hell did it fall on the floor?" the detective asked. "It was way over here."

Special wondered how the man kept his job. "Sweetie, I'll be right back." She snatched her purse from the table. "I have to go touch up my makeup."

"Aw, baby girl, your makeup looks fine. Let's get back to my special massage," he said, grinning.

Special opened her purse and pulled out a bottle of fluorescent pink nail polish. She reached across the table and placed it in front of the detective. "Maybe I'll let you touch up my toenails tonight," she teased.

Detective Coleman stared at the nail polish and a smile stretched from ear to ear. "I don't deserve you," he said, breathlessly taking a sip of his drink.

Special slid out of the booth and scurried past the ladies' room and into a tiny office. She found the club owner sitting behind a cluttered desk watching a battered-looking portable TV. A small copy machine sat on a coffee table next to a plaid love seat.

"Here're the copies." The club owner handed the papers to Special. "And this better not come back on me."

Special folded the six pages into quarters and stuffed them into her purse. "Thanks, C.J.," she said, giving him a big hug. "I owe you."

CHAPTER 33

Jefferson lay in bed, staring up at a ceiling he could not see in the darkened bedroom of the Residence Inn. LaKeesha was due back at work today and Jefferson was not looking forward to facing her.

He glanced at the digital clock on the nightstand. It was almost 5 a.m. He closed his eyes and tried to will himself to sleep. When that failed, he got up and jumped into the shower. After throwing on some jeans and a T-shirt and gobbling down a bowl of Frosted Flakes, he headed over to the worksite.

Propping his elbow on the desk and resting his chin in his hand, Jefferson gazed out the window at the approaching sunrise. He planned to act as if the whole thing had never happened when LaKeesha came in. He just hoped the girl didn't trip. But you never knew what to expect with women.

Stan walked into the trailer a short time later, carrying a bag of chocolate chip muffins. "You're here early," he said. He shuffled over to the coffeemaker and held up the empty carafe. "The first person here is supposed to make the coffee."

Jefferson shrugged and continued staring out into the parking lot.

"You not still trippin' about that mess with LaKeesha, are you?" Stan asked. "Just snap out of it." He took a coffee filter from the cabinet. "What you did ain't no big thang. A man deserves a little something on the side every now and then. That's the only way I've been able to survive fifteen years of marriage."

Jefferson scratched his chin. "Man, if I wanted to be out there banging a bunch of babes, I never would've gotten married. That gets old after a while."

Stan poured two pints of bottled water into the carafe. "You ain't even got five years under your belt yet," he said. "Wait until you've been on lockdown for ten or fifteen. You'll start seeing things my way."

"I doubt it," Jefferson said.

"All right. We'll see." Stan turned on the coffeemaker and walked over to his desk. "I just don't see messing around as any big deal." He removed a stack of invoices from an accordion folder. "If I find myself in a situation where some woman's willing to throw me some play, I ain't turning it down. I'm not some young stud like you. My options are few and far between."

Jefferson laughed.

"And besides, my wife knows the deal. If you asked Maria if I'd ever screwed around, she'd tell you, hell yeah. In fact, I was screwing Maria when I was with my first wife." Stan looked up wistfully. "Now, I *really* loved that woman. One of the sweetest, finest chocolate chicks I'd ever laid eyes on. But she didn't understand how things worked." He tugged his rising T-shirt back down over his stomach. "Now, Maria? I don't think she cares what I do as long as I keep it out of her face. She's a good old-fash-ioned Filipino who likes catering to her man. That's why I married her ass."

Jefferson walked over to the coffeemaker. "Man, some-times I wonder what planet you live on."

"Dude, I'm just a realist," Stan said. "And I'll tell you this, if I was running thangs, I could lower the divorce rate just like that." He snapped his fingers.

Jefferson poured coffee into two cups. "I know I'm going to regret this," he said, "but go ahead. Let me hear it."

"There should be a federal law that a married man should be able to get a piece on the side at least once every three months. That'll basically wipe out divorce."

Jefferson laughed. "And what about married women?" he asked, handing Stan a cup of coffee. "Would the same law apply to them?"

"Hell nah," Stan said. "Women don't even like sex that much after they hit forty-five or fifty. If God had meant for married women to screw around, he would've given 'em a penis. I wouldn't put up with a woman who messed around on me. It just ain't right."

"So if you found out Maria had some dude on the side, you'd leave?"

"Leave? Hell, no. I ain't going nowhere. I paid for that house. But I'd pack up her stuff and set it out on the curb. I need to know I can trust my woman. And, for me, keeping her legs closed is the ultimate demonstration of trust."

Jefferson took a sip of coffee and stared at his partner in bewilderment. "Man, please make sure you keep your crazy ass views to yourself when my wife's around."

"Like I said, my woman understands me. What I do on the side don't have nothing to do with her. Even if she had a body like LaKeesha's, I'd still be out there."

"Sure you would, Stan." Jefferson took a seat at his desk. "I think all the women you brag about having is only in your head."

"I'll have you know I was quite a catch in my day," Stan said. "I didn't always have this gut." Stan looked down and grabbed a handful of his stomach. "So don't be underestimating my skills with the women. I never told you, but remember that project we had last summer over in Carson?"

Jefferson nodded.

"Remember Linda, the short chick with the big ass who sat at the reception desk? I hit that several times."

"Man, you're lying. Why in the hell would she want you?"

"'Cuz I'm a very charming dude." Stan grinned. "And 'cuz I paid her rent for six months."

Both men laughed heartily.

"You're crazy," Jefferson said. "I don't know about Filipino women, but my wife's black *and* she's a lawyer. And she ain't having it."

"Hey, man, that was *your* mistake." Stan pulled a muffin from the bag on his desk and took a big bite. "Ain't no way I'd ever hook up with a lawyer. You could bring in the finest lady lawyer you could find and stand her butt naked right here in front of me and I wouldn't touch her. I swear if that chick who represented my first wife in our divorce walked in here right now, I'd strangle the bitch."

"You can't take out your hatred of her on all lawyers," Jefferson said.

"Oh, yes I can," Stan insisted. "That woman was the demon seed. I think she hates men so much, she'd work for free if she had to. You would've thought I'd cheated on her ass."

"Well, Vernetta's nothing like that," Jefferson said. "She's not a spiteful person."

"Hah," Stan said. "You let her ass find out about you and tenderonie, and you'll see the fangs come out. All women lawyers have 'em. The black ones have an extra set."

"I don't plan on Vernetta ever finding out," Jefferson said, though he wasn't completely sure he could keep that from happening. He turned back to the window, his face still plagued with worry.

Stan got up for another cup of coffee. "Just take my advice and forget about what went down between you and LaKeesha," he said. "'Cuz there ain't nothing you can do about it now."

Jefferson certainly could not argue with that. They finished their coffee, then headed outside.

CHAPTER 34

Shortly after eleven, Jefferson saw LaKeesha's car parked in the lot and rushed over to the trailer, hoping to talk to her alone. But when he opened the trailer door and their eyes met, he realized he did not know where to begin.

"Morning," LaKeesha said, only briefly looking up from the stack of invoices in front of her. Jefferson missed her customary *Hey, boss man* greeting.

"Morning," Jefferson replied. He walked over to a table at the rear of the trailer and spread out a blueprint. He stared down at it, but the lines all blurred together.

"Is everything cool with us?" Jefferson asked, briefly looking over his shoulder at LaKeesha.

She had on a clingy, cream-colored dress with black ankle boots. The dress accentuated every curve of her body. Jefferson turned back to the blueprint so he wouldn't get distracted.

"Everything's just fine," she snapped, but her curt tone said otherwise.

"I just want you to understand that what happened the other night can't ever happen again."

"You already told me that," LaKeesha growled. "I heard you the first time."

He looked over in her direction, taken aback by her attitude. He had said what he needed to say. Any other communication between them would be strictly work-related. "Did the Anderson Lighting bill get paid?" he asked.

Instead of answering him, LaKeesha strode over to Jefferson's desk, snatched a folder from a side drawer, then walked over and slapped it down on the blueprint.

Why was she acting like such a little bitch? He was just trying to make things right between them. He opened the folder and saw the word *paid* stamped across the top of an invoice in bold red letters.

"Where do you want me to order lunch from?" LaKeesha asked, her tone now distantly professional.

Jefferson felt his anger mounting. "I think you and me should go get some lunch," he said. "We need to have a little talk."

LaKeesha shrugged.

Jefferson glanced at his watch. "Let's try the Thai Palace up the street. If we leave now, we can get there before it's packed with the lunch crowd."

"I don't like Thai food," LaKeesha said sourly.

Jefferson's lips tightened. "Well, I do."

"So you're ordering me to go to lunch with you?"

"Yeah," Jefferson fired back. "I am."

LaKeesha grabbed her purse from the desk just as Stan walked in. "Hey, Stan, I'll get to that letter you wanted me to type when I come back," LaKeesha said. "Jefferson is making me go to lunch with him."

Stan gave Jefferson a confused look. "Man, you really think you should be—"

Jefferson held up his hand. "We'll be back in an hour."

Jefferson and LaKeesha walked the half block to the Thai Palace in silence. Once inside, they were shown to a large booth near the back of the restaurant and given menus.

"What would you like?" Jefferson asked, after he had finished perusing the menu.

"I already told you, I don't like this stuff. I don't even know what it is."

"I'm sure there's something here you'll like," Jefferson said. "You like chicken?"

"Yeah." LaKeesha pursed her lips and refused to look at him.

"You like shrimp?"

She huffed. "I like all meat."

He was about to tell her that shrimp wasn't meat but decided to let it go. "What vegetables do you like?"

"Broccoli and green beans."

When the waitress returned, Jefferson ordered curry chicken, shrimp fried rice, barbecued chicken, broccoli in oyster sauce and green beans in Thai chili paste.

"You trying to feed an army or what?" LaKeesha asked as the waitress walked away. Her voice still had a surly undertone to it.

"The portions aren't that big," Jefferson said. "Anyway, we can take whatever's left back for Stan."

LaKeesha started fidgeting with her napkin. Jefferson could see the girl's nipples through her dress. He took a sip of water and looked away.

"LaKeesha, I wanted to have lunch with you so that—"

"I know, I know." She raised her hand, palm out,

fingers splayed in an exaggerated sister-girl pose. "What we did was wrong. You're a married man. I'm too young. Yada, yada, yada."

Even though she was really pissing him off, Jefferson felt a twinge of sympathy for the girl. He apparently wasn't the first older man she had set her sights on.

"That wasn't what I was going to say," he continued. "First, I want you to know how much we appreciate the way you help us stay so organized."

LaKeesha shrugged and turned her head.

"You're the best assistant we've ever had. And I mean that."

LaKeesha tried not to smile, but couldn't help it. When Jefferson smiled back at her, she cut her eyes at him.

Jefferson paused to take another sip of water. He could not believe how nervous he felt. *She's just a kid.*

"And you were also nice enough to pick me up at the airport. Those hot toddies and that Sudafed worked because I'm feeling much better. So I want to thank you for that, too."

LaKeesha puckered her lips. "Aren't you going to thank me for that blow job, too?"

Jefferson felt heat warm the tips of his ears. He wanted to reach across the table, grab the girl by the shoulders and shake her. He had gotten himself into this situation and he would get himself out of it. He had to. If Vernetta found out what had gone down, she would not accept any of his excuses—the whiskey, his clogged sinuses, LaKeesha's forwardness—as mitigating factors. For Vernetta, infidelity, in any form, warranted the ultimate punishment. But he did not deserve to lose his wife over a five-minute blow job. And he was not about to let that happen.

"Have you always been such a tease?" Jefferson asked.

"Pretty much." LaKeesha smiled.

"Well, you really don't have to be. When the right man comes along, you won't have to throw yourself at him."

She tilted her head. "What if you're the right man?"

"I'm not." Jefferson did not try to hide his irritation. "And for the record, I want to apologize about everything. I shouldn't have let it happen."

"But you did," LaKeesha said brazenly. "And you enjoyed it. I could tell by the way you were moaning and rubbing my head. I bet your wife never sucked your dick that good."

Jefferson bit his lip and drew in a deep breath. This dangerous little girl in a grown woman's body had set a trap for him and he had walked right into it. He was itching to fire her ass, but he couldn't be sure that LaKeesha wouldn't do something vicious, like call up his wife. He needed some time to figure out exactly how to play her.

The waitress walked up carrying the first two dishes, the fried rice and the barbecue chicken.

Jefferson pressed his palms flat against the table. "I changed my mind," he said to the waitress. "We're taking our food to go."

CHAPTER 35

I stood at the podium facing Judge Lawrence Fetterman and tried hard to concentrate. "There are no material facts in dispute here, Your Honor. My client deserves summary judgment as a matter of law."

I had a pounding headache, which hurt more every time I opened my mouth to speak. That would be the last time I overdosed on piña coladas the night before an oral argument.

The judge leaned over to allow his law clerk to whisper something into his ear. I continued, although I knew it was a total waste of time. Fetterman was one of those judges who made up his mind based on the briefs. The oration of Shakespeare could not convince him otherwise.

"The plaintiff has no evidence that her gender had anything to do with her manager's decision not to promote her," I continued. I glanced down at my notes on the podium and tried to ignore the plaintiff's attorney, seated to my right, nosily ruffling papers. "I respectfully request that the court grant the defendant's motion in its entirety."

When I finished, I took a seat to the left of the podium. The judge raised his eyes over the rim of his bifocals and peered at my opponent. "Mr. Grant, the undisputed facts here demonstrate that your client was not the victim of sex discrimination. Do you have any evidence to the contrary?"

Donald Grant, a scrawny white man with a bad dye job, nervously stepped up to the podium. "Your Honor, my client deserves an opportunity to make her case before a jury and I think that—"

"That wasn't what I asked you, counselor. Ms. Henderson has demonstrated that your client had some serious performance problems. And over the last three years, her manager promoted two women who held the same position as your client. I just don't see any discrimination here, Mr. Grant? Do you have any evidence of pretext?"

"Well, not exactly, but—"

"Then my decision's simple," the judge declared, picking up his gavel. "Summary judgment granted. Defendant is awarded costs."

Grant looked stunned. "Your Honor, I—"

"I've ruled. Save it for your appeal, counselor."

I happily scooped up my papers from the defense table. Despite the Micronics debacle, at least my other cases were going well. As I headed out of the courtroom, I spotted a sight that caused my air of accomplishment to go stale.

"Well, well, well, counselor. Nice job in there," Hamilton said, walking up beside me.

"You're spying on me now?" I asked without slowing my pace. I had no idea whether Micronics still had somebody following him, but I did not want to take a chance of being captured in any more undercover photographs. I looked up and down the hallway, but did not notice anything suspicious. I increased my pace anyway.

"I wasn't spying," Hamilton said. "I had a motion across the hall and saw you go into Fetterman's courtroom. I got done early and decided to hang around and check out the competition."

I was practically jogging as we rounded the corner at the end of the hallway.

"Wait up," Hamilton called out. He had to lengthen his stride to catch up with me. "You need to slow down and savor your big victory."

"I have to get back to the office for a meeting," I lied.

Hamilton acted as if he hadn't heard me. "I got a call from your second-in-command telling me you'd been taken off the case and that she was running the show now. What's up with that?"

I was sure Haley had enjoyed delivering that news. "Look, I really have to go." I charged past him toward the bank of elevators.

Hamilton had not mentioned Karen Carruthers. It surprised me that the cat was still in the bag. I stepped into an already crowded elevator and Hamilton managed to squeeze inside just before the doors closed. When I exited on the first floor, he followed.

"You're just going to leave me hanging?" he asked.

"One of my other cases is heating up," I said. I was relieved to see the courthouse exit just a few feet ahead.

Hamilton stayed close, practically stepping on the back of my heels. I had almost reached the tall double doors that led to the street when my legs stiffened. *What if the photographer who'd been following Hamilton was waiting outside?* For all I knew Micronics could have hired somebody to follow me, too. I did an about-face.

"Hey, where're you going?"

"The ladies' room," I said. "See you later."

I rounded the corner and disappeared inside the nearest restroom. Since I did not have to use the bathroom, I touched up my eyeliner, reapplied my lipstick, then leaned against the sink and waited. If someone came in, I planned to dash inside one of the stalls since I would look pretty weird just standing there. After about five minutes, I cracked open the bathroom door and peered up and down the corridor. Hamilton was nowhere in sight.

I darted out of the courthouse, over to the parking lot across the street, praying that I didn't run into Hamilton before I made it to my SUV.

CHAPTER 36

Twenty minutes after ditching Hamilton, I was back at my desk. I got halfway through my voice mail messages before noticing the time. The O'Reilly & Finney Attorney Dining Room would be closing in ten minutes. I would have to hurry if I wanted to grab a quick salad.

Stepping off the elevator on the eighteenth floor, I felt uneasy. I had avoided eating in the Attorney Dining Room since my banishment from the Randle case, limiting my lunch options to the sandwich shop in the lobby of the building. I could handle facing the curious or chiding eyes of the lone associate or partner I ran across in the hallway or elevator, but I could not stomach confronting a whole roomful of them.

But I had nothing to be ashamed of, I reminded myself. I squared my shoulders, darted my chin forward and barreled through the door. The second I entered, a familiar voice, spewing enough hot air to send a helium balloon off into space, smacked me in the face.

"I'm handling most of the work on the Randle case now," I heard Haley brag. She sat at a small table for four, surrounded by three first-year associates, all male. If the looks on their faces had been any more obvious, they would have needed bibs to sop up the envy.

I stole a quick look around the dining room. Every table looked essentially the same. A sea of expensive ties, white skin and whiter shirts. The few female attorneys blended in so well, you would miss them if you failed to look close enough. Hispanic waiters dressed in imitation tuxedoes dashed about pouring coffee and picking up plates of half-eaten food, their presence effectively invisible to their all-attorney clientele.

"We're trying to get the case settled," Haley continued to boast between bites of lasagna. "It's just me and Joseph Porter on the case now, no senior associate. If it goes to trial, I'll definitely be second chair."

One of Haley's three lunch mates noticed me standing near the salad bar. He did not bother to give her a heads-up.

"I don't know the whole story about why Vernetta got kicked off the case," she went on, lowering her voice just a notch, "but rumor has it a little hanky-panky was going on between her and the plaintiff's attorney. Can you believe she would be stupid enough to be screwing an opposing counsel?"

Haley stuffed a piece of sourdough bread into her mouth at the same moment our eyes met. Like a car window rolling down at the press of a button, a bright shade of red blanketed Haley's face. I didn't know whether a lack of oxygen caused by the bread lodged in her throat or the shock at seeing me standing within earshot of her table prompted the change in hue. I hoped it was the former.

I snatched a pair of tongs from the salad bar and began

slapping salad fixings into a plastic container. I doused ranch dressing on top, signed my name on the billing register and stalked out.

As I stood in the hallway waiting for the elevator to arrive, I repeatedly punched the down button although it was already lit. *Screwing an opposing counsel?* I pounded the elevator button again. *Is that what everybody thinks?*

I thought about cornering Haley in her office and telling her off, but that would only make matters worse. I had to focus on the positives of my situation. Getting kicked off the Randle case was probably a gigantic blessing in disguise. Micronics was hiding something and when the case exploded, I didn't want to be anywhere in the vicinity. I also didn't want or need the hassle of dealing with Haley and Porter. Hamilton Ellis or Reggie Jenkins either. I had more than enough work to keep me busy.

The elevator doors glided open and I stepped inside and pressed the twelfth-floor button. Since my meeting with O'Reilly and Porter, I had tried my best to appear upbeat at work, but keeping up the facade was requiring more and more effort. Restful sleep still eluded me and an un-settled feeling kept my stomach perpetually tied up in knots. I had busted my ass for O'Reilly & Finney. Would this crazy allegation about me and Hamilton Ellis really blow my chances of making partner?

When I reached my office, I plopped the food down on my desk. I noticed that the message light on my telephone remained unlit. I had left a message for O'Reilly the day before, asking when he would have time for lunch. But he had yet to respond to my invitation. It was not like

O'Reilly to blow me off. The more I thought about what was happening to me, the angrier I got. If the firm was going to screw me over these ridiculous allegations, then somebody should tell me that to my face. Without giving it further thought, I headed for O'Reilly's office. When I got there, I found his door open.

"You busy?" I asked, peering inside.

"Never too busy for you, kiddo."

Then why haven't you returned my call?

O'Reilly got up to close the door, something he only did if we were discussing a sensitive case. He sat back down behind his desk and leaned back in his chair. "So how's everything going?"

"Maybe I should be asking you that," I said. I sensed an uneasy distance between us.

O'Reilly smiled, then picked up a gold pen from his desk and began twirling it between two fingers.

"Look, O'Reilly, I know partnership decisions are going to be announced in a few weeks, and I know you can't tell me anything," I said hurriedly, knowing that he was about to say exactly that. In reality, if you had a partner with some juice backing you—a partner like Jim O'Reilly—then the vote was nothing but a formality.

"I just want to make sure I'll be considered for partnership based on all of my work. Not just this Micronics fiasco."

"Of course," O'Reilly replied, his rigid smile contradicting his words. "I'm sure this whole thing'll blow over before you know it."

"O'Reilly, this isn't fair." I hated hearing the angst in my voice. "I didn't do anything wrong."

O'Reilly looked down at his gold pen. "Let's not forget that you could've settled this case for thirty grand," he said. "You were the one who made the decision to pursue your own interests over your client's."

My jaw tightened. "I didn't accept that settlement offer because based on the facts I knew at the time, I felt I could win the case at trial. And Porter, as well as the client, supported that decision. Micronics wanted to go to trial."

"Well, they certainly don't now," he said. "Kind of hard to prevail when your star witness is dead, don't you think?" There was nothing but condemnation in his voice. He sat forward and clasped his hands, a move that signaled the end of our conversation.

As I stood up, that unsettled feeling had disappeared from the pit of my stomach.

It now racked my entire body.

CHAPTER 37

I decided to leave the office early and do something to take my mind off work. I headed over to Magic Johnson's 24 Hour Fitness on Slauson to work off some of my frustration.

After thirty minutes on the treadmill and another twenty on the leg machines, I drove to the South Bay Galleria, hoping a little shopping might lighten my mood. I tried on four pairs of shoes at Nordstrom but none of them fit, which bummed me out even more. So instead of shoes, I bought a new Coach purse and picked up a Caesar salad at California Pizza Kitchen. On the ride home, I called Jefferson, but got no answer on his cell phone.

I climbed into bed around nine with a bag of microwave popcorn and a strawberry Snapple. I fell asleep halfway through the popcorn and fifteen minutes into *CSI*.

When the telephone rang at 1:47 a.m., it took a few seconds for me to gather my bearings. As the numbers on the clock came into focus, I felt a twinge of panic. A call this late had to be bad news.

I reached for the telephone on the nightstand and fumbled with the receiver. "Hello."

"Are you naked?"

The fear that had gripped me dissipated at the sound of my husband's deep voice. "Yeah," I said. "How 'bout you?"

"Yep. Straight up butt naked," Jefferson replied. "Wanna have phone sex?"

"Uh, it depends," I said. "Who is this?"

Jefferson laughed. "That wasn't funny."

"I miss you," I said softly. "I'll be so glad when your project is over."

"Me, too," he replied. "Now you know how I felt when you had to spend every waking hour in trial." His words were full of regret, not criticism.

"I guess I do." Neither of us said anything for a long, long while, happy to just share this quiet time, despite the miles between us. But I knew my husband. He had something on his mind. He worked so hard during the day that the only thing he wanted to do in the middle of the night was snooze.

"Is everything okay, Jefferson?" I asked.

"No, not really. We're way behind on the second phase." He yawned. "But how are you doing? They still got you off that case?"

"Yep." I started to tell him about my meeting with O'Reilly, but decided that for once, the conversation did not need to be about me.

"It was a sexual harassment case, wasn't it?" Jefferson asked.

"Yeah. Except it's the guy they fired who's suing the company, not the woman he harassed."

"What exactly went down?"

"He grabbed a woman in an elevator and tried to kiss

her. But he claims the company trumped up the charges because he was complaining about fraud."

"You believe him?"

"I didn't at first, but I'm not so sure anymore."

Jefferson yawned again. "What exactly *is* sexual harassment?"

I fluffed up my pillow and turned over on my side. Jefferson had never shown more than a superficial interest in the details of any of my cases before. He must've really been having a hard time sleeping, I thought. "Are you asking me for a legal definition?"

"Yeah, I guess so," he said.

"Well, there are two types, *quid pro quo* and hostile work environment harassment," I began. "*Quid pro quo* sexual harassment is when you condition an employment benefit upon a sexual favor. Like, *Sleep with me or you're fired.* Or, *I'll give you a promotion if you go out with me.*"

"Okay," Jefferson said. "But what about when there's none of that?"

"The other kind of cases fall under hostile work environment. That's when someone claims the harasser has made the working environment hostile, intimidating or offensive."

"How do you prove that?"

"It's not all that hard. Let's say something consensual occurred away from the workplace, but the relationship is over and now there's some hostility between them. And let's say the guy is her supervisor. Now when he looks at her the wrong way or criticizes her work because she doesn't want to sleep with him anymore, that can make her working environment hostile, intimidating or offensive."

"That's all it takes? Just looking at somebody the wrong way?" I didn't like the distress I heard in my husband's voice.

"I'm exaggerating a little," I said, "but I've seen lots of lawsuits based on some pretty flimsy facts. Anyway, most cases are settled."

"How much do they usually settle for?"

"Depends on the facts. I've settled some for as little as five thousand and one for as much as two hundred and fifty grand."

"What if the guy didn't do it?"

"It may not matter," I said. "It can cost upward of three or four hundred thousand dollars in attorneys' fees to litigate a case all the way through trial. And that's if you win. So if the plaintiff's willing to take a few thousand dollars to go away, then it makes sense to resolve the case short of trial—even if you think the case is bogus. It's a decision based on economics, not principle."

Jefferson didn't say a word.

"What's up, Jefferson? Why the sudden interest in sexual harassment law? Don't tell me one of your guys has done something stupid?"

"Uh...no." He hesitated. "Stan's...uh...cousin was accused of sexual harassment, but he claimed the woman made it all up. She was the one who came on to him, but lied and said it was the other way around. I couldn't believe the company would actually pay her off. But I guess based on what you just said, it's true."

"Probably," I said. "The conduct has to be unwelcome to amount to sexual harassment, but it's typically a case of he-said, she-said, and in my experience, the female victim is often the more credible of the two."

"That don't seem right," Jefferson said.

"Nobody said the law was fair," I replied. "Anyway, I don't want to talk about this stuff anymore. I really miss you."

"I miss you too, babe. Hopefully I can make it home in another week or so."

Jefferson was quiet for good long stretch. "Vernetta?" He almost whispered my name.

"Yeah."

"You know that I love you, right?"

"Of course I do."

"No matter what happens between us, that won't change. Ever. I can't imagine not having you in my life."

Jefferson's words made my eyes well up. "Are you sure everything's okay, Jefferson?"

"The only thing that's not okay is that you're not lying here next to me."

We hung up a few minutes later. I tried to get back to sleep but couldn't. After my husband's profession of his everlasting love, I should have felt like I was on top of the world. But instead, a dozen different scenarios were running through my head.

And not a single one was good.

CHAPTER 38

Rich Ferris sat in his black-on-black Lexus LS 460, as perspiration oozed from his pores. He reached for the package of tissues he kept in the car's side compartment and wiped his forehead. He wanted to at least look as if he had everything under control.

For twenty minutes now, Ferris had been sitting in a deserted area of the parking structure at the Del Amo Shopping Center off Hawthorne Boulevard. He glanced at the time on the dashboard—8:45 a.m. Cliff, a private investigator he knew only by his first name, was late. Again.

A knock on the window caused Ferris to jump so high he hit his head on the roof of the car. He pressed a button that unlocked the doors. Cliff slid into the backseat and Ferris relocked the doors.

"Do you have them?" Ferris asked without turning around. He wanted to get this over with so he could return to a normal life. He was not cut out for criminal activity.

"We've got a problem," Cliff said.

A wary sigh left Ferris's lips. "You could've told me that over the telephone."

Ferris glanced at Cliff in the rearview mirror. The man did not fit the image of a private eye, at least not the ones

Ferris watched on TV. He was short and lean and smelled like cigarettes. His nationality remained a mystery. Ferris surmised that he could have been anything from Iranian to Puerto Rican. As usual, he was dressed in a dark blue jogging suit. Ferris was certain Cliff had not jogged a day in his life.

"I'm going to need more money," Cliff said. "The documents are no longer in police custody. I'll have to hire a couple of guys to help me get them back."

Ferris fought the urge to turn around and face the man. "You told me you'd have no trouble getting them from the police!"

"Don't worry. I'll get them back," Cliff said. "They've been removed from the property room."

"What? By whom?"

"Some detective, I think. But I'm not sure yet. I have somebody working on that now. I'll call you with an update later today. But it's going to take some more time—and money—to get those documents back."

Ferris was ready to blow his top. He needed this problem resolved. Now. "Exactly how much time and how much money?"

"Another five thousand should do it. But that's in addition to the fifty thou you owe me once I deliver the documents."

Ferris inhaled. "I'll wire the money into your account. Just how much longer is this going to take?"

"I'll have a better idea of that in a couple of days."

Ferris closed his eyes. He had hoped to be able to deliver the documents to the CFO later today. The thought of facing him empty-handed terrified Ferris. Maybe he would call in sick.

"You need to make sure you get the originals as well as any copies," Ferris said. "We can't risk anybody seeing those papers."

"I got it," Cliff snapped. Without another word, he opened the back door and disappeared.

Ferris started the Lexus and eased out of the parking stall. He tried not to think about what would happen if they did not get those documents back. No amount of PR could explain them away. Micronics would be the focus of multiple government investigations and he, along with a long line of other executives, would end up in prison.

Ferris simply could not let that happen.

CHAPTER 39

By ten o'clock on the morning after Jefferson's late-night call, Special and I were zooming down the 405 Freeway in her 1995 Porsche Carrera, the top down, the warm air in our faces, blasting Mary J. Blige. The trip from L.A. to San Diego would take a law-abiding driver about two hours. With Special behind the wheel, we were on track to make the journey in just under ninety minutes.

"So when are you going to tell me why we're really making this trip?" Special asked, looking over at me with concern in her eyes.

I shrugged. "I just felt like seeing my husband."

"Girl, please. You call me at the crack of dawn and beg me to give up two vacation days so we can rush down here on a Thursday morning? What's the real deal?"

I had not told Special the whole story about my conversation with Jefferson the night before. I did not want to hear the unthinkable even from my closest friend in the world. But I knew she would eventually get it out of me.

I leaned forward to turn down the music. "Jefferson called me last night and started asking a lot of questions about the Randle case," I said.

She shrugged. "So?"

"At first, he acted like he was curious about the case, but then he started asking me some very pointed questions about sexual harassment law."

Special glanced over at me, then back at the road. "Did you ask him why he wanted to know?"

"Yep. He gave me some lame story about Stan's cousin being involved in a sexual harassment case. It sounded like something he just made up off the top of his head. I know my husband and I know when he's lying."

Special nodded but did not otherwise respond.

"Okay, give me your take on it," I said. I didn't like it when Special's lips weren't moving.

She shrugged again. "I think we just need to get down there and check everything out before jumping to any conclusions."

I chuckled anxiously. Now Special was the one holding back. "C'mon, I can take it," I said. "Tell me what you really think."

Special's expression darkened. "I'm thinking maybe Ms. LaKeesha filed a sexual harassment charge against Jefferson."

"Or maybe one of his guys," I added.

Special vigorously shook her head. "If it involved one of his guys, there would be no reason for him not to tell you about it."

I nodded, then gazed at the sparse traffic ahead. She was absolutely right. I pulled a bag of trail mix from my purse and began nibbling, even though I wasn't hungry.

"If you found out Jefferson was messing around, would you leave him?" Special asked a few minutes later.

I continued staring at nothing, but Special waited me out. "Yeah," I said. "I love him and I'd want to forgive him, but I don't think I could. Would you?"

"Probably," Special said. "If it was just a fling. With a good-looking brother like Jefferson, women are probably throwing it in his face all the time. So what if he got a little weak? All it is is sex."

"I wouldn't leave him because of the sex," I said. "I'd leave because he violated my trust."

"That sounds like something out of a sappy romance novel," Special said. "Women need to be more realistic. Men are wired differently. For them, sex is sex. They can separate it from love and trust and all that other mushy crap most women find important. I know, because I can. Most women can't."

"Well, I can't and I won't."

"And on top of that," Special continued, "men lose their minds when it comes to sex. How many powerful men have risked everything for the momentary pleasure of a five-second orgasm? I read somewhere that when their dicks get hard, something happens that cuts off the air supply to their brains."

I pressed my palm to my forehead. "Special, why don't you just—"

"No, I'm serious. I swear I read that someplace."

"Well, Jefferson better have a much better excuse than that," I said.

"Whatever happens, just don't overreact," Special warned.

"So you *do* think he's been screwing around," I said.

Special gave me a sympathetic look. "I didn't say that."

"No, but you might as well have."

She dropped her right hand from the steering wheel and squeezed my arm. "I'm only saying the brother's human. Just don't go down there looking for trouble."

I settled back in my seat and continued nibbling on trail mix I didn't really want. The Randle case had thrown a big wrench in my partnership chances, and now the other half of my world looked as if it might fall apart, too.

CHAPTER 40

We pulled into the dirt driveway of Jefferson's construction site right on schedule. I could see pockets of people at work all over the place. To the far left, what looked like a convenience store was close to being finished. The rest of the lot was dotted with structures in various stages of completion. It was amazing to think that in just a few weeks, the place would be an actual strip mall, packed with people.

We climbed out of the car and began walking in the direction of a trailer with the words Jones-Parks Electrical stenciled on the side. My pace slowed when we got a few feet from the trailer door.

"You okay, girl?" Special asked, placing a hand on my shoulder.

I was now having second thoughts about this surprise trip. Was I about to open the door to something I didn't want to know?

"Yeah, I'm fine," I said. I gingerly climbed the steps, then reached for the door, giving it a hard tug. When I opened it, I did not see Jefferson, but what I did see gave me pause.

The young girl standing near a table at the rear of the trailer was well built and attractive. Very attractive. A navel-ring peeked out from underneath her braless tank top and a tight denim miniskirt hugged her ample hips. She wore silver stiletto sandals, which made her long, muscular legs look even sexier. She did not have a body like Serena Williams. Her body looked better than Serena's.

"Hi, can I help you?" the girl asked.

Special responded before I had a chance to. "We're looking for Jefferson Jones," she said. "That's his wife." Special whipped a finger in my direction.

The girl smiled, then walked up to me and extended her hand. "Nice to meet you. I'm LaKeesha Douglas. Jefferson talks about you all the time."

Special was busy looking LaKeesha up and down. "I'm Special," she said, greeting her with a lazy half wave.

LaKeesha chuckled. "Special? Is that really your name?"

Special had heard that question on a daily basis for the past thirty-plus years, but she was suddenly perturbed to hear it coming from LaKeesha. "Yeah, it is," Special snorted. "Is that a problem for you?"

LaKeesha raised both hands. "Hey, I was just asking." She turned back to me. "I'll call Jefferson and tell him you're here."

I told LaKeesha we wanted to surprise Jefferson, so she picked up a walkie-talkie and asked him to come to the office for an important call.

"What exactly do you do around here?" Special asked.

Although Special had asked the question, LaKeesha directed her answer to me. "I help with the filing, return calls, run errands, keep the office clean. Whatever's needed."

Special strolled over to the back of the trailer and ran

her index finger across the countertop. "Guess you must've been too busy with the filing to clean up this week, huh?" Special raised her finger to her lips and blew away a puff of dust.

LaKeesha put her hands on her hips and shifted her body weight from one leg to the other. "I don't know what your problem is, but you just better be glad my grandmama taught me to respect my elders—even the rude ass ones."

Special dropped her red Prada bag to the floor. "You little heffa, I'll—"

Before I could get a word in, the trailer door squeaked open and Jefferson stepped inside. My husband looked from me to LaKeesha, then back at me again. I was certain that I saw terror in his eyes.

"Surprise!" I said, walking over and giving him a hug.

"Hey, babe," Jefferson said, pecking me on the lips. "You may not want to get too close to me. I'm kind of funky."

I hugged him anyway, and tried to ignore the dread that seemed to surge from his rigid body.

"What're you two doing here?" He let go of me and made a move to greet Special.

She took a step back. "Hold up, brother-in-law," she said, before he could reach her. "I'll pass on the hug until you've had a shower."

Jefferson grinned. "Nice to see you, too, Special."

He returned to me and threw his arms around my shoulders.

"You sounded kind of strange on the phone last night," I said. "So I decided a visit from me might do you some good."

LaKeesha was clutching her book bag, inching toward the door. "I'm finished with everything," she said to Jefferson. "I'll be in tomorrow to pay those invoices. Nice meeting you, *Vernetta*." She gave Special a nasty glare and walked out.

Jefferson eyed Special suspiciously. "What was that all about?"

"Nothing much." Special took a seat in a warped folding chair. "When did y'all start recruiting secretarial help from BET videos?"

Jefferson ignored her comment and gave me another kiss. "Hey, babe, I'm really swamped right now. It'll be a few hours before I can get out of here."

"No problem," I said. "I brought lots of work with me and I have a conference call at three. Give me your room key. We'll wait until you're done to go out for dinner."

Jefferson fished the key out of his pocket and handed it to me. Special, meantime, roamed around the tiny trailer as if she were the head building inspector.

"Hey, brother-in-law, you need to let me hook this place up. If you added a little color and a couple of nice prints on the wall, this dump might actually look like something."

"This is a construction site," Jefferson replied. "It's supposed to look like a dump."

"And while we're talking about office improvements," Special continued, "I think y'all need to adopt a dress code for your office staff. And make sure bras are on it."

Jefferson frowned. "Special, why don't you just mind your—"

I reached over and covered Jefferson's mouth with my hand. "We're leaving," I said.

Jefferson kissed me for the third time, then pointed a finger at Special. "Just hurry up and get her ass out of here."

CHAPTER 41

I got settled in Jefferson's suite at the Residence Inn, while Special checked into another room two doors away. While I prepared for my conference call, Special took off on a shopping spree.

The suite had a spacious living room with a fully stocked kitchenette. I sat down on the couch and spread out several folders on the coffee table. I had to go over some discovery responses with a manager who'd been accused of age discrimination. The call lasted about forty minutes and went well. I had just hung up when my Black-Berry rang.

I figured it was Special checking in, but it turned out to be Shelia, my secretary. What now? I thought. Were they asking Shelia to turn over my expense reports?

"I'm calling to report another Paris sighting," Shelia said, laughing.

The secretaries had given Haley the nickname "Paris," in honor of Paris Hilton, because she was constantly trying to be the center of attention.

"I just thought you'd want to know that Paris has been sniffing around your office," Shelia said.

"For what?" I asked.

"Not sure," Shelia replied. "I just came back from the restroom a minute ago and caught her walking out."

"Did she take anything?"

"Not that I could tell. When I asked if I could help with anything, she said one of the pleading files from the Randle case was missing and she thought it might still be in your office. But that was a bald-faced lie. I personally delivered all of the remaining files to her office myself, right after you were taken off the case."

"Then what was she doing in my office?"

"I have no idea," Shelia said. "But the girl looked as if I had just caught her shoplifting at Wal-Mart."

I sighed. I really did not need any more crap from Haley right now.

"And, of course, she asked me if I knew where you were," Shelia continued.

"What did you tell her?"

"Exactly what you told me to say. That you were out of the office on personal business. She tried to pump me for information, but I didn't give it up."

I stretched out on the couch. "Thanks for the info, Shelia."

"Wait, there's more," she said. "I went into your office after she left and I could tell that the girl had been snooping around. When I dropped off your mail earlier this morning, your desk calendar was on yesterday's date. After Haley left, it was open to today's date."

"That girl is going to give me a stroke," I said.

"Well, you won't be by yourself. She just went through her third secretary."

By the time I hung up, I was already debating whether

I should give Haley a call. Part of me wanted to let it ride. I was off the Randle case. There wasn't much trouble the girl could create for me now. But I needed to let her know that she should keep her nose out of my business. With some hesitation, I dialed her number.

"Hey, Haley," I said as cheerfully as I could when she picked up. "Shelia told me you were looking for me. Is there something I can help you with?"

"Uh…no, not really." I could tell she was surprised to hear from me. "I'm working on a motion in the Randle case," she said. "I was looking for one of the pleading files, but I found it. I didn't realize that my secretary had it at her desk."

Yeah, right. "What kind of motion are you filing?"

She paused. "Well…uh, since you're off the case, I'm not sure it's appropriate for me to be discussing it with you."

Whatever. "No problem," I said.

"Where are you?" Haley asked, trying hard to sound casual.

"I decided to take a personal day off," I replied.

"Yeah, your secretary told me. Is everything okay?"

"Yes," I said. "Everything's fine."

"Are you at home?"

That's none of your damn business! "If you need me for anything, you have my cell phone number. I gotta run."

I hung up without waiting for her goodbye. The girl probably wanted to know where I was so she could run and tell Porter. Was he using Haley to keep track of what I was doing? If the two of them were plotting against me, there wasn't really a thing I could do about it. I had come down here to deal with my husband. I needed to turn my energies back to *that* problem.

I walked over to the refrigerator and looked inside. I wanted a Diet Coke, but Jefferson did not believe in buying anything sugar-free or low in fat. I grabbed a regular Coke and returned to the couch. I wished I could shake the apprehension I felt at seeing the troubled look on my husband's face when he spotted me standing in the trailer.

I took a sip of Coke and started planning exactly how best to confront my husband about his big-breasted little assistant.

CHAPTER 42

Special meandered along the walkway at the Carlsbad Outlet Mall, her thoughts far from fashion.

A vivid picture of Jefferson's face when he first stepped inside the trailer was still etched in her mind. Horror, not happiness, shrieked from his eyes. Special did not want to believe it, but she actually thought something might have gone down between the girl and Jefferson.

Walking into Bebe, Special's eyes gravitated toward a pair of beige pants on the sale rack. She looked around for the dressing room, but didn't see it. Two salesgirls were busy chatting with each other.

"No such thing as good help anymore," she mumbled to herself. She found a red leather skirt that had been marked down twice and purchased both items in her size without trying them on. Bebe's clothes were usually a perfect fit.

After seeing nothing that wowed her in Barney's, she bought a slice of pepperoni pizza and a strawberry banana smoothie, then resumed her shopping. Twenty minutes later, she tossed her packages into her car and drove back toward the Residence Inn. She was less than a mile away when a sign in the window of a Radio Shack caught her attention. She made an abrupt U-turn and drove her Porsche into the Radio Shack parking lot.

It was just beginning to get dark by the time Special pulled into Jefferson's worksite. She was glad to find him alone in the trailer.

"I wish I could find a brother as hard-working as you," she said as she walked in carrying a small sculpture under her arm.

Jefferson stared at her. "What're you doing here?"

"I was out shopping and saw something I thought would brighten this place up a bit. She set the sculpture on his desk. It was close to eighteen inches high and depicted a jazz musician blowing a sax. "You like it?"

"Uh...yeah," Jefferson said, looking puzzled. "Thanks."

Special picked up the sculpture and walked over to the back counter. "It'll look great sitting right here where everyone can see it." She set it down, then stepped back to admire it.

When Special turned around to face Jefferson, his head was bent over a stack of invoices. She stared at him as if some admission might telepathically travel from his subconscious to hers. Special had always had a pretty cool relationship with Jefferson and it was hard coping with the disturbing thoughts that had been running through her mind all afternoon. If a man like Jefferson turned out to be a dog, there was no hope of her ever finding a decent guy.

"I'm about ready to pack up," Jefferson said, glancing up at her. "But I have to tell you, I'm too tired to go out to dinner."

"Vernetta couldn't care less about going out," Special said. "She only came down here to be with you. So if y'all just want to kick it together in your room tonight, that's fine with me. I can catch a movie."

"Thanks," Jefferson said.

Special walked up to Jefferson's desk. "Mind if I talk to you for a second?"

He stared at her guardedly. "Sure, what's up?"

"Your wife was a little stressed out about your phone call last night."

Jefferson's expression did not change, but he put down his pencil and folded his arms across his chest. "There was nothing for her to be concerned about. You know how Vernetta overreacts."

Special nodded. "Yeah, she does have a tendency to do that sometimes. But when your man's been out of town for several weeks, then calls you in the middle of the night professing his undying love, you tend to start wondering if he's got something to feel guilty about."

"I'll never understand how women think," Jefferson said, his face stoic. "I certainly don't have anything to feel guilty about, Special."

"I think maybe you might."

One corner of Jefferson's mouth turned upward, but a smile did not follow. Special could tell he was getting pissed, but she was not ready to back off just yet.

"Did Vernetta send you over here?" Jefferson asked.

"Nope. She thinks I'm out shopping."

"Then maybe that's where you need to be." He picked up his pencil and went back to his invoices. He took several pieces of paper from one pile and stacked them neatly on the left corner of his desk.

Special stayed planted just a couple of feet away. Jefferson looked up at her. "Since it seems like you plan on hanging around, why don't you have a seat, Special?"

She grabbed a chair and pulled it close to Jefferson's desk.

He looked her in the eye, started to speak, then stopped. She waited him out, hoping he was going to confide in her. For a second, though, she did not want him to continue. If he had some shocking admission to make, she wasn't sure she could handle it any better than Vernetta.

"I've known you for as long as I've known Vernetta," Jefferson began, visibly fatigued. "And I know she's like a sister to you and that you care about her a lot. In fact, I've always considered you to be like a sister to me, too."

Special smiled.

"And if you were my real sister sitting here talking to me, asking me what I think you're asking me…" His voice trailed off, then picked up again. "I'd tell you to mind your own damn business."

Special was taken aback by Jefferson's response but tried not to show it. She held up under his angry gaze for as long as she could, then got up and put the chair back where she had found it.

"Since Vernetta thinks you're out shopping," Jefferson said, "can I assume you don't plan on sharing this conversation with her?"

Special smirked. "If you don't have anything to feel guilty about, why're you concerned about my talking to her?"

"You just acknowledged that my wife has a tendency to overreact," Jefferson said.

Special nodded. "Nah, I don't plan to tell her about our little talk. She'd probably be more mad at me than you anyway."

Jefferson smiled for the first time. Special was headed for the sculpture when Jefferson quietly called out her name. She turned around to face him.

"I love my wife," he said, the look on his face so earnest that it scared her. "And I'd never purposely do anything to hurt her."

"So you're saying something happened, but it wasn't on purpose?"

Jefferson threw up his hands. "Damn! No, Special. That's not what I'm saying."

"Okay, okay," she said, backing off. The man was about to go ballistic. She continued to examine his face, praying that the sincerity she saw in his eyes was real. Anyway, she would find out soon enough.

Turning away from Jefferson so he could not see her hands, Special picked up the sculpture from the counter and pressed a tiny button on the right-hand side. The sculpture was equipped with a nanny cam video recorder. For the next forty-eight hours, it would record everything that went on inside the trailer. If something *was* going on between Jefferson and LaKeesha, the tape would tell all.

Special picked up her purse and was almost at the door when Stan walked in. As soon as he spotted her, his lips curled into a salacious smile and he made a beeline in her direction. Stan hit on her every chance he got, even though

Special's body language communicated that she thought the man was disgusting.

"How's the woman of my dreams?" Stan said, throwing a heavy arm across Special's shoulders. His big gut grazed her hip when he leaned in to kiss her on the cheek.

"I'm fine," she said, squirming free. He was funky, dirty and needed a shave. "I was just leaving."

"You don't have to go yet," Jefferson said with a facetious chuckle.

"Uh, yes I do." She stepped around Stan and grabbed the door handle.

"Hold on a minute, Special," Jefferson said. "Hey, Stan, can I trouble you to take Special out to dinner tonight so she won't have to spend the evening by herself?"

"Hell yeah!" Stan's big smile displayed a gold tooth that had lost its sparkle. "I've been trying to get a date with this hottie for I don't know how long. Baby, I'ma show you just what a good time is all about."

Special fired a nasty look in Jefferson's direction. "Thanks a lot," she said. "I'll be sure to return the favor."

CHAPTER 43

Champions Sports Bar on Century Boulevard near LAX was packed with boisterous patrons. Ferris anxiously rubbed his hands together, trying not to make eye contact with Nathaniel Hall, who was sitting directly in front of him, an arm's length away.

The CFO had a plane to catch and had ordered Ferris to meet him for an update on the Henry Randle situation.

Ferris silently counted at least fifty other customers in the bar and was glad to be surrounded by so many people. No one would possibly do anything crazy to him with this many witnesses, he reassured himself.

"So did you get the documents back yet?" Hall asked.

Ferris knew the question was coming, but his neck muscles still tensed at hearing the words. "Well, um, no. Not yet." Ferris's eyes darted around the room, which had flat-screen TVs on nearly every wall. "They…um…they haven't found them."

Hall's wrinkled fingers balled into fists. "What do you mean, they haven't found them?" the CFO hissed. He had a round, angry face, chiseled with thick age lines. A nervous twitch caused his right eye to blink uncontrollably. "I thought you said the police found the documents in Carruthers's car?"

"They did."

"Well?"

Ferris's heart began to beat erratically. "They're missing."

"What the hell do you mean, they're missing?"

Ferris cringed. "Our private investigator has a friend in the department who promised to get them back for us. But somebody else had already checked them out of the property room by the time he got there."

"Why would anybody else care about those documents?" Hall demanded.

"I'm not sure. An LAPD detective by the name of Coleman has them."

"Is he investigating the case?"

"Not officially."

"Then what in the hell does he want with those documents?"

Ferris noticed a couple at the next table staring in their direction. "Please calm down," Ferris whispered, leaning in over the table. "We don't want to make a scene."

"Don't tell me to calm down!" Hall said in a restrained shout. "You've botched this thing from day one. And just in case you've forgotten, your ass is on the line, too."

"I'm fully aware of that," Ferris replied, clutching his hands to stop them from shaking.

"What do you know about this Coleman asshole?"

Ferris wanted to lie and say he knew nothing, but the information Cliff had passed on about an hour ago would probably surface anyway.

"He's a close friend of Special Moore."

"What are you talking about? Who's Special Moore?"

"She's the best friend of Vernetta Henderson, that attorney at O'Reilly & Finney who was handling the Randle case. The one our investigator took the pictures of with Hamilton Ellis."

"And why do I care about this woman?"

"Because Coleman took her up to that street where Karen's car went off the road. They're apparently investigating the case."

Hall lowered his head until his nose almost touched the table. He began making a loud wheezing noise. Ferris knew Hall was an asthmatic and assumed he was in the midst of an attack. Just as Ferris was about to call for help, Hall's head bolted up and he reached for his Scotch.

Fear prompted Ferris to continue talking. "According to my source, Coleman is a bit of a slug. He's just hanging around waiting for retirement. He apparently has the hots for this woman, who considers herself an amateur sleuth. He told one of his buddies that he's humoring her by letting her think they're really investigating the case together." Ferris paused, afraid to deliver the rest of the information. "My source also tells me it's possible Coleman showed her the documents and may have even given her a copy."

The CFO slammed his glass on the table, which drew the attention of their waitress and several bar patrons. Hall lowered his voice, but the venom in it made up for the reduced volume. "You have to get those documents back. If they get into the wrong hands, we could all be in big trouble."

"I know, I know," Ferris said, closing his eyes.

"Where are we on the Randle case?" Hall demanded.

"We're hoping to get the trial date moved to give us some time to set up a mediation. But that hasn't happened yet." Ferris braced himself for another explosive display from Hall. "We've been trying to get it settled, but Randle's attorney, Hamilton Ellis, says he won't talk settlement with anyone except Ms. Henderson."

Hall drew in a breath. "If the guy only wants to deal with Henderson," Hall said, scratching his cheek, "then get her back on the case."

"What? How are we going to explain that?" Ferris asked.

"You figure it out," Hall barked again. "Hell, tell her we screwed up. Just do whatever you have to do to get the case settled. And get those documents back!" The CFO took another sip of his Scotch.

Ferris glanced around the bar again. When his sad eyes landed on a young Mexican-looking woman at the table to his right, she turned away.

"And find out why this Coleman guy has those documents. If anybody figures out what the hell they are, we're all going straight to jail. So you need to fix this. Now!"

Ferris did not say a word. How had he gotten himself mixed up in all of this? He wanted to ask about Karen, but was too afraid to even utter her name. He had tried to convince himself that her death had indeed been an accident, but the timing was simply too convenient for even him to buy that story.

Framing Henry Randle to get him out of the company had been a stupid idea. What had he been thinking? He should have stood up to them from the start. He was as much a victim as Karen.

This was all Henry Randle's fault, Ferris thought as he rubbed his forehead. The man should've just done his job and kept his complaints to himself.

Ferris had to get his hands on those documents. Too many careers were riding on it.

CHAPTER 44

Jefferson pulled his Toyota Tundra into the parking lot of the Residence Inn, squeezed into a space intended for a compact and turned off the engine. He hung his head and massaged the back of his neck. He was not happy about this impromptu visit from his wife and her busybody of a friend. He was already under enough stress with the project behind schedule.

The next couple of days would be all about playing it cool, he told himself. He just had to make sure Vernetta and Special headed back to L.A. without having another face-to-face with LaKeesha.

After their talk at the Thai Palace, LaKeesha hadn't tripped, but the female species was unpredictable. The girl could easily flip out and say something crazy to his wife. He could tell she had been just as uncomfortable in Vernetta's presence as he had been. He gathered that from her refusal to make eye contact with him and the fact that she left two hours before her quitting time. He was just glad LaKeesha had had the good sense to leave.

Jefferson climbed out of the truck and made his way toward the stairwell leading to the second floor. As he lethargically mounted the stairs, his feet felt heavier with each step. After Special's attempted inquisition, he knew he could expect more of the same from Vernetta. Unlike Special, Vernetta was not one to immediately move in for the kill. She liked to let things percolate, then pounce on him just when he thought everything was cool.

In retrospect, it had been a pretty stupid idea to call Vernetta in the middle of the night and quiz her about sexual harassment law. His wife was a lawyer. Of course his questions would send her suspicious mind spinning. For her to tear down here the very next day meant she definitely suspected that something was up between him and LaKeesha.

Jefferson paused at the top of the second-floor landing. The armpits of his T-shirt were soaked with perspiration. It was a few minutes after eight and almost sixty degrees, yet he was sweating as if he had just walked out of a sauna. He had to get it together before facing Vernetta.

He had already decided that he would admit to nothing and pray his wife did not see through him. Like his mother, Vernetta was a human lie detector machine where he was concerned. Both women could look him in the eye and tell when he was lying before the words even escaped his lips. But not this time. There was simply too much at stake.

The closer Jefferson got to his room the shorter his steps became. He did not like the idea of lying to Vernetta, at least not about anything important. But there was no way he could explain what had gone down with LaKeesha and expect Vernetta to be reasonable about it. Vernetta saw the world in very precise terms. Black and white. Good and bad. Right and wrong. What he had done would be nothing short of adultery in her eyes.

But from Jefferson's vantage point, he had just gotten a blow job. An unsolicited one at that. It was a minor infraction, not a felony. He did not deserve the death penalty and he planned to do everything in his power to keep from being dragged off to the electric chair.

He opened the door and spotted Vernetta asleep on the couch, wrapped in a thick blue bathrobe, curled up like a Siamese kitten. He liked watching her sleep. There was no question that he loved his wife. He could still remember the first time he'd made love to her. He had felt this strange emotion that he'd never experienced with another woman. The last time he could remember feeling anything even close was when Cynthia Hebron, the cutest girl in the whole fifth grade, had left a Valentine's card on his desk. A reappearance of that same inexplicable flutter in his heart was the primary reason he was a married man today.

Jefferson walked across the room, gripped the back of the couch with both hands and kissed his wife on the forehead.

Vernetta stirred, then her eyes blinked open.

"Hey, sleepyhead," he whispered.

Vernetta reached up to hug him, then kissed him on the lips.

Jefferson slumped down on the couch next to her.

"What time is it?" Vernetta asked.

"Just after eight," he said. "You eat yet?"

"Nope. I wanted to wait for you. Special told me you didn't feel like going out so I picked up some barbecue." Vernetta took Jefferson's right hand in hers and rubbed the calluses on his palm with her index finger. "You work this late every night?"

"Afraid so," Jefferson said. "I think I could use a beer." He got up, walked into the kitchenette and flipped on the light. He grabbed a Miller Genuine Draft from the refrigerator, popped it open and took a long swig.

"Special told me about you siccing Stan on her," Vernetta said, smiling. "She's going to be gunning for you in the morning."

Jefferson grinned despite the uncomfortable tension that saturated the room. He knew Vernetta was looking for the right entry point to commence her attack. He remained in the kitchenette, leaning against the counter.

"Are things going any better with your project?" Vernetta asked.

"Somewhat. At least we finally figured out where the problem is." He took a big gulp of beer.

More silence.

"LaKeesha certainly is a sight for sore eyes," Vernetta said. She yawned and retied her robe.

Jefferson inhaled and said nothing. *Here it comes.*

"Does she always dress like that?"

Jefferson took another swallow of his beer before responding. "Frankly, I'm usually too busy working to even notice how she's dressed."

"Is that right?"

Jefferson wished he could cut the conversation short. Or at least direct it to the left or right, rather than allow it to continue spiraling down the short, disastrous road on which it was headed. He knew his wife all too well. When something bothered her, she had to get it off her chest. And he would let her do that. He was the one who had messed up, so he owed her that much. But he wasn't confessing to shit.

"All your questions about sexual harassment last night got me a little worried," Vernetta said. "I started wondering whether you were asking me that stuff because you had gotten yourself into some trouble."

"I told you why I was asking." Jefferson stared off into space, afraid that if he looked over at his wife, his eyes might give him away.

"I know what you told me." Vernetta got up from the couch and joined him in the kitchenette. She rested her body against the opposite counter, facing him. Only a few feet separated them.

"The way that girl dresses, I'd say she was a sexual harassment case waiting to happen." Vernetta stopped to tighten the belt of her robe.

Jefferson shrugged. "Stan hired her. Not me."

"You certainly looked awful nervous when you walked in and saw Special and me standing there."

Jefferson turned away and set the beer can on the counter behind him, thankful to have a reason to break away from Vernetta's penetrating gaze. "You know what, babe? I'm tired as hell. And you standing here jamming me up like this ain't exactly what I need after working my ass off all day."

"If something's bothering me, I should be able to discuss it with you, shouldn't I?"

He chuckled in a way that he hoped conveyed how much this conversation irritated him. "Exactly what're you saying, Vernetta? You think I'm fuckin' that little girl? Is that what you wanna ask me?"

Vernetta stared back at him, sulking with her eyes. "I didn't say that. You just looked really nervous, that's all. That, combined with the fact that you called me in the middle of the night to tell me you'll always love me, no matter what. Just sounded to me like you had something to feel guilty about."

Jefferson chuckled again and reached behind him for his beer. "You know what? The next time I get the urge to tell you how much I love you—day or night—remind me to keep it to my damn self." He drained the beer can, then opened the refrigerator and grabbed a second one.

Vernetta buried her hands in the pockets of her robe.

"I hope you didn't come all the way down here just to jam me up over something that's totally in your head," Jefferson continued. "I thought you knew me better than that. I don't want that girl and she don't want my old ass. You're my wife and I love you. And the fact that you're standing here telling me you don't trust me is pretty messed up."

Vernetta seemed to be studying his face and Jefferson let her. Staring right back, remaining as expressionless as humanly possible. Vernetta finally grunted and stormed over to the couch.

Jefferson silently exhaled and took another sip of beer.

"You ready for me to heat up the barbecue?" Vernetta asked.

That was a good sign. At least she was still talking to him. He hated it when she gave him the silent treatment. "Let me take a shower first." Jefferson put the open beer can back inside the refrigerator, pulled off his T-shirt and headed for the bathroom.

Snatching back the shower curtain, he turned on the shower full force. He had just won round one. Vernetta was probably feeling guilty now for not trusting him. He hated turning the tables on her like that, but he had no other choice. He stripped off the rest of his clothes and stepped into the shower. He closed his eyes and relaxed as the warm water pelted his face.

When Jefferson reached for the soap, he flinched. Vernetta had slipped into the shower and was standing behind him.

"I didn't mean to accuse you like that," she said, placing a hand on his shoulder, motioning for him to turn around. "I'm sorry."

When he did turn around, he welcomed the sight of his wife's beautiful brown body, wearing nothing but a ridiculous-looking, polka-dot shower cap. She pulled him to her, a move that filled him with relief. Their conversation would be forgotten—for now. Jefferson fully expected that Vernetta would throw her suspicions about LaKeesha in his face for several days, maybe even weeks or months. He would have no problem dealing with his wife's snide comments about the girl. That was a punishment that fit the crime and he would happily do his time.

Jefferson pressed Vernetta even closer, enjoying the feel of her naked body against his. He was tired as hell, but the feeling of arousal rising up in him promised to wipe away all evidence of his exhaustion.

As his wife's soft lips brushed his chest with kisses, he thought about the incredible make-up sex they were about to have. And that made him smile.

CHAPTER 45

Whatever doubts I'd had about my husband's fidelity, or lack thereof, Jefferson had all but erased them. We had talked frankly about my concerns long into the night, and in the end, I had decided to heed Special's advice. I didn't need to go looking for trouble.

Friday morning, Jefferson and I ate breakfast at IHOP, while Special slept in. When Jefferson headed off to work, I made a few business calls, then worked out in the Residence Inn gym. Later in the day, Special and I strolled through the San Diego Zoo, had lunch at the Cheesecake Factory and caught two movies.

That evening, Jefferson took us to dinner at a seafood restaurant in the Gaslamp Quarter. Special had threatened to drive back home without me if Jefferson invited Stan along.

When I began packing on Saturday morning, I hadn't realized how hard it would be to leave. Jefferson walked out of the shower wrapped in a towel and lay down across the bed, watching me as I stuffed clothes and toiletries into my bag.

"I'm glad you came down," he said.

"Me, too. I wish we could stay longer, but Special has plans tonight."

Jefferson grinned. "Whoever the dude is, I feel sorry for him. Dating her has to be damn hard work."

I picked up a pillow and hit him with it. "Don't talk about my friend."

He slipped into his clothes while I wrestled with the zipper on my bag.

"I'll never understand why you women have to pack so much crap when you travel," Jefferson teased. "You were only here two days, but there's enough stuff in there for a three-week cruise."

"A woman likes to have choices," I said.

Jefferson grabbed my bag and I followed him out the door, toward Special's room. I knocked but got no answer. I knocked again, then glanced at my watch. We had agreed to leave at eleven o'clock and it was ten minutes after.

Jefferson turned around and peered over the railing two stories down. "Didn't Special park over there last night?" He pointed at an empty space in the left corner of the lot below.

I started to panic as I stared down at the spot where Special's car should have been. I pulled out my BlackBerry and dialed her number.

"I'm on my way," Special said before I could say a word.

"Where are you?" I asked.

"Had to make a quick run over to Jefferson's office. I lost an earring. But luckily I found it underneath his desk."

"Special, what were you really doing at Jefferson's office? Please tell me you didn't go over there to start anything with LaKeesha."

Jefferson opened his mouth to say something, but I held up my hand, cutting him off.

"I just told you," Special said. "I had to look for my earring. I was scared to death that I was going to run into that fat ass Stan. But thank God I didn't. I'm pulling in the driveway right now. Bye."

At that exact moment, Special's car zoomed into the parking lot below.

"Special went over to the worksite?" Jefferson asked as we headed downstairs. "For what?"

"She said she lost an earring and went over there to look for it."

"She didn't go over there to look for no earring," he said. "She probably went over there to finish her little beef with LaKeesha. But she doesn't work on Saturdays."

Jefferson had that same stressed-out look on his face that I had seen when I surprised him in the trailer. Once again, my stomach churned with doubt.

Special met us before we got to the bottom of the stairs.

"So, Special," Jefferson said, "why did you really go back to—"

She brushed past us, ignoring him. "Here," she said, stopping to toss her car keys to me. "Go ahead and put your stuff in the car. I'm already packed. I just have to grab my bag."

She continued up the stairs two at a time, then stopped at the top and called back to Jefferson. "Hey, brother-in-law, you need better security at your office. They just let anybody walk in. I could've stole something, but wasn't nothing in there worth stealing."

Jefferson started to respond, but I tugged at his arm. "Just let it go. If she was up to something, you'll find out soon enough."

When we got to the car, Jefferson tossed my bag into the backseat, then leaned against the passenger door and pulled me to him.

"Maybe this visit wasn't such a good idea after all," Jefferson said, holding me tight. "Now I'm going to miss you even more."

"Then I guess it *was* a good thing," I said.

Special jogged down the stairs and dropped her bag next to mine. "Okay, you two, break it up. You've got five seconds for one last kiss for the road. And please, no tongues."

Jefferson laughed, then promptly took me by the chin and gave me a long, wet kiss. "Call to let me know you made it back, okay?" he said, opening the car door so I could climb in. "And, Special, drive safely. You're carrying some very precious cargo."

"Ain't nobody more precious to me than me," she said. "I know what I'm doing behind this wheel." She started up the engine and slowly backed out of the parking space. Jefferson jogged alongside the car for a few feet, then waved goodbye.

As the Porsche sped northbound along the San Diego Freeway, I enjoyed feeling the fresh air grazing my face. Maybe I would buy myself a convertible when I made partner. Scratch that. *If* I made partner.

Special nudged my arm. "Girl, when did you become hard of hearing?"

"I'm sorry," I said. "Did you say something?"

"I was asking you if everything was okay between you and Jefferson."

"I guess so. I had a really good time. I'm glad we made this trip. Thanks for driving."

"So you're not worried that anything's going on with LaKeesha?"

"I don't know." I turned away. "I've never had a reason not to trust Jefferson. He's not the player type. Frankly, I have too much other stuff to think about right now to be worrying about him screwing around. For the time being, I'm just going to forget about it."

"I think that's a good idea," Special said. "So what do you think about Ms. LaKeesha?"

"I think she reminds me a lot of you. Except she's about two cup sizes bigger."

"Please! Can you believe a child with boobs that big has the nerve to walk around braless? I'm sending her ass a bra as soon as we get back."

"Special, you better not."

"She won't know it's from me."

"Special, don't!" I warned.

"Okay, fine," she hissed.

I turned off the radio and slipped in a John Legend CD.

"Let's hear it," I said, giving my friend a skeptical look. "Why'd you really go back to Jefferson's office?"

"I already told you. To look for my earring."

"Sure you did."

She smiled sheepishly. "And by the way, you owe me big-time for going out to dinner with that asshole, Stan. At least I had me some lobster. I couldn't believe he actually thought I was going to invite him into my room. That brother's delusional."

"I'm just glad Stan backed up Jefferson's story about his cousin being accused of sexual harassment," I said. "But I guess it really doesn't mean much. I'm sure Stan would certainly lie for Jefferson."

"I'm sure he would," Special said.

I sighed. "Like I said, I really don't want to think about this stuff anymore."

"Don't worry," Special said. "I got a feeling you'll find out soon enough whether anything went down." She looked over at me and smiled.

"Okay, Special, what do you know that I don't?"

"Nothing yet," she said with a smug expression, her eyes glued to the road. "But you never know what I *might* find out."

CHAPTER 46

Just after seven on Monday morning, I walked into the lobby of the O'Reilly & Finney building and spotted Haley coming out of Starbucks. I looked directly at her, but she pretended not to see me and headed in the opposite direction. I just hoped running into her this early in the morning was not an omen about how the rest of my day would go.

When I got to my office, I had a zillion e-mail messages to read and several phone calls to return, but no major fires to put out. After responding to a few e-mails, I scanned the Internet to see if there were any new reports concerning Micronics's GAP-7 Program and the crash of that transport plane in Iraq. But the story seemed to have run its course.

I worked until almost eight, then headed over to 24 Hour Fitness for a late-night workout. After forty-five minutes on the treadmill and one hundred sit-ups, I retired to the dry sauna.

I had the tiny wooden room all to myself for about twenty minutes. Then somebody invaded my space.

"Wow, it's really hot in here tonight," said an unfamiliar voice.

I was stretched out on an upper bench, lying on my stomach with my head facing the back wall. I did not appreciate the intrusion. I hoped my silence would communicate to my intruder that I was not in the mood for conversation.

"You're an attorney, aren't you?"

I did not bother to open my eyes or turn around to check out my sauna mate. I was too exhausted to care how this woman knew what I did for a living. I just wanted her to cut the small talk. I responded with a curt "Yes."

"And don't you represent Micronics?"

At that question, I perked up. Resting my upper body on my forearms, I turned to face the woman. She was African-American, probably in her late fifties, with speckles of gray throughout her short, stylish haircut. Her face looked vaguely familiar, but I could not place it. She had on a bright orange, one-piece bathing suit and was holding a paperback book. I only hoped she would start reading it.

"Look, let me be honest," the woman continued, apparently sensing my frustration. "I've been wanting to talk to you for a long time. My name is Norma. Norma Brown. I work in HR at Micronics. I'm an administrative assistant. I've seen you meeting with Rich Ferris. He's my boss. I've also seen you here a couple of times and I've been hoping to run into you again. I was too afraid to call your office. Tonight I finally got lucky."

I turned over on my back and closed my eyes. I knew precisely what was coming next. The woman was having a problem at work and wanted me to do something about it.

"I need to talk to you about the Randle case," she said, a little less timidly now. "There's some crazy stuff going on down there. The way they treated that man just wasn't right."

My eyes popped opened. The Randle case was the last subject I wanted to talk about. The best thing about my trip to San Diego was that it allowed me some time to think about something other than Henry Randle and Karen Carruthers. "I'm not handling that case anymore," I said.

"I just couldn't sit by and do nothing," Norma continued as if she had not heard a word I said. "I thought about calling Randle's attorney, but I'm not trying to lose my job or nothing. I figured since you work for the company, if you really knew what was going on, you might be able to do something about it."

The woman opened the center of the book and pulled out some papers that were folded into quarters. "I have something I want you to take a look at." She unfolded the papers and extended them to me.

I did not reach for them. "What's that?"

"It's a report about the Randle case prepared by one of our former attorneys. I worked with Mr. Randle for close to ten years. Ain't no way he grabbed that woman. And this report proves that he didn't."

"Where'd you get that?"

"Somebody left it on the copy machine and I made a copy of it."

"I can't look at that," I said. "And you could get into a lot of trouble for making a copy."

Norma looked both shocked and hurt.

I knew something was not kosher with the Randle case. And after Carruthers's death and the news story about that plane crash, my doubts about the case had only grown. But for all I knew, this could be another setup. I didn't buy Porter's story that Micronics was only surveilling Randle and his attorneys. I wouldn't put it past them to hire somebody like Norma to put me to the test.

A sun-starved white woman strolled into the sauna and flopped down on the bench next to Norma and started slapping lemon-scented oil on her arms and legs. After about two minutes of heavy panting, she left.

Norma folded the papers and placed them back inside the book. As she got up to leave, I began to feel bad about brushing her off.

"Look, I'm not sure what's going on," I said, just before Norma made it to the door. "But I agree with you. Something isn't right about that case."

I knew I was taking a chance, but I was dying to know once and for all whether Randle was being framed. Maybe the papers in Norma's hand could tell me. I climbed down to the lower bench.

"Why don't you sit back down?" I said.

A hopeful smile spread across Norma's face and she eagerly took a seat next to me.

"It's not a good idea for me to look at that report," I continued. "If anyone ever asks me if I've seen it, I want to be able to say I haven't."

Disappointment resurfaced on Norma's face. Her shoulders fell and she started to rise from the bench.

"No, wait," I said, gently touching her forearm. "I'm only saying I don't want to read it myself. Why don't you read it to me instead?"

CHAPTER 47

That same night, Special sat quietly in her hot-pink bedroom, perched on the edge of her king-size bed, contemplating a very important decision. Should she look at the nanny cam tape she had retrieved from Jefferson's office or toss it into the trash and forget the whole thing?

Special had debated that question for most of the day and hadn't gotten a lick of work done. While she didn't know whether she should look at the tape, there was one thing she was one-hundred-percent sure about. If she found out that Jefferson was screwing around with LaKeesha, she had no intention of telling Vernetta about it. She knew from experience that women did not like hearing from other women—even their closest friends—that their men were not all that.

After sitting there for a few more minutes, her curiosity won out. She said a quick prayer, then pressed the small tape into a special cartridge and slid it into the VCR machine underneath the TV at the foot of her bed. She positioned herself cross-legged on her Donna Karan bedspread and stared at the remote control for several seconds, giving herself one last chance to back out. She took a long, deep breath, then hit the Play button.

The first few seconds of the video were dark and grainy, then a much lighter static shot of the inside of the trailer came into view. The picture wasn't great, but Special could make out herself and Jefferson inside the trailer. Stan walked in a few seconds later. Special turned up her nose as she watched Stan kiss her on the cheek.

Once Special left the trailer, Stan started going on and on about what a good time he was going to have taking her out to dinner. A shiver went through her as she listened.

"Man, you think she'll let me hit it tonight?" Stan asked, slobbering with excitement.

"Forget it," Jefferson warned. "Special's way out of your league."

"You're underestimating me, my brother. If a man's willing to put enough cash on the table, he can get any woman he wants."

"Stan, you could put the entire Bank of America on the table and Special still ain't giving you none," Jefferson said.

Special smiled. "Whew! Thank you, brother-in-law!" she said out loud.

After a few more minutes of braggadocios talk by Stan, they both headed for the door. The tape went dark when Jefferson turned out the lights.

Special picked up the remote and fast-forwarded through several hours of video until the picture lightened up again. She shook her head at the sight of Stan walking into the trailer carrying three boxes of Krispy Kreme doughnuts. She zipped past him making coffee and studying some blueprints, but stopped the tape when

LaKeesha entered the trailer. She was wearing jeans and a green T-shirt, which she had tied into a knot at the waist.

Special grimaced. "That girl's breasts are going to be dragging the ground by the time she's thirty if somebody don't teach her ass to wear a bra!"

She watched in disgust as Stan stared at LaKeesha's chest, which LaKeesha pretended not to notice. When the girl bent over to get something from the refrigerator, Stan gawked at her ass.

"Old dog!" Special shouted at the television screen.

Stan gave LaKeesha some actual work to do, then left. Jefferson walked in about five minutes later.

Special picked up the remote and turned up the volume. The first thing she noticed was that LaKeesha and Jefferson seemed to be ignoring each other. Special hit the Pause button. She was certain Jefferson had not said hello to the girl when he walked in, but maybe she had missed it. She rewound the tape, hit Play again and listened more closely. She was right. Jefferson had not said a word to LaKeesha and LaKeesha had not acknowledged him either.

"Dang!" Special said, slapping her hand against her thigh. "Something definitely went down between them two."

As the tape continued to roll, Special noticed that every few seconds, LaKeesha looked over at Jefferson, as if she were trying to catch him watching her. Apparently irritated because he was not, LaKeesha walked over to Jefferson's desk. She stood in front of him, nothing but attitude on her face. Jefferson pulled a tablet from a side drawer and started writing, ignoring her.

"You know," LaKeesha said, "your wife didn't look nothing like I thought she would. She's cute and all, but I expected you to be with somebody much hotter. You can do a lot better."

Jefferson stopped writing. "I'm busy right now," he said without looking up.

"And her bitchy little friend with the stupid ass name, she has some serious issues."

Special hit the Pause button and hopped off the bed. "I should drive down there right now and whip that heffa's ass!" She closed her eyes, counted to five, then hit Play again.

"I was talking to one of my friends about you last night," LaKeesha said, smiling down at Jefferson. "She told me I should sue you for sexual harassment."

This time, Special hit the Pause button and fell back onto the bed. "No! No! No! No! No!" So Jefferson *had* screwed the girl. *How could he be so stupid?*

Special did not think she could handle watching the rest of the tape without a drink. She rushed into the kitchen and grabbed a bottle of chardonnay from the refrigerator. After removing the cork, she opened the cabinet to look for a wineglass, then changed her mind. She did not need a glass. She would probably have to drink the whole bottle after hearing what else LaKeesha had to say.

Back in the bedroom, Special sat down on the edge of the bed and hit the Rewind button. She listened a second time as LaKeesha told Jefferson that she should sue him for sexual harassment. Jefferson took a long time to respond. He started writing again, while LaKeesha leered at him. After almost a full minute, Jefferson slowly pushed his chair back from his desk and looked up at her.

"You can't sue me for sexual harassment, LaKeesha, because I haven't harassed you," he said calmly.

"I know you didn't harass me," LaKeesha said, smiling deviously. "But in a court of law, it's my word against yours. And who do you think they're going to believe? The cute, young college student or the older, married man whose wife is out of town?"

Special's mouth fell open. She hit the Pause button again. So Jefferson *hadn't* been with LaKeesha! *Thank you, Jesus!* Special was so relieved she wanted to cry. She took a long, sloppy chug from the wine bottle, almost choking as wine doused her blouse. When she was done coughing, she hit Play again.

Jefferson could only stare at LaKeesha, his face a mixture of anger and shock.

"This is what we're going to do," LaKeesha said, tossing a handful of braids over her shoulder. "I think I need a raise. Five hundred dollars a month ought to do it—for now. Otherwise, I'm going to call a lawyer and tell him I've been sexually harassed by my boss, who owns a successful electrical contracting company."

"But you don't have a case," Jefferson said, still playing it cool.

"I'll make one up," LaKeesha fired back, both hands gripping her hips. "So pull out that checkbook and start writing."

At first, Jefferson just sat there. Then he exhaled and

his whole body seemed to droop in defeat. He pulled some keys from the pocket of his jeans and unlocked the middle drawer of his desk. When Special saw what she recognized as a business-size checkbook, she jumped off the bed.

"You better not give that bitch a dime!" Special yelled at the television screen. She watched in horror as Jefferson scribbled across a check, tore it out of the checkbook and held it out to LaKeesha.

Jefferson got up. "Here's what we owe you, plus an extra week," he said, his voice angry, but not raised. "Now get your shit and get the fuck out. You're fired."

LaKeesha dropped her arms to her side, stunned. She snatched the check from him. "You think I won't sue you?" she screamed. "I will! I swear, I will!"

"Bring it on," Jefferson said. "I'm married to a lawyer, remember? And if you think she'll believe anything you say over what I tell her, you've got it all wrong. Now get out."

LaKeesha grabbed her book bag from behind Stan's desk. "My lawyer'll be calling you!"

Jefferson smiled at her. "Like I said, bring it on."

LaKeesha stormed out, slamming the trailer door behind her.

Jefferson sat back down, planted his elbows on the desk and clasped his hands. He closed his eyes and his lips started moving, but the tape did not pick up his words. If Special didn't know better, she could have sworn the man was praying. Jefferson got up after a couple of minutes and poured himself a cup of coffee, grabbed a long tube from the corner, then walked out of the trailer.

Special hit the Stop button on the remote control and took another long swig from the wine bottle.

"You did good, brother-in-law," she said, her pulse still racing from all the excitement. "You did really, really good."

CHAPTER 48

It took me by complete surprise when O'Reilly invited me for lunch two days after my trip to San Diego.

"How's it going, kiddo?" O'Reilly asked as he greeted me in the patio of the McCormick & Schmick's seafood restaurant across from our office building. He was already seated when I got there, but rose to give me a light embrace.

We engaged in small talk while browsing the menu. O'Reilly ordered a glass of white wine and his usual, the seafood salad. I ordered the same, minus the wine.

"So what's the real reason you invited me to lunch?" I finally asked. O'Reilly had barely spoken to me since my inquisition in his office just over a week ago. I was certain he had not extended this invitation just to shoot the breeze.

"What're you talking about? I don't need a reason to invite my favorite associate to lunch," he said.

My eyebrows fused in skepticism.

"Okay, Vernetta, you're much too smart for me." O'Reilly took a sip of wine. "I won't beat around the bush. Micronics wants you back on the Randle case."

I was momentarily stunned but quickly recovered. "Really? Even though they think I'm sleeping with the enemy?"

"C'mon, nobody thinks that. This was all a crazy mix-up. They realize now that nothing was going on between you and Hamilton Ellis. They really want the case settled and they think you can get the job done. We've tried to talk settlement, but Hamilton Ellis insists on dealing only with you. I told those boneheads at Micronics that they never should've taken you off the case."

Sure you did.

I suddenly remembered my conversation with Norma Brown and wanted to throw up. I had tried to convince myself that I had no obligation to report what she had told me since I was no longer handling the Randle case. But I couldn't even sell that faulty logic to myself. Even if I wasn't on the case anymore, I still had an ethical obligation to advise a client of the firm that one of its employees had unauthorized possession of a highly confidential legal memo.

The memo provided a clear explanation for Micronics's haste to resolve the case. It was a case analysis prepared by the General Counsel and addressed to the CEO, with a copy to Rich Ferris, the VP of HR and Nathaniel Hall, the Chief Financial Officer. It highlighted the obvious flaws in the Randle case, such as the lack of eyewitnesses to the incident, Randle's excellent work history, and the six white employees who'd engaged in sexual harassment that the company had not fired. Micronics's most immediate concern, according to the memo, was avoiding media attention concerning Randle's complaints of billing irregularities.

The memo noted that fifteen years earlier, the company

had been the target of a federal investigation that uncovered dozens of billing irregularities on a Navy contract. It was the kind of investigation that made great headlines, like a one-thousand-percent markup on a fifty-cent bolt. The media blitz and fines that followed sent Micronics's stock price into a high-speed nosedive. The memo warned that if the media picked up on Randle's allegations, it could prompt government investigators to take a closer look at not only Micronics's billing practices on the GAP-7 Program, but other programs as well.

The memo troubled me a great deal. It was yet another document that had been withheld from me. One that conclusively showed that Ferris knew about the other sexual harassment cases, but had lied to Porter about it. It also tended to support Henry Randle's claim that Micronics wanted him and his complaints of fraud hushed up. But had they actually framed him to achieve that end?

"How about it?" O'Reilly asked. He glanced past me to eye a tall brunette with legs up to her neck, wearing a skirt the size of a paper towel.

"This is a new one," I said. "I didn't know associates were allowed to pick and choose their cases." I felt like a rat trapped in a maze. If I reported Norma's conduct now, I would be chastised for not coming forward sooner, destroying any chance I had of making partner, if one still existed. If I refused to rejoin the case, the result would be the same. I would just have to keep my mouth shut and pray that Norma did, too.

"C'mon, Vernetta, don't give me such a hard time. We could order you back on the case, but I have too much respect for you as a lawyer to do it that way. The client made a mistake. They need you. The firm needs you."

Yeah, right. "Sure, O'Reilly, whatever you want." I took a sip of water.

"What I want is a little enthusiasm," he said.

"Well, it's hard to be excited about a case when the client accuses you of making out with the opposing counsel. Is Porter on board with this?" I asked.

"Yes, of course. He's looking forward to putting the entire case back in your lap. Haley's in over her head."

As the waiter walked up with our salads, O'Reilly stole another look at the brunette with the long legs. This time he made eye contact and smiled. The woman returned an even bigger smile.

"What's going on with the case now?" I asked.

"I understand there've been some significant developments. Haley was fishing around on the Internet and found some troubling information about Randle's background. And the Micronics Security Department went through some surveillance tapes and also came up with some useful stuff."

"Like what?" I asked, my interest piqued.

"I don't know all the details, but as I understand it, we're serving a motion to amend Micronics's answer to assert the after-acquired evidence rule." He glanced at his watch. "The motion is being served on Ellis and Jenkins right about now."

I had used the after-acquired evidence rule once before to get a wrongful termination case dismissed based on evidence discovered after the employee had been discharged. "The information Haley found must've been pretty good," I said.

"Apparently so."

"Is Micronics still willing to spend whatever it takes to settle the case?" I asked.

O'Reilly nodded.

"That can only mean they have something to hide."

"Name me one of our clients who doesn't have something to hide." O'Reilly reached for the basket of sourdough bread. "We just need to make the case go away. It's nothing short of a miracle that the other side hasn't found out about that woman's death yet."

I wanted to ask O'Reilly about the news reports concerning the GAP-7 Program, but thought better of it. My suspicion that there might be a link to the Randle case was nothing more than a hunch.

O'Reilly reached over and playfully patted my hand. "C'mon, Vernetta, this is no big deal for you. I'm sure you'll have the case settled in no time."

Being asked to return to the case, at least on the surface, seemed like a plus for me. But I could not shake a gloomy feeling that more bad news might be waiting in the wings.

"Does this mean I'm still on track for partnership?" I asked.

O'Reilly's lips curled into an evasive smile. "I don't recall anyone ever saying you were off track."

I tossed the same sly smile back at him. "Can I get that in writing?"

CHAPTER 49

"What kinda bullshit is this?" Reggie Jenkins screamed into the telephone.

I had rushed back to the office after my lunch with O'Reilly to take a look at the motion Haley had filed. Her Internet search had revealed that Randle had been convicted of felony burglary a month before he joined Micronics, some twenty-plus years earlier. Even more problematic for Randle, Micronics's Security Department had him on tape stuffing confidential documents into his briefcase.

Reggie must have dialed my number the second he finished reading the motion. I was surprised that he called me since he knew I'd been taken off the case. He had good reason to be upset about the motion, but the intensity of his rage startled me.

"Reggie, Reggie, temper, temper," I said. "I guess this means you'll be opposing the motion?"

"Absolutely!" Reggie shouted. "You know and I know those assholes at Micronics framed my client. Yet you have the nerve to file this bogus ass motion!"

"Look, Reggie," I said, "your client stole some confidential company records before he was terminated and neglected to mention that he was a convicted felon when he filled out his job application. If Micronics had known either fact, he would've been fired long before he grabbed Karen Carruthers in that elevator."

"My client never touched that bitch!" Reggie yelled so loudly I had to pull the telephone away from my ear. I was relieved that he had yet to mention Carruthers's death.

"Reggie, is that language really necessary? Can't we all just get along?"

"This ain't funny," Reggie snarled. I could almost see the smoke rising from his nostrils through the telephone.

"And if he did take any documents, it was only to prove that everything he was saying about the overbilling was true."

"Oh, so you admit your client stole the records," I said. "I guess that statement will back up the surveillance tape we have showing him stuffing documents into his little briefcase several months before he was fired."

Reggie began to stutter, but quickly regained his composure. "You know, my sistah," he said, his voice still raging with animosity, "I really don't understand how you sleep at night. The white boys over there are just pimping you, and you're too dumb or too naive to know it."

His words stung like a slap, but I refused to give him the satisfaction of knowing it. "You haven't said anything yet about your client's felony conviction." My tone was deliberately taunting. "And your defense to that is what?"

Reggie remained silent for longer than he should have. "Tell me something, Ms. Henderson, exactly how low do you plan to go? My client was barely out of his teens when that happened. He was in the wrong place at the wrong time. He asked a buddy for a ride and ended up in the middle of something he had absolutely nothing to do with. The judge knew it and the jury knew it. That's why he only got probation."

"But the fact remains that Micronics's employment application asks every applicant if they've ever been convicted of a felony. And your client intentionally lied about his criminal background. That's a material misrepresentation, which constitutes grounds for immediate termination. If he had answered the question truthfully, he never would've been hired in the first place. He was just lucky his conviction was too recent to have been picked up by Micronics's background check. So if he wants to scream fraud, he should stand in front of the mirror and do it."

I closed my eyes and tried to ignore the rancid taste rising in my throat. I wished there was some way to detach myself from my own smug words. *This is what lawyers do. Provide a vigorous defense for their clients.*

"I can't believe this!" Reggie said, yelling again. "Your boys have to go back more than twenty years to find a reason to justify terminating my client. What the hell does that tell you?"

That was not my problem. I needed leverage to get the case settled and Randle's felony conviction and his act of theft provided it. "The after-acquired evidence rule is a valid defense and Judge Sloan is going to grant our motion. So you may want to consider settling the case."

"Oh, so that's how you do it? Blackmail style?"

"Nobody's blackmailing you. I'm just suggesting we go back to the table. If you want, I can call the court and take the motion off calendar until we've had a chance to see if we can resolve the case."

"Screw that! Our position hasn't changed."

"I'm not sure Hamilton will feel the same," I said. "I heard he specifically wanted me back on the case precisely so that we could talk settlement."

"That was before you filed this motion. And anyway, this ain't Hamilton's case, it's mine. *I* call the shots. And we ain't settling. We're going to the mat on this one. Let's put twelve in a box and let a jury tell Micronics just how much this case is worth."

"You sure you want to do that? You and your client could very well end up with nothing."

"I'll take my chances," Reggie shouted. "I'll see your ass in court!"

CHAPTER 50

Reggie stared at the Micronics motion, then hurled it across the room. "This is some bullshit!"

He had never even heard of the after-acquired evidence rule. He turned on his ancient computer and tried to enter the Westlaw Web site to look it up. The message "access denied" appeared on the screen.

"Damn it!" he said under his breath. Cheryl had probably forgotten to pay the bill again.

He went to the Internet and typed in the Web address for FindLaw.com. He entered a series of search terms, but was not very adept at legal research and didn't find anything helpful. Running over to the narrow bookcase against the far wall of his office, Reggie cocked his head to the side and began scanning the spines of the books. He had never put much effort into building a decent law library. Instead, he kept up-to-date on new case law by attending seminars and reading newsletters. Over the last few years, however, he had failed to even do much of that. Being able to quickly settle most of his cases before they reached the motion stage made legal research unnecessary.

He finally spotted the book he was looking for, *Recent Developments in Employment Law*, which he had received at a seminar years earlier. When he snatched the book from the shelf, three others tumbled to the floor, kicking up a small cloud of dust. Reggie coughed uncontrollably as he waved the dust from his face.

He sat down and flipped to the index in the back of the book. He was surprised to find a whole section on the after-acquired evidence rule. Several cases were listed, but only one California decision—*Camp v. Jeffer, Mangels, Butler and Marmaro.*

As Reggie read the brief synopsis, he began to hyperventilate. The case was directly on point.

The Camps, a married couple, had been fired from a law firm for poor performance. They sued for wrongful termination claiming that they were really terminated because the wife had blown the whistle on one of the firm's partners, who had engaged in insider trading. After the lawsuit was filed, the law firm learned that both Mr. and Mrs. Camp had been convicted of a felony years earlier and had lied about it on their employment applications. The firm also discovered that before the couple's termination, they had stolen confidential documents to support their whistle-blowing claim.

In its motion to dismiss, the law firm argued that the couple had obtained their jobs under false pretenses and would have been terminated had the firm known about the document theft and the felony convictions. The motion requested that the Camps' complaint be dismissed and the court did exactly that. In explaining the rationale for its decision, the court stated:

The present case is akin to the hypothetical wherein a company doctor is fired for improper reasons and the company, in defending a civil rights action, there-after discovers that the discharged employee was not a "doctor." In our view the masquerading doctor would be entitled to no relief.

Reggie closed the book and pounded it with both fists. He was so angry his head was throbbing.

Had Reggie run the *Camp* case through the Westlaw database, he would have learned that it had been over-ruled. Later courts held that the after-acquired evidence rule could only be used as a means of limiting damages, not for a total dismissal of a case.

But Reggie didn't think any further research would do him any good. He was much too distraught after learning that the one case that could potentially make him rich was about to evaporate. He punched his intercom button, but Cheryl did not pick up.

Charging out of his chair, he flung open the door to his office. "Did you hear me buzzing you?" he yelled.

Cheryl was talking on the telephone and stroking her nails with a shiny gold polish.

"Hey, girl, I gotta go." She glared up at Reggie. "This man done lost his mind."

Holding the receiver between her thumb and forefinger so as not to smudge her wet nails, Cheryl dropped it back into the cradle. "I told you before, don't be shouting at me like that," she shouted back.

"I left my cell phone with Hamilton's number in it in my car," Reggie growled. "Get him on the phone for me. Now."

Cheryl took her time thumbing through her Rolodex.

Reggie walked up to her desk and hovered over her. When she finally pulled out Hamilton's business card, Reggie snatched it from her.

"Never mind," he said, running back into his office. "I'll call him myself."

CHAPTER 51

Reggie's tirade over the motion left me so rattled that I decided to leave work early. But instead of going home to my empty house, I called James, my law school buddy, and convinced him to meet me for a game of tennis in Fox Hills.

We had only been at it for thirty minutes or so when my energy began to wane.

"Stop playing like a girl," James yelled at me from across the court after I had missed an easy shot. He knew his sexist taunts would prompt me to hit the ball harder and aim my shots more accurately. I was innately too competitive not to take the bait.

I had arranged the game under the guise of wanting to get some exercise, but what I really needed was my friend's advice. I was quite conflicted about being reassigned to the Randle case. While part of me longed to jump back into the saddle and prove that I could successfully resolve the lawsuit, I feared that in a case this fishy, there was a good chance that something else would go wrong. I needed James's take on things, but I wasn't quite sure how much I should reveal to him.

After a series of long rallies, we took a break with the score at three games to one in James's favor.

"When're you going to tell me what's bothering you?" James asked, joining me on a bench that was badly in need of a coat of paint.

I smiled at him. "What makes you think something's bothering me?"

"Because lately you only invite me to play tennis when you're mad at your husband or stressed out about work. From the way you've been playing, I'd say it's probably both."

"If you weren't my friend, I'd hate you," I said playfully.

James got up from the bench, picked up his racket and took a few practice swings. "Slaughtered any unfortunate black victims of discrimination lately?"

I made a sucking sound with my teeth. James enjoyed kidding me about being a sell-out for defending big business rather than the working man, but I wasn't in the mood to be teased. "Please don't go there today, okay?" I was now having second thoughts about discussing my troubles with him.

"You're awful touchy this evening," James said. "Look, I know you're up for partner pretty soon and I also know how important that is to you. But despite all the wonderful stuff that partner said about you at that dinner Saturday night, you need to prepare yourself just in case it doesn't happen."

James had always been one of my biggest supporters. I didn't need to hear such pessimism coming from him. "Thanks for the vote of confidence," I said.

"I'm not saying it *won't* happen," he said, trying to backtrack.

"Then why even bring it up? I've worked my butt off and I deserve to make partner."

"I agree," James said. "You do. But life isn't always fair. Every law firm in America is talking about diversity these days, but that's all it is. Talk."

"You're always so negative," I said. "How are things supposed to change if no one is willing to give it a chance to?"

"I'm just looking at the facts," he said. "If all the white-shoe law firms like yours really wanted to have some black and Hispanic partners, they would be there. Instead they sit back and complain that they can't find any qualified candidates. At the same time, they welcome in truckloads of mediocre white boys, but expect anybody black or brown to walk on water."

"You're always talking out of both sides of your mouth," I said. "First, you criticize the law firms for not hiring minorities. And when they do, you attack the minorities who work there as sell-outs. You can't have it both ways."

"There's no real contradiction," James said. "I just don't think any minority who's racially conscious can survive for the long haul at a big firm. The law firm culture won't let them."

"That's not true," I insisted. "The more minorities the firms hire, the better it'll be for those who follow. And things *are* changing. Maybe not as fast as either of us would like, but there *has* been progress just the same. Remember Martin Miller? He graduated from Boalt the year before we did. He just made partner at Roosevelt & Womble's downtown office. And he's the third African-American partner there."

"Now that's an example of real diversity. There ain't nothing black about that brother other than his skin."

I wanted to sock James, but instead I opted to hit below the belt. "Yeah, you're probably right. I think he's married to a white woman, too."

His face went slack and I could tell that my comment smarted. But James wasn't about to let me know that. "You can go there if you want, but my being married to Melissa hasn't changed who I am. I'm probably even more committed to my people now."

"Whatever, James."

"Look, I didn't mean to upset you. I just want to make sure you understand that playing by the rules doesn't always work. Look at the way you're dressed."

James was really starting to rattle me now. "What's wrong with the way I'm dressed?" I glanced down at my outfit.

"You even look like a lawyer out here on the tennis court, dressed up in all your nice, bright white. You have on designer shorts *and* socks. How much did it cost you to have Kornikova's name on your shorts? Hell, this is the Fox Hills public tennis court, not Wimbledon. Nobody's gonna arrest you just because you're not dressed the part."

James was wearing his trademark cut-off jeans and a purple-and-yellow Lakers T-shirt.

Maybe it was the stress of everything I'd been through, but his critique had pushed me to the edge. Anger propelled me off the bench. "You know what? You're nothing but a hypocrite. You're only at the Public Defender's Office because you didn't have the grades to get a job at a law firm like O'Reilly & Finney, and we both know you wanted one."

I picked up my racket and slipped on the cover. "And you have some nerve trying to jam me up for going up against black plaintiffs. It must feel great to represent murderers and rapists."

"That firm has really got you uptight," James said, laughing.

"You're just jealous." I grabbed my towel and water bottle and stuffed them into my tennis bag.

"Oh, sure, I'd love to work fifteen hours a day, seven days a week, dealing with pompous, privileged white boys. You have the perfect life."

I spun around to face him. "Excuse me, but I'll gladly take my pompous white boys over those fake ass, do-good white folks you work with. Those white P.D.'s act so high and mighty because they're giving up big-firm salaries to defend blacks and Mexicans. But most of 'em aren't half as liberal as they profess to be. So don't give me that bull. Your ass wouldn't be living in Ladera if your wife didn't have a trust fund."

"Just calm down," James said, grinning. "You obviously haven't been getting any lately. I'm going to have to call Jefferson and tell him to get back home and hook you up. And forgive me for noticing, but you didn't have those bags under your eyes when we graduated from law school."

"Remind me to call you the next time I need a friend!" I snatched my tennis bag from the bench and turned to leave.

James jumped in front of me and grabbed me by the shoulders. "C'mon, Vernetta. Stop overreacting. You know I've got your back. Don't leave mad. Flash me that Compton smile."

I pulled away from him. "Get outta my face."

"See, that's why I don't deal with black women." James was laughing even harder now. "White women don't act like that."

James ducked just in time to miss the tennis bag that I had flung at his head. He was doubled over with laughter.

I had to walk past him to retrieve my bag.

"C'mon, homey, you need to lighten up," he said, still in stitches. "Let's go to Simply Wholesome. I'll treat even though you make three times my meager P.D.'s salary."

"Forget it," I said, storming off the tennis court. "Go have dinner with your rich white wife!"

CHAPTER 52

By the time I got home, James had left me three voice mail messages begging for my forgiveness. Frankly, I should have been the one apologizing to him. I was really on edge lately. I called him back and told him I was sorry for going off the way I had.

I showered, heated up some leftover pizza and was asleep by nine. When the telephone rang close to seven-thirty the next morning, I figured it was Special. Since Jefferson had been out of town, she had gotten into the habit of waking me up at the crack of dawn to share some inane gossip.

I grabbed the telephone from the nightstand on the third ring. "It's too early in the morning to be gossiping, so this better be good," I said, yawning.

"Please excuse me for calling so early." I didn't recognize the clipped, female voice.

I looked at the caller ID, but the number didn't register.

"I'm calling from Micronics Corporation," the woman said.

I sprang up in bed.

The woman introduced herself as the secretary to Bob Bailey, the company's General Counsel. She explained that Mr. Bailey needed to meet with me as soon as possible regarding the Randle case. Unfortunately, he was heading out of the country the following day and wanted to know if I could make it to corporate headquarters by nine. Although communicated in the form of a request, the urgency in her tone indicated that it was anything but.

I assumed that the General Counsel wanted a face-to-face meeting to personally smooth out my ruffled feathers. O'Reilly had mentioned that the overture would be forthcoming.

It took me only minutes to hop in and out of the shower. I put on my favorite black Tahari pantsuit with a white blouse for ultimate contrast. My coral earrings and matching necklace finished the ensemble. It was the most conservative outfit in my closet. I wanted to convey an unmistakable air of professionalism.

When I walked into Bailey's spacious office forty-five minutes later, a stormy tension smacked me in the face, causing my light mood to somersault into a dark cloud of panic. Bailey was sitting behind his desk, while Ferris, the Vice President of HR, occupied a chair off to the side.

Even before taking in the entire room, I felt the stoic presence of Joseph Porter, dressed in a polyester gray suit and a dated striped tie. He was sitting in a small chair facing Bailey's desk. His face was so flushed he looked three shades darker. Norma Brown sat only inches away from him, her head down, her hands cupped in her lap. She was the only one who had not looked my way when the door opened.

"Thanks for coming," Bailey said. "Why don't you

have a seat?" He pointed to an empty chair sandwiched between Porter and Norma. I stared at the chair as if it were the bull's-eye for a firing squad.

"We'd like to talk to you about this." Ferris snatched a document from Bailey's desk and waved it in the air.

I did not need to see the fine print to know that he was holding a copy of the memo Norma had read to me in the sauna. I glanced over at Norma, who still refused to look at me, just as I refused to look at Porter. I felt like I was trapped in a packed elevator with twenty people breathing their hot breath down the base of my neck. Maybe the room would stop spinning once I sat down.

I had yet to say a word. "I…uh…I need to go to the ladies' room first." I backed out of the room before anyone could object.

Frantically, I scurried down the long hallway like a victim in a bad horror flick searching for an escape route. I had not been in this area of the Micronics building before, but I knew that a restroom had to be close by. That was the law. One restroom per X number of employees. I was certain I had read that somewhere.

Just as I was about to turn around and begin my frenzied search at the opposite end of the hallway, I spotted a door with the familiar blue symbol and ducked inside. I stepped up to the nearest sink, gripped the sides with both hands and tried to catch my breath. I just stood there, my head bowed, my eyes tightly shut, my hands glued to the icy-cold porcelain.

If the sink had been made of mere glass, my hands would have been all bloodied by now, pierced with fragments of a material too weak to withstand such a desperate grasp. Talking to Norma about that document had been a big mistake. I should have left the sauna the minute she mentioned Randle's name. *What in the hell had I been thinking?*

Now they all knew. They knew that Norma had shown me the confidential document and that I had failed to report her misconduct. Their suspicions about my loyalties, or the lack thereof, had been undeniably confirmed.

This was not some oversight O'Reilly & Finney could ignore. This was an issue of ethics. There was no doubt now. I would not make partner. I would not even have a job. With O'Reilly & Finney or anybody else. Micronics would surely report me to the State Bar, which would probably mean a suspension or maybe even disbarment.

There was no way I could go back into that room. What would I say? I tried to think of a decent cover story but nothing came to me. What good was a lawyer who could not lie on demand? I was a disgrace to the profession....

I bolted up in bed. My satin nightgown was glued to my chest, soaked with perspiration, and my temples were throbbing with pain. *It was only a dream!* The digital clock next to my bed displayed 2:32 a.m. in bright fluorescent green. My head felt clouded and heavy. I grabbed the top sheet and pressed it against my sweaty face, mopping up the perspiration along my forehead. Plopping back down on my pillow, I tried to relax, but my heart refused to stop racing.

What if Norma *had* told someone about our conversation? There would be no way I could explain away my behavior. I just hoped the woman had enough sense to keep her mouth shut.

I hopped out of bed, put on a dry nightgown and walked into our spare bedroom that doubled as an office. I clicked on the light switch, turned on the computer and waited for permission to proceed. The next few seconds seemed to take forever.

Grabbing the mouse, I clicked on the Westlaw icon. I typed in my ID and password, then entered the California database until I got to the Code of Professional Responsibility, which proscribed the do's and don'ts for members of the California Bar. Almost instantaneously after typing the phrase *conflict of interest,* the screen listed dozens of matches. I entered a few more words to help narrow my search and quickly scrolled through each entry, slowing at relevant text.

Rule 3-310(B): Personal relationships with an opposing party or witness must be disclosed to the client. Norma was not an opposing party nor was she a witness. At least not technically speaking. And a single conversation certainly did not constitute a "personal relationship." Nothing I had done had violated that rule, I told myself.

Rule 3-500: "A member shall keep a client reasonably informed about significant developments relating to the employment or representation." Did knowledge of an employee's theft of a confidential document fit the definition of a significant development? It was not as if Norma had handed the document to Hamilton. No. The information about Norma's copying the document was not *significant.* It would not impact the outcome of the case.

I dumped my head into my hands. Who was I kidding? No matter what a given rule said, any halfway decent lawyer could find a plausible basis for asserting the exact opposite proposition. That was exactly what my three years of law school had trained me to do. Pick a side, any side, and defend it.

I said a quick prayer. Hopefully, after Reggie calmed down and discussed the motion with Hamilton, they would be calling me back singing a different tune.

If the motion to amend didn't convince them to fold, nothing would.

CHAPTER 53

At six forty-five the next morning, Special's yellow Porsche sped out of her underground parking garage and headed south on Buckingham Drive.

Cliff, the investigator hired by Ferris, was stationed outside in a white van. He started his engine and took off behind her but remained at least three car lengths back. He picked up his two-way cell phone. "All clear," he said tersely.

Inside the apartment building, two different men, dressed in dark blue handymen uniforms, emerged from the stairwell onto the third floor and headed in the direction of Special's unit at the far end of the hallway. They easily jimmied the dead bolt and were inside within seconds.

Cliff continued trailing Special as she sped down Green Valley Circle and made a left onto Centinela Boulevard. He was not worried about losing her. He had studied her routine for several days. It was Wednesday, so her first stop would be at Second 2 None, a beauty salon on La Brea, just south of Fairview. She would be there for at least an hour and a half. Then she would head downtown to her office in the Mellon Bank Building. On a rare occasion, Special returned home during the lunch hour, which was the only reason Cliff was trailing her. But it was really only a safety precaution. Justin and Paulie, the two men who had just broken into Special's apartment, would be done long before lunchtime.

Back on Buckingham Drive, Justin, an undernourished computer geek who could have been Steve Urkel's twin brother, was conducting an intense search of every inch of Special's apartment. If he found what they had been instructed to recover—the Micronics documents—a very big bonus awaited him. So he was highly motivated to do a very thorough search.

The other man, Paulie, a husky Norwegian, had a different task. His job was to make sure their visit left the occupant a very clear message: *You're playing with fire.* Paulie pulled a switchblade from his back pocket and dug it straight down the center of Special's newly reupholstered couch. He pulled out a handful of the cotton stuffing, tossed it onto the floor and made a second cut which intersected with the first, forming a perfect X. He attacked the two matching armchairs in a similar fashion, then walked around to the back of the couch and kicked it hard, causing it to crash into the coffee table, spraying glass across the room.

"Hey!" Justin said, tiptoeing into the living room. "Not so loud." He returned to the bedroom and continued opening drawers and dumping their contents onto the floor. He never understood how women could collect so much junk. He lifted the top mattress off the bed, disappointed to find nothing there but a pair of nylons. He kneeled to peer underneath the bed, and found it crowded with shoe boxes. He opened each one, then hurled it aside. He smiled when he removed the lid of a shiny black box.

Justin walked back into the living room carrying the box underneath his arm. "Look what I found." He held up a long vibrator with tiny prongs on the end for his partner to see. He switched it on and grinned. "Zoom, zoom!"

Paulie laughed. "Don't break it," he said. "She's gonna need the comfort when she gets home and takes a look at our handiwork."

Justin grinned again and went back to work.

Less than five miles away, Special pulled into a parking space in front of Second 2 None. She took a few seconds to touch up her lipstick before going inside the salon. Cliff drove his van into a strip mall directly across the street and parked between the Crab Pit and a mini-market. He had a clear view of Special's every move, thanks to the large picture window in the front of the salon. Using high-powered binoculars, Cliff watched as Special made her way to a shampoo bowl in the back.

He picked up his cell phone and chirped Paulie. "How's it going?" Cliff asked. "Find anything?"

It took a while before Paulie snapped, "Don't bother us. We're working."

Paulie slipped his phone into the front pocket of his overalls. He was standing in front of Special's handmade silk curtains. He seemed to take special pleasure in each swipe of his knife, as he ripped the curtains into shreds.

Justin rejoined him in the living room. "The documents aren't in the bedroom," he said, frustrated.

Paulie looked at his watch. "We've still got lots of time," he said. "We ain't leaving until we find 'em."

CHAPTER 54

Despite Special's hysterical telephone call shortly after seven o'clock that evening, nothing could have prepared me for the disaster scene I saw as I peered into her apartment.

Glass and debris littered the living room floor. Back issues of *Essence* and *O* magazines had been ripped apart and strewn around the room like confetti. Special's floor-length chenille curtains hung from the ceiling like strands of spaghetti.

I cautiously stepped across the threshold, struggling to find an empty space to place my feet. If a camera were rolling, it would have looked as if I were playing hopscotch in slow motion. I peered past the living room out onto the balcony and spotted Special wrapped in the arms of a man the size of a grizzly. As I got closer to the balcony, I could hear Special's low, sporadic sobs.

The minute she saw me, Special pulled away from the man and ran to embrace me.

"Girl, you see what they done to my crib!" she cried. I hugged her hard, which only seemed to make her sobs grow dramatically louder.

I looked over Special's shoulder at the huge man standing there staring at us. Since Special was too distraught to make an introduction, I did the honors. "I don't think we know each other," I said. "I'm Vernetta Henderson."

"Coleman. Detective Mason Coleman, LAPD," he said in a strong, official voice. He was a large, portly man and looked too old to be a cop. The lapel of his nice blue suit sported a crusty yellow stain that looked like mustard. He did not bother to extend his hand since Special and I were still entwined like a rope.

"What happened?" I glanced around the ransacked living room, still in disbelief. Maybe if I could get Special to talk, she would stop crying. "Did they take anything? Why would somebody do this?"

"I just hope it don't have nothing to do with that dead secretary," Detective Coleman said.

Special stopped mid-sob and pulled away from me. She gave Detective Coleman a dirty look and began twirling a loose thread on the hem of her blouse. "Hey, let's go inside," Special said, her voice hoarse from crying.

"No, wait a minute." I grabbed Special by the elbow. "What's he talking about? What dead secretary?" I looked first at Special, then at Detective Coleman.

"Well," Special began, then paused to let out a long, dramatic sigh. "I've—I mean we've been kind of looking into Karen Carruthers's murder." She moved closer to the detective, stepping over a piece of broken glass that used to be part of her coffee table.

"What murder?" I silently cautioned myself to remain calm. I looked around for a place to sit but couldn't find one. "Who said Carruthers was murdered?"

"That's what we were trying to find out," Special said. "Don't be mad, homey. I did it for you."

"Excuse me?" Anger had replaced my concern.

"I just wanted to find out the real deal. The police found some documents in Carruthers's car and Detective Coleman let me take a look at 'em. And I think—"

"What?" I turned to stare at Detective Coleman. "What in the hell possessed you to do that?"

A stupid grin spread across the detective's face as Special smiled up at him. I glanced down at my friend's shoeless feet. Each toenail was painted a bright fluorescent pink.

"You're both nuts!" I yelled.

"Well, at least let me tell you about the documents that woman had in her car," Special pleaded.

"I don't want to know about the documents."

"No, just listen. We—"

"I said I don't want to know!" I shouted. "I'm back on the Randle case now. What if somebody thinks I'm involved in what you did? This is not a game, Special. Look at your place. This is serious!"

"I know, I know," she said. Her voice grew shaky again, as if she were about to commence another crying spell. "I think I should go home with you."

I was worried about Special's safety, but I was not in the mood for a full-time houseguest. "Wouldn't you feel safer at your parents' place?"

"Girl, you know I can't go there. My mama'll be all up in my business. Just let me stay with you for a few days until the police figure out who did this."

I inhaled. It was probably best if Special did stay with

me. At least I would be able to make sure she didn't do any more snooping around. "Fine. But on one condition. Could you please let the police handle this from now on?"

"You got it," Special said. "This is scary."

"I'll take over from here, ladies," Detective Coleman said in a take-charge voice. "Special, do you have those pictures we took at the accident scene?"

Special blasted Detective Coleman with another nasty look.

"Pictures! Accident scene!" I looked at Special and then at Detective Coleman. "You actually took her to the accident scene? Couldn't you lose your job behind that?"

Detective Coleman stared down at the floor. "Well—"

Special jumped to his defense. "I just wanted to see if there were any skid marks where that woman's car went off that road," Special said. "And there weren't. That's because they just ran her ass off that cliff."

I threw up my hands. "Micronics is my client! All this *help* you guys are trying to give me is going to cost me my job!"

Special folded her arms and sulked. "You know I got your back."

"You got *my* back? Look around this place. You need to be worried about your own back!"

"Don't worry, Vernetta," Detective Coleman interrupted. "I have those documents under lock and key."

I rubbed my eyes. I had no more faith in him than I did in Special. He deserved a starring roll on *America's Dumbest Cops*. He had no business getting her involved in this. "Let's just start cleaning up this mess so we can get out of here."

"That'll have to wait until we can get some pictures and fingerprints," said Detective Coleman. "A couple of officers from the burglary unit are on their way over."

"Fine, then. Let's go," I said to Special.

"Wait. I have to go get my clothes." Special ran into the bedroom and in seconds walked back into the living room dragging two large Louis Vuitton suitcases that she had apparently packed before I got there.

Exactly how long was she planning on staying?

She smiled seductively at Detective Coleman. "Sweetie, can you give me a hand?"

He obediently lumbered to Special's aid as if he were hypnotized by the mere sound of her voice.

"Those won't fit in your Porsche," I said.

"They're not going in my car, they're going in yours. My nerves are too bad to drive right now. You can bring me back to pick up my car in the morning."

I had no energy left to protest. I pulled my keys from my purse and followed the two of them out the door.

CHAPTER 55

As we drove east on Slauson Boulevard toward Baldwin Hills, Special was unusually quiet, a trait she rarely exhibited during waking hours.

Regret began to tug at me. Special was only trying to help. Maybe I had been too rough on her. "You okay, girl?" I reached over and squeezed her hand.

Special responded with a weak smile. "Yeah, I'm fine."

"Everything'll be okay. You have renter's insurance, don't you?"

"Nope. I cancelled the policy two months ago. I've been paying renter's insurance for a zillion years and never needed it." She seemed to be on the verge of tears again.

"Well, don't worry about it right now." I squeezed her hand again.

"I just wish they hadn't taken my laptop. That's where I had all my information about the documents and the murder."

My bout of empathy instantly morphed into frustration. "Didn't you hear anything I said at your place? You don't need any notes because you and your detective friend are through with your little investigation. You just better pray this was a random burglary."

Special looked over at me and bit her lip. "I have something else I need to tell you."

I tightened my grip on the steering wheel and tried to mentally brace myself.

"Promise you won't get mad," she said.

"Just tell me." I was scared to imagine what else Special could have done.

"Okay," she said, scooting over closer to the passenger door. "I have a copy of those documents they found in Carruthers's car."

"You what?" I screamed. "I thought Detective Coleman said he had them. How'd you get a copy?"

"Girl, there's not a man alive who can keep Special Sharlene Moore from getting what she wants. He doesn't even know I have 'em. Anyway, you should be glad. This is our insurance policy. If they try to mess with us, at least we got the documents for bargaining power."

I felt flush. "You're absolutely nuts! This is not some TV cop show! Somebody just vandalized your apartment. And the same person may've framed Henry Randle *and* killed Karen Carruthers. Do you understand that? Somebody is dead. D-E-A-D. Dead! And they could very well want you dead, too!"

Special looked away.

"Where are they?" I asked.

"What?"

"You know what. The documents."

"I have them."

"I know that! Where the hell are they?"

"Right here in my purse."

Instead of turning left onto Overhill Drive, I pressed down on the gas pedal and sped through the yellow traffic light. Then I abruptly hit the brakes and swerved into the parking lot of La Louisanne's, a popular neighborhood restaurant and nightclub.

"Good move," Special said. She unhooked her seat belt and flung the door open. "I could definitely use a Long Island iced tea." Special was halfway out of the car before she noticed that I had not moved. "What's the matter? Aren't we going in?"

"I only pulled in here to keep myself from running off the road," I snapped.

"Girl, I don't understand why you're trippin' so hard." Special pulled the door shut. "I'm telling you, you're going to need some insurance if them white boys start messing with you about partnership."

I pressed my head against the headrest and massaged my temples. "Special, you're scaring me, okay?" This time my tone was gentle and full of concern. "You have to give this up. What you're doing could have very dangerous consequences."

"Girl, nobody even knows I've got these documents."

"What do you mean, nobody knows?" I shouted. "How do you know those documents aren't the reason somebody just tore up your place? For all you know, somebody could be watching us right now."

Special grabbed the rearview mirror, turned it in her direction and scanned the parking lot behind us. I was actually glad to see fear in Special's eyes again. I needed her to understand that this was serious business.

"Remember that investigator who took the pictures of Hamilton and me outside Little J's?" I said.

Special's eyes widened. "Ooh, good idea! You're going to hire him to find out who broke into my place?"

"No!" I wished I had some Advil because Special was giving me a massive headache. "Can you just be quiet for a minute and let me finish. I didn't tell you at the time because I didn't want you to go off, but that investigator had a picture of you, too."

This revelation did not elicit the response I had hoped for. There was outrage, not fear in Special's eyes. "They had the nerve to take a picture of me? I'm suing them for invasion of privacy. I can't believe you didn't tell me!"

"You're not suing anybody for anything. Nobody has an expectation of privacy in a public place."

"Well, I'm gonna—"

"Look, Special, I'm just trying to get you to understand that if a major corporation like Micronics hired a private investigator to follow people and take pictures, this has to be some pretty serious stuff."

"That's because they're up to no good."

"You're probably right," I said. "But please, just swear to me that you'll forget about trying to investigate this case. Karen Carruthers is already dead. I really don't want anything to happen to you."

"Okay, but only if you do me one favor."

"What?"

"Just look at these documents," Special pleaded. "Nobody'll know you looked at 'em except you and me."

The Micronics documents posed yet another ethical

dilemma for me. Hell, I had already stepped way over the line with Norma. "Give 'em here," I said.

"See, I knew you'd—"

"Just give 'em to me and don't say another word. And hurry up before I change my mind."

Special hurriedly pulled the documents from her purse. I quickly scanned the six pages. "They look like engineering documents," I said. "But they might as well be in German. I have no idea what this stuff means."

"Well, they've definitely got something to do with Micronics because the company's logo is on every page. See?" Special leaned over and pointed at the small Micronics symbol.

"And they also have the words *company private* stamped on them," I grumbled, "which means we have no business looking at them."

"I know, but I can't shake the feeling that these documents are at the center of this whole thing with Randle and that dead secretary. Don't you know anybody who can tell us what they mean?"

"No, I don't. So let's just—" I paused. James's wife was an Assistant U.S. Attorney. She had recently prosecuted a senior engineer at Boeing for embezzlement, and had also majored in electrical engineering at MIT. Maybe she could help.

Despite my nagging reservations, I started my Land Cruiser and headed back west up Slauson. Every few seconds I looked in the rearview mirror, then checked both side mirrors. I was apparently much more rattled than even I had realized.

"Why are we going this way?" Special's voice was infused with fear. "You're not taking me back home, are you?"

"I know somebody who might be able to tell us what these documents mean."

A flood of excitement filled Special's eyes. "Really? Who?"

"Just wait and see," I said. "And, please—let me do the talking."

CHAPTER 56

Less than five minutes later, we pulled into the driveway of a spacious ranch-style home on Shenandoah Street in Ladera Heights. The house stretched almost twice the length of every other home on the block. A narrow rainbow of flowers lined one side of a lawn plush and green enough for a *House & Garden* cover spread. A Lincoln Navigator and a BMW were parked side by side in the driveway.

"Who lives here?" Special asked as she unlocked the passenger door.

"James," I said.

"Dang! He's living hella large off that white girl's trust fund. But how is that Uncle Tom brother going to help us?"

"Stop calling him that. We're here to talk to Melissa, his wife."

I jogged up the driveway, while Special grudgingly dragged up the rear.

The housekeeper, an older Brazilian woman, opened the door seconds after I rang the bell and greeted me with a hug. Special, still grumbling to herself, followed as Ana led us down a long marble hallway that opened into a sunken den almost as large as Special's entire apartment.

"Dang," Special said after Ana had left to find James.

"If marrying a white babe'll get me a crib like this, I might have to check out the lesbo scene."

I pinched her on the arm.

"Ow! That hurt!" she said, rubbing her arm.

"Then hush," I said. "Don't you know how to whisper?"

A large picture window took up most of the east wall of the room. If it weren't so smoggy, the Hollywood sign would have been visible in the distance.

Special walked over to check out the view. "I can't believe they have a live-in housekeeper!" she said, astonished. "They ain't even got no kids. That's just lazy."

"Please be quiet!" I whispered. "And if you can't do that, at least lower your voice."

"Yeah, whatever."

"And please be nice to Melissa." I did not waste my time asking Special to be nice to James.

"Okay, okay. I'm cool with her. But you know I can't stand James's ass. He has some nerve thinking he's too good to date black women."

"Special, I'm not playing. If you—"

"Hey, Vernetta," James said, walking into the room. He hugged me with honest warmth, our tennis spat long forgotten.

"You remember Special," I said.

"What's up?" Special said flatly.

James nodded in her direction. Neither made an attempt to hug or shake hands.

"Want something to drink?" James asked.

Special perked up. "I could use a glass of wine. What kind do you—"

"No, we're fine," I said, cutting her off. "We're here for business."

We all sat down. James and I on the couch, Special in an adjacent club chair. After swearing James to secrecy, I pulled out the Micronics documents and began giving him the background information. I left out some of the key details, like Carruthers's death and exactly how Special had obtained the documents. There was no need to drag James and his wife all the way into this thing just yet.

James listened without comment, then stood up. "Let me go get Melissa."

As soon as he left, Special began strolling around the room, her hands clasped behind her back. "Yeah, they're living real high on the hog." She stopped to examine a huge lithograph over the fireplace. "They spent some big bucks on this." Special's nose was so close to the glass frame she left breath prints on it.

"And how would you know that?" I said. "Didn't you buy all of your artwork on the corner of Crenshaw and Adams?"

Special stuck out her tongue. "Excuse me, but I took a semester of Art Appreciation at USC. So I do know a little something." She strolled over to the opposite side of the room and picked up a small sculpture sitting on a three-foot metal base. She held it high over her head so she could examine the bottom. "They paid some serious money for this, too."

"Special, please sit your butt down!" I begged. "And I'm serious. You better be nice to Melissa."

"If you ask me to be nice to that girl one more time, I'm gonna scream." Special flopped down into the chair and crossed her legs. She leaned over to get a closer look at a framed photograph of James and Melissa sitting on an end table.

"Girl, they look like Clarence Thomas and Marge Simpson," Special exclaimed. "Thank God they haven't reproduced yet. But they might get lucky. Some of the homeliest zebra couples make the prettiest babies. I think God feels guilty for making ugly people."

"Special, I'm not playing with you. You better—"

"Hi, everybody!" Melissa bounced into the room right behind James and gave me a frail hug.

She had short black hair that obviously had not seen the hands of a hair stylist in months. The age lines around her eyes made her look slightly older than James, even though she was three years his junior. She was wearing jeans, an oversized sweatshirt and the hardened look of a criminal prosecutor.

"You remember Special," I said.

Melissa extended her hand. "Nice to see you again," she said cheerfully.

Special reached up to shake Melissa's hand but did not bother to stand up.

"James already filled me in," Melissa said. "Let's see the documents."

CHAPTER 57

I expected to hear the low beeping of the burglar alarm when I opened my front door. But when I walked past the living room and into the den, I was surprised and a little perturbed to find Special sprawled across my Ethan Allen couch snoring like a foghorn.

It had been four days since Special moved in and our roommate arrangement was getting old fast. I noisily dropped my purse on the coffee table, causing Special to jump to her feet.

"Girl, you scared me!" Her hair was matted to the left side of her head and mascara was smeared underneath her right eye.

My face tensed as I took in my normally immaculate den. The grease stain on the arm of the couch hadn't been there when I'd left that morning. A Chinese take-out container sat in the center of the wrought-iron coffee table next to a coasterless wine cooler bottle. Two half-open shoeboxes and a Nordstrom bag were strewn across the floor nearby. Jaheim's voice floated from the stereo, but could barely be heard over *The Fresh Prince* rerun on the flat-screen TV.

Special yawned and sat up. "You're gonna have to start

calling me on my cell to let me know when you're coming home. You know how jumpy I am lately."

I definitely could not put up with my friend's paranoia—not to mention her sloppiness—much longer.

Special propped up her feet on the coffee table. Her toes were still sporting that gaudy pink nail polish.

"I see you weren't too worried about somebody following you at the mall," I said, staring down at her new purchases.

"Girl, you know how much shopping relaxes me. The four hours I spent at the Beverly Center today was the first time I've been able to relax since they tore up my apartment."

"I thought you were trying to save money to buy some new furniture," I reminded her.

"I needed this spending spree to help me with my emotional equilibrium. Shopping can do that, you know."

I kicked off my shoes and sat down on the far end of the couch. I wanted to watch the local news but I knew Special would complain if I changed the channel. I did not enjoy feeling like a guest in my own home.

After a few minutes of "The Fresh Prince," I traipsed into the bathroom, doused a hand towel with hot water and pressed it against my face. When I removed the towel, I nearly leapt two feet off the ground, startled by Special's presence in the doorway.

"You're almost as jumpy as me," Special said, chomping on a half-eaten egg roll. My eyes followed the crumbs that fell from Special's mouth to my newly shampooed Berber carpet.

"Did Melissa get back to you about the documents?" Special took another sloppy bite of her egg roll.

"Yeah, but she has no idea what they are," I replied. "She wanted to show them to this engineer she knows, but I told her to hold off. We need to be careful who we drag into this."

"Isn't there anyone else you trust who can look at them?"

"Yep." I blotted my face with the towel and reached for a bottle of moisturizer.

"Who?" Special asked anxiously.

"Bradley Davis."

"That fine-ass lawyer you used to call me up and brag about every time you had sex with him?"

My face scrunched up all by itself. "I did not call you every time I had sex with him."

"Oh, yes the hell you did. And every single time you sounded like you'd just gotten off the Matterhorn at Disneyland. That brother was definitely rockin' your world. I remember because I was jealous as hell. What does he know about engineering?"

"He used to be a computer programmer and he handles a lot of engineering-related patent lawsuits."

"You better hope Jefferson doesn't find out."

"Jefferson has nothing to worry about. I don't want anything to do with Bradley."

"Yeah, whatever," Special said. "I know you love your husband and everything, but you ain't never given me any indication that Jefferson was putting it down like Bradley."

"Maybe I don't tell you *everything*. Anyway, let's change the subject."

"Fine with me. You're the one who brought him up."

I brushed past her and headed into the kitchen. Special stayed close on my heels like a hyperactive puppy.

"So when is Bradley going to look at 'em?" Special asked.

"I have a meeting at his house the day after tomorrow."

Special's hands flew to her hips. "Why didn't you tell me? I know you weren't about to go over there without me."

Actually, that had been my plan. I stopped in my tracks when I got to the doorway of my kitchen. Dishes were piled up in the sink, the trash can lid was askew and there were three balled-up paper towels on the counter.

"Special, we have a trash can and a dishwasher," I complained.

"I was going to clean up before I went to bed," she said in a monotonous whine.

I pulled open the refrigerator and reached for the bottle of cranberry juice. The quart I had bought two days earlier barely had a drop left. I held up the empty bottle and eyed Special.

"Girl, I've been really thirsty lately," she said. "I'll hook us up with some groceries when I get paid in two weeks. I just maxed out all my credit cards."

Two weeks? If Special was still here in two weeks, then *I* would be the one moving out.

CHAPTER 58

The following afternoon, Jefferson stepped across the threshold of his Baldwin Hills home and froze in place. His overnight bag fell to the floor and he stared at his living room in amazement, certain that he had somehow parked in the wrong driveway and entered the wrong front door.

The place resembled the bedroom of a delinquent teenager. A big brown stain on the rug near the stereo caught his eye first. Clothes were strewn across the arm of the couch and an empty Starbucks cup and an open bag of Nacho Cheese Doritos occupied one of the end tables. He peered into the kitchen and could see a stack of dirty dishes on the countertop.

Two days after Special had moved in, Vernetta had called him in a tirade, complaining about her best friend's sloppiness. Jefferson figured she had been exaggerating. But now, seeing everything for himself, he realized that Vernetta had actually downplayed the situation.

"C'mon in, man," Jefferson said to Stan, who closed the door behind him. "You'll have to excuse the mess."

They had driven to L.A. just for the night so Stan could surprise his wife for their wedding anniversary. It would be another couple of hours before she got off from work. Stan headed straight for the kitchen and opened the refrigerator.

"Man, doesn't your wife eat?" Stan called out from the kitchen.

"Yeah, but only if it's from a take-out container," Jefferson yelled back. "I'll order some pizza." He picked up a stack of mail from the sofa table near the front door and was going through it when he heard the doorknob turn.

Special let out a frazzled yelp when she saw Jefferson standing in front of her. "You scared me to death!" She clutched her chest. "I was about to pull out my Mace."

"Hello to you, too, Special," Jefferson said, returning to the mail. "Shouldn't you be at work?"

"I left early so I could clean up before Vernetta got home," she said, still rattled. "When did your wife turn into such a neat freak?" Special walked into the living room and picked up the Starbucks cup but ignored the Doritos bag. "Are you here to surprise her?"

"Nah. She's on her way home right now, so you better get to work. We're heading back in the morning."

"Who's we?"

"We is me, your long lost lover boy!" Stan sloshed out of the kitchen chomping on an apple. "How you doing, sweetness?"

"You know what?" Special scurried from the living room, over to the front door. "I just remembered an errand I need to run." She grabbed the doorknob and pulled it open, then shrieked again.

A bearded Hispanic man in his early twenties was standing in the doorway. Special ducked behind Jefferson for cover.

"I didn't mean to scare you, ma'am," the man said. "I have a package for Jones-Parks Electrical."

"That's for me," Jefferson said. He set the mail back down on the sofa table and reached for the clipboard the messenger held out to him. After he scribbled his name, the man handed him a large white envelope and left.

"I wonder what this is?" Jefferson tore open the envelope. "None of my mail for the business should be coming here." Special peered over his shoulder, hoping to get a look at what was inside.

Jefferson pulled a thick document out of the envelope. When his eyes focused on the words in the upper left-hand corner of the page, trepidation seized his body. *Law Office of Benjamin Wallace, Attorney for LaKeesha Douglas.*

The reality of what he was looking at took only seconds to register. "Shit!"

"What is it?" Stan asked, talking with his mouth full.

"It looks like LaKeesha's suing y'all," Special announced.

Jefferson stuffed the papers back into the envelope, walked into the living room and slumped down on the couch. Stan had all but convinced him that LaKeesha's threat about suing him for sexual harassment was just the temporary wrath of a scorned woman. And Jefferson had gladly put the whole LaKeesha saga behind him. He told Vernetta that they had decided to lay LaKeesha off because the project was winding down. That news had seemed to please her, and to his relief, she had not asked him another question about the girl.

Stan took another bite of his apple. "Aw, man," he said, "you gotta—"

Jefferson raised his hand. "Just be quiet, Stan. Don't say another word." He turned to Special. "Stan and I need to talk privately about this. Weren't you just about to leave?"

"I was," she said, "but now I think I should hang around. At least until Vernetta gets here."

Special joined Jefferson on the couch and held out her hand. "Let me see them papers. What's that little heffa suing you for?" Special made a move for the envelope, but Jefferson pulled it out of her reach.

"Special, this is a private matter that I need to discuss with my business partner. Why don't you just run along?"

"C'mon, brother-in-law, you know Vernetta's going to tell me everything anyway. If it's something really bad, you might as well tell me first so I can help you break the news to your wife."

Jefferson's brain was a muddle of confusion. He was about to be the target of a nasty sexual harassment lawsuit. There was no way he could keep it from Vernetta. If he tried to hide it and she found out later, that would only make matters worse. Special's reaction would be a preview of Vernetta's. He reluctantly handed Special the envelope, then slumped farther down on the couch, closed his eyes and started praying.

Jefferson did not need to read the document to know what it said. It probably recounted every dirty little detail of what had happened in his room at the Residence Inn. Considering how mad LaKeesha had been when he fired her, it would not surprise him if she had made up a bunch of extra stuff.

When he finished praying, Jefferson looked over at

Special, studying her face. She didn't seem all that disgusted, but Jefferson knew he wouldn't be that lucky when Vernetta read that document. He hung his head and started to pray again.

"This ain't that big a deal," Special said, stuffing the papers back inside the envelope.

Jefferson stared hard at Special, trying to make sure she wasn't playing with him. When he saw that she was not, he almost wanted to hug her. If Vernetta reacted this calmly, he was going to start attending church every Sunday for the rest of his life. Hell, he might even become a deacon or join the men's choir.

"But there's some good news and some bad news," Special said, handing the envelope back to Jefferson.

His cheeks expanded with air. "I'll take the good news first."

"It's just a workers' comp case," Special said. "A stress claim."

Jefferson wanted to jump for joy. When he had first opened the envelope, he had been too stunned to read any of the words past LaKeesha's name at the top of the page.

"Half the people I work with have filed stress claims," Special went on. "Including me. You got workers' comp insurance, don't you?" Special asked.

Jefferson nodded in disbelief at his good fortune. LaKeesha had apparently thought better of suing him for sexual harassment after he reminded her that his wife was a lawyer. His workers' comp insurance would take care of her stress claim without him even having to think twice about it. They'd pay her some chump change and it would be a done deal.

Stan whistled. "Man, you are one lucky dog."

"Why is he so lucky?" Special asked suspiciously.

Jefferson frowned at Stan and abruptly stood up.

"Uh—we were late paying our workers' comp insurance," Jefferson said, trying to think fast. "If she had filed this case a week ago, we wouldn't have been covered."

"So what's the bad news?" Stan asked.

Special stared up at Jefferson. "Well," she said, "LaKeesha's stress claim is based on sexual harassment. What's that all about, brother-in-law?"

Jefferson slid the document out of the envelope and flipped to the second page. His eyes burned as he scanned the words. *Hostile and intimidating working environment...forced to engage in sexual conduct...severe and pervasive sexual harassment.*

Jefferson tried to speak, but couldn't. His lips were sealed shut from both rage and fear.

CHAPTER 59

As Jefferson read LaKeesha's allegations, Special examined his shocked face with quiet amusement. She very badly wanted to tell the man that she possessed a smoking gun that would completely torpedo the little home wrecker's case. But she couldn't do that without getting herself in some serious hot water. Jefferson would just have to sweat it out until she could figure out the best way to use her secret nanny cam tape.

"This is a bunch of lies!" Jefferson shouted. Thick veins of fury protruded from the left side of his forehead. He stuffed the document back into the envelope and hurled it onto the couch. "I didn't force that girl to do shit!"

Whoooaaa! Special pounced off the couch and faced Jefferson. *Didn't force her? What was that about?* "I thought you said nothing happened between you and LaKeesha?" Now Special was the one experiencing distress.

Jefferson massaged the back of his neck. "That's what I said."

"Nooo," Special said, her heart beginning to palpitate, "you said you didn't force her to do anything. That's totally different." Special glanced over at Stan. He looked even more troubled than his business partner.

Jefferson walked over to the window, then absently marched back to where he'd been standing. "Well, that's what I meant," he said. "People shouldn't be able to get away with making up stuff like this." Jefferson fell onto the couch and Special sat down next to him.

Special didn't know what to think. But Jefferson's denial didn't make sense. "A man who'd been falsely accused would've said, it never happened," she said. "Not, *I didn't force her.*"

Jefferson threw up his hands. "Special, this is all a bunch of bull. I swear it is. This thing has got me so mad, I don't know what I'm saying. But I'm telling you, everything written on that page is a bunch of lies. I'll swear to *that* on the Bible."

"Okay, okay," Special said, feeling a little better. Her mind went back to the videotape. When LaKeesha had threatened to sue for sexual harassment, Jefferson told her she didn't have a case and LaKeesha had clearly said she would make one up. Maybe Jefferson really was so upset that he didn't know what he was saying.

She gave him a sisterly pat on the back. "Don't worry about it, brother-in-law. It'll all work out."

And she planned to make absolutely sure that it did. She just had to figure out a way to divulge her secret evidence without letting Jefferson or Vernetta find out that she had installed a nanny cam in Jefferson's office. Neither one of them would be happy about that.

Jefferson closed his eyes. "I hope Vernetta acts as calmly as you do about all of this."

"I can guarantee you she won't," Special said.

Jefferson slumped down even farther on the couch and leaned his head over the back. He stared up at the ceiling for a while, then turned to Special.

"I need a really big favor," he said.

Special's eyes narrowed. "I'm listening."

"I don't want you to mention this to Vernetta." He rubbed the back of his neck for the umpteenth time. "It'll just stress her out. She's under a lot of pressure because of that Micronics case and being up for partner. She doesn't need to be worrying about me being sued, too."

Special gave him an incredulous glare. "Do you know how mad your wife would be if she found out that I knew LaKeesha was suing you for sexual harassment and didn't tell her?" Special said.

"Just let me handle it," Jefferson said. "I'm going to tell her that LaKeesha filed a workers' comp case. I just don't plan to mention the sexual harassment part."

"Dang," Special said. "You sure look awfully worried. You sure nothing went down with that girl?"

"I told you," Jefferson said. "It's all a bunch of lies."

"So," Special said, "you want me to lie to my homegirl, huh?"

"I'm not asking you to lie to her. I'm just asking you not to bring it up."

Special paused. She was in complete agreement with Jefferson. Vernetta really was wigging out behind all the crap over the Randle case and the possibility of not making partner. She didn't need anything else to add to her stress level. But Special wanted to let Jefferson stew a bit.

"So what do I get outta this?" she asked.

Jefferson exhaled. "What do you want out of it, Special?"

She tilted her head sideways and pressed her index finger to her cheek. "Let me see…. I gotta think about it."

They heard the sound of a car approaching and Stan waddled over to the window and peered through the curtains. "Well, y'all ain't got a lot of time to negotiate," he said. "Vernetta's pulling up right now."

Jefferson moved closer to Special. "So are you with me on this?"

Special smiled and continued to mull over his request.

At the sound of Vernetta sticking her key into the doorknob, Jefferson snatched up the envelope, slid it underneath the couch and walked toward the front door.

He grabbed his wife in a bear hug as soon as she stepped inside, kissing her as if he might not have another chance to. "I really missed you, babe," he said.

"Wow," Vernetta said when he finally released her. "I guess I should send you out of town more often."

"How're you doing, Stan?" Vernetta walked over and gave him a hug, then leaned forward and peered into the kitchen. "Uh, Special, don't you have some work to do?"

"Yeah, yeah, yeah," Special said, rising from the couch.

But all four of them just stood there as silence saturated the room.

"Did I walk in on some confidential conversation or something?" Vernetta asked.

Jefferson laughed. "Nah, girl. We were just sitting here waitin' for you to get home. Come here." He pulled her close again, smothering her with another hug.

Special made a move toward the kitchen, then stopped

and looked back at Jefferson. He stared at her over Vernetta's shoulder, his eyes pleading. She noticed a big half circle of perspiration under each of his armpits. Brotherman was definitely sweating bullets, Special thought.

She was enjoying the feeling of power she had over Jefferson, even though she knew the man was being falsely accused. But her job was to look out for Vernetta. Her buddy would flip out if she ever laid eyes on that that workers' comp lawsuit and all the lies LaKeesha was telling.

Special gave Jefferson a thumbs-up and hoped he could read her lips.

I got your back, brother-in-law.

CHAPTER 60

"I'm serious this time." I sternly wagged my finger inches from Special's nose. "I'm not putting up with your craziness tonight. You better behave."

"Why're you always jumping down my throat?" Special swatted my finger out of her face. We were standing on the doorstep of Bradley's Manhattan Beach condo and I was tired and irritable. I had stayed up late with Jefferson and spent the day in a long, frustrating deposition.

I was about to ring the buzzer when the door swung open and Bradley pulled me into his arms. His greeting was far more intimate than it should have been. He was wearing a Sean John velour jogging suit. The jacket was completely unzipped, revealing a tanned, muscular chest.

"You remember my friend Special," I said, awkwardly pulling away from him.

"Nice to see you again." Bradley shook Special's hand and led us inside. "Have a seat in the den. I gotta run back into the kitchen and finish preparing some snacks for us to munch on."

"Dang!" Special said as our feet sank into Bradley's plush white carpet. "Does everybody you know have a big-ass crib?"

The enormous, stark white room had an artistic feel to it, as if it belonged to an architect or an artist. Sparse in furniture, but classy in style. The ten-foot couch, oval coffee table and twin club chairs were all snow-white, as were the walls. Huge floor plants and multicolored sculptures and paintings added a colorful but elegant contrast.

"I know this brother must've hired an interior decorator to hook this place up." Special stepped up to the fireplace. "And I wouldn't be surprised if this fireplace worked by remote control."

"Special, please stop acting like you haven't been nowhere before." My frustration meter was already inching toward the red zone.

Special peered through the French doors, out onto a balcony overlooking a sea of lights. "This brother's got an incredible view!" She walked out onto the balcony, closing the doors behind her.

"I asked my brother, Trent, to drop by," Bradley bellowed from the kitchen. "He used to work for DynaTech Software. I figured he might be able to help."

"Thanks," I said.

Special came back inside a few minutes later and walked right past me down a narrow hallway, peering into each room along the way.

"This crib is slamming!" she whispered, glancing back at me, still seated in the den. "But I wanna see his bedroom. I know it's pimped out."

"The bedroom's upstairs so forget it," I said. "Just get back over here and sit down."

"I'm coming," she said, continuing to take her sweet

time. "I know you're married and everything, but you might wanna consider keeping this brother on the side 'cause I would love to be chilling up in here on a regular basis."

I closed my eyes, exasperated. "Special, can you please sit down before Bradley comes back?"

"Stop being so uptight." Special finally sashayed back into the room. "I'm sure he don't mind me looking around. You know that boy still wants to get with you, don't you? That's why he left that jogging suit unzipped, showing off all five of his chest hairs."

Bradley rejoined us carrying a silver tray with four wineglasses, deviled eggs, wheat crackers, pepper cheese and a bottle of merlot.

"How's life at O'Reilly & Finney these days?" Bradley asked. He placed the tray on the coffee table, then poured wine into three of the four glasses.

"Just fine," I said. I felt no obligation to provide any specifics about all the professional drama I had experienced lately. I picked up a piece of cheese. "How's everything going with you?"

"I'm hanging in there." Bradley crouched down on the floor and rested his back against an ottoman. "We just got this huge case for a major defense contractor. I'm the lead associate on the case and—"

The doorbell rang just in time. Bradley enjoyed nothing more than pontificating about his boring patent cases.

"That's got to be Trent." Bradley hopped up and headed for the door.

"Who's Trent?" Special took a sip of wine at the same time she reached for a deviled egg.

"Bradley's brother," I said.

Special's eyes lit up. "Really? Does he have a big-ass crib like this, too?"

Before I could respond, Trent and Bradley walked into the room.

Trent was tall and muscular and had the kind of versatile, clean-cut looks intended for television commercials and billboard advertisements. He could have advertised anything from a Mercedes-Benz to multi-grain cereal. Mr. All-American Mandingo.

Before Bradley could introduce him, Special rose from the couch and took charge. "I'm Special," she said, extending her hand.

"Excuse me?" Trent replied, taking Special's hand in both of his.

"I'm sorry," Special giggled girlishly. "My name is Special, and it's spelled just like it sounds."

"Well, nice to meet you," he said. "I have to say, you're the first *Special* I've ever met."

"And I don't think you'll ever meet another one." She smiled and slipped her hands into the back pockets of her jeans.

"And this is Vernetta." Bradley intimately threw his arm across my shoulders, pulling me close to him. I squirmed free and reached out to shake Trent's hand.

"Nice to finally meet you," Trent said. "I've heard a lot about you."

Bradley crouched back down on the floor. "Okay, let's get started. How can we help?"

"Let me pour you some wine," Special said to Trent in

a sweet, sultry voice, ignoring Bradley's attempt to get down to business. She filled one of the wineglasses and walked around the coffee table to hand it to Trent, even though she could have just as easily passed the glass to him without getting up.

"I hate to drag you guys into this," I began, "so I'm not going to go into the whole long story. I'm just hoping you can take a look at these documents and tell us what they are." I pulled the papers from my purse and handed them to Bradley.

"We think they're some kind of engineering documents," Special volunteered.

Bradley reviewed the first page, then handed it to Trent.

"So, Trent, what do you do?" Special asked. Her legs were daintily crossed and her hands cupped her knee.

"I'm a struggling writer-slash-director-slash-producer." He looked up from the papers and gave her a warm smile. "But I'm also working as a production assistant at Paramount Studios to pay the rent until somebody options one of my scripts."

"Yeah," Bradley teased, "he gave up a promising career as a software engineer in hopes of becoming the next Spike Lee."

Trent turned to face his brother. "Okay, big bro, after I direct my first movie, don't ask me for tickets to the premiere."

"That's so exciting," Special gushed. "Brains and creativity, too."

Special's mindless chatter was making me antsy. "How long did you work as an engineer for DynaTech?" I asked.

All I cared about was whether he had the expertise to decipher the documents.

"About five years," Trent said, still studying the papers.

"Hey, Trent, do you ever run into any stars down at the studio?"

Before he could answer, I interrupted. "Which way is the little girl's room?" I asked. I had to get Special alone so I could tell her to put a lid on it.

"Don't act like you haven't been here before," Bradley said playfully. "Down the hallway on the right."

"Special, why don't you join me?"

Special looked perplexed. "I don't have to pee," she said, then put a hand to her mouth. She hadn't meant to use such an unladylike word in Trent's presence.

I gave up and took off for the bathroom alone. I needed to think up a way to get her to turn off the charm so Trent could concentrate on the Micronics documents.

When I returned minutes later, Special was still at it. It had been a while since I'd seen her pour it on this strong.

"Trent, may I refill your glass for you?" Special asked.

"Thanks, but I'm fine. I'm hanging out with my friends Michelle and Curtis later tonight, so I better not drink too much." His perfect teeth glistened when he smiled.

I stole a side glance at Special. If the mention of a female friend was meant to deter her, it had no impact whatsoever. Special thrived on competition.

"Where do you usually hang out?" Special asked.

"I really don't have a favorite spot," Trent replied. "Tonight we're having dinner at The Abbey."

"The Abbey? I've never heard of it." Special nudged me with her elbow. "You heard of it?"

"Sounds vaguely familiar," I said, trying to place it.

"Where is it?" Special asked.

"West Hollywood."

Special gave me a furtive look that only the two of us could decipher: *The brother's into white chicks.* But I knew my girl. She would consider it an honor to help Trent find his way back to the hood.

"Well, I'll definitely have to drop by there sometime."

Bradley had a disconcerting expression on his face. "Let's just get back to the documents," he said impatiently. "What do you think, Trent?"

"They look like ATPs," he said finally. "Except these documents are a lot more complex."

My forehead creased in confusion. "English, please."

"ATPs—Acceptance Test Procedures. At least that's what we called them at DynaTech. They probably call them something else at Micronics, but it's basically the same thing. Once a product is finished, it has to pass a series of tests to make sure it can actually do everything it's supposed to do."

I pointed to a column on the second page. "What do these numbers mean?"

"They're test results. It looks like whatever product they were testing failed in five of the twelve categories."

"How can you tell that?" I asked.

"The first column is usually the threshold number." Trent leaned forward to hand me one of the pages. "If you go down the list of numbers in the second column here, you'll notice that every number is higher than the threshold number except in five of the twelve categories. Any number lower than the threshold number is effectively a failing grade."

I paused to study the page. "But the numbers aren't even off by much. This one is only off by one-hundredth of a point."

"That might be a small number to you," Trent said, "but in the world of engineering it could add up to major problems."

A thought came to me. "What if somebody forges a copy of these documents?" I asked.

"Why would somebody want to do that?" Special asked before Trent could respond.

"To cover up the failed testing," I said. "What if instead of turning in these documents—the original ATPs—someone created new ones with all passing scores?"

"That's it," Special blurted out. "That's why they killed that woman. I bet you anything she was blackmailing them with these documents! That's why they murdered her ass!"

CHAPTER 61

Bradley eased himself off the floor and sat on top of the ottoman. "Hold on a minute," he said apprehensively. "You never said this had anything to do with murder."

I wanted to stick a sock in Special's mouth. "That's because I didn't want to get you guys that deeply involved," I said apologetically. "And we don't really know that these documents have anything to do with murder. Or that anybody was even murdered."

Trent made a T-formation with his hands. "Time out. Everything I just said is all conjecture."

"But it makes sense," Special said.

For once, I agreed with her. "But we still don't know exactly what project they pertain to," I continued. "The plaintiff was complaining about overbilling on Micronics's GAP-7 Program."

"Do you know anything about it?" Trent asked.

"It's a navigation system for a military aircraft." I looked down at the page Trent had handed to me. "But there's no indication that this document has anything to do with that program."

"Wait a minute." Trent moved to the edge of his chair. "About five years ago Micronics won this huge contract to build a super-advanced navigation system for an Air Force plane designed specifically for low flying in combat zones. It was going to have an extremely high-tech encryption system. The contract was worth hundreds of millions of dollars. All the big computer software companies submitted bids for it."

"What's *encryption* mean?" Special asked.

"It's a process for encoding information," Trent continued. "We all use some form of it every day. Like when you send an e-mail, or enter a computer password or punch in your pin number at an ATM machine. The product Micronics was working on, however, was about a thousand times more sophisticated."

"You think these documents could pertain to that project?" I asked.

"I have no idea," Trent said. "I just remember that there was a lot of hype surrounding the bidding for the contract. I think Micronics's stock went up ten points the day the Air Force announced that the company had won the bid. If these papers do pertain to that project, I could definitely understand why somebody might want to keep any failing test results a secret."

"But that seems pretty risky," I said. "Why give the Air Force something you know won't work?"

"Actually, it may not be a risk at all," Trent explained. "Even though these papers show five failing test scores, it just means that the component didn't meet some arbitrary threshold level, not that it won't work. It's like when you take your car in for a smog test. Just because the car doesn't meet the state's threshold requirements doesn't necessarily mean you're polluting the air."

"But it still seems stupid to take that kind of risk," I repeated.

"Maybe. Maybe not. Redoing just these five failed tests—which are only off by fractions—could involve tens of thousands of lines of software code, which could take months or even years to retest. There's tremendous pressure to deliver the project on time. If you don't, the government will definitely remember that the next time they have a contract to award. Then you have to tell them the precise nature of the problem. But you may not even know what's wrong or how to fix it. When it hits the newspapers that Micronics is having trouble with the project, the company's stock will almost surely plummet. So there's really a whole lot at stake."

I nodded. Trent's theory definitely sounded plausible. "I know this is all just speculation," I said, "but it's the best explanation we've come up with so far."

Bradley held up a hand. "Just make sure you leave our names out of it."

The room remained silent until the doorbell rang again.

"That's probably for me," Trent said. He started to rise when Bradley waved him back to his seat. "I'll get it," Bradley said.

"I guess we get to see what Barbie looks like," Special muttered.

When Bradley walked back into the room, the smile returned to Special's face.

Standing behind him was a tall, brown-skinned man

who was almost as good-looking as Trent. He was wearing black jeans, cowboy boots and a tight-fitting Lycra shirt that showed off every protruding pec and bulging biceps God had so kindly bestowed upon him. He had to be a professional body builder.

Special leaned over to me. "If Trent refuses to take the bait, this brother wouldn't be a bad consolation prize," she whispered. "Hell, I might even suggest we make it a threesome."

"Hey, everybody, this is Curtis." Trent rose to greet his friend. They embraced, then lightly pecked each other on the lips.

Special let out a loud gasp and simultaneously grabbed my knee in what was definitely a reflex move. Everyone pretended to ignore her outburst.

"I guess you guys don't need me anymore," Trent said. "Nice meeting you, Vernetta. Special. Hope everything works out okay for you two."

Trent placed his arm around Curtis's waist and the two of them walked out of the room.

CHAPTER 62

As soon as we said our goodbyes and Bradley closed the front door of his condo, Special let me have it.

"How in the hell could you just sit there and let me hit on that boy when you knew his ass was gay?" she yelled. "You're supposed to have my back!"

I was laughing so hard I had to bend over to hold my stomach. "I didn't know he was gay," I said, barely able to get the words out. "I thought The Abbey might be a gay bar. But I wasn't certain."

"You didn't have to be one-hundred-percent sure. Two percent would be good enough for me." Special hurled a look to kill my way. "I don't know why I didn't figure it out the minute he mentioned West Hollywood. I guess because he was so damn fine I couldn't bring myself to even consider the possibility that he might be gay."

Special stalked off ahead of me and I had to jog to catch up with her. I was still laughing so hard tears were streaming down my cheeks.

"I thought I was going to pee on myself when that fine ass Trent put his lips on that man." Special cupped her forehead. "My gaydar needs to go into the repair shop for a serious overhaul."

As we climbed into my SUV, I faked a cough to keep from bursting out laughing again. "Let's just forget about it, okay?"

"Easy for you to say," Special steamed. "You weren't the one looking like a fool in there."

I put the key in the ignition and pulled off. "I'm not sure what I should do next," I said, returning to my problem. "I'll bet anything Trent's theory is right. And I also bet Carruthers found out about those failed ATPs and somebody killed her because of it."

"I'm glad to hear you finally admit that I was right," Special said with satisfaction. "I told you that woman was murdered. Does Randle's lawsuit mention anything about the ATPs?"

"Not a word. I doubt he knows a thing about them. If he had, Reggie would've put it in the complaint. Or at least Randle would've mentioned them during his deposition. It wouldn't make sense not to."

"But from everything you've told me, Randle might've actually been set up," Special said. "So if it wasn't over the ATPs, then what?"

"I wish I knew."

We rode the rest of the way lost in our own silent thoughts. About twenty minutes later, I turned off Slauson Boulevard onto Buckingham Drive. "Hey, why're you turning here?" Special said.

"This is the street you live on, isn't it?"

"I'm not ready to go back home yet," Special moaned.

"Girl, you know I love you to death, but it's been almost a week since the break-in. I think it's time for you to get reacquainted with your apartment. Your place is all cleaned up now and your landlord even installed a new security system. If you don't go back home soon, you might develop a phobia about living alone."

Special rolled her eyes.

"Why don't you call your detective friend with the foot fetish?" I said. "He'd probably be willing to station his big body on guard duty right outside your door tonight. Or better yet, invite him in and let him paint your toenails again."

"My car's at your house," Special complained. "How am I going to get to work in the morning?"

"You still carpool with your neighbor sometimes, don't you? She can either take you to work or drop you by my house in the morning to get your car. If she can't, call me in the morning and I'll come get you."

"But all of my clothes are at your house."

"Don't even try it. You took half of your clothes back home after we cleaned up your place, remember?"

I pulled up in front of Special's apartment building but kept the engine running.

Special did not open the door. "This is cold-blooded. I'm scared to stay by myself."

"You want me to take you to your parents' house then?"

Special threw open the door and sulked up the walkway.

Before she reached the lobby door, I rolled down the passenger window, leaned over and called after her. "Hey, I forgot to tell you. Jefferson wants you to meet his cousin, Darnell. He just moved here from New York."

Special stopped and did a theatrical, model-like turn, then took her time striding back to the car.

"I'm only going to stop being mad at you long enough to get the 4-1-1 on Jefferson's cousin," she said. "So spill it."

"He's thirty-eight, tall and athletic, and very, very fine. On top of that, he's dark chocolate just like you like 'em."

She was nodding her head and smiling. "Sounds like a nice draft pick. What does he do?"

"He's an investment banker for Morgan Stanley. He's transferring here to head up their Century City office."

"Okay," Special said, still smiling with delight, "you're completely forgiven for kicking me out of your house. When you planning to hook us up?"

"It's been a while since Jefferson had a home-cooked meal, so I was thinking about planning a cozy dinner for the four of us. Jefferson's project should be slowing down in another month or so."

"A month? Girl, I don't wanna wait that long. This is L.A. He could be engaged and married by then. You know how desperate the women are in this city. I need to move in for the kill. Immediately."

"Let me talk to Jefferson and find out when he's coming home again," I said.

"No need," Special replied. "We don't need any chaperones. Just give him my number." She paused. "Scratch that. Why don't you get me his number? I'll call him up and welcome him to L.A. *Special* style."

CHAPTER 63

I was sitting at my desk the next morning, trying to figure out what to do about the information from Trent, when Rich Ferris called. My intuition told me it was no coincidence.

"Ms. Henderson, good morning." He sounded just as phony as he always did. "I'm calling for an update on the Randle case."

"Everything's pretty much on target," I said. This was the first time I had spoken to the HR exec since I'd been reassigned to the case. Making small talk with Ferris was always awkward. Like trying to slow dance wearing ankle weights.

"Have you had an opportunity to speak with Mr. Ellis about settling the case?" he asked. His tone was cautiously polite.

"No, not yet. As you know, we filed a motion to amend Micronics's answer to add the after-acquired evidence defense. If the motion's granted, Randle's potential damages could be significantly reduced. Reggie Jenkins wasn't very happy about it. To be honest, he went a little berserk. Anyway, I'm very hopeful that he'll be interested in talking settlement once he cools off."

"Well, exactly when do you think that will be?" Ferris asked sternly.

"The filing deadline for their opposition brief is just a few days away. I told them I would take the motion off calendar if they wanted to discuss settlement. I expect to hear from them any day now. They're probably just waiting until the last minute."

"Let's hope so," Ferris said.

He apparently had no more questions but seemed reluctant to end the conversation.

"Well...please keep me informed." Ferris sounded overly polite, but in a forced way.

"I sure will."

"Anything else happening on the case?" Now his tone was casual, as if he were chatting with an old friend.

"Not that I'm aware of. Is there something going on that I should know about?" I asked.

"Uh, no. Not that I can think of," Ferris stammered. "I just want to make sure we're communicating about every phase of the case."

You're fishing. You want to know if I know about those documents Karen Carruthers had in her car. "You know everything I know," I replied.

After a few more seconds of silence, I decided to test the waters. "It was really too bad about Ms. Carruthers."

"Yes," Ferris said. "What a horrible accident." There was a nervous edge in his voice.

Accident, my ass. "What exactly happened to her?" I asked.

"As I understand it, she lost control of her car and drove off the road. Mulholland can be pretty treacherous."

"What was she doing up there? Didn't she live in Long Beach?"

"I'm not exactly sure," Ferris said.

"Was something wrong with her car?"

"I have no idea."

"It's just so unfortunate," I said.

I could hear Ferris twisting about in his chair. I was just sorry that I wasn't there to watch him squirm.

"If this case ends up going to trial," I said, "the jury isn't going to like the fact that Randle won't have a chance to confront his accuser."

"If you do your job and get the case settled, it'll never get to a jury." His statement sounded very much like a threat.

"I'll do my best," I said, maintaining my cool. "Is there anything else?"

Ferris mumbled something under his breath, then said a brusque goodbye.

Although I felt I had the upper hand now, I also felt a tinge of trepidation. What if Ferris knew that I had a copy of those documents? Whatever they were. Would somebody be ransacking *my* house next?

I closed my eyes and inhaled. I was convinced that Ferris was somehow mixed up in all of this. I only wished I knew how.

CHAPTER 64

To my relief, Hamilton called just minutes after I hung up with Ferris. I was more than glad to hear from him, even it meant enduring a tirade from him, too. But he didn't go off the way Reggie had. After a short, pleasant conversation, I agreed to meet him at his office to discuss settlement.

By ten o'clock, I was sitting in the foyer of Hamilton's swank office in Century City. Walking into the lobby made me feel like I had stumbled onto the set of some TV show. O'Reilly & Finney was a pretty classy place, too, but Ellis & Dunlop was one hundred percent L.A. chic. The walls were creamy beige and you could see the entire city from the twenty-foot windows that encircled the lobby. A dramatic winding staircase with a stainless-steel railing took up one corner of the entryway.

Hamilton met me in the lobby and escorted me to his office. The first thing I noticed when I stepped inside was the ego wall behind his desk. Ego *billboard* probably would have been a more accurate description. There were two poster-size pictures of Hamilton on the football field during his Bruin and Raider days, as well as smaller pho-tographs of him with every prominent politician, celebrity and professional athlete you could think of. An eight-by-ten of Hamilton and the Governor smoking huge cigars caught my eye, but I purposely gave the wall only a passing glance and admired the view from his window instead. I could tell from the way he lingered near the wall that my feigned disinterest disappointed him.

I headed for a chair in front of Hamilton's desk, but he placed his hand on my back and steered me in a different direction. "Let's have a seat over here," he said, pointing to a red suede couch that had to be ten feet long. "Much more comfortable."

He sat down on one end, facing me, and stretched out his arm along the back of the couch. A tall, busty brunette in a low-cut sweater walked in carrying a sterling silver tray. She placed it on the coffee table in front of us. The tray held Waterford crystal glasses filled with ice, two bottles of Evian water and an array of muffins, croissants and scones. *He had to be kidding.*

"Well, before we get down to business," Hamilton said, "don't you have something to thank me for?"

"Do I?" I had no idea what he was getting at.

"When I heard you'd been taken off the case, I figured something was up. So I told your little cohort that if Micronics wanted to settle the case, I would only deal with you. I figured letting you get the credit for wrapping everything up would be a nice feather in your cap before that partnership vote."

"Oh, yeah," I said. "I guess I do owe you a thank-you." I wasn't so sure though that what he had done was actually a good thing. In fact, I'm sure some people at the firm would view his request as proof that something had indeed gone on between us.

"Like I said before, if the partnership thing doesn't work out at O'Reilly & Finney, we could use someone with your skills. Using the after-acquired rule was a pretty cold move. No one's ever sprung that one on me."

"Thank you," I said.

"Not many attorneys have what it takes to be a trial attorney," Hamilton said, his hazel eyes glued to my chest. "I can tell you get off on trying cases just like I do."

I wanted to tell him that there wasn't anything about me that was even remotely similar to him, but now was not the time to piss him off. "Thanks for the offer, but I'm here to talk about settling the Randle case, not my career. So let's get to it."

He took a white terry-cloth towel from the top drawer of the end table to his right and bent down to buff the toe of his left shoe. "You really believe Micronics fired my client for sexual harassment?" he asked as he moved over to his right foot.

"Hamilton, I didn't come over here to argue the evidence. I know your version of the facts and you know mine. None of that has changed. Let's hear your number. If we're in the same ballpark, I can have a settlement agreement in your hands this afternoon."

"Oh, so you've got it like that?" He placed the towel back in the drawer. "You're telling me you have full authority to settle this case without having to make a bunch of telephone calls."

"Within reasonable limits."

"What do you call reasonable?"

I laughed. "My client is the defendant. I'm not opening the bidding."

Hamilton grinned. I could tell that he very much wanted to settle the case, but he also enjoyed toying with me.

"How long did it take you to build up that steel shell of yours, counselor?" he asked.

I looked up at the ceiling as if I were mentally calculating the time. "About three years from the time I graduated from law school, give or take a month. You like it?"

He smiled. "See, that's why I don't date lawyers. Much too hard to deal with."

The man was getting on my nerves and I was finding it difficult to keep it in neutral. "Since I have no plans to date you either, that shouldn't be a problem."

"And you black women are the worst. Y'all are on the attack all day at work, then come home at night ready to bust a brother's balls, too."

"Please tell me you didn't have me drive all the way over here just so you could share your views on black female lawyers."

"You're right," he said. "Forgive me." He moved to the edge of the couch, letting his hands dangle between his knees. "I'll put my cards on the table. My client's tired of fighting. He can't find another job as long as his employment record shows that he was terminated for sexual harassment. He's been in Atlanta helping out with his father's dry cleaning business to make some cash, but it's been rough. So first, Micronics has to agree to change his personnel file to state that he voluntarily resigned so he'll be able to get another job."

"Done," I said.

Hamilton grinned. "Okay, cool. This might be easier than I thought. We also want Micronics to foot the bill for Randle's medical coverage for two years."

Two years' medical premiums would total about fifteen thousand dollars. I could easily live with that, too, but I did not want to seem like a push-over.

"How about this?" I said. "Micronics will agree to pay Randle's medical premiums for two years, unless he gets a new job that provides the same level of coverage he had at Micronics. Then we're off the hook."

"Just like a woman," he said chuckling. "Always trying to get blood out of a turnip. Fine. I'm sure my client will buy that."

"So what's your number?" I asked.

Instead of responding to my question, Hamilton picked up an Evian bottle from the tray, slowly unscrewed the cap and poured the water into one of the crystal glasses. He took a sip, then looked at me.

"One million dollars," he said. "My client wants one million dollars."

CHAPTER 65

I didn't react at first. Then I realized that Hamilton wasn't kidding and my heart sank.

We both smiled at each other for a few tortuous seconds. My smile was meant to camouflage my distress. If he was starting out this high, I had my work cut out for me.

"C'mon, Hamilton," I said, "let's get serious. What's your *real* number?"

He straightened his tie. "You just heard it."

"If the judge grants our motion," I said, "you wouldn't get close to that, even if you were lucky enough to win at trial."

"Judge Sloan's not granting that motion and you know it. The man loves me and he's still irritated with you for not settling the case for peanuts when you had the chance. When the jury hears about that white guy who grabbed some woman's titty and still kept his job, they'll know that Micronics discriminated against my client and they're going to pay him handsomely."

"Tell me something," I said. "How did Reggie find out about those other cases?"

"It wasn't that hard. People talk. One of Randle's co-workers heard about the other cases from an employee in

HR who was pretty upset about what had happened to Randle. And we'll definitely be calling her as a witness."

I assumed he was talking about Norma Brown. She probably had no idea that she would have to testify. My breath caught. If that happened, my conversation with her would surely be revealed.

"I thought you were putting your cards on the table," I said, even more motivated to settle the case. "You can start at a million, and I can start at ten or twenty thousand and we can go back and forth for the next two hours, wasting each other's time. Let's skip all the pretense. Tell me what you really want to settle this case."

"A million dollars," he said again. He stood up, picked up a folder from his desk and sat back down. "I asked one of my paralegals to get me some of the recent jury awards in race discrimination and whistle-blowing cases reported in *Verdicts & Settlements*. Let's see what we have here." He shuffled through the pages. "Two million. One-point-five million. Ah, this one is ten-point-three million. Shall I go on?"

Despite my unlimited settlement authority, there was no way I could go back to my office and tell Porter that I had settled the case for a million dollars. I needed to resolve it for a much more reasonable sum if I was going to get past the humiliation of botching the original settlement opportunity.

I snatched my purse from the floor and got up. "Why'd you have me come down here if you weren't serious about settlement?" I was angry and I didn't care if he knew it.

Hamilton was also standing now. "I wanted to meet with you face-to-face so I could look you in the eye," he said, locking gazes with me. "I'm a pretty good judge of character. I knew your eyes would tell me the real deal."

"What the hell are you talking about?"

"I just wanted to know if you really believed Micronics's lie about my client assaulting Karen Carruthers in that elevator."

"So what're my eyes telling you?"

"That you don't believe a single word of it. You're just doing your job."

I willed my body not to show any sign of emotion. "Is that right?"

"And I would also bet good money that this case has been messing with your head since the day you took it." Hamilton reached down for his glass and took a sip. "I checked you out. You're pretty solid."

"And just how did you *check me out?*"

"I've got my connections. You grew up in Compton. Working-class parents. You were vice president of the Black Student Union at USC. Even in law school you were a bit of a black activist. I was quite impressed."

I narrowed my eyes. "Thank you."

"Black folks who understand what being black represents can do what the white man pays 'em to do, but they can't do it *and* sleep at night. It's called having a conscience. And my research tells me you've got one."

Hamilton looked very satisfied with himself.

I wasn't certain how I should respond. I could reassert that my client had done nothing wrong, but I wasn't sure

I could do it with the necessary amount of conviction. I was pretty decent at telling lawyer lies—saying what needed to be said for the sake of the case. But lying about my personal feelings wasn't exactly my strong suit. My ethical obligations to my client, of course, prevented me from saying what I really thought about Randle's case. Hamilton was right about me. And he knew that I knew he was right.

He raised his glass to his lips and took another sip. "Okay, okay, have a seat. I'll make you another offer. A serious one."

We both sat down, though I did so with great reluctance.

"How's your girl, Special?" he asked.

I knew he was stalling, and I welcomed it. "*My* girl? I thought she was *your* girl?"

"I wished she could've been." His tone was wistful. "Dealing with that babe was like trying to date ten women. She's hot and everything, but she's way too high maintenance for me."

Hamilton paused and leaned closer to me. "But the girl is real. It would kill her to sell out a brother for the white boys. White boys who only care about how much money they can make off you. What are they billing you out at, three-fifty, four hundred an hour?"

"You trying to sidetrack me with a guilt trip, Hamilton? You're a partner in this firm. You telling me you don't make money off of your associates?"

"Touché," he said.

I picked up the other Evian bottle from the tray and took my time opening it. "So, Hamilton," I said, giving

him the warmest smile I could muster under the circum-
stances, "are you going to make me a real settlement offer
or continue to sit here playing head games?"

CHAPTER 66

Special typed the Web address for PeopleFinder.com on her office computer and waited.

She was growing increasingly concerned about Vernetta, who was stressing out more and more every day about not being able to get the Randle case settled. Special couldn't help her best friend with that particular lawsuit, but she was confident there was another one she could put to rest.

Grabbing a handful of Nacho Cheese Doritos from the bag on her desk, she waited for the Web site to appear. She had not done a lick of work all morning, her thoughts consumed with the plan she was about to put into motion. She had almost talked herself out of it, but the whole thing with LaKeesha had been bugging the hell out of her. What she was about to do was definitely the right thing. Vernetta didn't need this crap. Neither did Jefferson.

When the PeopleFinder Web site finally popped up, Special clicked over to the appropriate page, then typed in *San Diego* and *LaKeesha Douglass*. She held up two crossed fingers as she stared hopefully at the screen. The computer took a while to complete its search, then the words *no match* appeared.

"Shoot!" Special reached for the can of Pepsi next to her computer monitor and took a swallow. She had already tried directory assistance. Maybe she could locate LaKeesha's telephone number through San Diego State University, assuming the girl was actually a student there, which Special seriously doubted. But convincing some admissions clerk to release a student's personal information would require some real maneuvering. Of course, she could have searched the Telecredit database, but she wasn't trying to get her ass fired for misusing company records.

She continued staring at the screen, then decided to try another PeopleFinder search. This time she typed LaKeesha's last name using only one *s*.

"Bingo!" Special yelped when three names appeared on the screen. Only one of them listed a San Diego address. She wrote down the information on a Post-it note, then reached for her phone. She dialed the area code, then dropped the phone back into the cradle. She didn't want the girl to have her work number. Special dug her cell phone out of her purse.

"She not here," a kid's voice replied after the first ring. The child could not have been older than four or five.

"Do you know when LaKeesha will be back?" Special asked.

"Nope. She in college."

"Is there anybody else there I can talk to?"

The kid must have dropped the phone to the floor. "Nana, telephone!" Special heard him yell.

When Nana came to the phone, Special explained that she was calling from a temp agency and was trying to contact LaKeesha about a job interview. The woman gladly gave up LaKeesha's cell phone number.

Special checked the time. It was close to eleven, so there was a good chance LaKeesha would be in class. A flutter of hesitation hit her as she dialed the number. She shook it off when LaKeesha answered on the fourth ring.

"This is Special Moore," she said, "I'm—"

"I know who you are," LaKeesha spat into the phone. "How'd you get my number?"

"Don't worry about that," Special said sweetly. "I was just calling to give you a little warning. That workers' comp case you filed is bogus. And if I were you, I would drop it."

"You have some nerve calling me," LaKeesha huffed. "Ain't nobody scared of you. You call my number threatening me again and I'll sue you, too."

Special remained poised and professional. "If you don't drop your case, you're going to be facing charges for perjury, filing a false claim and a whole lot of other stuff." Special wished she knew some more legal-sounding words to throw at the girl, but she couldn't think of any.

"I don't know what you're talking about," LaKeesha said smugly. "I'm about to get *paid*."

"I'm talking about you trying to blackmail Jefferson."

"You're trippin' and I don't have time for this."

"Well, hopefully you have time to listen to this." Special hit the Play button on her microcassette tape recorder and held it up to the phone.

I know you didn't harass me. But in a court of law, it's my word against yours. And who do you think they're going to believe? The cute, young college student or the older, married man whose wife is out of town?

"How did you…? Where did you…?" LaKeesha struggled for words.

"Don't worry about how I got you on tape. Just know that I do. And like I said, you'd be smart to drop your little fake ass stress claim."

Special wished she could see the girl's face. "As it stands right now, Jefferson doesn't even know I have this tape. But if you don't dismiss your case, I'm giving it to him and he'll be turning it over to his lawyer." Special waited a beat. "They put people in jail now for filing fraudulent workers' comp claims. You might wanna ask your attorney about that."

She could tell from LaKeesha's labored breathing that the girl was in shock, but the jolt did not last long.

"I wonder how Jefferson would like it if I called up his wife and told her how her little Goody two-shoes husband let me give him head," LaKeesha said coolly. "I bet you that's not a lie. Why don't you put *that* on tape?"

LaKeesha's words hit Special like a blow to the head. She tried to recall the rest of the conversation on the videotape. There was nothing about *that* on the nanny cam tape. Then Jefferson's odd denial came back to her and it all made sense. *I didn't force that girl to do shit!*

"Oh, so you don't have nothing to say to that, do you?" LaKeesha said snidely. Now she was the one on the offensive. "I guess Jefferson forgot to mention how much he enjoyed letting me suck his dick."

Special reached for the Pepsi can and drained it dry. She

was standing up now, one hand gripping the cell phone, the other one grasping her hip. "You know what?" she said slowly, her voice cool and collected. "Your word choice is very, very interesting. *Let me give him head.* Not, he came on to me, or he asked me to give him head, or he tried to get with me. But *let me give him head.* That obviously means *you* came on to *him.* What brother wouldn't be happy to have some ho' throwing it in his face? Women like you are the reason brothers can't do right even when they want to. Tell me something. How many dicks did you suck this week?"

"I don't have to take this shit from you, you old ass bitch!"

"Old!" Special shouted. "I look younger than you do. And if I were you, I'd find myself a better role model than Monica Lewinsky."

"Fuck you!" LaKeesha yelled, and the phone went dead.

Special crunched up the empty Pepsi can, then tossed it across the room, missing the trash can by a mile. She fell back into her chair, satisfied that she had gotten her point across. Then her thoughts went to her best friend. If Vernetta found out about her husband's little tryst with LaKeesha, she would absolutely freak. Within seconds of meeting the girl, Special could see that LaKeesha was up to no good. How come Jefferson didn't see that?

"Men are such knuckleheads," she said out loud.

Special wasn't all that good about keeping secrets this juicy, but she was going to lock up this little tidbit and throw away the key. The girl had all but admitted that she had come on to Jefferson, not the other way around. The man did not deserve a divorce behind this one little misstep. Special just hoped that was all it was.

"Whew!" Special said, "preventing injustice is hard work." She dropped her cell phone back into her purse and zipped it up. She was going to pick up a tuna sandwich at Subway, then run over to the mall on Broadway to do some shopping. Retail therapy always calmed her nerves. Luckily, she had just gotten a new credit card in the mail. Starting next month, she was going to get her financial house in order and stop spending so much.

She was almost at the door when she remembered a very important message that she had forgotten to deliver to LaKeesha. She sat down behind her desk, took out her phone and hit the redial button. This time, LaKeesha's voice mail came on. Special tapped her fingers on her desk as she waited for the message to finish playing.

"I'm calling back because I forgot something I wanted to say," Special began, her voice as snotty as she could manage to make it. "And you should take this advice in the helpful spirit in which I'm giving it. Your boobs are entirely too big for you to be prancing around without a bra on all the time. If you don't start strapping 'em down, you're gonna have two pancakes flapping against your chest by the time you're thirty. So after your next class, you need to take your ass to Target and buy yourself a bra."

Special closed her cell phone and smiled. Mission accomplished.

CHAPTER 67

I spent another thirty minutes trying to convince Hamilton to reduce his settlement demand. He finally lowered it to $800,000 but refused to budge from there. When the haggling began to make my head hurt, I gave up and returned to my office.

To my surprise, Hamilton called me just after lunch and offered to settle the case for $600,000. After about ten more minutes of telephone negotiations, we agreed on $475,000, the value of Henry Randle's salary, bonuses and benefits for a three-year period.

When we were done, I quickly typed up the settlement agreement and faxed it to Hamilton's office. He asked for a few minor changes, then said he planned to fax it to Reggie and to Randle in Atlanta. He promised to call me with any additional changes before noon the following day.

With that done, I picked up the telephone and called Ferris. He was overjoyed about the settlement. The only question he asked was whether the agreement contained a strong confidentiality clause preventing Henry Randle from talking about his allegations of fraud or any other aspect of his employment with Micronics. I assured him that it did. Ferris asked to be notified when I had the signed agreement in hand.

The fact that Ferris didn't balk at the hefty settlement amount only bolstered my suspicions that Randle had been set up, that Carruthers's death was no accident and that whoever killed the woman wanted those ATPs very badly. I was also convinced that Special's apartment had been vandalized for the same reason. The Micronics documents were now safely hidden at my house. The very thought made me shudder.

I retrieved some empty boxes from the file room down the hall and began packing them with documents from the Randle case. The faster the documents were cleared out of my office and sent off to storage, the easier it would be for me to put the case behind me. In no time, I had filled up three boxes and was about to ask my secretary to bring in two more, when something stopped me and I sat back down behind my desk.

As much as I hated to admit it, Hamilton's caustic remark about me selling out a brother weighed on me. Maybe there was some clue in the file that I had overlooked which might help me confirm once and for all whether Henry Randle had been framed. I began perusing every document in the three storage boxes, hoping to find something, anything, that I had missed.

The name Bill Stevens jumped out at me as I flipped through the correspondence file. I had never spoken to the Micronics attorney who handled the case before it was transferred to O'Reilly & Finney. Maybe he would have some theory about what had really happened.

I needed to talk to Stevens as soon as possible. Once I received the signed settlement agreement, I would have no reason to continue my investigation. Not that I actually had a valid justification for doing so now. I dialed Micronics and asked for the Legal Department.

My call was answered by a woman who sounded like a teenager. "How may I help you?" the woman asked.

"I'm an old friend of Bill Stevens," I explained. "I understand he recently left the company. Could you tell me where he's working now?"

"We aren't allowed to disclose personal information regarding our employees," the woman replied stiffly.

"I understand that," I said, "but I don't think this qualifies as personal information."

The woman was not easily pushed. "Well, whatever it is, we don't give it out. Since you're an old friend, maybe you can find out from another old friend where Mr. Stevens is working."

"Thanks for your help," I said, my sarcasm thick.

"No problem."

I hung up the telephone, but really wanted to slam it down. Maybe I should've been honest and identified myself as an attorney for the company. No. I could not run the risk of my inquiry getting back to Ferris.

I pulled up the Martindale-Hubbell Web site and searched for Stevens's name. The nationwide attorney directory still listed him as in-house counsel for Micronics. It would be a waste of time to check any of the other legal directories since they were not updated until the beginning of the year.

I heard a light knock on my door. Haley was standing there with a vacant look on her face.

"What can I do for you?" I asked, trying not to appear as disgusted as I felt at the sight of the girl.

"Uh…I…uh…I just wanted to know if you needed help with anything on the Randle case." That aura of superiority no longer surrounded her.

"No thanks. I have everything under control."

I was about to tell Haley the case had been settled, but thought better of it. Knowing her, she would run off to Porter's office and claim that *she* had resolved it. I planned to advise Porter when he returned to the office later that afternoon.

Haley inched her way closer to my desk. "Are there any other cases I can help you with?" she asked. I was not used to her sounding so timid.

"Nope. All my cases are already assigned."

Shelia told me that the other senior associates were avoiding Haley like the plague, the kiss of death for any associate. If none of the senior attorneys wanted to work with you, you had nothing to bill and without billable hours, O'Reilly & Finney had no use for you.

Haley had made the mistake of focusing all of her energies on trying to impress the partners and no one else. It had pleased me to learn that I wasn't the only associate Haley had crossed. In another case, she failed to pass on some important information to a senior associate who, unbeknownst to Haley, was drafting a discovery motion directly related to the evidence she was hoarding.

When the partner on the case returned from an out-of-town trip three days later, Haley proudly shared the news she had discovered, expecting to make herself look good. By that time, the motion—minus the crucial information—had already been filed with the court.

Instead of applauding Haley for her keen investigative skills, the partner gave her a long lecture on the importance of teamwork. The speech ended with a blunt warning that if she ever pulled a stunt like that again, she would be fired.

Haley opened her mouth to speak, then stopped. "Uh, I just wanted to…uh…"

I almost felt sorry for her. Almost.

"Yes?" I said, anxious for her to spit out whatever she had to say, then skedaddle.

"About that day in the attorney dining room when you overheard me talking about the Randle case. I just wanted to apologize. I shouldn't have been passing along gossip like that. I knew that stuff about you dating Randle's attorney was a stupid rumor the minute I heard it."

Haley's eyes were appealing for forgiveness. But I was not feeling particularly priestlike. "Just forget about it," I lied. "I have." *And if you believe that, I have some prime swampland for you in Compton.*

"If something comes up that you need help with, just let me know." She gave me a hopeful smile. "I have some free time now."

I hear you have a whole lot of free time. "Thanks for the offer. I'll call you if I need anything." I watched Haley's shoulders sag as she turned to leave.

"Hey, wait a second," I called out, just as Haley had stepped into the hallway.

She dashed back inside, her blue eyes a shade brighter.

"While I was off the Randle case, did you conduct any other interviews?"

"Just one," Haley said. "I spoke to Bill Stevens, the former in-house attorney. I interviewed him over the telephone."

My ears perked up. "What did you find out?"

"He didn't come out and say it, but I got the impression he thought the allegation of sexual harassment against Randle was a little fishy. Would you like me to go over my notes with you?"

"Definitely."

"Okay," Haley said, excited about the prospect of having some work she might actually be able to bill. "I'll go get them."

"Hold on," I called out as Haley was about to skip away. "How'd you find him?"

"I looked him up on the State Bar Web site," she said. "I figured if he was still practicing law in California, he'd be registered with the Bar. He's working in-house for a small software company headquartered in Seal Beach."

I nodded. "Good thinking," I said. *Score one for the second-year.*

CHAPTER 68

After reviewing the notes of Haley's conversation with Stevens, I called him up. He agreed to meet with me at his office at three.

Stevens was a short man with a bronze fisherman's tan and a scruffy beard. A stiff smile never left his face. He met me in the lobby of his building and led the way to his office.

"So is this an official or unofficial visit?" he asked, closing the door.

I knew Ferris would not appreciate my being there, especially now that the case was all but settled. So I sidestepped the question with the proficiency of a two-term congressman caught on camera with his pants slumped around his ankles.

"As I told you on the telephone, I'm representing Micronics in the Randle case. I don't know how much you remember about the case, but—"

"Oh, I remember it well." His smile broadened.

I couldn't figure out if his expression had any special meaning since his lips were permanently etched in a half circle.

"What makes it so memorable?" I asked.

"Oh, it was just one of those cases you don't forget."

This was going to be like pulling teeth. Lawyers always made the most difficult witnesses. "Well, why was this one so unforgettable?"

"Because it's the reason I'm sitting here, instead of in the office I had for over ten years at Micronics."

"Are you saying they fired you over something related to the Randle case?"

"They didn't fire me, but they might as well have. When I began asking questions about the case, they suggested that I might like to take a separation package."

"What kind of questions were you asking?"

"I pointed out that there were other employees who'd engaged in sexual harassment but had not been fired. But nobody wanted to hear it."

"Was this before Randle was fired?"

"Sure was."

"What did they say when you gave them the information?"

Stevens shrugged. "I just got a clear message that I should keep it to myself."

"Did somebody actually tell you that?"

"Not in so many words, but that was the message I gleaned."

"Can you tell me who?"

"I'd rather not say." Stevens's eyes expanded. "If I didn't know better, I'd think you were here looking for information to help Henry Randle, not Micronics."

"It's important to know all the facts of your case—good and bad," I said. "I don't like surprises at trial. I'm just trying to get to the truth."

"You can't handle the truth!" Stevens said, doing a terrible Jack Nicholson impersonation.

I didn't laugh.

"I'm sorry," he said, embarrassed. "Just a little movie trivia to lighten things up."

I decided to stop beating around the bush. "I'm concerned that Randle's claim about being set up may have some merit. What's your opinion?"

"I never found a definitive answer."

"But what do you think?"

"It doesn't matter what I think. It only matters what a jury thinks."

I stared at him, annoyed. "Well, is there anything you can tell me about the investigation that might not be in the case file?"

There was a long, painful stretch of silence. Stevens seemed to be carefully weighing his next words. "Maybe."

"I'm listening," I said.

Although we were behind closed doors, he lowered his voice as if he were afraid of being overheard. "You didn't get this from me."

"Okay," I said.

"I think Rich Ferris, the VP of HR, had a thing for blondes. One strawberry-blonde in particular."

At first, I didn't understand what Stevens was getting at. Then it dawned on me. "Are you saying he was involved with Karen Carruthers?"

"Let's just say they had a pretty close relationship."

I tried not to show my surprise, but I was certain that I had failed. "But he's married, isn't he?"

Stevens nodded. "He certainly wouldn't be the first married man to have an affair."

"How do you know this?" I asked.

Stevens shrugged again. "Just take what I said as fact, not speculation."

"Are we talking about an intimate relationship?"

He nodded again.

"But he approved Randle's termination. The fact that he was dating the complainant would've been a clear conflict of interest."

"Exactly."

"So you *do* believe that Henry Randle was set up."

"Once again, Ms. Henderson," Stevens said, "what I believe is not important."

CHAPTER 69

By one o'clock the following day, I had not heard from Hamilton regarding the settlement agreement. I checked my e-mail every thirty minutes or so, hoping and praying nothing had gone wrong.

I had just returned from the ladies' room when Haley walked in.

"I was just wondering whether I might be able to help you prepare your opening statement for the Randle trial," she said eagerly.

The girl was really hurting for work, I thought. She needed to bill at least one hundred eighty hours a month. More than two hundred if she wanted to stand out. I had already advised Porter about the settlement, but I wanted the signed agreement in hand before announcing it to anybody else.

"Thanks," I said, "but I have everything under control."

Haley exhaled and took a seat in front of my desk even though I had not invited her to sit.

"I was just about to run downstairs and get a sandwich," I lied, hoping she would leave.

"There's some food left over from the Labor Department lunch," Haley said cheerfully. "I can go grab you a sandwich."

"No, you don't have to do that. I can—"

"I don't mind." Haley was out of the door before I could finish protesting. She returned almost as fast carrying a turkey sandwich, pasta salad and a can of Diet Coke.

"I only brought you a Diet Coke because I've seen you drinking it before. I...uh...I'm only telling you this because I don't want you to think I'm trying to say you need to lose weight or anything." Haley laughed.

"Thanks, Haley. I really appreciate your doing this." *Now can you leave?*

As hard up as Haley was for work, she would probably try to bill the client for her little errand. I made a mental note to double-check her time sheet to make sure she didn't.

Haley stared at me as I ate. When I took a second bite of my sandwich, Haley closed the door before taking a seat. She started to speak but paused as if unsure of herself. "I guess I kind of got off on the wrong foot at the firm. Everybody hates me."

Maybe if you weren't such a pompous little witch, you'd have a friend or two around here. "Nobody hates you," I said. The lie rolled effortlessly off my lips.

"Yes, they do," she said, "but thanks for saying that." Haley looked down at her hands. Her nail polish was badly chipped and her fingernails were bitten down to the nub. She pulled a long curl out of her face and smiled at me. The girl was making a real pitch for sympathy, but I wasn't buying it.

"Before I got to law school, everybody I knew told me I'd never make it as a lawyer because I was too shy," Haley said. Her voice sounded small and childlike. "Including my own mother. You have no idea how awful it is to have a judge for a mother and a political consultant for a father. All they cared about was making sure that I didn't do anything to embarrass them. They demanded that I be perfect at everything."

I could hear her right foot tapping the floor.

"All through law school, I practiced being assertive. I always volunteered in class, took on any student leadership role I could get and tried to act assertive and superconfident, even though I was shaking inside." Haley stopped talking and looked at me as if she needed to hear some words of support.

I took a big bite of my sandwich to avoid having to say anything. I found it amazing that anybody with Haley's looks and brains could be insecure.

"But I was determined to show my mother that I could make it as an attorney," Haley continued. "And after spending so much time acting like somebody who had it all together, it began to feel natural. People were attracted to my new, gregarious, confident personality. But when I got here, it kind of backfired. I guess it was a bad idea to use TV lawyers as my role models," she said with a nervous laugh.

I could see now that Haley's arrogance masked a deep-seated insecurity, but I still didn't feel all that sorry for blondie. "One of the principles I live by is to treat other people the way I'd like to be treated," I said. "And that extends to everybody. Even the folks in the copy room. You never gain anything by being rude to people."

"I know, I know," Haley said. "I really screwed up and

now I'm paying for it." She started peeling the nail polish from her ring finger.

"Just put everything behind you," I said. "Memories fade fast around here." That lie was more for my benefit than Haley's.

For the next few minutes, Haley shared other personal details of her upbringing. When she was done, I had a mental image of Haley's mother as Faye Dunaway in *Mommy Dearest.*

"What do you think about the Randle case?" I asked, wanting to discuss something less depressing.

"I think some of the company's actions are pretty suspect," she said.

"Does it bother you to have to defend a suspicious case?"

"No, not at all. That's what I get paid to do."

"You'll make a great lawyer," I said.

"Thanks. I'm really trying to be."

Haley didn't realize that my statement was not intended as a compliment. We chatted for a few more minutes.

"Thanks," she said again as she was about to leave.

"For what?"

"You're the first person who's been nice to me since I got here."

I didn't want to give the girl the impression that we were on the road to friendship, so I just took another bite of my sandwich.

"Well, if you have anything I can help you with, don't hesitate to ask," Haley said.

"I won't." I was glad she was finally leaving. As she walked out, I tossed the remains of my lunch into the wastebasket underneath my desk. Just then, my intercom buzzer sounded.

"You have a visitor in the lobby," Shelia said.

I glanced at my calendar to make sure I had not forgotten some appointment. "Who is it?"

"Detective Mason Coleman with the LAPD. He says it's extremely urgent."

I began to get excited as I waited for Shelia to escort Detective Coleman into my office. Maybe he had some information about the ATPs. I had settled the Randle case and perhaps Detective Coleman was now about to hand me some more good news. I was definitely on a roll.

When the detective walked in, he was wearing the same suit he'd had on at Special's place. That crusty mustard stain on his lapel was now a very noticeable shiny spot.

"Nice to see you again." I rose to greet him. "What did I do to earn this unscheduled visit?" I wanted to be cordial, but I also wanted to let the detective know that he couldn't just drop by unannounced, even if he was the LAPD.

"I think you better have a seat."

"Wow, is the news that good?" I asked, returning to my chair. "Don't tell me. You've figured out who vandalized Special's apartment and you've solved the Carruthers case, too."

"Not exactly." He looked away, then got up to close the door. "It's about Special."

"What now?" I braced myself for a shocker. "Please don't tell me she's still snooping around in the case after I told her to cool it."

Detective Coleman stuffed himself into one of the chairs

in front of my desk. "Special's been hurt. She's in intensive care at Centinela Hospital."

"Oh, my God!" I blasted out of the chair, covering my mouth with both hands. "What happened? Was she in a car accident? Is she okay?"

"Please calm down. Somebody broke into her house again last night. She was beaten up pretty bad. Stabbed in the neck and chest multiple times."

"Oh, my God!" I fell into my chair. "Oh, my God! I never should've made her go back home. It's all my fault!"

"No. You can't think like that." He sounded as distraught as I felt. "I'd be glad to drive you over to the hospital."

I grabbed my purse and was out of the door before Detective Coleman could hoist his enormous body out of the chair.

CHAPTER 70

Entering Special's hospital room and seeing her lying there unconscious rendered me totally numb. Her barely recognizable face was bruised and swollen, and her neck and chest were patched with bandages.

I walked over and embraced Special's parents, who were standing on the far left side of Special's bed.

"I don't understand why somebody would do this," Velma Moore cried, turning back to Special and stroking her limp hand. "Why would somebody want to hurt my baby?"

Although her eyes were swollen with grief, Special's mother was still as immaculately dressed as ever. Her linen skirt was much tighter and shorter than the average fifty-five-year-old woman would have been comfortable wearing. A matching tam, tilted to the side, revealed only a glimpse of her honey-blond dye job. Her bright orange earrings, from the same set as her necklace and bracelet, dangled from her ears like two miniature sweet potatoes. Her two-inch heels did little to heighten her petite, five-foot frame. A strong whiff of Chanel No. 5 encircled her like an invisible hula hoop.

"What did the doctor say?" I whimpered, unable to control my own tears.

"Her lungs collapsed," Milton Moore said quietly. His words were barely audible, as if he were mumbling to himself. I had never heard his normally booming voice sound so feeble. "But my baby's a fighter like me. She's going to be fine."

Special's father was almost seventy, but he had the physique of a man almost half his age. After years of his wife's nagging, he had finally started dying his naturally silver-gray hair. He insisted, however, on leaving his bushy eyebrows untouched. At six-four there was no question about where Special had inherited her height.

"The doctor said they're moving her out of intensive care as soon as she wakes up from the anesthesia," Special's mother said.

I walked around to the opposite side of the bed and moved a wisp of hair from Special's forehead. "You can't leave me, girlfriend," I sniveled. "You have to hurry up and get well."

Detective Coleman remained planted near the door until I remembered to introduce him. When I mentioned that he was with the LAPD, Special's parents began pelting him with questions he could not answer. *When did it happen? Who found her? Did anybody hear anything? Why would somebody do this?*

I torpedoed a sharp look at Detective Coleman to make sure he was not about to volunteer any unnecessary information. Special had never told her parents about the earlier break-in for fear that they would have pressured her to move back home with them.

When I could no longer bear to look at my friend's motionless body, I walked out into the hallway and pressed my face against the nearest wall. The initial flash of cold felt good. I pulled my BlackBerry from my purse and dialed Jefferson's number. When I heard his voice, I tried to speak, but only sobs escaped from my lips.

"Babe, babe, what's the matter? Did something happen at work again?" Jefferson asked in alarm. "Are your parents okay? Please stop crying and talk to me."

"No, no. It's…it's Special," I blubbered. Only the sturdiness of the wall kept my body from collapsing into a heap on the floor. "She's at Centinela Hospital. Somebody broke into her apartment and stabbed her. She's in intensive care."

"What?" The panic in Jefferson's voice mirrored mine.

"And it's all my fault," I sniffed. "She wanted to stay with me but I made her go home. She'd be okay if she'd still been at our house. It's all my fault!"

"No, no, listen to me," Jefferson said. "You can't blame yourself."

"Yes, I can! I shouldn't have made her go home. Jefferson, I need you. I'm scared."

"Just calm down," Jefferson said. "I'll be on the next plane back home as soon as we hang up."

CHAPTER 71

By nine o'clock that night, I was sitting across from my husband at our kitchen table, sipping cranberry juice, my nose runny and red. I had spent the last hour telling Jefferson everything about the Randle case, including my theory about the ATPs and Carruthers's death, as well as my newest suspicion that Micronics probably had something to do with the attack on Special.

When I finished, Jefferson had a look of complete shock on his face. "This sounds like something out of a movie," he said. "I can't believe you guys didn't let the police handle this."

He reached across the table and grabbed both of my hands and kissed them. "I'm not going back to San Diego until I know both you and Special are okay."

"I'll be fine," I said. "I know your project is in a crunch right now."

"No, I'm staying right here with you," he insisted, "at least until all of this blows over. But there's something I need you to do. You have to go into work tomorrow morning and tell O'Reilly everything you just told me."

I felt nauseous. "I can't do that. They'll fire me for sure!"

"Babe, this is some serious stuff you just told me. These

people aren't playing games. I don't want anything to happen to you. I love you."

"I love you, too."

He stood up and pulled me into his arms. "I know it doesn't seem like it now, but everything's going to turn out fine. But you have to report what you know to the firm and to the police. And when I say police, I'm not talking about this Coleman dude."

"I know, I know," I said. "But maybe if I confronted Ferris first, I could find out who attacked Special."

Jefferson gently squeezed my shoulders and leaned back so he could look me in the eyes. "No way," he said firmly. "All this detective work you and Special have been doing is nuts. It's bound to get you both killed. I won't have that. You have to talk to O'Reilly."

"I know, I know," I said again. "But how am I going to explain why I didn't come to him earlier?"

"Let's just worry about that in the morning. Right now you need to get some sleep." Jefferson placed his arm across my shoulders and guided me to the bedroom.

Just as I sat down on the edge of the bed, I heard the faint ringing of a telephone. I dashed back into the kitchen, determined to grab my BlackBerry from my purse before my voice mail picked up the call.

"Hey, what's…what's…happening, homegirl?" Special's words came out haltingly, in a voice that sounded as if it belonged to a ninety-year-old woman.

"You have no idea how good it is to hear your voice," I said. Tears started to flow again. "How are you? You had me so scared."

"Girl, you know I...ain't leaving this earth until I get a look at Jefferson's cousin," Special said in a measured, raspy voice. "That man might be my future husband."

We both chuckled weakly. "Is there ever a time when you're not thinking about some man?"

"Hell, no," Special said.

"How are you really? Are you in pain?"

"I've got stitches up the...wazoo, but I'm not really in that much pain." The hoarseness in her voice indicated otherwise. "I have a...a machine with a little remote-control gizmo. The minute I feel even a twinge of pain, I can just press a button and boom. I'm as high as a kite. Technology is a mutha, ain't it?"

I laughed again.

"And I even lucked up and got me a male nurse." I heard Special grunt. "And he's quite a hunk. I swear to God..." Her voice trailed off. I could tell it was a major struggle for her to speak. "He looks just like that fine brother who used to play for the Pittsburgh Steelers, Jerome Bettis. But after that thing with Trent, I need to be extra careful. And he's a nurse, so that's already one strike against him."

"Well, don't get too used to him because I want you back home. And when I say home, I mean home with me. I'm so sorry I made you go back to your apartment."

"Girl, this isn't your fault." Special cried along with me. "You told me to stay out of it. I should've listened to you."

"You were only trying to help me," I sobbed.

We both boo-hooed in unison for a while.

"Anyway," Special managed to say between sobs, "I

don't even remember what happened. The doctor said it's possible I may never remember."

"Don't cry," I said, ignoring my own advice. "You're going to be fine."

"I know I'm lucky to be alive," Special said. "But, girl...tell me the truth. How bad did they mess up my face? They won't bring me a...a mirror, and they won't let me get out of bed so I can see for myself."

"Your face is fine."

"It feels hard and swollen and no matter where I touch it, it hurts. I bet they scarred me for life!" Special's sobs were now interspersed with hiccups.

"No, they didn't. You're still the finest woman in L.A."

"You're just saying that."

"No, I'm not. You just have a few bruises that need time to heal. That's all. I swear. I'll even bring you a mirror tomorrow. Okay?"

"Promise?"

"Promise. Now why don't you get some sleep?"

"Okay, girl, but don't forget that mirror. And make sure you don't let Jefferson's cousin hook up with some other babe while I'm in here recuperating."

"I'll tell Jefferson to put him under house arrest," I said, chuckling. "I love you, girl."

"I love you, too."

CHAPTER 72

The next morning, I paced the short length of my office until my feet went numb. I fully intended to keep my promise to Jefferson and tell O'Reilly everything, but each time I picked up the telephone to dial O'Reilly's extension, I felt like I was having a panic attack.

And it didn't help my state of mind that I hadn't heard back from Hamilton regarding the settlement agreement. Maybe Hamilton was having a hard time reaching Randle. I thought about calling him, but I didn't want to let on how anxious I was to wrap up the case.

I quietly rehearsed what I planned say to O'Reilly as I paced between the door of my office and my desk. I reviewed which facts were essential to include and which ones I could conveniently leave out. I also tried to anticipate any questions O'Reilly might ask. Like, *Why didn't you come to me earlier?* For that one, I still had not thought up an acceptable response.

Just before ten, I decided to run down to the Starbucks in the lobby, hoping a dose of caffeine would boost my confidence. I'd only eaten half of a banana for breakfast, but I was too nervous to think about lunch. I had pulled a five-dollar bill from my purse when the phone rang. The caller ID showed my home telephone number.

"I've been waiting for you to call me," Jefferson said when I picked up.

I sat down on the edge of my desk. "I haven't had a chance to talk to O'Reilly yet," I said before he could ask. I neglected to mention that I had not even called his secretary to make an appointment.

"You *are* going to talk to him, right?" Jefferson's question was more like a command.

"I promised you I would."

"And you're going to do it today, right?"

I paused. "Yeah, if I can catch him."

"Why don't you call him right now? Tell him it's an emergency."

I was near tears again. "I don't know what to say. This is going to end my career. I just know it."

"Right now I'm more worried about your life than your career. If they fire you, you can find another job. You're an excellent lawyer."

"I won't be able to find another job if I get disbarred."

"That's not going to happen."

"How can you say that?"

"Because I can. You haven't done anything to get disbarred for. And if they do disbar you, I'll go down to the State Bar and kick everybody's ass."

I chuckled. "Stop making me laugh. I don't want to laugh right now."

"If I don't hear from you soon, I'm coming down there and you know you don't want me to do that. No telling what could happen if I run into that little rent-a-cop again."

"You better not come down here, boy."

"Then you better go take care of your business. I got your back, babe."

I hung up and dialed O'Reilly's extension. When his secretary told me he would be out of the office all morning, my whole body exhaled. I made an appointment to see him at two.

After returning to my office with a Caramel Macchiato, I picked up a copy of *California Lawyer* and tried to read a story about some public interest lawyer who had eight foster children. I read the same sentence three times, then tossed the paper aside. I knew it would be useless to try to do any work. My concentration level was nil. Maybe seeing Special would give me the courage I needed to face O'Reilly. I grabbed my purse and headed out of the door.

Thirty minutes later, as I pulled into a parking space at Centinela Hospital, my BlackBerry rang. When I answered, the sound of Hamilton's voice thrilled me.

I wondered if he had heard about Special. I doubted that she would want to see him, so I decided not to tell him what had happened to her.

"You know, counselor," he began, "I should be amazed, but I'm not. Seems you've been withholding some very important information from me and my client." His voice was both calm and hostile.

I felt a hot tingle all over my body. "What're you talking about?"

"Don't you think your star witness's death was something you should've disclosed to me? Did you really think I wouldn't find out that your client put a hit out on her?"

"A hit? C'mon, Hamilton. That one's a stretch even for you."

"Well, that's exactly what my sources are telling me."

"Your sources are misinformed," I said. "Karen Carruthers died in a car accident."

"Why would you expect me to believe that when you don't believe it yourself?"

"Talk to the police," I said. "They'll tell you what happened."

He chuckled sarcastically. "Come now. You don't trust the cops any more than I do. But I don't have a lot of time, I'm on my way in to court. I was calling regarding our tentative settlement agreement?" Hamilton said.

"There was nothing tentative about our agreement, Hamilton. We had a deal."

"*Had* is right. All bets are off. That agreement isn't binding until it's been signed by your client and mine. You almost pulled one over on me. I'm just lucky that one of my paralegals happened to hear about Carruthers's death from a friend of hers who works at Micronics."

"Now what?" I asked. "You're upping your demand?"

"You got it. This case is looking a whole lot better to me right now. Call me back when your client's ready to write a check for ten million dollars."

CHAPTER 73

I turned off the ignition and just sat there, too emotionally drained to move. Only thoughts of Special's well-being gave me the strength to climb out of my Land Cruiser.

By the time I reached the hospital lobby, an achy muscle spasm had started hammering away at the base of my neck and my temples were throbbing in pain. I sat down on a circular couch to the right of the information desk. I had to get myself together before I got to Special's room. That girl could read me better than anybody.

Once I felt sufficiently composed, I asked the receptionist for directions to the gift shop. When I got there, they didn't have any tulips so I opted for a huge bouquet of white roses. After handing the clerk my credit card, I remembered my promise to Special.

"Do you have any hand mirrors?" I asked.

The woman reached behind the counter and handed me a large oval mirror with a short handle. "How about this one?" she asked.

I held the mirror inches from my nose, carefully examining my own face. One side reflected a normal image, while the other provided a greatly magnified view. I knew Special was going to flip out when she saw her battered face, even though her bruises would surely heal. The mirror would definitely reveal far more than Special needed to see right now.

"Never mind." I handed the mirror back to the woman. "You can go ahead and ring up the flowers." The small MAC compact in my purse would have to do.

I stepped out of the elevator and trekked down the hospital hallway, the bouquet of roses fanning out in all directions, obstructing my view. I had to peek to the left or right every few steps to make sure I was not about to mow anyone down.

I walked past the empty nurses' station and was inside Special's room before I realized it was empty. To my surprise, there were no signs of life in the stark space. The bed was freshly made, the curtains drawn and the nightstand cleared away. I rushed back to the nurses' station, still struggling to maneuver the enormous flower arrangement.

"I'm here to see Special Moore in room 710, but she's not there."

"This is intensive care. You can't just walk into a patient's room and you can't bring flowers in here," the nurse scolded me. "Didn't you see that sign on the wall?" she said, pointing.

I gave the sign a quick glance. "I'm sorry." I set the flowers down on the counter. "I didn't see it."

The nurse gave me a skeptical look and picked up a clipboard from the counter.

"Is Special okay?" I asked, trying to read the chart upside down.

The nurse slowly flipped through the pages attached to

the clipboard, in no apparent hurry to answer my question. I tried to calm myself, but my mind kept racing to the worst. "Is everything all right?" I asked again.

"Ms. Moore is fine," the nurse replied. "She's been moved to the fifth floor. Room 517."

I was about to ask why, but remembered Special's mother saying that Special would be moved out of intensive care once she came out of the anesthesia. I closed my eyes and massaged my temples between my thumb and forefinger. I needed to relax. Special was going to be fine.

I hoisted up the flowers and headed back toward the elevator. When I made it to the fifth floor, I was disappointed to find room 517 empty. But this time, I was certain that I was in the right place. The bed was unmade and a plastic cup and pitcher of water sat on the nightstand next to a colorful bouquet of tulips and copies of *Essence, Star* and *People.* I placed the flowers on the window ledge and went looking for the nurses' station.

"I'm here to see Special Moore in room 517," I said to the first nurse I spotted. "She's not in her room. Is she having some tests or something?"

The nurse paused for much too long. "Are you a member of the immediate family?" she asked.

"Yes, she's my sister," I said without missing a beat.

The nurse briefly averted her eyes.

"Is something wrong?" I silently cautioned myself not to overreact again.

When the nurse placed a hand on my shoulder, I thought I was going to lose it. "I'm sorry," she said, "there were some complications. They rushed Ms. Moore back into surgery about fifteen minutes ago."

My legs buckled as if someone had kicked them out from under me.

The nurse grabbed me by the arm, holding me up. "Miss, are you okay?"

"What kind of complications?" I said, barely able to speak.

"You'll need to speak with her doctor for that information." The nurse had genuine empathy in her voice. She walked me over to a small chair near the nurses' station. "I think there're some other family members in the hospital chapel. Would you like me to go get someone for you?"

"No. I'll be fine," I said, too stunned to cry. I sat there for another minute or so, then dragged myself out of the chair.

"How do I get to the chapel?"

CHAPTER 74

I lethargically made my way to the first floor. My body felt abnormally light, as if I were floating along the hospital corridor using somebody else's legs.

The interior of the hospital chapel was a comforting contrast to the bland white walls outside. A warm amber glow hovered over the entire room. Imitation stained-glass windows and flickering candles wrapped the room in serenity. Eight rows of pews bordered a narrow aisle that led to an altar crafted in teakwood.

I spotted Special's parents sitting in the front row entwined in each other's arms.

As I took a step toward them, I felt a hand on my shoulder. When I turned around and saw my mother's face, I collapsed into her arms.

"Why did I have to hear about Special from Mrs. Moore and not from you?" My mother's soft whisper both chided and comforted me.

"I didn't want to worry you and Daddy." My voice broke as I tried, but failed, to hold it together. "I'm so glad you're here. Mama, I'm so scared." Tears stung my eyes.

"I know, baby, I know." My mother hugged me tightly.

"But everything's in God's hands now. We just have to have faith. Let's sit down."

We slid into the last row, still unnoticed by Special's parents. My mother swallowed my hands in hers, closed her eyes and started to pray in a low, fervent voice. "Father God, right now, we need the kind of strength only you can give us."

I squeezed my mother's long, wrinkled fingers and marveled at how eloquent she sounded whenever she talked to God. For years, I had watched her summon His presence in prayer meetings at church, during telephone conversations with one of her prayer partners or during her early morning meditations.

When my mother finished praying, we walked to the front of the chapel to greet Special's parents. Just then, a nurse entered. "I'm looking for the family of Special Moore," she softly called out.

Milton and Velma Moore scurried to the back of the chapel. My mother and I followed close behind.

"Your daughter's out of surgery," the nurse said. "And she's back in ICU."

"Can you tell us how the surgery went?" Special's father asked.

The nurse pursed her lips and drew in a breath. "I'm sorry. You'll have to talk to the doctor."

"Oh, my God! Oh, my God! Something went wrong!" Special's mother gasped. She buried her head in her husband's chest. I tightened my grip around my mother's hand.

"She didn't say anything went wrong, Velma," Special's

father said, hugging his wife. He turned back to the nurse. "Can't you tell us anything more?"

The nurse looked away. "If you'd like to follow me, I can page your daughter's doctor. He can give you an update."

Special's parents rushed out of the chapel behind the nurse.

"Mama, why don't you go with them?" I said weakly. "I'm going to stay here a little while longer."

My mother hesitated. "Please, Mama, go on. I'll be fine."

"Okay, Netta." She took me by the chin and wiped the tears from my cheeks with her thumb. "Don't worry. God is going to take care of Special."

"I know," I said, hugging her again.

When she left, I walked to the front of the chapel and knelt before the altar. I tried to speak, but sobs replaced my words. Audible prayers had always been awkward for me. I closed my eyes, clasped my hands together and hoped that God could hear my desperate thoughts. There was no way I could make it without my best friend. God could not let that happen.

I had no idea how long I had been kneeling at the altar, but when my knees began to ache, I got up and headed out of the chapel. I stopped near the elevator and dialed home. When I heard the answering machine pick up, I hung up and dialed Jefferson's cell phone. His voice mail message began to play and I hung up again, too weak to talk. I waited another few seconds, then decided to send him a text message. I wasn't sure what to write, so I just typed *Call me. ASAP.*

I pushed the elevator button, intending to head up to ICU, but when the doors opened, my feet felt like two cement blocks. All of a sudden, the sterile hospital smell made me dizzy. I needed some air.

Heading south toward the hospital entrance, I walked through the automatic glass doors into the blinding midday sun. I wasn't paying attention to where I was going and almost mowed down an elderly couple. I found an empty bench and sat down. I made a halfhearted attempt to do some deep-breathing exercises, but I couldn't concentrate. When a young man in a green smock joined me on the bench and lit up a cigarette, I moved to another bench, away from the smoke. Before I could get comfortable, I felt gripped by fear.

Maybe they're coming for me next! I glanced up and down the street at the stream of cars and people passing by. My body began to tremble as my eyes darted from left to right. I walked quickly back to the lobby, turning to look over my shoulder every few seconds.

A middle-aged Hispanic woman sat behind the information desk, but the lobby was otherwise empty. I slumped down in a wide blue chair and started to sob again. I had no idea how much time had passed when I abruptly stopped crying.

I can't let Micronics get away with this! I hurried outside, trying to remember where I had parked. I had only taken a few steps beyond the glass doors when terror took control of me again and I bolted back inside. I could not shake the feeling that someone might be watching me.

"How do I get to your emergency room from here?" I asked the receptionist at the information desk. I did not bother to wipe the tear stains from my face. The woman was no doubt used to seeing distraught people.

"Go down that corridor and make a left after the bank of elevators on the right," she said, her voice as soothing as her eyes.

Trotting down the corridor, I kept looking back over my shoulder every few steps. Once I was certain no one was following me, I dashed inside the emergency room, which was crawling with worn, sad-looking black and brown people.

I scanned the room and spotted glass doors that led out to the street. I zigzagged my way through the crowd of waiting patients, almost tripping over a toddler. When I got outside, I saw exactly what I had hoped to find.

"Do you take American Express?" I asked, walking up to a lone cab and opening the back door.

"Sure do," the driver said, sensing a big fare.

"Good. Take me to the Micronics headquarters on Sepulveda as fast as you can."

CHAPTER 75

Jefferson stepped out of the shower and heard the beep of his cell phone, signaling a new message.

He wrapped a towel around his waist, walked into the bedroom and grabbed the phone from the nightstand. He scrolled through his missed calls and saw that Vernetta had called him from her cell phone but had not left a message. The light on their home answering machine also showed a new message. When he hit Play, all he got was a dial tone.

Then Jefferson noticed that he had a new text message. Dread rocked him when he read what Vernetta had written. *Call me. ASAP.* He sat down on the edge of the bed and dialed her back.

By the time her voice mail picked up, Jefferson's pulse rate had doubled. The outgoing message seemed to take forever to finish. He gripped the edge of the nightstand as he waited. "Hey, babe, I was in the shower when you called." He made a concerted effort not to sound as worried as he felt. "What's going on? Call me back when you get this message."

Jefferson called Vernetta's office and left the same message, then got dressed and tried to watch TV. Vernetta should have finished her meeting with O'Reilly by now, he thought. He assumed that her text message meant that things had not gone well. He walked into the kitchen to fix himself a bowl of Frosted Flakes, but only found Shredded Wheat. He doused the cereal with sugar and wolfed it down while watching ESPN highlights.

He picked up the house phone and listened for a dial tone to make sure it was working, then checked the charge on his cell phone. Almost an hour had passed now. *Why hadn't Vernetta called back?* Jefferson dialed her office again. This time he got her secretary.

"I'm trying to find Vernetta. Have you seen her?"

"No," Shelia replied. "And I'm beginning to get worried. She scheduled a two o'clock meeting with the Managing Partner and didn't show up or call. That's not like her."

"Did you talk with her this morning?" Jefferson asked.

"Yes, but just for a second. She was already in when I got here, but a few minutes later, she took off without saying anything. I figured that maybe she went to the hospital to see Special."

Special! How could he have forgotten? She had probably taken a turn for the worse. "That's probably where she is," Jefferson said. "I'm going to head over to the hospital right now."

"When you hear from her, please have her call me," Shelia said.

"I will," Jefferson promised.

He grabbed his keys, jogged out of the house and drove as fast as he could over to Centinela Hospital. Every few minutes, he said a prayer for Special. By the time he pulled his Chrysler 300 into the parking lot, he was so revved up, he felt like he had run five miles at breakneck speed.

He pulled into the first empty space he saw and jumped out of his car. His heart all but stopped when he spotted Vernetta's Land Cruiser parked two rows over. That meant she was okay, but her rushing over here and skipping out on her meeting with O'Reilly only confirmed that Special was not.

As he approached the information desk to find out Special's room number, he saw Vernetta's mother coming down an adjacent hallway.

"Have you seen Netta?" she asked, gripping him in a warm hug. Her voice was heavy with worry. "I've covered every inch of this place trying to find her."

"She's not with Special?" Jefferson said.

"We haven't seen Netta since we left her in the hospital chapel over an hour ago. I can't imagine where she could be." She wrung her hands.

"I just saw her Land Cruiser in the parking lot," Jefferson said, trying to comfort her. "So she's got to be around here somewhere. How's Special?"

"Oh, Lord. Not good. Not good at all. She's in a coma." Vernetta's mother pressed both hands to her cheeks. "But God answers prayers."

Jefferson assumed Vernetta was somewhere in the building. She probably just needed some time alone. He pulled out his cell phone and tried to call her again, but she still didn't pick up.

"Something's not right," Vernetta's mother continued, still shaking her head. "It's not like Netta to disappear like this. Lord, Lord. First, somebody attacks Special for no reason and now my baby's missing."

"Don't worry. Vernetta's fine." Jefferson gave her shoulder a firm squeeze. "Why don't you head back up to Special's room while I go find her?"

"Dear God, please let my baby be all right," her mother murmured as Jefferson marched off.

Jefferson called Vernetta's cell again, but she still didn't pick up. After finding the hospital chapel empty, Jefferson checked the cafeteria, the gift shop and the waiting rooms on nearly every floor. When he walked into the waiting area near the intensive care unit, he found Vernetta's mother and Special's parents sitting with Detective Coleman.

Jefferson expressed his sympathies to Special's parents, then introduced himself to Detective Coleman. "Could we speak outside for a minute?" Jefferson asked.

The detective followed him a few yards away from the waiting area. "Vernetta told me the whole story last night, including the stuff about the Micronics documents," he said, once they had come to a stop several yards down the hall. Jefferson's tone was subtly berating.

"Yeah," Detective Coleman replied, shoving his hands deep into the pockets of his pants. "This is definitely one big mess."

Jefferson folded his arms and leaned against the wall. "I hate to even say this, but I think something may've happened to Vernetta," he said. "She sent me an urgent text message over an hour ago, but she's not answering her cell and I have no idea how to send a text message.

Her Land Cruiser's still in the parking lot, but I can't find her anywhere in the hospital."

Deep folds of dread lined Detective Coleman's mammoth face. "Let's go take a look at her SUV. It might tell us something."

CHAPTER 76

Jefferson and Detective Coleman rushed up to Vernetta's empty Land Cruiser and peered inside. The detective examined the windows and got down on his hands and knees to look underneath.

"There're no signs of a break-in," he said, pulling out a small tablet from his back pocket and jotting down some notes. He placed both of his hands on the hood. "And the engine is cold."

Jefferson used his key to unlock the doors and climbed into the driver's seat. Nothing appeared to be out of place. Jefferson was slowly becoming unglued. "This is crazy. Where the hell is she?" He hopped out and slammed the door.

"Don't worry, man, everything's going to be fine." Detective Coleman reassuringly placed his hand on Jefferson's shoulder.

Jefferson shook it off. "Is it?"

The detective cautiously backed up.

"What the hell were you thinking getting Special all wrapped up in this bullshit?"

The detective's cheeks expanded with air and he slowly exhaled. "Look, man, I had no idea it would turn out like this. Special wanted to play detective, and I was just trying to humor her. If I'd known—"

"If you'd known? Man, what were you thinking? You took her to the accident scene and you gave her copies of those Micronics documents."

"Copies? I never gave her any copies. I showed 'em to her, but I didn't give her any copies."

"Well, she has some because she gave 'em to Vernetta. That's exactly why she's lying up there in a coma. And now Vernetta's all up in it, too. I just hope whoever's looking for those documents doesn't know that Vernetta has 'em."

Detective Coleman's mouth gaped opened. "Man, man, man," he said, walking in circles. "I didn't mean for this to happen. My career is over!"

"Your career? Nobody cares about your goddamn career!" Jefferson shouted. "If something happens to Vernetta, your career is the last thing you need to be worried about."

The detective's shoulders went rigid and he seemed prepared to ward off a blow.

Jefferson pounded his right fist into his left palm.

"Look," Detective Coleman said, "we should just concentrate on trying to find Vernetta. Let's go back inside and canvass all the floors again. This time, we need to talk to people. Somebody had to have seen her."

That was the first decent idea that the man had come up with, Jefferson thought. Detective Coleman took out his tablet again. "Do you know what Vernetta was wearing?"

Jefferson tried to think. He had walked Vernetta out to her car earlier that morning, but had not paid much attention to what she'd been wearing. "A burgundy pantsuit with a pink blouse," he said, hoping he was right.

The detective asked for her height, weight and a few other identifying traits. "Okay, you talk to the woman at the information desk and then stop by the gift shop," Detective Coleman ordered. "I'm going to try to find Security. Then I'm calling a couple of my buddies at the station for some backup."

CHAPTER 77

I jumped out of the cab and stormed into the Micronics lobby. I wanted some answers and I was going to get them.

I had called Ferris's secretary from the cab and told her I needed an emergency meeting with her boss regarding the Randle case. When she started to explain that he was unavailable, I told her I was already on my way over and that I would wait in the lobby until he *was* available. As she started to protest, my BlackBerry went dead. I couldn't even remember the last time I had charged it.

A thirty-something African-American woman with long braids greeted me with an odd look when I walked up to the Micronics reception desk. "Are you okay?" she asked. "You don't look too good."

I noticed my reflection in the decorative mirror behind her chair. My foundation was blotchy and missing in spots and both of my red, swollen eyes were smeared with dark patches of mascara.

"Bad day," I said, digging into my purse for my make-up bag. "I'm Vernetta Henderson and I'm here to see Rich Ferris."

While the receptionist called Ferris's office, I took out

my MAC compact and stepped off to the side to touch up my makeup. The quick fix did little to improve my appearance. I dropped the compact back into my purse and started rehearsing in my head what I planned to say to Ferris. I wasn't sure exactly how I should play him. There was no way he would willingly admit to any wrongdoing. If this trip was going to be worth my while, I would have to be slick about it.

I felt a presence behind me and whirled around, but no one was there. My eyes crisscrossed the lobby. Two middle-aged white men in dark suits were conversing in one corner. A thin Asian woman was standing near the window talking on a cell phone. I looked through the wall of windows that lined the front of the building. Nothing appeared out of order in the parking lot out front. I exhaled, but I was still on edge.

From the direction of the elevators, I saw Ferris's assistant stalking toward me. Kathryn Phelps looked like a 1960s schoolmarm. She had a severe bun perched on top of her head and was wearing a flower-print blouse and a skirt that fell well below her knees. She did not extend her hand or offer me any greeting.

"Mr. Ferris has a very busy schedule," she hissed. "Unannounced visits are quite inappropriate."

"I fully understand that, but this is extremely important." I was purposely making an effort to be more cordial than I'd been on the telephone during the cab ride over.

Kathryn glowered at me, but her attempt at intimidation had no effect. "Come with me," she said curtly.

I followed her to the elevators, and once inside, I

tracked the elevator light as it moved from floor to floor. I hoped no one would delay my mission by stopping it to get on.

As we neared Ferris's office, I spotted Norma Brown sitting in a small cubicle. We had not seen each other since our conversation at 24 Hour Fitness. There was a brief display of terror in her eyes.

When we reached Ferris's closed door, his secretary pointed at a waiting area with two cube-shaped chairs. "Please wait here."

I took a seat, grateful for a moment to compose myself. Before I could get my thoughts together, Kathryn walked out of Ferris's office and motioned for me to enter. I would just have to wing it.

"I hope you're here to deliver that signed settlement agreement." Ferris's smile was as taut as a rubber band. I could tell that my impromptu visit displeased him.

I took a seat without answering him. He slowly sat down as well.

"I'm here," I said, "because we have a problem with the settlement. I just got a call from Hamilton Ellis." I paused and swallowed. "He's backing out."

Ferris's eyes expanded into silver dollars and his face hardened. "What?" He sat forward in his chair. "Why? Did they find out about Karen's death?"

Karen? Not Ms. Carruthers? I nodded.

He pounded the desk with his fist.

"It gets worse," I said.

Ferris's harsh brown eyes bore into mine.

I intentionally waited a beat. "He thinks Ms. Carruthers was murdered...that somebody at Micronics put a hit on her."

Ferris pounced out of his chair. "That's insane!"

Is it? Hamilton's claim was so outrageous that Ferris should have simply dismissed it with a laugh. His over-the-top denial told me that there had to be some truth to the charge.

"This is ludicrous. We were willing to pay those clowns nearly half a million dollars to settle that case. What the hell do they want? Maybe it's time for me to get involved. Perhaps I can talk some sense into those idiots."

"I'm not sure that's a good idea." I crossed my legs and fiddled with the strap of my purse. "It would be out of the norm to receive a call from the client. That would only signal that Micronics is running scared."

Ferris returned to his chair.

"Mr. Ferris," I said, "is there anything else about this case that I need to know?"

"I don't know what you're getting at, Ms. Henderson."

"I need to be honest with you," I said. "Something about this case just seems fishy to me."

"Don't tell me you believe this craziness about a hit?" he said, aghast.

"Frankly, I don't know what to believe." I wasn't sure where I should go next, but I had to push the envelope. Regardless of the consequences. "Do you know for sure that no one at Micronics had anything to do with Ms. Carruthers's death?" I asked.

"That question is completely insane." Ferris stared at

me with pure disgust. "How can you even ask me such a question?"

"It's my job to ask questions."

"Well, I'm telling you that one is completely inappropriate."

But you haven't denied it. "And Randle's charges about fraud on the GAP-7 Program. No truth to that, either?"

"Ms. Henderson, your questions make it clear to me that you aren't the right attorney for this case," he sneered. "I guess we made a big mistake reassigning you to it."

"Mr. Ferris, it's my job to dig for the facts. All of them. And I just can't shake the feeling that Micronics is hiding something. And if I'm going to defend this case properly, I need to know what that is."

"Ms. Henderson, I would feel much, much better if you operated on facts, not feelings."

I was not about to let Ferris intimidate me. "I have to be the first to admit that I'm an emotional wreck right now. I came here from Centinela Hospital. My best friend was attacked in her apartment and severely beaten. She's fighting for her life right now."

I saw a flicker of recognition in his eyes that scared me. *Did he already know about Special's attack?*

"I'm sorry to hear that," Ferris said. "But I don't understand what that has to do with me or this case."

I wanted to mention the ATPs, but I wasn't ready to play my trump card just yet. "My friend—her name's Special Moore—was captured in one of those pictures your investigator took. She was dating Hamilton Ellis,

Henry Randle's attorney. I'm just wondering if her attack could be connected to this case?"

"I have no idea what you're talking about."

I decided to take a different approach. "Mr. Ferris, let's go off the record. If you confide in me, I swear I'll maintain your confidence. And if you are involved in any way, I promise to do all I can to help you out of this."

I thought I saw relief in his eyes, but it vanished as quickly as it had appeared. "There's nothing I need help out of, Ms. Henderson. As I told you from the start, Randle's claims are a bunch of lies."

His eyes veered toward the crystal clock on his desk. "I'm afraid we're going to have to cut this conversation short. I need to advise the CFO that the settlement is off."

"Why is the CFO even involved in this case?" I asked.

Ferris stood up. "I need to get going, Ms. Henderson. And you should know that I'll be giving Joseph Porter a call after my talk with the CFO."

I took a few seconds to gather myself. I was on the brink of losing it and I didn't care if I did. My best friend had nearly been beaten to death and this guy probably had something to do with it.

"So you're going to have me taken off the case again?" I asked.

Ferris folded his arms. "Well, what would you do in my situation?"

"Mr. Ferris," I said, pulling my purse higher on my shoulder, "I would never *be* in your situation."

CHAPTER 78

I marched out of Ferris's office, asked his secretary to call me a cab, then took the elevator down to the lobby. When I pulled out my BlackBerry to make a call, I remembered that I had no charge left. The first thing I was going to do when all of this was over was buy a separate cell phone with a decent battery life.

Glancing around the lobby, I spotted a bank of pay phones and darted in that direction. It was time for me to reach out for some help. My hand trembled as I punched in James's number.

"I think I know what those Micronics documents are," I said in a hushed voice the minute James picked up. My eyes welled up again and tears began streaming down my cheeks. "And Special's been hurt, and—"

"Slow down, slow down," James said. "Are you okay?"

"No, I'm not okay." I wiped tears from my face with the heel of my palm. "You won't believe what I've been through in the last twenty-four hours."

"Calm down. Just calm down."

Talking ten miles a minute, I told him about the attack

on Special and my hunch about the Micronics documents. "I really need your advice about what I should do next."

"Where are you?"

"I'm at Micronics headquarters." I suddenly realized the foolishness of having this conversation on a lobby pay phone. Someone in this company had tried to kill my best friend over the very documents that were now hidden at my house. No telling who was listening in.

"I need to get out of here," I said. "Can you meet me somewhere?"

"Sure," James said. "Just name the location."

I tried to think of a suitable meeting place. If someone was after me, they would be less likely to act if I were surrounded by lots of people. "How about the Starbucks in the Ladera Center?"

"Good choice," James said. "I'm just finishing up with a witness interview at the Inglewood Courthouse. I can be there in twenty minutes."

"Okay. It'll probably take me a little longer than that. I'm waiting for a cab right now."

I glanced at my watch and realized that I had missed my meeting with O'Reilly. But I didn't have time to think about him right now. I did, however, need to call my mother. She was probably worried to death after I disappeared from the hospital without a word.

Jefferson was another story. He was expecting an update following my talk with O'Reilly. But if I told him that I'd gone to Micronics to confront Rich Ferris, he would be all over me.

"I need you to do me a favor," I said to James. "First, call my mother on her cell phone and tell her I'm okay. Then I need you to call Jefferson. If I call him, I'll have to explain where I am. And if I do that, he'll go nuts."

CHAPTER 79

Ferris waited for what he thought was sufficient time for Vernetta to board an elevator, then walked briskly to the CFO's office on the far side of the fifth floor. He brushed past Nathaniel Hall's secretary and barged straight through the CFO's closed door.

"We no longer have a settlement in the Randle case," Ferris said, closing the door behind him. He was anxious and winded. His words eked out between shortened breaths of air.

Hall's eyes hooded over, but he didn't speak.

Ferris walked closer to Hall's glass-top desk and quickly recounted snatches of his conversation with Vernetta.

"How in the hell did you let this happen?" Hall began pacing the length of his office, but stopped at the window on his third go-around. "Hey," he said, pointing below, "isn't that her?"

Ferris looked down at Vernetta standing in front of the Micronics building and nodded. "My secretary just called a cab for her. It apparently hasn't gotten here yet."

Hall snatched his cell phone from his desk, dialed a number, then paused, covering the receiver with his hand.

"You don't need to hear this," he said. "Perhaps you should leave."

"What are you doing?" Ferris said, alarmed. "Nobody else needs to get hurt."

"You can leave," Hall ordered. "Now."

Ferris crept out of the CFO's office and walked sluggishly back to his own. When he got there, he parked himself at the window and stared down at Vernetta, still standing in front of the building. He prayed that she wasn't next on the list, but he knew that was exactly what Hall was arranging at this very moment. He reached for a cord, pulling the blinds shut. The lack of sunlight seemed to cause the walls to close in a foot or two.

He rubbed his eyes and wished that he could wake up from this nightmare. As he eased into his chair, his thoughts traveled back to the day his own greed and stupidity pulled him into this whole, deadly scheme.

About three weeks after Henry Randle first complained about fraudulent billing, Ferris was called to the office of the GAP-7 Program Manager. When he arrived, the Program Manager, Dean Timmons, and the CFO were already seated at a circular conference table.

"How can I help, gentlemen?" Ferris said cheerfully. He pulled out a chair and took a seat across from them. He assumed that the men had some high-level HR problem requiring his assistance.

"We have reason to believe that you've been involved in an inappropriate relationship with another employee," Hall charged.

"What?" Ferris said, completely taken aback.

"Are you having an affair with an employee by the name of Karen Carruthers?" the CFO demanded, barely allowing Ferris time to process the first question hurled at him.

Ferris's back went erect. They were trying to intimidate him and he was not going to let that happen. "No, I'm not!"

"Well, these pictures certainly say otherwise." Timmons tossed a handful of photographs onto the table. "I wonder what your wife would think of these," Hall said.

Ferris picked up the pictures, his hands trembling with rage. The color snapshots showed Ferris and Carruthers dinning at Spago's, embracing in the lobby of the Carlsbad Four Seasons Hotel, holding hands on Rodeo Drive.

"What business is it of yours?" Ferris finally said. "My personal relationship with Ms. Carruthers does not violate company policy."

"Well, these certainly do." Hall placed a stack of papers on the table.

Without reaching for them, Ferris recognized the documents as copies of his expense reports.

"I'd say it was against company policy to steal company funds, wouldn't you agree?" The CFO picked up one of the pages. "Let's see...we traced one, two, three dummy corporations back to you. It seems you wrote quite a few company checks to these nonexistent companies. And then there were dozens of unauthorized business trips. You hit Vegas several times last year."

Hall tossed the page at Ferris and picked up another one. "And you stayed in some pretty fancy hotels and restaurants in San Francisco. We calculated at least ten thousand dollars in personal gifts, like those diamond earrings you bought at Saks last Christmas. Counting your generous gifts, the trips and the payments to the phony corporations, we've found close to ninety-five thousand dollars in unauthorized expenses over the past two years. But then, our investigation isn't finished yet."

Ferris opened his mouth, but the only communication came from the shock in his eyes.

"I'd call this fraud, wouldn't you, Dean?" the CFO said, turning to the Program Manager.

"Sounds more like embezzlement to me," Timmons retorted.

They allowed Ferris to sit in shock for a good thirty seconds, then told him that if he wanted to keep his job and avoid a prison stint for embezzlement, he would have to convince Carruthers to help them with a scheme to get Henry Randle out of the company.

Ferris tried to tell them that the plan was ridiculous, that it would never work. But they refused to listen. The CFO feared that Randle's complaints would eventually prompt a government audit of the program. Something Micronics could not allow to happen.

Everything was already planned out, Hall explained. Randle would be fired for sexually harassing Karen Carruthers. They anticipated that he would file a wrongful termination lawsuit, but defending his case would be preferable to allowing Randle to continue making noise about the GAP-7 Program. And if he claimed his firing was in retaliation for blowing the whistle about the GAP-7

Program, the sexual harassment allegation would severely undercut his credibility.

Ferris had no choice but to go along with the scheme. If they dug deep enough, he knew that they would discover that the sums he had stolen during his tenure with the company totaled hundreds of thousands of dollars.

That same evening, Ferris took Carruthers to dinner—this time, on his own dime—and told her about the company's discovery of his expense reports, but left out their concerns about the GAP-7 Program. She agreed to go along with the scheme, but only to keep him out of jail. Later, after the lawsuit was in full swing and she had been deposed, she had called Ferris in tears, saying that she could not go through with it. Ferris managed to calm her down, then reminded her that she had already given her deposition—which was the same as testifying under oath. Now she, too, could end up in prison. And not only for perjury, but for being a part of the entire conspiracy against Randle. The possibility that *she* might have to do time suddenly trumped Carruthers's concerns about Henry Randle.

For several weeks, everything had been going along just fine until Ferris screwed up and told Carruthers far more than she needed to know. In a moment of weakness, prompted by his own guilt about what they had done, he foolishly told her the whole story, at least everything he knew. He explained how Micronics's top executives were worried about Randle's allegations of fraud. At that point, Ferris still had no idea exactly what an investigation of the GAP-7 Program might reveal.

But then Carruthers did something extraordinarily

stupid. She called Ferris and threatened to expose their little scheme unless Micronics paid her a hundred thousand dollars. At first, Ferris had just laughed. When you only made thirty-two thousand dollars a year, a hundred grand probably felt like hitting the lottery. But Ferris was not laughing days later when she increased her demand to a million dollars, claiming she now had documents that proved Micronics was guilty of providing false information to the Air Force about the GAP-7 Program. She claimed to have gotten the documents from the Quality Manager on the program, whom she now happened to be dating.

The CFO was not pleased when Ferris passed along Carruthers's demand. It was only then that Ferris had learned about the ATPs and the real reason Micronics was so anxious to avoid a government investigation. The GAP-7 Program was both behind schedule and over budget and had run up against several minor mechanical flaws. Retesting the failed components would take years to complete. If that news leaked out, the company's top executives feared that Wall Street analysts would immediately downgrade Micronics's stock, jeopardizing other programs and reducing the value of the executives' stock options by millions of dollars.

So the decision was made to ignore the failed tests scores and move forward. Phony ATPs were submitted to the Air Force, stating that the super high-tech navigation system had passed every single test with flying colors.

Recalling the string of events made Ferris want to heave. And the situation was far worse now because the

GAP-7 navigation system was being blamed for the crash of that transport plane in Baghdad.

Ferris pressed the back of his head against his soft leather chair and closed his eyes. Karen was gone and Vernetta's friend had been brutally attacked. Special Moore was not supposed to have been hurt. Ferris had ordered Cliff to search her apartment for the ATPs one more time. They knew that she had copies of the documents because they had been scanned into her laptop computer, which they'd taken during the first break-in. She had also written extensive notes about the documents on her laptop, though it was clear that she had no idea what they really were. The woman's apartment had been empty for days. They were not expecting her to return home that night. And when she walked in on Justin and Paulie ransacking her apartment again, Paulie just went nuts.

Ferris knew that Vernetta would be next. He hurried over to the window and peered through the blinds. He watched with relief as a cab pulled up and Vernetta headed toward it.

His ethical side knew that he should pick up the telephone right now and warn her. But the other side—the survival side—said that doing so would put his own life at risk. Everything would all work out, Ferris told himself.

It had to.

CHAPTER 80

I was relieved to finally see a yellow cab roll to a stop in front of the Micronics headquarters building. "Take me to the Starbucks in the Ladera Shopping Center," I said as I climbed into the backseat. "It's at the corner of Centinela and La Tijera. Just go straight up Sepulveda and make a right on La Tijera."

The cab driver nodded.

Even though my confrontation with Ferris had not elicited the information I wanted, his reaction convinced me that my concerns were much more than a hunch. I tried to plot my next move. Was there some way to unravel this mess and still keep Special and me out of it? Hopefully, James would know what to do.

It did not take long before my thoughts traveled back to Special. I needed to call the hospital to see how she was doing. I fumbled inside my purse for my BlackBerry, then remembered that it had no charge left. I closed my eyes and said another quick prayer. *Special is going to make it. She has to.*

Snapshots of all of the events in my life that Special and I had shared together appeared before me like a slow-motion filmstrip. We had endured so much. There was no way God could take a life as vibrant as Special's so soon.

As the cab sped through an intersection, I glanced mindlessly out the window, watching the passing buildings but not really seeing them. After a few minutes, I realized that I did not recognize my surroundings. The cab was not on Sepulveda *or* La Tijera. I strained to read the street signs as we moved swiftly along.

"Where are we?" I asked with growing concern. "This isn't the way I asked you to go."

"Too much traffic on Sepulveda," said the driver, a wiry black man. "I took a shortcut."

I tried to roll down the window, but the electric switch didn't work. I lowered my head to get a better view of the passing street signs. We were on Lincoln Boulevard, which was west of where I wanted to go. *This wasn't a shortcut!*

Something inside my brain finally clicked into gear. "Let me out of here," I yelled. I reached for the door handle, but there wasn't one. I turned to the opposite door. No handle there either.

"Where are you taking me?" I demanded. "Stop this car right now!"

The cab made a sharp left into the parking lot of what looked like an abandoned bowling alley. I had to get out. Now! My heart pounded furiously as I scanned the backseat for something I could use to break the window. The cab came to an abrupt stop and I raised my right foot, poised to pound it against the window. Before I could, the door opened and a hulk of a man grabbed me by the ankle, pulled me toward him, then pushed me back across the seat with such force that my head crashed into the opposite door.

Pain rippled through my body and I had to struggle to remain conscious. "What's going on? Let me out of here!"

I shrank against the door as the man slid into the backseat next to me. He slammed the door shut behind him, then reached over and grabbed me by the neck, shaking me furiously. I grabbed his wrists and tried to pull his hands away, but that only made his grip around my neck tighten.

When I let out a feeble scream, he released my neck, but grabbed both of my wrists in one of his enormous hands, then slapped me hard across the face several times.

"Shut up and sit still," the man said.

My face went numb with pain. His grip around my wrists was so tight that I could feel my wrist bones scraping against each other. With his free hand, the man pulled a gun from his pocket and stuck it deep into my stomach.

"You and your little friend have some documents that don't belong to you," he said. "And I want them back."

CHAPTER 81

Jefferson, James and Detective Coleman had been sitting outside Starbucks for nearly forty minutes.

"Vernetta should have been here by now," Jefferson said, pounding his fist on the wrought-iron table. "Something's wrong."

The worried look on James's face silently affirmed his concurrence with Jefferson's statement. Something was *very* wrong. He scanned the busy parking lot of the Ladera Center hoping to spot a cab with Vernetta inside. James still could not believe the story he had heard from Jefferson and the detective. He didn't understand why Vernetta had not told him the full story behind the documents when she'd first brought them to his house. But his mounting anxiety over her safety allowed him to put that aside.

James stood up and was about to head inside for a cup of coffee, but changed his mind when he saw that the Starbucks was packed with people. A long line of customers stretched from the counter to the glass door. To the left of the line, college students, bent over laptops and thick textbooks, occupied every available seat. Outside, on the east side of the building, a small group of black men were crowded around tables watching two chess games in progress.

"I told her not to take her ass down there!" Jefferson fumed as James rejoined them at the table. "She's so damn hardheaded!"

"I'm waiting to hear from one of the patrol cars I sent over to Micronics," Detective Coleman said confidently. He was gobbling down his second piece of lemon pound cake.

Jefferson glared at him. "Like I said before, you just better hope Vernetta doesn't get hurt."

"This isn't exactly a good time to be passing around blame," Detective Coleman replied, taking a sip from his Banana Coconut Frappuccino.

"Well, you make sure you let me know when the time is right because I have a whole lot of shit I wanna say!" Jefferson yelled.

The detective lowered his eyes. "Don't you think I'm worried about Vernetta, too?"

"Based on what you said in that hospital parking lot, it sounded to me like your muthafuckin' career is the only thing you're worried about."

"C'mon guys," James interrupted. "This isn't helping. I hate to say it, but Jefferson's right. Vernetta should've been here a long time ago. Considering what happened to Special, we have to assume she's in trouble."

Jefferson sat forward, planting his forearms on the table. "I can't just sit here," he said. "We need to do something."

"I don't know what we *can* do," James said. "There's still a chance she's just held up in traffic."

Jefferson checked his watch. "What traffic? There's no major traffic around here."

James and Jefferson stared at each other, while Detective Coleman stuffed another piece of pound cake into his mouth.

"If these guys were bold enough to break into Special's apartment twice and nearly kill her the second time, we have to assume they'd have no qualms about snatching Vernetta in broad daylight," James said. "Maybe they got to her before her cab arrived."

The sound of the *Bad Boys* theme song rang out from Detective Coleman's cell phone. He finished chewing before pulling the phone from his breast pocket. "Detective Coleman here."

Jefferson drummed his fingers on the table.

"That was the patrol car I sent over to Micronics," the detective said, closing his phone. "No sign of Vernetta or any cab."

Jefferson reached into his pocket and pulled out his keys. "I don't know exactly what I'm going to do," he said, "but I can't just sit here and do nothing."

CHAPTER 82

I sat cowering in the backseat of the cab as the man spat into my face. "We want those documents your nosy little friend stole. And if you have any copies, we want those, too."

"I don't know what you're talking about," I wailed.

I had never felt this kind of fear before. It paralyzed my brain, rendering me totally unable to think. The man was still holding my wrists in a makeshift vice and my hands were numb from the lack of circulation.

I have the right to remain silent was the only thought my brain was able to process.

"Do you hear me?" the man said gruffly. "Where are the documents? We know your friend has them because of the information we found on her laptop. So where are they?"

I made eye contact with the driver, who peered at me from the rearview mirror. He looked too young and clean-cut to be involved in a kidnapping. I stared back at him, my eyes begging for his help. But he looked as scared as I was.

"I don't know what you're talking about," I said again.

I tried not to think about the gun still pressed into my stomach. I was totally ignorant about weapons. When the police rescued me, I wouldn't even be able to tell them what kind of gun it was. Was it a revolver? A semi-automatic? I had heard rap songs talk about Glocks, but I had no idea what a Glock looked like.

I decided to concentrate on my attacker's face so I would at least be able to pick him out of a lineup. I studied him as if I were a portrait painter, making mental notes of any and all distinguishing traits. He had pale, white skin and a thick nose, and I surmised that he was probably Norwegian or Swedish, although he did not speak with an accent. Right below his left eye, he had a fresh two-inch scar. His tan polyester pants and white shirt brought back images of my ninth-grade civics teacher. I closed my eyes and tried to commit the faces of both men to memory. I refused to consider the possibility that I would not survive this ordeal.

"If you want to make this hard on yourself, we can do that." The man leaned in close enough for me to know that his last meal had included onions.

I could tell that he was about to blow a fuse.

"I'm sure my friends have called the police," I said, surprised at my bravado. "They're probably looking for me right now."

The man laughed arrogantly. "That really frightens me."

I glanced over his shoulder. We were parked behind the bowling alley, and it was definitely abandoned. Nothing looked familiar. They could do anything they wanted to me back here and no one would hear or see.

The man set the gun on the floor, out of my reach, and grabbed me around the neck again with one hand, still holding my wrists with his other. His beefy fingers pressed so deep into my throat I couldn't even muster a scream. I was certain I was about to take my last breath when the driver intervened.

"Hey, Paulie! Let her go!" he yelled. When Paulie didn't let go, the driver reached over the front seat and tugged at the man's forearm. "Paulie, cut it out! We can't kill her. We have to get those papers back first!"

First?

Paulie, who seemed to be in a trance, finally released his grip and I gasped for air.

"This little cunt thinks we're playing." He reared back and slapped me across the mouth with his open hand. This blow didn't hurt as much as the others, probably because my bruised and swollen face had been anesthetized by the previous blows. I tasted my own blood as it dripped from my lips onto my silk blouse.

"Maybe we should beat her until she gives us what we want." Paulie slapped me again, sending my head crashing into the window. "Or maybe we should make a trip to Centinela Hospital and finish off her friend."

That threat snapped me out of my pain-filled silence.

"Okay," I cried out, trying my best to shrink away from the man. "I'll give you the documents! Just don't hurt Special!"

CHAPTER 83

The cab rolled to a stop in front of my house and the driver jumped out and opened the back door.

Paulie pushed me out of the backseat and yelled at the driver. "Get out of here, but don't go far. I'll call you as soon as I get the documents." We were barely out of the cab before it sped off.

I wobbled up the driveway leading to my house with Paulie so close on my heels I could feel the gun nudging my spine. I glanced up and down the street, praying that somebody would detect the fear in my eyes or the bruises on my face before we made it inside. I looked at the house to my left and stared at the closed kitchen window. *Where in the hell was Mr. Robinson?* I thought about trying to yell out to him, but the gun stuck in my back muted my vocal cords.

The rest of the block, as usual, was quiet and deserted. That's what I got for living on a street where people minded their own business. In my parents's neighborhood in Compton, somebody would have noticed the huge white man escorting me up the driveway and instinctively known that something wasn't right.

Paulie ushered me through a side gate and into the

backyard. He snatched the keys from my purse, letting a tube of lipstick, a hair brush and my wallet tumble to the ground. "Which one is it?" he demanded.

I tried to think up some way to keep from going inside, but my brain failed me. When Paulie shouted at me again, I pointed to a silver key. Still holding the gun on me, he stuck the key into the door but had a hard time getting it open. When he finally did, he shoved me inside with such force that I fell to my knees and slid across the kitchen floor.

I screamed, but the man did not seem to notice or care.

"I don't have time for any more crap. Give me the documents!"

I gripped the edge of the kitchen countertop and pulled myself up. I wasn't sure whether it was me or the room that was spinning. The familiarity of my kitchen provided some comfort, but not enough to erase the hopelessness of my situation. My eyes scanned the room for something I could use as a weapon. My turkey-carving knives were in a drawer next to the stove, only inches away from me. But there was no way I could grab one of them without the man blocking my path.

After the first break-in at Special's apartment, I had talked her out of buying a gun. This experience only confirmed that having a gun was useless. Even if I had owned one, it would have been locked away in my bedroom closet, of absolutely no value to me now.

"Where're the documents?" Paulie grabbed my arm and dragged me from the kitchen into the den. He sounded even more agitated.

I was trying to stall as long as I could. I knew that once

he had the papers, he would have no further use for me. "I think they're in my office," I said.

"They better be. I'm tired of playing games, you little cunt!" Paulie backhanded me across the face and I fell to the floor, landing on my right shoulder. He grabbed the back of my neck, pulled me to my feet and thrust me toward the hallway leading to the bedrooms. My knees ached and I did not think I would be able to walk without assistance. I knew exactly where the documents were, but I was in no rush to give them to him. I stumbled into the office and pretended to search through a stack of papers on my desk.

Paulie came up behind me and punched me in the side. I fell to my knees again, which were now blistered and bloody.

"Stop stalling and give me the fuckin' documents!" He pulled a cell phone from his left pocket and put it in my face. "I can call somebody right now and have them run over to Centinela Hospital and finish off your friend. Is that what you want?"

The thought of somebody attacking Special as she lay unconscious in her hospital bed hurt me far more than any of the blows I had just taken. "They're in my bedroom," I blubbered, crouching on all fours now. "I swear they are."

"They better be!" He snatched me by the hair, dragged me into the bedroom and flung me onto the bed.

"Get 'em!" he said, standing in the doorway.

Realizing I had no other choice, I pulled the top drawer of the nightstand all the way out, turned it over and tossed it onto the bed. A large envelope was stuck to the bottom with masking tape.

"Hand it here!" Paulie shouted. He remained just inside the open doorway, still holding the gun on me.

I ripped off the tape and handed him the envelope. He snatched it from me and smiled for the first time. His teeth were varying shades of gray. He pulled the pages out of the envelope and quickly scanned them.

Noticing that he had lowered his gun, I took a step back, hoping to make it to the closet to grab a hanger, a belt buckle, anything I could use as a weapon.

He took out his cell phone and hit the chirp button. "I got 'em," he said. "Get back over here."

Before I could make my move, the bedroom door hurled forward, plowing into the side of the man's face, causing his gun to fly out of his hand.

I just stood there, frozen in blissful amazement as my handsome husband jumped out from behind the door, tackled the much larger man to the ground and pounded him into unconsciousness.

Jefferson picked up the man's gun, then got to his feet. He reached out and corralled me in one of his arms, muffling my cries. I pressed my face against his chest and clutched at his T-shirt.

"Hey," Jefferson finally said, breathing heavily. "I thought you said you wouldn't be needing me to punch anybody out."

EPILOGUE

"Knock, knock," I announced as I pushed an empty wheelchair into Special's hospital room. "Guess who's here to take you home?"

Special grinned when she saw me enter the room. "Girl, aren't we a sight for sore eyes?"

Special's neck and chest were still covered in bandages and the bruises to my face had not completely healed yet. "You ain't never lied," I said, smiling.

She gingerly sat up in bed, which still wasn't easy for her. "You have no idea how glad I am to be getting the hell up out of here. Before you take me to my parents' house, we have to make a stop at Fatburger. The cooks in this hospital don't even know how to spell Lawry's seasoning salt."

I laughed. Special was finally back to her old self again and that made me incredibly happy. I helped my friend swing her legs over the side of the bed. Although she was still moving slowly, her prognosis for a full recovery was excellent. And her beautiful face barely had a scar to show for her ordeal.

In the days following my husband's daring daylight rescue, my life had changed dramatically. The first thing

I did was thank my neighbor, Mr. Robinson. He had been watching from his bedroom window and knew something was wrong the minute that cab screeched to a stop in front of our house. He called the police, then reached Jefferson on his cell phone. Jefferson got there just seconds after the cab had pulled away. I still don't know how he managed to climb through our bedroom window without us hearing him. I was just thankful that he had.

The Randle case eventually settled for $475,000, the sum Hamilton and I had originally negotiated. Hamilton only accepted the offer because Judge Sloan granted our motion on the after-acquired evidence rule. Even if Randle had won at trial, his damages would have been significantly reduced because of his application fraud and document theft.

One-third of the settlement went directly to Randle's two attorneys. Hamilton had agreed to bill only for the hours he had actually spent working on the case, which left Jenkins with a take of well over $100,000, his biggest recovery ever.

I could have tried to settle the case for less, but I was not motivated to save Micronics one dime since I later confirmed that Henry Randle *had* been set up. He eventually found a job working for an electronics company outside Atlanta, earning almost as much money as he had at Micronics.

For several days, the Micronics story led the local news as well as CNBC and the network news shows. At least eight Micronics employees, including Ferris, the CEO, the CFO, the General Counsel and the Program Manager, were indicted on sixteen counts, including securities fraud, conspiracy and attempted murder concerning the attack on Special. The minute the story broke, Micronics's stock nosedived to a fraction of its original value. Ferris cut a deal guaranteeing him probation, and to show his appreciation, he sang like a canary with a recording contract.

A homeowner who lived on Mulholland Drive later came forward and told police that a car had been pursuing Karen Carruthers when her Mustang went off the road. Some of the news reports surmised that the indictments against the Micronics execs would soon be amended to add accessory to murder to the counts. Federal prosecutors were also planning to charge the company's executives in the deaths of those twelve U.S. soldiers in Iraq.

The full extent of Special's or my involvement in exposing Micronics's fraud never hit the press. The LAPD's top brass did not want the public to find out about all the rules breached by one of their veteran detectives. Rather than face an internal investigation, Detective Coleman quietly retired.

A week before the partnership announcements were made, O'Reilly walked into my office and closed the door. The gloomy expression on his face told me he had bad news.

"This is going to be pretty tough for me," O'Reilly said, taking a seat, "so I guess I'll just spit it out. Your name won't be submitted for partnership this year."

I did not allow time for O'Reilly's words to sink in. "And why is that?" I asked.

"It's been a bit of a rocky year for you, kiddo." He forced a smile. "But don't worry, this is only a temporary setback."

"I didn't do anything wrong, O'Reilly," I said. "Micronics engaged in misconduct, not me."

"Yeah, I know, I know," he said. "We just need a little time for memories around here to fade. That's all."

"Are you telling me I'll definitely make partner next year?"

"Vernetta, you know there're no guarantees with the law."

"I'm not talking about the law, O'Reilly." I refused to let him off the hook. "This is business." The look in my eyes demanded a straight answer.

Instead of giving me one, O'Reilly looked away.

"You're the Managing Partner of this firm. You're telling me you don't have the power to give me that guarantee?"

"Vernetta, you know I can't do that. I've already said more than I should've. I didn't want you to be surprised when we made the partnership announcements tomorrow. Just give us another strong year and I'm sure everything'll work out just great."

Looking back, I was surprised at how calmly I had reacted to the news. I had poured everything I had and then some into becoming O'Reilly & Finney's first African-American partner. The news that it was not going to happen, at least not now, left me more disappointed than angry.

I now had some important decisions to make about my career. The most significant one was whether to remain with the firm. Luckily, I did have other options. One of my favorite law school professors was now dean of the USC Law School. An assistant professorship was mine for the asking. Working in-house for a corporation, joining another law firm, including Hamilton's, or even starting my own law practice, were also viable career moves.

For now, I just wanted to spend some quality time with my husband and help nurse my best friend back to health. Haley was babysitting my cases while I was out of the office and was trying her darnedest to be my new best friend, but I wasn't having it. The word around the firm was that she probably wouldn't last another six months.

I reached for the duffel bag I had brought with me to collect Special's belongings and pulled out a brightly colored, floral-print sundress that buttoned up the front.

"What's that?" Special scrunched up her face as if she had just sucked on a lemon.

"I bought you a new dress. I tried to find something in your closet that would be easy for you to slip into, but I couldn't find a single thing that didn't have spandex in it."

"That's ugly." Special stared at the dress as if it might bite her. "Who'd you buy that for, my grandmama? I ain't wearing that. Somebody I know might see me."

"You're kidding, right?" I laughed. "If you don't wear this, just what're you going to wear out of here?"

She grabbed the dress from me and held it out in front of her for a better look.

"Where'd you buy this thing, the Goodwill? When have you *ever* seen me in a floral print dress? I have an image to think about. I can't wear that." She tossed it onto the bed.

"I bought it at Nordstrom," I said. "And it cost me eighty dollars. If you don't put it on, I'll make sure you never lay eyes on Jefferson's cousin."

Special sulked for a few seconds, then snatched up the dress. "I'm only doing this because there's a man involved," she said. "And if he's not as fine as you say he is, you're taking me back to Nordstrom and buying me three dresses."

I smiled at my crazy friend. "You've got a deal."

"How's your husband doing?" Special asked.

"He's fine. That project in San Diego should be wrapped up in three more weeks. And oh, I forgot to tell you, after they laid off LaKeesha, she filed a workers' comp case stress claim. She barely worked twenty hours a week. Can you believe that girl's nerve?"

"Really?" Special said.

"Yeah, but for some reason, she suddenly dropped it," I said.

"That doesn't surprise me at all," Special said, grinning. "I told you that girl had some major issues."

"Jefferson's been coming home every weekend," I continued. "And he's been insisting that we go to church every Sunday. I almost fainted last week when Bishop Blake opened the doors of the church and Jefferson got up and walked down that aisle. I still can't believe it. I've been trying to get him to join West Angeles ever since we got married, but he always claimed organized religion wasn't for him."

Special smiled. "You've got yourself a good man, girlfriend."

"Yes, I do," I said as a gust of emotion snuck up on me. "He rushed up here the minute I told him you'd been hurt. And God knows what would've happened to me if he hadn't jumped out from behind our bedroom door."

Special eased herself off the bed, and with my help, slipped into her new dress.

"You look marvelous," I said. I had never seen my friend in anything that allowed her skin that much breathing room.

"Yeah, whatever," Special replied, sitting back down on the bed.

I scooped up her get-well cards and magazines and stuffed them into the duffel bag. I was headed toward a vase of flowers sitting along the window ledge, but Special stopped me.

"My mother took the rest of my flowers home," she said. "I'm leaving those for one of the nurses. She snuck me some chicken sausage from Woody's Barbecue yesterday."

"You could've gotten that woman fired," I said.

"I know, but I was desperate for something besides watery soup and strawberry Jell-O, and you were nowhere to be found."

Once I had everything packed up, I sat down next to Special on the bed. I could see that everything she had gone through had suddenly hit her.

"You okay?" I asked.

"Yeah, I'm fine." Special's voice softened. "It's weird to think about it, but I was almost a goner. I'm pretty blessed to be able to walk up out of here."

"Yes, you are," I said, realizing that I was equally blessed. I held out my arm and helped Special into the wheelchair. I hung the duffel bag on the back of the chair and pushed her into the corridor.

I waited while Special thanked the nurses for taking such good care of her. When she was done with her goodbyes, I steered the wheelchair toward the bank of elevators at the end of the corridor.

Special gazed up at me. "Thanks for always being there for me," she said somberly.

I gave her shoulder an affectionate squeeze. "Ditto."

I looked away as my eyes began to moisten and a big lump settled in my throat. I did not want to set off another crying spell.

By the time we reached the elevators, we had both perked up.

"Now getting back to Jefferson's cousin," Special said as I rolled her to a stop. "You claim he's really fine, right? Well, I just need to know. Is he sophisticated fine like Denzel or roughneck fine like Ice Cube?"

BOOK CLUB QUESTIONS FOR *IN FIRM PURSUIT*

1. Did you consider Vernetta a sellout for representing Micronics Corporation?

2. Could you defend a client if you suspected that the client might be guilty?

3. Do you think Jefferson should have been honest with Vernetta about LaKeesha?

4. If Jefferson had been honest with Vernetta about LaKeesha, how do you think Vernetta should have reacted?

5. Do you think Special was a traitor for going along with Jefferson?

6. What's the best way to deal with a coworker like Haley? Confront her or cautiously watch your back?

7. Why do you think men like Stan hold such contradictory and sexist views about women?

8. Do you think high-level executives who act unscrupulously have inherent character flaws or could any highly principled person be persuaded to act unethically if put in the right situation?

9. Why (other than money) are some people willing to sacrifice their own personal values and fulfillment to climb the corporate ladder?

10. What did you like/dislike about *In Firm Pursuit?*

Pleasure SEEKERS

Part of the Hideaway Legacy

A sizzling, sensuous story about Ilene, Faye and Alana—
three young African-American women whose lives are
forever changed when they are invited to join the
exclusive world of the Pleasure Seekers.

Rochelle Alers

NATIONAL BESTSELLING AUTHOR

"Fans of the romantic suspense of Iris Johansen,
Linda Howard and Catherine Coulter
will enjoy [*Pleasure Seekers*]."
—Library Journal

Available the first week of January wherever books are sold.

sepia™

A special Collector's Edition from
Essence bestselling author

KAYLA PERRIN

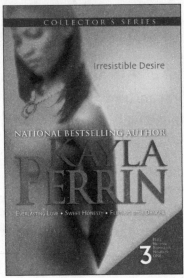

Three full-length novels

From one of the most popular authors for the Arabesque series comes this trade paperback volume containing three classic romances. Enjoy warmth, drama and mystery with EVERLASTING LOVE, SWEET HONESTY and FLIRTING WITH DANGER.

"The more [Kayla Perrin] writes, the better she gets."
—*Rawsistaz Reviewers* on *Gimme an O!*

Available the first week of January wherever books are sold.

KIMANI PRESS™
www.kimanipress.com

KPKP0530107TR